A DOLLY MYSTERY

DOROTHY DUNNETT

Moroccan
Traffic

Farrago

This edition published in 2023 by Farrago,
an imprint of Duckworth Books Ltd
1 Golden Court, Richmond, TW9 1EU, United Kingdom

www.farragobooks.com

First published by Chatto & Windus Ltd in 1991

Print ISBN: 978-1-7884-2421-9
eISBN: 978-1-7884-2422-6

Cover design and illustration by Nathan Burton

Have you read them all?

Treat yourself again to the first Dolly novels –

Tropical Issue
Make-up artist Rita Geddes travels to Madeira in search of who killed her mentor Kim-Jim, and needs all her nerve to succeed.

Rum Affair
Tina Rossi, a famous coloratura soprano, has come to Edinburgh to sing – but finds a dead body, and her lover Kenneth gone missing.

Ibiza Surprise
When Sarah Cassells, recently trained as a chef, hears of her father's violent death on Ibiza, she refuses to believe it's suicide.

Turn to the end of this book for a full list of the series, plus – on the last page – the chance to receive **further background material**.

1

'Bifocal spectacles!' shouted my mother, coughing heavily over her daisy-wheel printer. 'Now my daughter wastes her time on some self-employed painter with no index-linked company pension?'

The dog in the next house began barking.

I took off and hung up my coat. This is my welcome, arriving bombed-out from my office. I yelled, 'He paid for my lunch. He fed me better than you do.' I have strong, healthy lungs. I don't know where I could have got them from.

She is a devil, my mother. She went on shrieking from inside the sitting-room. 'And so this painter goes blind? What happens to you and the children?' The printer volleyed out some professor's closely spaced argument (she types for a living) while I shut the door and looked about for my supper.

I have no children; and after the events of that day, I shouldn't have counted on Johnson to father them. Whoever fathered my children would receive my mother as mother-in-law within a few skid-marked weeks of the pregnancy test. My widowed parent, with her business training cassettes and her annotated back numbers of the *Woman Executive Quarterly*. My mother, who has taken, for the sake of my career, seminars on everything from The Team Management Wheel to (providentially) a teach-in on Plans for Disaster. My mother is fat and fifty and nosy. I hate her.

I knew of Johnson Johnson, of course, before he came to the office that morning. I'd drafted the letter that commissioned him to paint the Chairman in oils. I'd drawn up the company cheque with four zeros on it. After that, I'd gone on vacation (Treasures of France: singles and retired people welcome), and forgotten all about Mr J. Johnson. Until I returned, fit and fresh to serve my company.

It is a well-paid position, that of Executive Secretary to the Chairman of Kingsley Conglomerates. Their central office in London is a four-storey building in tasteful caramel glass. On the third floor are the Chairman's suite and the boardroom, fitted with leather, mahogany and romantic photographs of electrical domestic machinery. Beyond that is an outer office occupied by me, by Sir Robert's Personal Assistant and by Trish, our personal typist. When I am not there, Trish looks after the Chairman.

I enjoy healthy holidays away from my absorbing and interesting work. If I were to dislike holidays (which I don't), it would be because of what I might be missing. When I got back to the office that morning, I saw at once that the Special Board Minutes had gone, and the Acquisition Sub-committee Minutes were absent, and so were a few other files my mother suggested I look at. Even the boardroom was locked. Then I noticed that the morning mail had also vanished, which meant that Sir Robert's PA had got into town even faster than I had.

If he knew I was after his job, Val Dresden didn't show it that morning. Emerging from Sir Robert's room with the post, he came across in his usual manner. 'Who do I see? Wendy back in the Wendy-house! *Divinely* tanned, and a new lacy ruffle. Were the beach boys too luscious?' He bent at the hips and gave me a deep, humming kiss on the cheek. He had changed his colour rinse and his aftershave. Trish, who had only just sauntered in, sat down and began to fix her hair, surveying us both through her mirror. She was wearing a designer top and real pearls. RWT, Dresden calls her when chatting her up. It stands for Rich White Trish, and she likes it.

I said, 'The beach boys are always lovely in Paris. So what's been happening? Sir Robert is early?'

Val flipped some mail on my desk, covered with ticks and scribbled instructions. 'Slept in the office last night. Don't go rushing in, sweetie: he's shaving. Wants to be fresh and pretty, does Bobs.' Sir Robert thinks the world of Val Dresden.

The diary smelt of chocolate and described Sir Robert's engagements in Trish's large childish writing. I flipped through the two weeks I'd sacrificed.

There was no direct mention of the company I was looking for. Our favourite stockbroker had been in and out, and a man from our corporate lawyers; and our biggest institutional shareholders had each been given a slap-up Savoy Grill Room luncheon. A boardroom lunch had been held, and attended by the new head of our corporate money consultants. In between, the traffic among our own senior staff seemed to have been about normal.

There were quite a lot of social engagements, some with Lady Kingsley but more often without. She was away at the moment and hadn't gone, then, to last night's big affair at the Oppenheims'. Sir Robert had. It was down in the diary. Which explained, of course, why the Chairman had slept in the office. He had had a night on the town without Charity.

The diary, of course, said nothing of that. It produced, for today, a single early date to receive a J. Johnson, and then nothing till lunch with a banker. So why Val's smirk, and fresher and prettier? Then I got it. I remembered who Johnson was.

As I've said, the Board had decided to honour its Chair with a portrait. Sir Robert, who always liked quality, had chosen the artist at the top of all the lists discreetly provided. He didn't know he was going to regret it. Johnson Johnson sent to say he couldn't accept Sir Robert at all for six months. Courted, he conceded that he could make a start sooner, but not away from his studio. Shamefully seduced, he finally named a day upon which he could begin work on the portrait on Sir Robert's own premises, subject to interruption without previous notice; early resumption not guaranteed.

Chairmen are a separate breed. I would have sent him a three-line dismissal, but Sir Robert told me he would ring Mr Johnson himself. And he must have used all his charm, for work had begun, Val Dresden informed me, and Sir Robert was thrilled with the likeness, and could be heard to kiss it in greeting each morning.

'What's it like?' I asked, shutting the diary.

'Nobody knows,' Val Dresden said. 'The boardroom's locked, as I'm sure you found out, and I'm told the priceless canvas is shrouded. Dear old things; Trish claims they're using it to watch video nasties.'

I picked up the mail and got on with my work. I was glad when Reception rang, and I was able to buzz through to Sir Robert, and tell him Mr Johnson was here.

The Chairman sounded pleased that I was back. 'Wendy, my dear! How splendid! Did you have a good holiday?' He has a nice voice. He won all his directorships and an early constituency with the help of that fizzing enthusiasm. That, and his flamboyant size, and his rebellious hair, and his ear for mimicry, and his ability, at the right time, to knock off and have fun with the boys. And the girls.

I said, 'A very good time, thank you, Sir Robert. If you aren't quite ready, I could offer Mr Johnson some tea while he's waiting.'

'Do that,' he said. 'Then come into the boardroom. You and I must have a session, if the great man, of course, will allow it. The smell of oil paint doesn't bother you?'

It didn't bother me. I lobbed a smile of fake triumph at Val and Trish as I told them. Beneath was a smile of real triumph. I was going to see the Chairman's oil before they did.

Down in Reception, there was no one but a tweedy man with black hair, a shapeless satchel, and an expensive Burberry heaped up beside him. He was printing doggedly on a doubled-up crossword. When he began to look up, there was nothing to see but two lenses, separated by a nose which had once been reset. Presently his glasses inclined, and he saw me. 'Mr Johnson?' I said.

The great man gazed at me. I realized he was used to Val, or to Trish. I said (Handling Callers with Confidence and Care), 'I'm Wendy Helmann, Sir Robert's Executive Secretary. Would you care to come up?'

He rose, bringing coat, bag and newspaper to the door with more agility than I expected. He said, 'Work-out at the Veterans' Athletic Club. You've been on holiday. Nice to be back?' His accent was the same as Sir Robert's, but with nothing hearty about it.

If I was surprised, I took care not to show it a second time. *Nice to be back?* Very few people say that, outside situational interviews.

'The first day?' I said, smiling. I am not my mother. I knew at once he was Casual Old Money. At the lift, I added, 'I'll begin to enjoy it tomorrow.'

'That's right,' he agreed. I heard, but no doubt misinterpreted, a trace of approval. The lift began to ascend. He said, 'Who was the boudoir-eyed stud I met last time? Valentine somebody?'

I began to realize then that he was enjoying an idle hour drinking blood. I said, 'I don't know, Mr Johnson. Perhaps you met Mr Dresden, the Chairman's Assistant. He would paint very well.'

'He thinks so,' said Mr Johnson. 'And Vampirella?'

The words floated out through the lift doors, which opened to reveal Valentine Dresden, lingering beside Trish's desk in his voile shirt and a cloud of citrus top-notes and a further new double cloud of resentment. 'And a very good morning to you both,' said Mr Johnson, in exactly the same tone of voice. 'The boardroom? Or am I too early?'

He didn't mean it. He meant he was exactly on time, but the Chairman wasn't waiting to greet him. I said, 'Could I offer you a seat for five minutes? Sir Robert had to work late last night, and slept in the office. He asked me to offer you tea.'

'Too kind, but I never drink before painting,' said Mr Johnson. 'Why don't I go through to the boardroom and start?'

'Don't you need Sir Robert?' said Trish. Trish is forward because of her upbringing; a nuisance not worth correcting, since she never stays anywhere long.

He said, 'Not if Miss Helmann will sit in his jacket.'

He seemed to be serious. Trish said slyly, 'Wouldn't Mr Dresden be better?' Dresden went sallow. It was interesting. I'd thought they were sleeping together.

Mr Johnson Johnson inhaled. He said, 'But is Mr Dresden's aura quite right? And really, the young lady's attributes would be wasted. So what is left but the resourceful Miss Helmann?'

We all got it. Val was scented, Trish was bosomy and I could bring him tea when he wanted it.

My mother has trained me in body language. I received the key to the boardroom from Dresden, and walked without haste to insert it. I opened the door at the second try. Mr Johnson didn't hurry me.

He said, 'Why should I bore you with advice? There's decaffeinated coffee, or early retirement. You want to see the Chairman's picture?'

I followed him slowly in. It was there, covered up on an easel. At the other end of the room stood Sir Robert's chair and his jacket. The door to his bedroom and office was shut. It was time to deal with Mr Johnson. Comfort, Question and Listen; I knew what to do when insulted. I said, 'Mr Johnson, may I ask you a question?'

He thought. He nodded. My mother, baiting me, looked just like that.

I said, 'Why do you paint, if you don't like it?'

He thought again. 'Good question,' he said. 'Look, and tell me the answer.' And he lifted and dropped back the sheet on the portrait.

The boardroom is proofed against sound. You could hear the low hum of the heating, and the creak of a chair, and the nearly inaudible click of the quartz clock. There was nothing to say. I said, 'I'm sorry.'

'Thank you,' said Johnson Johnson. 'Want to watch? Sit there, and don't talk.'

'You don't need the jacket?' I said.

'Not particularly,' said Mr Johnson. 'Quite enjoy someone breathing in the same room. Even fire and brimstone. Now shut up, there's a splendid young lady.'

Ten minutes later, Sir Robert bounded in. 'Ah, Johnson, you're working. Can you forgive me? Wendy dear, can you find us some coffee? What do you think of this, then? After five sittings?' He wore a fresh shirt and tie and dark trousers. His waist was solid, but there was no flabbiness anywhere. He picked up and slipped on the jacket which I had not been required to wear. I had not been required to do anything but stand and watch paint being slapped round a palette and placed, without pause, on the canvas by someone who was not like my mother at all.

I said, 'It's a very good picture.'

'Good?' said Sir Robert. 'My dear girl, that portrait will be on the centre wall of this year's Academy. You're a genius, old boy. Charity will say the same when she sees it.'

The genius said, 'You got back all right then?'

'Boring party. Yes. Didn't know you knew that crowd?' Sir Robert said. 'Slept here last night, as a matter of fact.'

'I thought you might,' said the genius. 'Who can claim to know a financial consultant except other financial consultants? Fiddler's bidding, in fact. Muriel phoned me. Her people and mine are old friends. Nice girl, Muriel. Lucky chap, Oppenheim.'

'You're absolutely right,' said Sir Robert.

Working late, I had said. Mr Johnson didn't bother to look at me, and I didn't look at Sir Robert. I got out, fast, for the coffee.

Although I brought him a cup, Mr Johnson refused again. I thought he wouldn't care for me to work while he painted, but he simply hooked out a chair by his easel and I sat down with a notebook. The Chairman talked, had a break, and then talked again. Only during the final half-hour did Mr Johnson make a suggestion. 'Now I have a touch to do to the mouth. All right, Sir Robert? Miss Helmann?' And Sir Robert smiled and stopped speaking, while Mr Johnson took up the running.

Chatting was, I suppose, part of his job, and he knew Sir Robert's interests by this time. He knew a surprising amount about cricket and racing, and had quite a stock of anecdotes about acquaintances from Sir Robert's various quangos. He knew about Charity's passion for paintings and horses. I supposed he knew what to expect if and when he ever met Lady Kingsley.

At the end, he put down his palette, threw his fistful of brushes on the trolley and stepped back, his eyes on the canvas. He said, 'Well, that's about it. Two-thirds done: the right stage to leave off, although I must say I'm sorry. It's really coming along.' He stood absently folding a rag.

I sat where I was, watching the Chairman's smile fade. He said, 'Leave it? Until when?'

The bifocal glasses turned. 'Where are we? Spring… summer… Resume in September, perhaps?'

'I beg your pardon,' said Sir Robert gently. He rose in the controlled way he has, put one hand in his pocket and strolled towards Mr Johnson. He said, 'We discussed the possibility of an interruption; I remember that very well. But not, my dear chap, what the shop floor might describe as a walk-out. You are proposing a gap of seven months without warning? A little steep, wouldn't you say?'

Johnson frowned. 'Disappointing, of course. But there it is.' He shook his head, tossing tubes into his box. 'These things happen.'

'Not in my boardroom, as a rule,' Sir Robert said. I had heard him say it before, with the same look on his face, and the same pleasant tone in his voice. He continued, 'I have a feeling you want to go on with this as much as I do. There's a way around everything. What can I do to help matters?'

'Paint six portraits?' said Johnson, with all the indifferent charm of a Customs officer. He unscrewed a final tin and soaking a cloth, used it to banish the paint from his fingers. Then he looked up, perhaps struck by the silence.

He said, 'Perhaps you've forgotten. This is the risk you accepted. I have a client who reserved the right, long ago, to make his own priority appointment. He rang me last night and made it.'

'For tomorrow?' said Sir Robert. He sat down in a chair and leaned back. 'For every day this week and next? I thought a professional spaced out his sittings.'

'For March,' said Johnson. 'And I have three other commissions to finish beforehand. You, and those who booked later than you will, sadly, have to wait till September. But in time for next year's Academy, certainly.'

He had laid hands on the easel and was turning it thoughtfully. The blue daylight of London glittered on the wet picture, and Sir Robert's eyes fastened upon it. He rose without shifting his gaze, and thrust a hand, as before in his pocket. His own face looked back as if from a mirror, full of a vigour so piercing that flesh and blood seemed to spring from the canvas. The fit, heavy body. The amused, clean-shaven face with years of explosive living caught in every line. It was two-thirds done, as Johnson had said. A third was only blocked in.

'But of course,' Johnson said, 'if art and trade can't agree, don't let's quarrel. Take back your fee and I'll scrap it. You will, after all, have wasted as much time on the thing as I have.'

Sir Robert's hand hung at his side. I watched its fingers curl and then stretch. He had just realized he was face to face with a monopoly. He had opened his mouth when Val Dresden jerked the door open. Val said, 'Bomb threat, Sir Robert, I'm sorry. We have to get out of the building.'

He sounded sorry all right. He'd heard the row through the door, and was dying to know who was winning. Sir Robert's hand subtly relaxed. He said, 'What a bore. My dear fellow, I have to apologize. Perhaps we can continue when this is all over?' He made for the door, and we followed. The alarm was warbling by now, and I could hear a confusion of voices and whistles, and footsteps thudding down stairs and through passages. I scooped up my handbag and hurried.

A voice, socio-economic group A, said, 'You're well-drilled, Miss Helmann. Does this happen often?'

Mr Johnson jogged at my side like a billboard. Between his two outstretched arms he was grasping the cause of the dispute, wet side outermost. I said, 'This is the first time really since Christmas. We wait at the end of the street unless it's raining. Twice, Sir Robert sent everyone home.'

'Nice,' said Mr Johnson.

'Except the personal staff, of course,' I said. 'He has the Rolls driven up to the cordon and we stay until the security sweep has been finished.'

We'd got to the foyer when Sir Robert pushed his way back to Johnson's side and noticed he'd rescued the painting. He said, 'My God, I'm impressed, but in fact there's no danger, old boy. Happens regularly. Hang about for a clean bill of health, and then we'll have that chat over a noggin. Why not wait for me over there? It's a good hotel. And it's cold, standing about in the roadway.'

'I don't mind,' said Mr Johnson. 'Was it a phone threat you had?'

'The police are tracing it,' said Sir Robert. 'The usual rubbish. A bomb will go off in an hour unless we arrange to hand over a million. I feel rather insulted. You'd think they'd value us a little bit higher.'

'So you hand over the million?' said Mr Johnson. We had reached Sir Robert's car.

My chairman laughed. 'Christ, you know better than that. A lot better. Don't worry. Name your price, and we'll meet it.'

Mr Johnson stopped walking. He said, 'I have named my price. I may cancel the contract, but I have no need to alter it.'

'What did you think I was saying?' the Chairman said quickly. 'All we both want to do is finish the bloody picture. It's the best you've ever done. You know it. I know it. I'm trying to help you finish it, so quit trying to slam me down, will you?'

Inside the car, Val Dresden was taking a phone call. He opened the door. 'Sir Robert! The threat's been repeated. They think there *is* a bomb in the building.'

I stood outside, and watched the Chairman dive in and grab the car phone. Mr Johnson watched him as well, the painting resting gently reversed on the road. The ambulances and fire engines arrived. Behind the cordon, I could see the rest of the staff, and sightseers, and residents. Occasionally one of the executives would come over to speak to Sir Robert, and be introduced to Johnson Johnson who was holding court by the boot of the Rolls.

Flattery was doing him good. Presently, he was so far softened up that he would step forward and shake hands with anybody. Then I saw Sir Robert stiffen and, looking round, realized who was coming.

It was too late to prevent an encounter. Sir Robert assumed a welcoming smile. 'Ah, Morgan. Dreadful bore, isn't it? Johnson, may I introduce our newest director? Mr Morgan and his team have just joined Kingsley Conglomerates.'

He didn't say more. He didn't actually say, 'This is the Bummer of the Year; give me a week and I'll fix him.' But you could tell he hoped Johnson got the message.

He probably did, from the way he shook hands. In his own design room, according to rumour, Mr Morgan favoured T-shirts with bracelets and denims. For a visit to HQ he had found a peculiar suit with a hole in one elbow. His pigtail was the same. Mr Morgan said, 'Heard of you. Can I? Or do you make a small charge?'

'Feel free,' said Mr Johnson, and turned the canvas for Mr Morgan to look.

'Wow!' said Mr Morgan. His jet-black eyes didn't blink. 'Wow, that's tubular.'

'Thank you,' said Johnson. 'It's a personal best. What do *you* make?'

'I'm into microchips,' said Mr Morgan. He hadn't removed his eyes from the paint. 'I've got low arousal. It's better than women.'

'If you say so,' said Mr Johnson. 'I hope they've given you nice golden handcuffs.'

'Brother,' said Mr Morgan, 'in the matter of shackles, I am not in your league. Why have you stuck yourself with this stuff?'

Mr Johnson looked at him calmly. 'You joined a conglomerate.'

'I promised my teacher,' said our newest director. 'Soon as I got out of Remand School. So what's your problem with blue pigments? Permanence.'

I stared at them both. Johnson Johnson said, 'Yes, permanence. Why?'

'I've done some work on that. Ring me some time. Not now: I'm going on holiday.'

'You're into chemistry, too?' said Mr Johnson.

'You name it. Pays the bar bills. Better get back. Blue's a bugger,' said Mr Morgan, and threw himself lithely into the crowd which was still milling about, rubbing its arms and staring towards Kingsley Conglomerates.

Which, ten minutes later, blew up.

The flash came first: then a bang that deadened my ears. The glass flying out of the windows looked like a broken kaleidoscope. It began to fall in the empty street, together with lumps of concrete and tangles of metal and other rubbish. We were too far away to feel much of the blast, or the heat that followed as the fire took its hold. Sir Robert scrambled out of the car, followed by his silent PA, shivering in his voile shirt. The driver was gripping the wheel fit to break it. Those executives I could see were all pale, and the girls in the crowd were mostly screaming except those like Trish, who were patently thrilled.

Sir Robert said '*Christ!* Police, security, dogs, and they can't defuse a bomb on a plate with a ticket on it. Have they brought down the whole fucking building?' Unlike the other faces, his had turned scarlet.

You could see nothing now but black smoke with a glare of red flame in it. But I had caught that single instructive glimpse: the flash of glass buckling and jumping along the third floor. I said, 'It's the boardroom floor only, I think.'

For us, it wasn't bad news. Blast-proof safes protected all the company papers. Apart from expensive leather and curtains and carpets, the third floor held little of capital value. Even the portrait was safe. I looked again at Johnson Johnson who was holding it.

Staring upwards, he looked properly stunned. But his first reaction, when the bang came, had been different. It had been one of raw and unmistakable anger. Then, observing me, he'd said, 'Shit,' in a mild voice.

It wasn't my place to speak, and I didn't. The management announced Crisis Procedure. I waited, notebook in hand, but Sir Robert gave all his orders to Dresden. Then he came quietly over and asked me to take care of a particular problem.

I can't pretend I was pleased. You don't get blown up every day, and I was going to miss the excitement. On the other hand, the personal success would be mine, and not Dresden's. I agreed, and left him, and crossed to the car to phone my mother.

I got my mother's recorded voice on the answer-phone. I had to wait all through the familiar rasp, and the place where she unstuck her fag to cough better. Mr Morgan, peering into the car, said, 'What's up? No one at home?'

Because of the pigtail, his hair had stayed neater than anyone else's, and he was neat in build also. He had a bony face and a nose like an osprey's. From three inches away he looked what he was, in his thirties. I wondered if he guessed that the Chairman, having seen off the bomb, would immediately wade into his low-authority clothing.

'I left a message,' I said. 'On the answer-phone. My mother will get it.'

'Go home, angel,' he said. 'Nothing here for nice kids with mothers.'

I didn't need to explain why I couldn't. Sir Robert approached. 'Wendy, Mr Johnson is waiting. We really can't let him cart that wet canvas home single-handed. Help him as much as you can. And get warm. Have something to eat. There's no hurry: Dresden will manage quite splendidly.' His voice bounced off a newly stopped taxi into which Mr Johnson was easing his picture.

'What?' said Mr Morgan, as anyone might. But Sir Robert merely put a warm hand on my shoulder and propelled me into the taxi with Johnson. I went, for I knew what he wanted. The other third of his portrait, finished pronto.

Sir Robert usually gets his own way. In due course Mr Johnson thanked me for helping, and dutifully asked if he might take me to lunch. Even knowing all I now know, dutiful is still the word I would attach to Johnson Johnson. He was being perfectly dutiful to someone.

Hence (as I was to find out long after) our lunch table was already booked. Booked for himself and for me, a full twenty-four hours before it all happened.

2

We dropped the picture off at Mr Johnson's apartment, which had a marble entrance with bay trees and two porters who seemed to know all about handling wet paintings. Then we went to his club, which had two Jags, a Porsche and a pale blue vintage Sunbeam inconspicuously parked in the forecourt.

I have learned all I need to know about etiquette: I expected there would be a Ladies' End to the dining room, and there was. I was quite nicely dressed, and accustomed to conferences, where you have to walk about with older men. I noticed the people we passed were quite a lot younger than Mr Johnson, and I thought that perhaps he had picked one of his sportier clubs. Walking through, I heard members greet him, but no one offered to join him. They possibly thought I was a personal friend. Or they may not have wanted to join him. Cosy was not what I would have called Johnson Johnson. He had a social distance zone the size of a car park.

And his club was nothing to write home about. When we got to the table, the menu wasn't even in French. I chose pâté, sole and the cheese board. The great man plumped for soup, mince and pudding, ordered a stingy two glasses of claret, and ate while I thanked him for his hospitality. 'Think nothing of it,' he said. 'I hate to hear of nice girls getting the sack. Would you like to dispose of the whole subject now, or are you keen to get me pissed first?'

I thought of my mother, and the world's largest library of aids to self-improvement. Among my mother's cassettes were quick-help assessments of Extroversion, Introversion and Neuroticism, with in-job analysis measures designed to tap critical on-the-job behaviours.

The authors hadn't met Mr Johnson.

I had absorbed four professional ways of saying 'I'm angry' and my client had used them all up in one morning.

I said, 'You want to finish that painting. I know Sir Robert. I thought I might suggest an accommodation.'

'I tell you what,' said Mr Johnson. 'Suppose you suggest it over the pudding, and we actually eat our first two courses in peace. Why didn't you go to university?'

He made me nervous, being so unpredictable. I could, of course, have told him the answer. Because my mother didn't believe in universities, that was why. Because my father had died street-stupid the way he was born, always with a new idea for a new business that would start paying the rent. Business people didn't succeed by going to university, my mother said. I agreed with her. I said, 'I'm keen on business. For a girl, a good secretarial training is often the best way into management.'

'What fascinates you about management?' said Mr Johnson. 'Getting to the top? Starting up on your own? Or earning the means to do something quite different?'

He moved in the same circles as Sir Robert. He knew Daniel Oppenheim. He knew chief executives and investment brokers and bankers. I said, 'I like doing things well, and seeing things happen. I may not reach top management, but I can enjoy giving loyalty and good service along the way.'

He handed me salt, and took back the butter. He behaved exactly like a man entertaining a lady guest of his choice. He said, 'Well, that's the stock answer. What's the real answer?'

'That is the real answer,' I said.

'Is it?' he said. 'I'm not going to propose you for a new job, you know. Or discuss your capabilities with Sir Robert. I expect, in any case, you know enough about Kingsley's to make it worth while digging in. Or aren't you interested in what they are up to?'

I said, 'Of course I am. To help the Chair, you have to know what his policies are. But you can't expect me to talk about that.'

'I don't. I'm not even getting you drunk. What car do you drive?' said Johnson Johnson.

It's a second-hand Volkswagen. I'm not ashamed of it. When I told him, he finished wiping his lips and put down his napkin. He said, 'Well, that settles that. You aren't into insider trading.'

15

I was furious. My suit might not come from Hardy Amies or wherever his women shopped, but it was a nice one. And not every EA can afford any car. I nearly retorted that if I wanted to go into insider trading I could do it tomorrow. It was pretty well true.

I didn't have the nerve to get up and go, but he must have read my expression. He said, 'Have I paid you a back-handed compliment? I'm sorry. I'd forgotten how the feminine mind works. May I move on to what I actually wanted to say to you?'

Now I looked him in the face, I saw what he was really like. He was without personality. His nose had been broken and reset with a discretion that gave it no distinction at all. His mouth was too spare to convey anything. His eyes, behind glass, possessed no radiating lines of good humour. Even his hair, surprisingly black, conveyed no puckish clue to his actual mood, as Sir Robert's did. Sir Robert's face was full of bantering lines, and his lips were beautiful. I said, 'Please say what you want. I'm your guest. I don't need to answer you.'

'As you remind me,' he said. 'But here we are. Let's see if there isn't something useful to be got out of it. You're not exploiting your job, no: of course you're not. You're ambitious. I'm sure you enjoy doing things well. So do I. But every now and then, I ask myself whether the thing I'm doing well is worth doing. And sometimes the answer is no, I'd be better doing something quite different. For example, I expect that you've picked up some languages?'

I wondered what made him ask that, as well. I said, 'Of course: doesn't everyone? We couldn't go into Europe without.'

'But you don't want to chuck business and go in for interpretation, or travel? Where did you go on holiday, for example?'

I shot a glance at him, but his face displayed no special cunning. He didn't expect me to say Kashmir or Bali. I described my two weeks with the Treasures of France. He asked quite intelligent questions, and I was careful with the way I pronounced things.

We were into the pudding and cheese before I realized how I'd been diverted. I broke off. I said, 'You promised a serious talk.'

I expected a put-down. I drew on my training to prepare for it. The Implications of Being a Woman had been no help at all, despite Sir Robert's obvious expectations. My host laid down his spoon with a certain mulishness rather than anger. He said, 'It's all right; it was a rather large pudding. So let's talk about Sir Bob's bloody portrait. You *thought you might suggest an accommodation.* So, fast-forward: such as?'

It was time for my pitch. The tables around us were empty, although at the other end of the room a few flushed youngish men were emitting bursts of occasional laughter. From time to time, one of them waved at our table. Mr Johnson paid no attention.

I said, 'The portrait deserves to be finished. Also, we'd like it exhibited this year as a business asset. We know you can't come to us. But Sir Robert would come to you to be painted in whatever time you could spare from your client. At his own expense, and wherever you say. With a little good will, surely that would be possible?' A man from the rowdy table had risen. He was young, blond and built like a Saxon gasometer.

'Clients, plural,' said Mr Johnson. 'I have to paint more than one person. And you've put it very nicely, but no, I'm afraid it wouldn't be possible. My sitters are not in this country.'

'That needn't matter,' I said.

'To Sir Robert Kingsley?' he said. 'Miss Helmann, you know and I know that his diary must be full to December.'

'No,' I said. 'He and Lady Kingsley were planning a vacation in March. Where are your sittings to be?'

He never did answer. Before he could speak, the gasometer was standing before us. Close to, in every sense, he was staggering. I was aware of leather and buckles and suntan; of rippling sand-coloured hair, and eyes fringed with white lashes like woodlice, their gaze wholly directed at me. The vision said, 'Who is she, J.J.? Come on! We've all put down a tenner.' Sandhurst and Army, I thought. Cheek and Old Money again, but this time not so casual.

'Go away, Seb,' my host answered. It was quite pleasant, like Sir Robert's voice in the boardroom.

'Not a hope, old pal,' said Seb. 'We heard you scored with a wench in the Balkans.' He was still examining me. 'Are you from the Balkans? And wasting your charms on a shark from the Navy? What's your name, darlin'?'

The great painter stirred. 'Miss Wendy Helmann of Kingsley Conglomerates,' he said. 'Meet Colonel Sebastian Sullivan, sportsman. Amateur sportsman.'

'Bloddy hell!' said Sebastian Sullivan. He was Irish.

'Amateur,' Mr Johnson repeated. 'If you were a real one you'd get the hell out.'

'No,' said Colonel Sullivan. He was swaying slightly. He said, 'Hey!'

'Yes?' said Mr Johnson.

Colonel Sullivan said, 'Does she work for King Cong?'

'Who?' said Mr Johnson.

'Kingsley Conglomerates,' I said calmly. 'It's what they call us.'

'It's what they call Bob Kingsley,' said Colonel Sullivan. 'And if she works for him, she's never come from Yugoslavia. She's not Balkan, and I've lost me bloody tenner.'

'I'm British,' I said. It's what I always say.

Colonel Sullivan pulled out a chair and sat down. He said, 'So whose girlfriend are you?'

Mr Johnson gazed at him. 'Mine,' he said with some distaste. 'At the moment. Colonel, your guests are getting fed up.'

I don't know about getting fed up. The remaining two men at his table had stopped drinking and were watching us with apparent difficulty. One was young and raunchy like Sullivan. The other wore a smart leather jacket over a button-down shirt and pink tie. As we looked, leather jacket got up, steadied, and began to come over. His round face was not improved by a crewcut, and he'd had a lot more club claret than I'd had. Seb Sullivan jerked his thumb at the table. 'You know Gerry,' he said. 'And the approaching skinhead is Pymm, a visiting scribbler from our Canadian colony. Ellwood, Mr J. Johnson.'

The skinhead, arriving, heard the introduction and said, 'Ma'am!' to me, and 'Sir!' to my host. I should have said he was an American.

'Delighted,' said Mr Johnson. 'Goodbye.'

'I'm not going,' said Colonel Sullivan. 'And you can't go: you haven't finished your disgusting Spotted Dick yet.' He frowned, looking at me. 'If she's not from the Balkans, what would you suppose the poor girl is doin' here, then?' His accent was getting more Irish.

'Attempting to finish her rather cold luncheon. We are refugees from an unfortunate incident at Kingsley's. I've been painting Sir Robert.'

'What colour?' said the buttoned-down man with the crewcut. He put his arm round the Colonel's shoulders, mimed a short burst of laughter and straightened.

The Colonel winced. He said, 'Hang about. Wait just a minute. Didn't Kingsley's blow up this very morning? Send all the lovely washin' machines back to their Maker? So what will the big boss do now?' He was looking at me. His eyes were blue, and not as glazed as I'd expected.

'She doesn't know,' said Johnson Johnson. 'And if she did, she wouldn't tell you. Miss Helmann, have you heard of Black & Holroyd, Public Relations?'

I had, from Sir Robert. Public relations are important in the City when one company means to merge with or take over another, and the biggest firms employ experts to interpret their plans to the public. Public Relations Consultants have a nose for what will please the important fund managers. Some go further. Some employ investigators whose sole job is to undermine the opposition. Undermine, terrify or persuade it. Black & Holroyd were one of the most successful PR firms in the business. Looking at Mr Sullivan, I thought I could guess what he was good at. I wondered if my host knew. I let him tell me.

'Seb and Gerry,' explained Mr Johnson painstakingly. 'Management and Acquisition PR Consultants. Mr Ellwood Pymm, as you've heard, represents the hounds of the Canadian press. Anything you say about Kingsley's will not only go straight to the City, it will find its way to radio, newspapers, television and five rival companies, not to mention very likely the police. You have been warned.'

'So lost the masterpiece, have you?' Seb Sullivan said. He sounded disgustingly pleased.

'No,' said Mr Johnson.

'What?' said Ellwod Pymm with some sharpness.

I said quickly, 'The portrait's safe, but not finished. That's why I'm here. To persuade Mr Johnson to complete it.'

'Why, don't you want to?' said the Colonel to our oil-painting genius, who was staring at me without much expression.

'Mr Johnson says he has to fulfil a commission abroad,' I informed him.

'Have you?' said Colonel Sullivan to Mr Johnson. 'Or are you simply fed up with the glorious Cong?' He turned to me again. He had a lot of gold in his teeth. 'Come on, let's have the dirt about Bobs. What's he like in the office? What's he like out of the office? After three wives, don't tell me he's fading?'

'He isn't,' said Pymm. He had sobered enough to finish our plate of choc mints and was wiping his lips with his wrist. 'Guess who was in the T & Q the whole of last night? *With*—'

The T & Q is a well-known London night club famed for its hostesses. I knew Sir Robert sometimes went there. I've seen Val come from Sir Robert's room in the morning and wink, the empty hangover glass in his hand. Most great men have their weaknesses. I tried to stare down Ellwood Pymm but Mr Johnson interrupted him anyway.

'You don't need to answer,' Mr Johnson said tartly to me. And to Sullivan: 'Yes, I'm working abroad; and no, I've nothing against Sir Robert or Kingsley Conglomerates.'

'They've got Mo Morgan,' Sullivan said. 'And that can't be bad news. He wouldn't take a job without a golden back-up commitment.'

'Seb,' said Mr Johnson. 'She isn't going to talk about Mo Morgan's terms of employment.'

'Or about MCG?' said Seb Sullivan wistfully. 'Beauty salons? Cosmetics? There's a whisper going about that the MCG directors have caught a small chill, and wish they hadn't gone to the market. Come on, J.J. Let me ask her if Kingsley's wouldn't like to take over a bargain-price middle-range business that uses lots of lovely big washing machines? A hint is all that we ask. You've got stocks. She's got stocks. One of Seb's little tips might do you a world of good one of these days.'

I couldn't have spoken. I sat gazing at Sullivan, and heard Mr Johnson answer him with impatience. 'One of Seb's little tips might blow up the rest of Kingsley's one of these days, and Miss Helmann with it,' said my host, the genius, getting rid of his pudding. 'Right. Enough. Miss Helmann, can I take you downstairs for coffee?'

I didn't want coffee. I wanted to get away from Colonel Sullivan, but my conscience wouldn't let me. I knew there was mileage in him yet. I said, 'I don't mind, Mr Johnson. Everyone tries to pick up information. But if the Colonel's your friend, maybe he'd help change your mind.'

'His?' said Sullivan. 'Darlin', you're talking Naval Reserve. If they change their minds, they get bloody dents in them. Change his mind about what?'

'About this painting,' I said. 'It's really got to be finished, and it only needs two or three sittings. Sir Robert will follow him anywhere.'

Sullivan grinned. Sullivan said, 'Anywhere? Australia, for example? Where are you travelling to, my dear two-timing pal? I hope it's nowhere sordidly cheap.'

'It doesn't arise,' said Mr Johnson. His voice was dry, but he didn't seem unduly offended. 'I shan't have time for Sir Robert.'

'Won't you?' said Sullivan. He lay back. 'Come off it. I've known you take four clients a day.'

Mr Johnson said, 'I've *got* four clients a day.' He and Sullivan stared at one another.

Then Sullivan said, 'Well, go on, Leonardo. I take it you're painting a group. Or wait a minute – ' He stopped. He said, 'I know where you're going.'

'I doubt it,' said Mr Johnson. He said to me, 'Are you ready?'

I was, but I took a long time to collect my handbag and put down my napkin and begin to get to my feet. Ellwood Pymm watched me with interest. Seb Sullivan continued to gaze with a knowing expression at Johnson. He said, 'I heard you were off to join Dolly. So *that's* your game.'

'If you say so,' said Mr Johnson. 'These days, I'll paint anything. Now, do you think we could find our coffee in peace? Miss Helmann's to get back to her bomb site. If you're all that keen, I'll join you down at the bar in a minute.'

You could see some kind of chain reaction taking place in the Irishman's mind. He brightened. 'That's what I came over to tell you. I'm rallying,' said Colonel Sullivan. 'Not in the bar, on the Continent. Gerry's co-driving the Sunbeam.' He waved to his rear. I

21

had forgotten Gerry. Gerry, his head on the table, was sleeping. The Colonel said, 'That's how I knew about Essaouira.'

'Good,' said Mr Johnson. 'Out. Till later.'

The Colonel looked offended, then enlightenment spread over his bronzed and regular features. He said, 'You're not going there to paint, not a bit of it. You're slipping over there for some sleaze on the side, and I've gone and buggered it up. Will you accept me apologies?'

'Willingly,' said Mr Johnson. He offered no contradiction. 'Make them from the other side of the room. Goodbye, Sebastian.' He watched the booted figure stagger away in a miasma of alcohol. He said, 'I've heard of passive smoking, but passive drinking is something again. He's almost civilized, when he's sober.'

I said, 'He's very young to be a colonel.' Mr Pymm, after hesitating, was picking his way back to his table.

'He's very young for almost everything,' said Mr Johnson. 'He used to race cars for a living. You must, I'm afraid, have a very poor impression of this club. Perhaps you don't really want coffee.'

I didn't. I was choking with nervous tension, not to mention a new and unexpected anxiety arising from the conversation I'd just heard. With difficulty, I remembered the portrait. I said, 'The meal was lovely, but I'd better get back. Mr Johnson, what am I to say to the Chairman?'

'I don't know. I didn't go on the right courses,' said Mr Johnson regretfully. 'But I suppose you could say that you did your best, but I was ideologically resistant, and fobbed you off with my foul-mouthed companions.'

He produced a quirk that in another man might have come to term as a smile. 'In fact, I've enjoyed it: I hope you did. Tell him I listened to all you had to say, and that it isn't your fault I refused him. In fact, if he rings, I'll be happy to tell him myself. Will you do that?'

I said I would.

'And you are warm and fed, I hope, and fortified for the climb up the pioneer curve. You aren't married?' said Mr Johnson.

It seemed rather late to make that particular inquiry. 'No. I have a mother,' I said.

3

Most of what I'd said to Johnson Johnson was true: I wasn't into insider trading. I did, however, happen to know a lot more than I should of the inner strategy of Kingsley Conglomerates. I like to have my ear to the ground. And, as my mother frequently said, I wasn't going to understand policy management until I had seen policy management actually working.

The Saxon-Irish gasometer had mentioned the rumour about the company called MCG, and I knew it was more than a rumour. Kingsley's not only wanted to take them over, they'd already fluttered their eyelashes, and MCG hadn't undone a button. Which wasn't going to stop Sir Robert from trying again.

It isn't wise to let your boss know all you know: it leads to suspicions like Mr Johnson's. On the other hand, there was advice I could give that no one else in Kingsley's could; not even Val Dresden. I was tempted at first to go home, but I might find nothing at home but the answer-phone. So, after a few well chosen calls, I set off resolutely to confront the Chairman, and climb the greasy pole of creative success. The pole my stupid father made greasier.

Sir Robert was sprawled in his shirt-sleeves at the company flat, talking to his finance director and the company secretary, also jacketless. One or other of the three phones kept ringing. They all noticed I'd come, and soon realized that there were a number of phone calls I could deal with, and finally that they all wanted coffee.

Eventually the executives left to go back to base, currently a floor in a hotel where all the top management were installed, along with Property Management, Personnel and PR. Val, as I'd hoped, was busy shuttling between them. The telephones would be scream-ing there, too, and I trusted he was having a nice time, and had remembered to send a reassuring message to the Chairman's wife Charity who, as ever, had a horse racing somewhere.

Then Sir Robert was alone in the flat, and able to turn and say, 'Well. We still have a business, and part of the business is the Chairman's delightful public image. How did you get on with Johnson?'

I knew the mood he was in from the tone of his voice. I tried to convey absolute calm. There are three trusted methods.

I said, 'He's a difficult man, but I think you may just get your portrait. He's broken the contract, and not because of a client. He's going abroad for entirely personal reasons, and I'm quite sure, if you rang him, you could persuade him to resume sittings.'

'Dear me. Twist his arm?' said Sir Robert. He yawned sudden-ly, shaking his head. 'I don't know, Wendy, if it would really be worth it.'

'It would,' I said. 'And not only because of the picture. May I make a confession?'

He looked at me without pleasure. Then he slowly stretched up his arms and, bending them, nursed the back of his head in his palms. His striped shirt fitted smoothly into his waistband. 'I don't think I have the strength for a confession. But if you must, make it.'

I told him.

Halfway through, he lowered his arms. At the end, he picked up a pencil and played with it idly. He said, 'So you know quite a lot about our little dabble in hairdressing. Why are you telling me, Wendy?'

'Because it came up at the lunch with Mr Johnson,' I said. 'We met a Colonel Sullivan who works for Black & Holroyd. He knew MCG were in trouble. He asked if Kingsley's were interested.'

'And you said?' said Sir Robert. The pencil had come to rest.

'Nothing. But I thought you should know.'

'Yes,' said Sir Robert. 'I'm glad you told me. How did you learn what we were doing?'

I said, 'I read files. I probably shouldn't. But I love the firm. I want to help, if I can. That's why I told you.'

'I think I believe that,' said Sir Robert. 'In fact, I know I do.' He tossed down the pencil and sinking back, smiled at me ruefully, his legs outstretched, his hands loose on the arms of his chair. The neck of his shirt was unbuttoned. He said, 'It's my fault, really, isn't it, Wendy? I should have trusted you with all this long ago. And of course Colonel Sullivan's right: MCG are ideal for our purposes. The salons would give us a new market for all our washing and drying equipment. The firm is well run: the problems are recent, and all on its cosmetic side. But as it happens, that's enough to make its share-holders restive, and give us an opening. We want that new outlet.'

'And if you owned MCG, it would help service your debts?' I said cautiously. 'The loans you raised to set up Mr Morgan's division? In which case—'

'Yes?' said Sir Robert. His head had levelled, compressing his jaw.

'—I wondered if you meant to resume the talks secretly when you and Lady Kingsley went on vacation? Because if so, the portrait would make a very good cover.'

'The portrait?' said Sir Robert. He had forgotten about it. He said, 'Johnson. Yes. Where was he going?'

'He's going to Essaouira,' I said. 'It's a place on the Atlantic coast of Morocco. He isn't going to paint. He's meeting a woman called Dolly.'

'Who is she?' he said. He looked irritated rather than amused.

'I don't know. Apparently Mr Johnson has a number of lady friends. But if you and Lady Kingsley stayed where he could reach you, he could finish the painting, and you could court MCG without causing more rumours.'

I waited. He said, 'Yes. Yes, that would be possible.'

I knew it would. I knew how often he used these short trips to camouflage business. I said, 'There is something else. It might scupper it, or it might be a help.'

'Yes?' he said. He had pulled himself to the edge of his seat and picked up the pencil again.

I said, 'The PR man, Colonel Sullivan will be over there too. He goes about with a vintage car crowd, and every year they arrange a foreign rally. I've checked. This time it begins at Rabat, spends three

25

days partying at Marrakesh, and ends in the south after ten days. They don't touch Essaouira. Now, the Colonel's inquisitive. On the other hand, he knows you want Mr Johnson to finish the portrait, and the fact that you haven't altered your plans may well put him off the scent. I don't know.'

'I don't know either,' said my chairman. He pushed both hands through his hair, which stood up in spikes like a boy's. He said, 'You're an amazing girl, Wendy. What shall we do? I must think about it. I shall, of course, and you will hear what we decide. You can probably help us. Not that it's the only problem we have.'

'I know,' I said. 'The bomb. They haven't caught anyone yet?'

'Well,' said Sir Robert, 'the only person they've caught can't tell them anything. They've found one of the bastards in the wreckage. He must have blown himself up.'

I thought of us all standing there, and the silly conversation with Mr Morgan. I said, 'Who was he?'

'Nobody knows. They asked me to go and look at him. Not very nice.'

'No,' I said. I waited.

He said, 'The point is, they also asked me to open the safe and take our private papers away. I suppose they wanted to check they were in order.'

'And they weren't?' I said.

'Oh, they were,' said Sir Robert. 'But they weren't quite the way that I'd left them. I happened to know exactly how the papers were lying.'

He would. He'd spent the night in the office. Part of the night, anyway. I said, 'You mean the safe was secretly opened and closed by someone during the bomb scare? Then the same someone was caught by the explosion? Who could he have been?'

'The minion of somebody,' Sir Robert said. 'There are agents around who are prepared to spy for anyone who can pay them. Anyone with an interest in the stock market. A rival company. A potential target. Or the opposite: a raider sizing up possible victims. Maybe this attempt was the work of one man, and his information died with him. But maybe it didn't. We'll only know by watching the market.'

I wondered if he was right. I thought he probably was. I knew about the security measures the company took against hacking and tapping and listening. Every firm did the same.

He got up and stretched, opening his shoulders, and stood rubbing one sleeve with his hand. I stood also. He said, 'About the files. I'd have worried if it had been anyone else, and of course it wasn't in order. That said, you've turned in a very shrewd piece of work, and I can see there might be more you could do for us. We'll certainly talk about this again. But meantime, there's only one rule. I don't need to tell you, my dear. You don't discuss these things outside the company.'

No one has a voice, or a smile quite like his. I reassured him.

My mother *is* the company, practically speaking.

Presently he put me into a taxi, and I picked up the Volkswagen and drove myself home to Ealing to assuage the anxiety everyone assumed my mother was suffering. The trouble was, I had a much greater anxiety than she had. I had to tell her that I had told Sir Robert we knew all we knew.

She would kill me.

She didn't kill me at once, because she was smoking and feeding the printer. Because she was late with her thesis, the sitting-room wasn't full of the usual neighbours, and she contented herself with routine questions, at the pitch of a bull seal with asthma. Why had she to rely on the answer-phone to tell her her daughter was living? Did this firm not send a policeman to break the news to a worrying mother? And if her daughter was living, why did she not present herself on television, when the cameras were all over Kingsley's? All day, the neighbours had rapped on the door. Was I deformed, that I couldn't be photographed?

I supposed it would have made her day if I'd been photographed charred in the ruins. I explained, in a low scream, that I'd been at lunch with Johnson Johnson. I started on an introduction to the rest of my news, but what chance did I have against my mother's lungs, and my mother's professional daisy-wheel? I noticed, approaching the printer, that it was composing a speech on geriatrics and the demographic revolution. As I passed it, the machine buzzed along

27

backwards, concluding the author's case before stating it. My mother banged down a plate of frizzled lasagne and sat herself opposite, her arms as nearly crossed as she could get them. A cup of very strong Turkish tea stood before her. 'You tell me about Johnson,' she commanded.

I was happy to talk about painting. I described the rounds in the Great Portrait Battle, and she listened in relative silence. Her eyes, when not shut against cigarette smoke, are large, black and heavily ringed. On the printer, the speech rolled up a space, zapped a dot, delivered three lines, and rolled up another few inches of silence. At the end, she delivered her verdict. 'You did all right, Wendy. Shot him tight close-probe questions, fixed your aspiration level and stuck to it; thought out your Min and Max Positions and was all set to Walk Away and Come Back. But he outsmarted you. You didn't make him want the job.'

'He didn't want the money,' I said. 'After the Chairman...'

'He didn't need the money,' she said, banging the pages of *Who's Who* before her. 'Look at them schools. Ex-Navy. Yachting Clubs. You needed to find something else.'

I thought I had something else. I thought he really wanted to finish that portrait. I remembered something he'd asked me that I hadn't asked him. I said, 'Is he married?'

'You don't know?' my mother screamed. 'One wife, died years ago.'

'Years ago?' He hadn't looked as old as all that. I read the *Who's Who* upside down. He wasn't as old as all that. He was still in his thirties, if barely. And (not in *Who's Who*) he had a Balkan girlfriend and a mistress called Dolly. I started to say so. My mother said, 'Cut your losses. He was tricky. Your job is to—'

Which was as far as she got. The lights went out. The printer sighed and was silent. My mother yelled 'Mo!'

The answering voice was one I realized, madly, I recognized. It said, 'When did you last have these fucking wires checked?'

'Why, checked?' said my mother. 'They've never gone bust before. You said you was an electrician?'

Exuding annoyance, Mo Morgan came in, with a torch. His pigtail had come undone. He was in his shirt-sleeves with his tie off.

He looked like a hand-knotted Dacian rug. I said, 'Mother. This is Mr Morgan. One of Kingsley's executive directors.'

'Hell, I know that,' said Mrs Doris Helmann, my mother. 'Came to say you was all right, in case I heard of the corpse. Any body you knew? Not that Valentine Dresden?'

The note of hope in her voice would have smitten an ox. Mo Morgan said, 'Mrs Helmann, it wasn't. But the life or death of Val Dresden is the least of obstacles in your little girl's way. Do you have a 13-amp fuse?'

'Cupboard behind, third shelf up, fourth box from the left. You work in washing machines?' said my mother. She knew. She knew very well that he was an electronic designer who could write his own ticket, and did.

I could hear him scrabbling about, occasionally swearing. After a bit, all the lights came on, blinding us. The printer whined into life, and the speech rattled out its clinching argument; produced a space, and then two snaps which might have been someone's initials. The telephone rang. From two rooms away, Mo Morgan yelled, 'Your telephone's ringing!' My mother, sitting with her arms almost crossed, didn't get up. I went, and after some time, came back.

My mother and the newest director of Kingsley's were seated on either side of the fire, consuming strong Turkish tea and wet halva. I said, 'That was the Chairman.'

'He phones you at home?' my mother said. 'He carries your number?'

'He wanted to thank me,' I said. 'Mr Johnson has changed his mind. He thinks he can manage the portrait, if Sir Robert can come to Morocco.'

'Morocco?' said my mother distantly.

'Yes,' I said. 'Mr Johnson has a yacht there.' I couldn't understand it, myself. *Dolly* was the name of his yacht. He had planned a holiday on his yacht and Sir Robert had talked him into finishing his commission. It was good news, of course.

My mother said, 'There are yachts in the Sahara? I believe you. Arabs, camels, palm trees and yachts. And there is snow in the Sahara. I believe this Mr Morgan as well. He goes there every year.

Ice picks, crampons, to the desert. I believe you all. Hell freezes over.'

She was looking at Mr Morgan, who went on chewing halva, undisturbed. 'You never heard of the Atlas mountains?' he said. 'And all those beaches? Casablanca? Tangier? Agadir? Where's Johnson put this yacht of his?'

I didn't know Mr Morgan was going to Morocco. I didn't know what to say. It seemed to me that Morocco was getting too crowded. On the other hand, he was a director. 'The yacht's at Essaouira,' I said. 'Sir Robert will stay in Marrakesh, and Mr Johnson will come inland to paint him.'

'Two hours' journey each way. Bully for him,' said Mr Morgan. 'I'd rather climb Toubkal.'

'He climbs the same mountain every year,' said my mother, pouring tea. 'This shows little initiative. Is climbing bad for the bowels?'

'Terrible,' said Mr Morgan. His big-nosed face, surrounded by half-pleated hair, looked like that of an Afghan hound in a drizzle. 'And I don't eat properly either. You could send me off with some food.'

'A fine pressed ham, I make,' said my mother. 'Wendy will tell you. But what is the use? You drink like a haddock.'

'I have problems,' said Mr Morgan. His eye, roving, fell on the copies of the *FT* and *Forbes* and *Business Management*. He said, 'Someone's doing an MBA study course?'

'Wendy,' said my mother triumphantly. 'You have problems, you take them to Wendy. You lament the erosion of student competence in oral and written communication, analytical thinking and interpersonal development? I give you Wendy.'

'Thank you,' said Mr Morgan with moderate gratitude. He said to me, 'You into company tactics?'

'Is she?' said my mother. 'Look at this MCG mess? Have Kingsley's gone about that the wrong way or not?'

'Mother,' I said.

He didn't query the reference. He didn't look surprised or suspicious. 'They sure have,' he said promptly. 'What would you have done in their place?'

I sent out wild signals. My mother paid no attention. She said, 'You want to acquire a nice little company, do you woo the shareholders before you've made love to the management? Do you talk about asset-stripping – are you crazy? You get hold of their figures. You sort out their discounted cash-flow: profit before tax and interest; piles of non-cash little addbacks. You judge their discounted terminal value. Then you stalk them like a sweet cat: lots of good food and drink; high class invites; tickets to premieres, boxes with private toilets and unmarried ladies with titles. Yes,' said my mother. 'That Sir Robert Kingsley got written out of the will, and deserved to. But Morocco. Yes, if he could tempt that firm to talk in Morocco, he might have a second chance.'

Mr Morgan's large wistful eyes looked inquisitively from me to my mother. He said, 'You think they'll meet in Morocco?'

'Ask Wendy!' my mother said.

By sheer chance, today I knew more than a fully fledged Executive Director. I said, 'Sir Robert plans to meet their Finance Director in Marrakesh. At the Mamounia where he's staying I suppose.' I saw my mother's eyes on me. I lowered mine.

'Lucky MCG,' said Mr Morgan. 'Lucky everyone else. I usually sleep in a tent.'

'You haven't been invited?' said my mother, releasing my gaze rather thoughtfully. 'Never mind. You have my ham, Mr Morgan. I'll make you a goulash.'

'No one's going to be invited,' I said. 'Not from the Board. Sir Robert wants to keep it all very quiet.' I paused. I knew I couldn't keep it from my mother much longer. I said, 'All he needs is someone to take notes and send messages for him. He's asked me to go.'

'To Morocco?' said my mother.

'To the Mamounia?' said Mr Morgan. 'Will you send me a take-away?'

I knew my skin was red. 'To a nice hotel, but just a holiday one. It'll seem as if I'm on holiday. We mustn't look like a team.'

'You and Sir Robert a team?' said my mother, with fondness. It sounded like fondness. She knew that, for all this to happen, I had told the Chairman all that I knew.

'You and Sir Robert and Lady Kingsley a team?' said Mr Morgan. Compared to my mother's, the gleam in his eye was quite virginal. He said, 'You know, I'd like to go to those meetings? After all, I'm on holiday too. Would Sir Robert object?'

'You're on the Board,' said my mother. 'You get fresh bread where you stay?'

'Not as good as yours,' said Mr Morgan. My mother got up. He added, 'Wendy?'

'Yes?' I said. My mother was making up sandwiches for a director whose salary ran into six figures.

Mr Morgan was frowning. 'A nice girl like you, on your own. The Chairman needs to send someone with you. An aunt. A girl friend. Your mother.'

My mother looked up. So did I. He went on talking. Eventually he got to his feet, and she handed him the sandwiches and walked him to the door where she stood, buttoning him into his coat. She came back without him. She was glowing. 'There is a boy I would have been glad to call son! He said it himself. He said I should go with my child to Morocco. Tomorrow he speaks to Sir Robert. Tomorrow he tells us what happens, when he comes to deal with the plumbing.'

'Mother?' I said. 'You know who this Mo Morgan is? He is an inventor. He had the best OEM design company in Europe, and Kingsley's bought him over and presented him with an international division of his own, with all the money he needs for new processes. He has friends, colleagues, contacts, family. Why is he here fixing your bed-blanket?'

'Because you never have time, and he don't want to see an old woman fry,' my mother said, clearing the table. 'Family? None. He lives in a flat: a service company cleans him on Thursdays. Friends? He sees them all day: they all work with him. That little inventor, he wants nice food and a mother. You'd do better with him than this man who is blind with the yacht.'

'At the rate we're going,' I said, 'he's likelier to ask you than me to be the first Mrs Morgan. Don't be crazy. Mothering he may think he needs, but he's not deranged enough to need it in Ealing.' I'd been to look in the bedroom. He'd fixed her blanket, rewired her bedlamp, set the digital clock and propped up the bad leg of the bed. The gas cooker had recovered its pilots. On the wall, where he'd forgotten them, were three yellow stickers covered with drawings. I imagined they were ideas he'd had while he was working. I said, 'You don't suppose that after a hard day in the stratosphere he plans to relax by reclamping your ballcock?'

'So what does he want?' said my mother, sitting down and switching the television on to full volume. She didn't say a thing about blowing the gaffe to Sir Robert.

I realized she had dismissed the fact as now unimportant. I realized I was telling her nothing about Mr Morgan she hadn't already worked out. This is the trouble with our relationship. I said, 'He wants a personal line on Sir Robert?'

'Maybe,' said my mother.

I thought. 'He wants to pick up shopfloor gossip on Kingsley's?'

'Maybe,' said my mother.

'And he likes your cooking,' I said. 'But you're not damn well coming to Morocco. And Sir Robert won't let him in either.'

'Are you joking?' she said. 'Whatever that brainbox wants, Kingsley's can't afford not to give him.' Behind the smoke, I thought she was smirking.

She could smirk. The Chairman wasn't running a package tour. I could see myself in Morocco. And Sir Robert. And Charity. I could see Sir Robert gratefully clinching his deal while, from his boat at the seaside, Johnson Johnson blindly commuted to finish his portrait. But Mr Morgan and Mother I couldn't see.

My mother could. My mother stubbed out her broken-kneed gasper. 'Me and Morgan and Johnson. It'll happen, Wendy,' she said, coughing absently. 'Change gives Birth to Leaders. You pour us two nice Cockburn's Aged Tawnies while I fix us some travel insurance. Them Tuaregs is a shower of Vikings.'

4

I flew with my mother to Morocco. As she informed me (and the rest of the passengers), we travelled above France, Spain and either the Mediterranean or the Atlantic, since Morocco, being in the north-west corner of Africa, is bordered by both. As we landed, she noticed a camel. Although expecting a camel, she was rendered temporarily silent, and kept briefly in that condition by the fact that in Morocco the officials speak French. We had, as it turned out, a great deal to do with officials.

I prefer not to think of the two weeks before we left England. In malign and orderly succession, Mr Morgan came to fix the plumbing, announced he was leaving for Toubkal and departed, carrying a ham and a polythene bag full of goulash, both of which were confiscated, as we later learned, by the Customs. Mr Johnson withdrew from communication and presumably also set off, money no object, eventual destination Essaouira. Sir Robert, in a brief conversation, suggested that, at Kingsley's expense, I should take my sick mother on vacation to Marrakesh. The suggestion had been Mr Morgan's since, after all, I had just come back from one holiday. It was the first hint I'd been given that the Chairman and Chief Executive of MCG had actually agreed to meet Sir Robert privately in Marrakesh. And I, his EA, was the person chosen to go with my chairman. Not Paul or Frank or any of our top men whom everyone knew, but me, with my sick mother. That was the malign bit.

The news of my sick mother spread round our temporary office at Hendon, and was not entirely believed. My coffee was delivered unsugared by Trish, and amusing dialogues about Beau Geste and Ealing took place between her and Val Dresden. Jokes about Morocco Bound and Humphrey Bogart occurred to nearly everybody: I grew very tired of Sam's tune. I spent a lot of overtime with Paul Pettigrew, being made to memorize figures, and memorize ways of transmitting fresh figures. I learned more than I had ever known before about the affairs of the Kingsley company, and what was known of the affairs of our target. I didn't think of MCG as our victim. I thought of it as an enhancement and rescue operation. When I got home, I rehearsed it all with my mother.

Just before we flew out, Sir Robert called me in and spoke quite seriously about my hard work, and what a lot it meant to him personally. He added that, as I knew, Lady Kingsley would be in Morocco with him, and if I received a note from her, I was to respond to it. In this way, I should have an excuse to be present at meetings. Lady Kingsley was quite willing to do this but would not, of course, attend the meetings herself.

After that he paused and said, 'And there's something else you should know. The chap they found dead by the safe. Remember?'

I wondered what he was going to say. Up till then, the body had never been identified. Sir Robert said, 'I've just heard from the police. He wasn't killed by the bomb. He was shot before it went off. He'd been murdered.'

In our office. In the *boardroom*. Seminars don't cover this sort of thing. I said, 'Why?'

Sir Robert shook his head. 'Terrorists are unstable people. The police posit a quarrel, an accident.'

It seemed likelier to me that the murder had to do with the safe-breaking. I nearly said so. Then I realized what he was really telling me. The police didn't know that someone had been through our strategy files, because Sir Robert had said nothing about it.

I thought about it, although not for long. I could see that there were several good reasons for silence. A witch-hunt for a culprit might upset the precious MCG meeting. He wouldn't want a suggestion of leaks, which might shake Kingsley's position in the market. And he didn't have a compulsion to track down the villain for there was no sign that any use had been made of the figures. Perhaps because the man who meant to use them was murdered.

There was, of course, the matter of justice to be considered. But I thought the police could get on with it quite well without Sir Robert's help or mine at this juncture. I said, 'I understand. Well, thank you for telling me.'

Sir Robert said, 'There's a little more to it, Wendy, than that. Overseas, there may be other attempts to interfere with us. You've worked so unstintingly that I hesitate even to say it. But I have come to wonder if you wouldn't be safer staying in London.'

I said, 'No one else knows the figures. There isn't time.'

'I know enough to settle things broadly. I should go alone,' said Sir Robert. 'You shouldn't have to run into danger. And there's the risk to your mother as well.'

I looked at him in amazement. His own mother had worn out five husbands.

I said, 'My mother feels as I do. The bottom line is the company's welfare.'

'Wendy,' he said. 'If you really think so.' He looked a little shaken. Upper management, even today, don't always recognize how far executive training has come. I went home, and packed, and refrained from saying anything about murdered safe-breakers until our plane was irretrievably airborne. There is a bottom line. There is also a sub-bottom line; and I didn't want to explore it. My mother and I left, resolutely, for Morocco.

We didn't have long to wait for the unpleasantness. It began at Marrakesh, when a Customs search at the airport revealed a radio-cassette player we weren't supposed to have, plus thirty cassettes ranging from *Corporation Finance and Take-over Strategy* to *How to Turn Sales Mice into Tigers*. My mother had packed everything needed to send me up the corporate ladder and get us both jailed. The authorities were rigid with suspicion even before they got to her gas escape hood and her biomagnetic regulator bracelet and her packets and bottles against paratyphoid A and B, TB, gamma globulin (hepatitis and tetanus), and a sure fix for polio and malaria. When they penetrated to her anti-AIDS outfit at last, they just laid out the syringes, the needles, the sutures, and sent for the police. It was just as well I speak French.

After the British consul arrived, we were allowed away with a warning and sent off to our hotel with the courier, who had gone very silent and didn't have the intellectual equipment, anyway, to handle my mother on an expense-paid trip to the land of the Desert Song.

By that time, it was dark. It was nevertheless warm when we finally got into a taxi and began driving through flat, lightless land from the airport. When we suddenly stopped, I saw we had caught up with a lot of other taxis and cars and horse-drawn vehicles and donkeys and people, who all seemed to be waiting. My mother put down the window, letting in a hubbub of noise, and some flowery smells, and some less than flowery. I could see – I knew it by now – a police uniform. My mother said, 'Oh my God: they're going to body-search us again. You know I put my girdle back on inside out? You know that's bad luck?'

My mother's Strong Control girdles are shaped like beer barrels: they must have had to send for a cooper. I said, 'Why are we waiting?'

The driver turned round. He said, with reproof, 'The King passes.'

At the time I was surprised. I looked out of the window. I saw, far back on the road from the airport, a black line of US stretch limos, making their way to the city. The motorcade hummed slowly nearer. A posse of motorcycle outriders came up and passed, followed by two limousines, both totally darkened. Behind them was a third, lit from within, in which a figure leaned back, amiably waving. There followed a fourth, also lit, which contained men in European dress, conversing together.

One of them had black hair, a cracked nose and glasses. Also a tailored dark suit, with classic white shirt and neat tie. I wouldn't have recognized who it was, except that the cavalcade slowed, and I saw him quite clearly in profile.

Johnson Johnson, who might have a yacht on Essaouiria but who was not, it was clear, safely sharing it with a friend. J. Johnson who, bitchily, must have been telling the truth from the start. He had claimed to have a portrait commission, and it was all too clear now that he had. He must be painting the Moroccan royal family.

I tapped my mother's unyielding arm. I said, 'That's the man I had lunch with two weeks ago.'

'The King?' said my mother, with interest. She didn't mean it. Her eyes were fixed on the bifocal glasses.

'Just about,' I replied. I felt disturbed. I said, 'He must be staying in Marrakesh, same as we are. Now what do I do?'

My mother said, 'You're telling me that sharp item in the suit is your painter? What you do, Wendy, is zilch. He don't suspect that you're here: he don't need to find out that you're here. End of problem.'

'That is the King's cavalcade,' said the courier.

'Yes,' I said.

'You have a friend in the King's cavalcade?' said the courier caustically.

'Just one of the great English portrait painters,' said my mother, before I could kick her.

There was a silence inside the car, if not outside, where the traffic, blaring, was beginning to move again. The driver said, 'The papers say that in honour of the Anniversary of the Enthronement of the Monarch, the royal family are allowing themselves to be painted. By an English painter.'

My mother pulled her arm out of my grasp and said, 'Well, that's him. Johnson.'

'You know this Johnson?' said the courier cautiously. His veins had begun to lie down. 'Yet you do not stay at the Hotel Mamounia?'

Sir Robert and Lady Kingsley were about to stay at the Hotel Mamounia. For several hundred pounds per night less, my mother and I were staying at the Hotel Golden Sahara: poolside restaurant, sight-seeing facilities and a display of Berber dancing and horsemanship on Mondays and Thursdays. I said, 'Mr Johnson has a yacht at Essaouira.'

The driver and the courier digested this information.

'Maybe,' said the courier at last. 'But it is several hours from Marrakesh to the sea. He will have a suite in the Mamounia. It is the custom.'

My mother patted my hand. 'You think Sir Robert can't handle this? Of course he can. And what interest has Mr Johnson in City affairs? None. You told me.'

I knew all that. I was there when Mr Johnson brushed off Ellwood and Seb with a shovel. I was also there when Mr Johnson saw Kingsley's blow up, and was angry. I wondered if Mr Johnson would have recognized the corpse by the safe. I thought, next time I spoke to Sir Robert, I might mention it.

At the hotel, I found two messages waiting. One, from Lady Kingsley, asked in terrible writing if I would come to the Mamounia next day at four to take tea with her. The other, from Mr Morgan, was addressed to both my mother and me, and simply said he'd called and was sorry to miss us. I said to my mother, 'I thought he was climbing Toubkal?'

'He must have climbed it,' she said. 'We've got the morning free then tomorrow? I'm going to see some viable Arabs.'

Unfortunately, I knew what she meant by viable Arabs. She meant Omar Sharif, Peter O'Toole and the Desert Song version of Batman. I gave her the guide-books, to let her see they weren't in the index. I promised to take her to the Romantic Old Town in the morning, to inspect the Assembly of the Dead and the souks. I unpacked before going to bed. That is, I unpacked everything but the Kingsley MCG papers that Sir Robert had entrusted to me, which I left tidily locked in the suitcase. If there were villains about, they would be rifling Sir Robert's luggage, not mine. I thought I was in command of the situation.

Next morning I rose, shared a five-course breakfast (extra) delivered (extra) by room service at the behest of my mother, and bought the only newspaper remaining in the hotel shop. It was in French. Postponing the Assembly of the Dead by mutual agreement, I read it by the pool at the feet of my mother, who was bestowed on a lounger with her Sony Walkman clamped to her ears. The cassette-cover lay in her lap: *Overcome the Credibility-Robbers in your Speech-Patterns.* She said, 'Them foreigners over here: they play football, then?'

I followed her gaze to the newspaper photograph. I said, 'That's the Crown Prince of Morocco and the President of FIFA and the Wali of Casablanca attending the opening ceremony of the Africa Cup along with Mrs Daniel Oppenheim and her husband. Next to it is a picture of the opening of Horse Week at the Royal Polo Club:

the foreigners over here also ride horses. Next to that is the opening match for the Royal Tennis Trophy...'

'You don't need to push it,' said my mother. 'They're an energetic little kingdom, I grant you. But what about all them sad-looking little boys in that picture? Someone nicked all their tickets?'

'It's all in honour of the Festival of the Enthronement,' I said.

'Well, they don't look happy, poor little mites,' said my mother. She bent closer, and I laid a casual arm over the caption. A shadow fell on it. A once-heard transatlantic voice said, 'Miss Helmann? Miss Wendy Helmann, that's right?'

Pug-faced, crew-cut and peeling: Mr Ellwood Pymm of the Canadian press, last seen in Johnson's club, having lunch with the liquidized Seb. I dispatched an inclination to gape, frown or scream. I said, 'Mother?' This is—'

'Ellwood Pymm, the *Express* of Toronto,' he said. 'Met your lovely daughter in London. I can't believe it. You're on vacation?'

He was even wearing a tie. 'You're not?' I said.

'Comes with the job,' said Ellwood Pymm. 'Boys and girls imbibing the spirit of Morocco to take back to the wonderful listeners and readers in Canada. Six jerks from the press, and six radio. You like the hotel?'

'So far,' I said. 'How long are you staying?' With some adroitness, my mother had concealed the cassette case on the cloth-covered piste of her lap. Its successor lay on the grass: *Be Ready to do Handsprings to Resolve Each Perceived Service Failure.*

Ellwood Pymm said, 'I guess long enough to see all those monkeys perform in the square. We're off to the ski slopes this morning. What's the place called? Johnson said we mustn't miss it.'

'Johnson?' I said.

The skin on his nose was flaking off like pink coconut. He said, 'The guy who lunched you in London. He fixed a deal with Kingsley to finish the portrait. You know?'

'Of course,' I said. 'I didn't know Johnson had arrived. Does he ski?'

'Search me,' said Ellwood Pymm. 'But he says there's no snow and a great hotel that specializes in Canadian rye. He says if we play our cards right, we could stay there all day. Have you ever spent a day on mint tea?'

'Arabs drink it,' said my mother. 'And they saw off the French. What's Canadian rye done for you?'

'Well, it keeps the Scots out of the bars,' said Ellwood. 'I don't suppose, Mrs Helmann, that you'd allow your lovely daughter to come with us to Asni? She'd be perfectly safe. Twelve nice boys and girls, and a swimming pool, Johnson says.'

My mother gazed back at Ellwood Pymm, with her olive face and round, ringed black eyes and hand-painted head-scarves and three layers of King's Road ethnic caftan hefted over her girdle. Even in one hour in the shade, she had darkened like a Polaroid film. She said, 'I remember what it's like to be young and pretty and a bee round a honeypot. Of course, take Wendy away. Don't think of me. We was going to the Assembly of the Dead and the souks. Another day, we will go. If I am well enough.'

I looked at Ellwood Pymm and he looked at me. I said, 'I'm afraid...'

He had lovely American manners, when he was sober. He said, 'Mrs Helmann, of course I wouldn't deprive you of Wendy. Some day, if I may, I'll come and take you both out. Meanwhile, you look after yourselves. You go to the souks. You know the lingo?'

'No,' said my mother swiftly.

Ellwood Pymm said, 'Then why don't I lend you a phrase-book? You let me have it back when you're finished. Don't thank me. Have a wonderful day! This is an amazing old country.'

I took the handbook he was holding out. It was entitled *Making Arab Friends for Your Company* and meant that, whether I wished it or not, he and I were going to have another encounter. My mother looked emotionally grateful. I gave him a smile full of muted appreciation. He lifted the straw hat he had been carrying and prepared to move off. His eyes fell on my forgotten newspaper. 'Poor little sods,' he said, with compassion. 'Now that sure wouldn't occur in Toronto.'

To reach the walled town of Marrakesh, it is necessary to pass through the wide modern streets of the French city, built during the Protectorate and sunnily Western in style. Between the palms, the orange trees and the marigold beds of the boulevards, horse-drawn victorias full of red tourists are jammed between yellow taxis and droves of snarling Motobecane Vespas Super Bleu ridden by determined veiled women in glasses. At my request, our little taxi dropped us in the shopping quarter, where my mother, before meeting Omar Sharif, required to buy modern postcards.

The market in the Boulevard Mohammed V has not only postcards but a display of every kind of comestible likely to appeal to a middle-aged matron from Europe. My mother, who in motion resembles a baboushka on ball-bearings, rolled semaphoring from alley to alley, pausing before double-beds glaring with citrus fruit. She examined slopes of leeks, onions and radishes, passed by artichokes and wheeled round bins of walnuts and almonds, crates of straw-berries and hanks of asparagus tips like embroidery. She inspected a cave of flowers packed from floor to ceiling with roses, lilies, iris, freesias. She arrived at the fish and the meat, the brass, the copper, the handbags of sewn hide and bought twelve colourful postcards, arguing over the price. Someone said, 'You in trouble again?'

It was Executive Director Mo Morgan, in his pigtail and a terrible T-shirt, with a shopping-bag full of Kodak wallets over his forearm. My mother handed one postcard back. 'Now I need only eleven,' she said. 'You finally got bored, climbing that mountain?'

'Mrs Helmann,' he said. 'Nothing could be as fascinating as your company, but you're talking bullshit. Come along and have coffee, and I'll show you some pictures of Toubkal.'

I said, 'Mr Morgan. Does Sir Robert know you're here?'

He looked at me and smiled. His face was so narrow he had a mouth like a split in a pea-pod. He said, 'Don't worry, darling: I'm legitimate. I'm even attending the MCG meetings. At Sir Robert's request.'

My mother said, 'I said to Wendy. They won't refuse you nothing: not after that outlay. Will this coffee be safe?'

'Does it matter?' said Mr Morgan. 'You're supposed to be sick, in any case.'

Outside, it was hot. We passed the pharmacies and the jewellers, and the shops selling Dior and Chanel and really good briefcases with sensible handles which I wanted to go back and look at, for one of the things they don't teach you on executive courses is how to manage your handbag and briefcase while you get round the door of a toilet. We then arrived at a corner café with a bright orange canopy and many white and green tables and chairs, occupied by black-moustached gentlemen. Mr Morgan took us inside, and gave us coffee in tumblers. Then he and my mother discussed the time-switch on her washing machine while I watched the daily life of your ordinary Marrakesh citizen.

Stout, curly haired men passed in open-necked shirts and cable-knit sweaters. There were women in heelless slippers and trousers carrying white bundles about on their heads, and boys with trays of fine pastries, and women in short skirts and fishnet tights and high heels and handbags. There were robed mothers leading small children stuffed into bright padded tracksuits. There were men in white caps and smart djellabahs with briefcases; and babies carried by children, their bare toes appearing under their elbows. There were donkeys with panniers, and pedal-bikes with bunches of gladioli riding pillion, and invalid cars, and, stationary on the other side of the road, a powder-blue exquisite Sunbeam surrounded by dozens of people. I said, '*Look.*'

Mr Morgan spoke. He said, 'Now that's a nice pair of legs.'

He was just trying to needle me. I said, 'I saw that car in London. It belongs to Seb Sullivan.' I suddenly glimpsed, among the dark heads, a quantity of rippling sandy hair above a mighty pair of shoulders straining through a safari shirt. I said, 'There *is* Seb Sullivan.'

'Is that a surprise?' said my mother. 'He was to be in the vintage car rally. Three days of partying in Marrakesh. You told me.'

Mr Morgan was looking from my mother to me. He said, 'I'm missing something? Who is Seb Sullivan?'

'Public Relations,' I said. 'He and his co-driver Gerry Owen belong to Black & Holroyd, registered sneaks.' I had got up on my chair. I got down again suddenly. 'He's coming here. And look who's coming with him.' It was not Gerry Owen.

Mr Morgan climbed his chair as if it were Toubkal. He said, 'Hey, that's the painter guy Johnson. I promised to help with his blues.'

I pulled him down so fast he landed on the floor tiles. I said, 'I'm sorry, but I don't want him to see us. Can we get out the back?'

'I wouldn't recommend it,' said Kingsley's Executive Director. 'We could sit under the table, but the shoeshine boy'd flush us out in a moment. You mean if they see us, the share price will fall?'

'Roughly,' I said.

'I guess,' said Mo Morgan thoughtfully. 'Then we'd better stay where we are. Turn your chair. Mrs Helmann, tell us what they are doing?'

My mother sat with her robed knees apart, and gazed out to the pavement. She said, 'That's a beautiful man.'

'Johnson?' I said. I knew it wasn't. I didn't know that she had suddenly found the Red Shadow: in the world, you simply don't think of PR in these terms.

She said, 'You brought up in a zoo? Has a life in business destroyed your sense of symmetry? This Colonel Sullivan is sitting down with the painter. The painter is wearing a jersey from Oxfam.'

I had seen it. In place of the svelte suit for royal occasions, Mr Johnson had relapsed into bags and a ruinous sweater, with an open shirt collar which someone had ironed very nicely. His watch had cost, I reckoned, a tenth of a painting. Crossing the road with Seb Sullivan he had looked browner than I remembered. His hair hadn't been recently combed, and if once he had been at odds with Seb Sullivan, he was so no longer: they seemed extraordinarily relaxed, and even joking together. I wondered what about. I said, 'Never mind. Go on. What are they doing?'

My mother would have made a good boxing commentator. 'They've ordered beers and a coffee. They're talking. They've sent for a *Figaro*. That lovely man is having his boots shone.'

They had tried to shine Mr Morgan's shoes too, but he wore dirty sneakers. All the same, he had tossed them a coin, and they had thanked him, smiling. A child wandered in and performed a short, spinning dance, revolving briskly so that his cap-tassels whipped. Mr Morgan tipped him as well. I said, 'Do you always throw away money?'

'Here, I do,' said Mr Morgan. 'They think alms are important. Carry some cigarettes and a purseful of dirhams, and you'll be surprised at the difference. Also, a word of Arabic helps.'

I remembered Ellwood Pymm's book. I was about to mention it when an old woman tottered into the café and began to follow the beaten track to our table. Her face beneath the black drapes was creased like the top of my coffee, and she carried a polythene bag in one claw. I waited for my neighbourhood philanthropist to pull out his dirhams and fulfil the old country custom. Instead, she leaned over his shoulder and popped into her bag the wrapped sugar he'd left in his saucer. Then she moved on to the next table and did likewise.

Twisting round, we watched her get nearer Johnson and Sullivan. We watched her stop by their table, and Sullivan detain her with a hand on her arm, and Johnson rapidly unwrap a coarse block of sugar and taking his pen, write something on the sugar paper. Then he rewrapped it and gave it to her smiling. Along with it went a packet of dirhams. I saw them. We all saw them. Mo Morgan said, 'What was that?'

'I don't know,' I said. 'But I'd like to know.'

'Then you follow her,' said my mother. 'Or you are afraid. Or you have no sense of what is necessary.'

'Or we don't want to leave you, Mrs Helmann,' said Mr Morgan.

'In a café? In the French quarter of Marrakesh, with taxis passing before us? You are speaking to Wendy's mother,' my mother said.

I saw Mo Morgan hesitate. I didn't hesitate. I said, 'Come on. Leave her the bill. If we don't get out now, then we'll lose her.'

To his credit, he came. We slid out of the café. We mingled with the throng on the pavement, briefly held up by a heap of live turkeys. The small black figure hurried on, aiming south-west. I said, 'That's the way to the Assembly of the Dead and the souks.'

'So what is the Assembly of the Dead?' said Mo Morgan. He still carried his bag, in which were his holiday snapshots. He said, 'It is just the square Jemaa-el-Fna where all Morocco comes to do business, and then spends the afternoon and evening having a ball, if you will forgive the understatement. And what are the souks to a stout-hearted woman? They are crowded, that is true. It is easy to get lost in them: that is true also. But they are no more than the quarter of the old Arab markets, where things are made and sold and bartered. She'll exchange the sugar for something she needs.'

'She'll exchange that message for something she needs. Think!' I said urgently. 'Johnson is painting Sir Robert. Sir Robert is setting up an extremely sensitive deal. Seb Sullivan earns his living sussing out secrets. Don't you see it matters who Johnson is writing to?' As I spoke, I could hear myself panting. I was wearing a nice cotton dress and strap sandals, and my heels were blistering already.

'Of course I do,' said Mr Morgan. 'Mind you: it must be a very small message. Hardly room for more than a line and the Black Spot.'

'Room for an assignation,' I said. The woman, speeding up suddenly, staggered off round a corner. 'Or he could have slipped a note in his dirhams.'

'So he could,' said Mo Morgan. He spluttered. 'But who is he trying to meet, remembering there is such a thing as the telephone? The man who planted the bomb in the boardroom? The guy who killed the guy who planted the bomb in the boardroom? The Old Lady of Threadneedle Street in bed with Smith and Dow Jones, diabetics?' He calmed and said, 'OK. Let's see where she goes. And then I'll show you my pictures of Toubkal.'

Just then we wheeled round the corner. The pavement was empty. It took a moment to spot our old woman beside a line of parked bicycles. As we strolled hurriedly forward she unlocked one, hoisted herself into the saddle, and disappeared billowing into the traffic, her sugar-bag bumping the handlebars. Mo Morgan swore, for once, in genuine surprise. Then he hailed a small mustard taxi and shouted, '*Suivez la bicyclette!*' to the driver.

The driver stared at him. I hauled out Ellwood Pymm's American–Arabic phrase-book and opened it. The first column said:

My name is Joe.
You are very beautiful.
I love your eyes and your long hair.
Would you like some Pepsi-Cola?

There was nothing about following bicycles. Mo Morgan said patiently, in English, 'Follow that bicycle!' and with a grinding of gears, the taxi did.

5

It is quite a long way from the high life of the French café quarter to the Place Jemaa-el-Fna. We passed the Place du 16 novembre and the Place de la liberté and then suffered the full cultural shock of two wizened water-carriers in chenille tasselled hats who blocked the path of the taxi and tried to sell us some water. We had got to the Romantic Old Town. So had our quarry, who could be seen disappearing in the distance across a paved area the size of four football pitches filled with buses and tourists.

'The Assembly of the Dead,' said Mo Morgan. 'There they are, walking in file with their guide-books. Come on.' He peeled off notes for the driver and got out, spinning some coins in the air, which the water-carriers caught in their cups. Ahead, the old woman got off her bicycle, handed it to a child who seemed to be waiting, and disappeared behind hedges of tourists. We followed.

It was extremely hot. We were cursed in French, German and Japanese and occasionally in French. We ran into, and out of, a raft of professional beggars. We attracted the attention of the proprietors of a row of ramshackle kiosks selling Cartier watches, Adidas sneakers and Lacoste sports gear. We trotted round a circle of rapt men and boys listening to a turbaned story-teller who had learned his trade in Movietone News. We passed another rapt audience around a white-bearded man sitting with one large, bare clean foot round the back of his neck. As we went by, he shot his second foot straight in the air, then crossed it over the other like scissors. Under his rucked-up shirt he wore snow-white neatly pressed trousers. Behind him, to the sound of a drum, a man was charming a snake under a canopy, his motor bike parked just behind him.

There was a circle round two slapstick comedians knocking each other out with plastic mineral bottles, and a body-building stall, and a box of monkeys, and a man selling teeth. We passed the tea-break facility, where nameless stews simmered over charcoal and market punters in robes sat in rows sucking up soups. There were Europeans on one of the benches, playing a board game with several Arabs amid a litter of shish-kebab sticks and orange juice. Among them I saw a couple of women. One of them had bright orange hair and dark glasses under a tall woollen hat clearly bought off a water-carrier. Before I could so much as mention it, Mr Morgan said, 'Oh ho.'

Our old lady had come to a halt in one of the few uncrowded spots in the square. We stopped, concealed by the throng, and stood watching her. She sank to her knees.

She wasn't praying. She was consulting a man sitting cross-legged on a carpet with some lined paper before him. Before him also was a bottle, a ruler, some pens and two unlit candles. Crouching before him she spoke, and he answered. More than that we couldn't see. Then she scrambled to her feet, and before we could move, darted across the square at full speed and vanished.

This time, she had gone for good. We wasted ten minutes winding round further lines of shuffling tourists, and Mr Morgan even took himself into a café in case, he said, she had gone to collect some more sugar. When he didn't come out at once I went in myself, and found him in a room with eighty Moroccans watching football on TV. It turned out to be another tense game in the Africa Cup, with the Elephants of the Ivory Coast teamed against the Hearts of Oak players from Accra. Although the other viewers complained, Mr Morgan allowed himself to be extracted quite peacefully, announcing, *'Je donne un lèger avantage aux Elephants.* Haven't you found her, then?'

I hadn't, but I'd had a bright idea. I said, 'That man she stopped and spoke to. Let's ask him.'

'Using your Arabic phrase-book?' said Mr Morgan. He had delayed for the purpose of trying on round knitted hats.

'Yes, using my phrase-book,' I said. I had the page open already. 'Did you hear that man say *Assalamou AlaiKom* to you? There it is. *"Assalamou AlaiKom,* Hi".'

'He said "Hi"?' said Mo Morgan. He bought the cap, and the man said 'Hi' in Arabic again, and Mo said it back. He said, 'It figures. All Western culture comes from the Arabs, they say. Let's try your man on the ground.' We turned back.

I thought at first that the man with the candles had gone, but he was merely surrounded by tourists. A guide with an umbrella was explaining that educated natives like this earned their living as scribes, writing letters for the illiterate. I said, 'Listen. That's what he was doing!'

'Writing?' said Mr Morgan. Several tourists hissed to us to shut up.

'No. *Reading,* of course. Whatever Mr Johnson had written, she couldn't read it. Such as, an address.'

Phrases of German annoyance floated over our heads. Mo Morgan said, 'Now that I call brainy. Let's ask him.' And he pushed his way forward and said, 'Hi!' in Arabic. Then we tried to ask, in French and Arabic, what we wanted to know.

We were not popular. The guide wanted to complete his dissertation. The tourists wanted to hear him and take photographs. The scribe wanted to please everybody and get paid in full for doing so. Someone seized Mr Morgan by the pigtail, and he turned round and swung a fast punch, impeded by his knitted cap, which had been levered over his eyes. The crowd swayed, and someone kicked over the ink. The scribe wailed, and three burly men pushed their way into the circle and stood behind him glaring, as if about to begin the Polovtsian Dances. A voice in beautiful German said, 'Ladies and gentlemen, behind you the acrobats are about to arrive to be photographed. Please come this way.'

Even the guide with the umbrella looked bemused, and gradually everyone turned and began moving off in the opposite direction. The German speaker, addressing himself to the three burly gentlemen, said, 'Forgive me, but I think a performance is expected. Be assured. Your friend will come to no harm.'

I was amazed. The three men bent and spoke to the scribe who was lifting dripping papers and moaning. We waved them irritably away. The three acrobats left. The scribe was left alone with me, Mo Morgan and the German speaker, who proved to be a brown, curly haired man in dark glasses wearing a genuine Lacoste T-shirt, baggy shorts and sneakers as dirty as Mr Morgan's. I had seen him before. He was one of the row of Europeans who had been sitting eating along with the traders. He said, in English as beautiful as his German, 'Hallo. I hope you don't mind. But that sort of nonsense can develop quite quickly. Can I help you? I speak a spot of Arabic and some French.'

Mo Morgan was quicker than I was. He said, 'Brother, you can help me that way any time. Let me ask this fellow something, and then I'll stand you a drink.'

'Perhaps I can ask him?' said the man. I had thought he was German, but now I wasn't so sure. 'What do you want to know?

I wouldn't have told him, but Mr Morgan did. He said, 'We're trying to contact a friend. It's a long story, but he gave his address to an Arab lady, and a few minutes ago, we think that she asked this man to read it. If he could recall what it was, we could go there.'

'No problem,' said our rescuer fluently. He spoke fast to the scribe who, muttering, was shaking out several stained letters. At the same time, our chevalier laid on the ground a small but opulent stack of old dirhams. The scribe ceased muttering and spoke, glancing with pleasure at the donor and hatred at us. Our rescuer turned.

'You're right. Someone asked him to decipher an address, and he's written it down. There it is. Do you know how to reach it?'

We didn't. Mr Morgan said, 'We'll find out, don't worry. Meanwhile, I owe you.' He had pulled out some money, and I let him.

The other man said, 'Not a bit of it. Look. It's not far. I'll take you. We can have a drink some other time.' He smiled and said, 'You're English too? My name is Rolly. Here with some chums, trying not to make a film.'

'Wendy and Mo,' Mo Morgan said. 'I'm climbing, she's here with her mother. *Not* making a film?' We were walking to the far end of the square.

'Actually, we are making a film, at Ouarzazate. In the south. If you climb, you probably know it. Nice cheap film studios; snow; mountains; sand. It needs scenes in Marrakesh and the director's going spare, trying to avoid the dyed wool and the chimps and the snake-charmers. Not my headache: I'm just an accountant. Here's your place.'

There were several openings off the end of the square, some of them wider than others. He had turned into a street lined with low shops and houses which opened into a small market place, its centre laid with blue plastic and heaped with ordinary things like babies' bootees and small children's clothing. He approached a pair of closed doors and banged on them. After a while, Mo Morgan banged too, and they both went round the back and returned.

If this was where the old woman had brought the sugar-lump message, then she hadn't been able to deliver it. The place was closed. And there was no sign of the old woman anywhere. Rolly, ever courteous said, 'Your friend isn't there. I'm so sorry. But at least, now you can come back another time. Look. It's really bloody hot by this time. We've got an awful sort of lodging nearby. Why don't you come and have a drink there? We'll send out for the odd bun if you're hungry. Or Rita's always got food in the house.'

'Your wife?' I asked politely. He wasn't young, but he had the sort of confident style that Val Dresden would give up his locket for.

'Rita? I wish she was. No,' he said. 'Make-up technician by trade, and a hanger-on otherwise like myself. Natural den-mother to a film-crew of hopeless eccentrics. Do come. It's just along here.'

We had no reason to worry. We went.

For quite a while the alley remained sunny and open, although the nature of the trading had altered. We passed a row of lacquered sheeps' heads, the flies buzzing about their taut skulls. Then presently, our path narrowed and darkened: the first manifestation of the souks. Here, the crowds were all Arab, and the cubicles lining our passage were workshops. Deep in their recesses men smoked and drank tea and played cards, worked and talked and glanced at us as we passed. There were smells of leather and sawdust and cannabis. A boy, sitting outside his shop, turned the leg of a chair with the help of his hands and his toes; a veiled woman took a jar from a fountain and hurried away; the open door of a mosque, heavy with stucco, afforded a glimpse of prostrate forms and heavy carpets.

A drum-beat, half-heard under the noise became insistent and threatening. From round the next bend in the souk approached a slow procession of men, women and children, their faces impassive. They carried, glinting with spangles, life-sized figures on poles. The figures were headless: drooping ferns hung from the neck sockets. The man called Rolly held us back with his arm as the crocodile made its way past, its drums beating. From inside the shop at our backs came a tinny, thunderous roar. The Africa Cup was flickering on.

I didn't like it. I didn't like not knowing what was real, and what was being done for the tourists. I looked at Mr Morgan for reassurance and saw that he, too, had lost his small smile. Then he saw me and winked, and tucked my hand into his arm and kept it there when we began moving again. He was short, but he had a lot of big muscles. Then Rolly said, 'So here's our little inglenook. Sorry about the surroundings: they drove a souk right past the front door. Do come in.'

The alley had widened. Instead of unbroken shops and ramshackle dwellings, a high wall ran along on our right. In its centre was a small postern, and a pair of closed double doors wide enough to admit a film van, or a fairly large car. Our new acquaintance unlocked the small door and, stepping through, revealed a fair-sized paved patio with a fountain playing drunkenly in the centre. I hesitated, but Mr Morgan, nodding, persuaded me through. While we looked about, the man called Rolly shut and locked the small door behind us. Then he turned, lifted his head, and yelled, 'Rita!'

The inglenook surrounded three sides of the patio and rose to two storeys, and in some places to three. At middle-floor height ran a wooden gallery, reached by a set of narrow carved steps. Behind the pillars that upheld the second storey were handsome peeling grilled windows and a few open-leaved doors leading to a variety of unspecified apartments. Loud rock music poured from one of the windows. As we watched, an orange head poked from another. It belonged, unsurprisingly, to one of the ladies from the Place Jemaa board-game and shish-kebab party. Instead of dark glasses, she now wore a pair of enormous rose-coloured spectacles, pushed to the end of her nose. Our escort addressed her. 'Two nice English guests with a thirst. What's on offer?'

'Depends how English they are,' she said shortly. She disappeared.

The man Rolly slapped his own forehead and grinned at us. 'She's from Scotland. Don't hold it against her.'

My mother's cassettes came into my mental focus. Coping with a Blank Mind might have helped, had I been going to speak. Mo Morgan disentangled his arm and, ceasing to stare, trained his attention on Rolly. He said, 'Man, we ought to be treating you, not the other way round. Have you rented this place?'

'Knowing him,' said the voice of Rita, 'He probably won it in a cheap carpet speculation. Didn't I see you in the square?'

She stood in the door, surveying us. She was short and made like a gymnast, her legs encased in brilliant gauchos. I had put her down as a girl but close to, in the sunshine, she looked nearer Rolly's age than my own. Beneath her touched-up natural red hair, her make-up was bold verging on the outrageous. She suddenly grinned. 'They're English,' she said. 'Got in trouble?'

'Not their fault,' said the man Rolly. 'Mo is in Morocco to climb, and Wendy is here with her mother. They're thirsty.'

'So you said,' said the small orange lady. 'Well, come in. The chaps are looking at rushes: we'll get some peace for a while. What are you climbing?'

The kitchen was tiled and cool, with an ancient refrigerator in one corner from which she produced plates of jellied meat and a bowl of cold soup and some pastries. She cut up French bread, the rings on all eight fingers sparkling. Mr Morgan said, 'But you've already eaten. We mustn't trouble you.' In that company, he looked nearly normal.

The woman said, 'We only go to the square to meet pals and fleece them. Watch Rolly. He'll have two dinners any day. What, then?' She threw back the question again. She had brought out bottles of beer and a jug of orange juice, and dropped cutlery on to the table. Mr Morgan didn't reply, but as we sat, he leaned over and put his plastic bag on the table before her. She laid down plates and glasses and sitting down, pulled the bag over and opened it. Inside were all the Kodak wallets. She pushed her spectacles up, picked out one and took out the photographs.

We ate, served by Rolly, while she looked at them. When she'd finished the pack, she rapped Rolly's arm and held them out to him. Then she shifted her gaze to Mr Morgan. 'You're not in films?'

With a face like a lupin, Mo Morgan was not, I should have thought, God's most obvious gift to the cinema. He hesitated and said, 'No.' Beneath it, you could tell he was flattered.

The man Rolly in his turn was leafing through photographs. He said, 'By God.' After a while, since I hadn't said anything, he turned and said, 'Have you seen these?' And when I shook my head, 'Then have a look. They're not your ordinary snaps.' He held one towards Mr Morgan. 'Where the hell were you when you took that shot?'

On Toubkal. I could have told him. I took the snaps, which turned out to be studies of rock, sky and snow, taken from pinnacles. I like pictures of people, myself, but I could see that these were of a nice colour, and sometimes consisted of very long views, which meant he must have climbed quite high to take them. I said, 'Very nice.'

The man Rolly took them from me gently and then waited while the orange lady looked through the next lot. When he got them he muttered, 'Tizrag. The Tizi n'Ouadi.' He broke off and said, 'You did the east face of Anrehemer in March?'

'Do you know it?' said Mr Morgan. 'It was a bit tricky. Nice descent.'

'No. I don't know it,' said our rescuer. 'But I know someone who did it once in late winter. He said he'd only done three things worse in those conditions.'

'Do I know him?' said Mr Morgan.

It was the woman Rita who said, 'No.' She said it shortly, as when she had said it depended how English we were. The man Rolly glanced at her, as if in warning. Then they laid down the pictures, and got Mo Morgan to talk, without excluding me. After that they answered questions about the film, an epic which had run through three different directors, and about which the man Rolly was sardonic and the cooking-lady full of definite views. They appeared to get on well together, although she told him off a few times and we all helped with the washing-up at the end. For an accountant, I thought he was very patient.

Just before we took our leave, our host asked Mr Morgan's permission to tip the photos all out on the table and look at them again. With the woman, he pored over them. They had already asked all about his lenses and stops. The cooking-woman said, 'If you want to try your hand at cinefilm, give Rolly a call. He could put you in touch with a studio. Or you should publish.' She put them back in the bag. 'Waste of time to put those in a drawer.'

Mr Morgan said, 'I know, but I've got other interests. If I get the sack, I'll come back and ask you. It was a great lunch. I don't know how to thank you.'

'Oh, we'll see you around,' said the accountant. He saw us to the door, yelling back to the woman to stay until he returned. She retorted, and he turned to us, grinning. 'Let her out once alone, and she'd never find her way back until Christmas. But she's a bloody good cook. So. You'll get to the square by going through there, and you'll find plenty of taxis. If you want to call in again, here's my card, with this address added over it. I hope you track down your friend?'

'What?' said Mr Morgan. He was looking at the card.

'The one whose address you had lost. I hope you find him in. Or her. Or whatever. Nice to meet you,' said Rolly, and shut the door.

We stood being pushed about in the souk, and Mo Morgan didn't move. I said, 'What's wrong?'

He didn't say anything. He just held out the card. On one side, written in pencil, was the address of the house we'd just left. Printed on the other side was a London address under Rolly's full name: *Roland G. Reed, BA, MA, LB, Financial Director.* And below that was the name of his employer, which was the MCG Company, plc. Or otherwise, the firm we had come to take over.

I didn't speak. Morgan said, 'We've been bloody hijacked.'

Roland Reed, Financial Director. He'd washed up the dishes. I said, 'He can't be. He's helping someone work on a film.'

'A hobby, no doubt,' said Mo Morgan. 'The same line I was shooting, come to think of it. *I take good pictures, but I have bigger concerns than all that crap, buster.*' His eyes, for the first time since I'd known him, were unfriendly.

I said, 'He didn't know who we were.'

'The hell he didn't,' said Sir Robert's Executive Director. 'That's the man Sir Robert had the first meeting with, the one that failed. That's the man he's come to Morocco to meet. He picked us up deliberately.'

I said, 'How could he know who we were?'

'How? Johnson and Sullivan,' Mr Morgan said. 'They sent the woman and fooled us into following her. They knew MCG hung out in the Place.'

I thought he was wrong. The café had been dark. I was sure neither Johnson nor Sullivan had seen us. And why should Johnson or Sullivan interfere with the affairs of Kingsley Conglomerates? Out of mischief?

I said, 'But if Roland Reed knew who we were, why give us his card?'

Mr Morgan's eyes, nearly black, were looking into space. Then he shrugged. 'One upmanship? We'll meet him – when is it? – at this afternoon's so-called tea party. He knew we'd know soon enough who he was. Maybe he wants us to worry about Johnson and Sullivan. Or it has to be Sullivan. You said Sullivan had his eyes on MCG. He could cause trouble.'

I looked at him. When he'd wired my mother's house, I'd thought he wasn't director material. I said, 'There isn't much time.'

'No,' he said. He stirred. 'You're right. Let's get to the square. You go back and see your mother's safely home from the café. I'd better get to Sir Robert.'

I said, 'What will you tell him?'

And Mo Morgan said, 'What we've just said. We don't know any more than that meantime. But I think you need to watch out. Something's happening, and it could be a bastard.' He pulled out a notebook and scribbled in it. He had big-jointed iron-hard fingers. He said, 'That's where I'm staying. Don't pass it on, there's an angel; I don't want Sir Robert on top of me. It's a small hotel that caters for climbers. I have friends there if you run into trouble. All right, Wendy?'

'All right,' I said. I was relieved. I felt satisfied. He was really Upper Management all the time.

*

56

There is no more expensive hotel in Morocco than the Hotel Mamounia, Marrakesh, where, under guise of a four o'clock tea party, the Chairman of Kingsley Conglomerates, his self-invited Electronics Director and I were to meet and persuade another company towards a friendly take-over.

Churchill stayed in the Mamounia, which adheres to the walls of the old city of Marrakesh. It is built like a large Moorish palace, full of fountains and tiles, carved stucco work and terrazzi and flowers. There are seventeen acres of tropical gardens, fifteen suites and nearly two hundred bedrooms.

I was glad I had left my mother behind at the Hotel Golden Sahara with my Arab phrase-book and Ellwood Pymm, whose party had just returned from a successful visit to the hotel with the Canadian rye, thus avoiding a handball final, an art exhibition, and a reception held for the competitors in the Grand Rally of the Voitures de Collection, 1900–1940, among whom were Colonel Sebastian Sullivan and his co-driver Gerry.

The present whereabouts of Johnson Johnson was not mentioned, but at the rate the Anniversary of the Enthronement of the Monarch was generating activities, I wouldn't have been surprised to hear of him anywhere, except that I trusted it wouldn't be at the Hotel Mamounia at four p.m. that afternoon.

Because of Ellwood Pymm, I'd been able to tell my mother nothing except that I'd had a nice time in the Romantic Old City. It was Ellwood Pymm who said, 'With a boyfriend! Did I hear all about that! Was I jealous? How come you make a boyfriend so quickly?'

It sounded innocent enough, but he was a journalist, and he had friends in Wall Street, I remembered. I said, 'I met someone I once knew in London. Where are you going tomorrow?'

Ellwood Pymm fished out his programme. 'There's a choice. Swimming. Polo. The Africa Cup. Lecture on the Pathology of the Knee. Le Gala International de Boxe. The Africa Cup.'

I said, 'I saw it on TV.'

'Try and miss it,' said Ellwood Pymm. 'Half their trainers come from English football clubs. The stands are full of coaches talking African dialects full of Liverpool swear words. Jimmy Auld's daughter is here.'

My mother said, 'We know that. There was that photograph in your paper this morning, Wendy. Mrs Daniel Oppenheim and her husband.'

I said, 'Mrs Daniel Oppenheim is the daughter of a football coach?'

'It happens,' said Ellwood Pymm. 'I must say the news nose became twitchy when I saw the Oppenheims had also flocked to Morocco. But there you are. The God Football. Nothing sinister.'

I said nothing. I hoped my ignorance would count as a plus. I hoped my face wasn't showing my feelings. For Mr Daniel Oppenheim, finance consultant, had dined with Sir Robert – and Johnson – the night before the explosion. And I knew, and perhaps Ellwood Pymm also did, that Daniel Oppenheim, before he set up for himself, had headed the prestigious firm of corporate finance experts who advised the Board of Kingsley Conglomerates.

I put my briefcase into a shopping-bag, and walked into the marble halls of the Mamounia. I wandered up steps and through arches and past a long, mirrored pool and into a Moorish kiosk surrounded by shops with six-foot malachite vases in the window. I trod on carpets, and past deep-cushioned chairs round a fireplace. A boy in a red tarbush and a white high-collared tunic came past ringing a bell and waving a board about as if it were a painting. I thought it was time to go up. I asked for Sir Robert's suite, and Lady Kingsley came down to meet me.

Sir Robert is a big man, and she was a big woman to match. Like all his wives, she was an excellent hostess with lots of money, lots of energy and several strong alternative interests, including the opposite sex. All of this was not much of a secret, but neither of them ever suffered from nasty gossip because they were popular, and even their philandering seemed somehow healthy. Also, Charity was a very good horsewoman, who worked her own stables, bred hounds and won competitions in which she quite often risked her neck. She had her own circle of friends, and kept a good business table for her husband. Now she said, 'My dear Wendy: how delightful to see you! How is your mother? Come upstairs and tell me all about it. How good of you to leave her for a little!'

She led me to the lift, attracting quite a lot of attention in a tailored safari suit and a lot of pearls and gold chains. She never wore make-up, and her hair was greying and her face like fine leather, but her features were marvellous. She had never called me Wendy before, but of course it was all for the cause. The suite, when we came to it, was full of silk rugs and marble, and had a balcony that looked over the pool. The pool had a stand of palm trees in the middle. Sir Robert rose and said, 'Wendy! How kind of you to come!'

He was dressed formally, too, in a navy club blazer and flannels, which flattered his weight. His hair was stuck down and his eyes didn't quite match his smile. Behind him sat Mr Morgan, now in a short-sleeved shirt and old shorts and passable shoes. A lump of hair had fallen over his face: it moved when he lifted his brows at me. The look said Problems, Problems, and I believed him. Then Lady Kingsley said, 'Well, that's it, then? I'd better leave you. How *is* your mother, Miss Helmann? Well, I hope.'

'Very well, thank you,' I said. I had spent a lot on a nice cotton suit with a strapless top under it. I could be an Executive Secretary or someone taking tea at the Mamounia or even someone sunbathing at the Mamounia, if things had been different. But with Mr Roland G. Reed on the way, no one knew what to expect.

Lady Kingsley departed gracefully to what appeared to be a private dining-room, where I could see an easel set up on the balcony. It reminded me of something, and I resolutely dismissed it. The door closed behind her and Sir Robert said, 'Since tea is here, we might as well have it. Mr Reed will be here in five minutes. Wendy, the papers?'

I gave them to him, along with two curling fax messages already decoded. He had others, I saw, on a table, including an envelope that must have come from London by courier. We hadn't risked bringing Paul Pettigrew, but he was in touch with our accountant all right. He didn't waste time, either, on preliminaries. 'Wendy, today we re-open the talk if possible in general terms, without troubling too much about figures. Mr Morgan has agreed to leave most of the running to me. You'll be introduced simply as my confidential secretary. He may not want formal notes taken. In that case, memorize what you can.'

I nodded. In my dispatch-case was a small recording machine, ready to activate. I hoped Mr Morgan wouldn't hear it. If MCG agreed to contemplate an offer from Kingsley's, then Mr Morgan's innocence, his talent and his eccentricity might, I thought, be one of our assets. Or even his photographs. I said, 'Mr Morgan told you what happened this morning?'

Sir Robert glanced at his Board member, and then at me. 'Yes. There is something about that I have to tell you both. I think it should wait until after the meeting. Meanwhile, from what you say, there seems to be some chance that your meeting with Reed was coincidence. Since he treats it that way, then we should. I gather that, when you met, there was no discussion of company business?'

Mo Morgan said, 'No, I told you. They didn't ask what we did, and we didn't even mention our surnames.'

Sir Robert said, 'Then I think you should put it all down to sheer chance. For the moment.'

I didn't argue, but I thought it preposterous. It didn't explain what Johnson and Sullivan thought they were doing, sending a message to a house that was closed. I hoped there would be time to return to the puzzle. Sir Robert said, 'Anyhow, there is nothing in it to worry you, Wendy. You simply tell him the truth: that you realized for the first time who he was when you read the name on his card. It is what Reed himself says that will interest me.'

He turned and finding a newspaper on his chair, flung it out of the way and sat down. He was less cool than he seemed, and I was sorry the news I had brought couldn't wait. I said quickly, 'Sir Robert, you know there is a party of Canadian journalists in town? Ellwood Pymm is among them. The man I met lunching with Colonel Sullivan. The special festival seems to have brought them.'

'Another coincidence?' said Mr Morgan. There was a little piano. He wandered over and sat down before it, his brown knees apart. He looked at Sir Robert, and I saw Sir Robert's lips tighten. I had meant to tell, too, about Daniel Oppenheim, but suddenly thought better of it. There is a limit. As Cassandra found, there is a limit.

Then the door opened, and Mr Roland Reed was announced and walked in, with our eyes riveted upon him.

Being of the same stamp as Sir Robert rather than that of Mo Morgan, he had changed out of shorts and into a shirt and tie with expensive pants in fine, pale material. His briefcase and shoes were Italian, his watch plain, and strapped with black leather. His curly brown hair had been brushed, and his smooth brown face wore a look of pleased inquiry. His gaze travelled round us and back to the Chairman. He said, 'Sir Robert. I'm glad to see you. I'm even more puzzled. These are friends of yours?'

Sir Robert shook his hand, smiling. 'I knew it was a small world, but I'd never have guessed this would happen. Do you realize how they felt, when they read your card and saw who you were? Let me introduce Mr Morgan, one of the most prestigious Executive Directors of Kingsley's. And this is Wendy Helmann, my invaluable Executive Secretary. If I'd known you were going to feed them, I should have invited myself to the banquet. Please sit. We are very happy to see you.'

He indicated a place on the settee, and Morgan and I reseated ourselves. Mr Reed remained standing. He said, 'If they'd intro-duced themselves, I should have telephoned you like a shot. How extraordinary.' He stared at Sir Robert.

Sir Robert said, 'Well, you were amazingly generous, both with your help and your hospitality. I long to hear about this film you are making. Do please sit down.'

Roland Reed said, 'You really didn't know who I was?' Still smiling, he was speaking to Morgan.

I sat on the edge of my seat. I could see Sir Robert's mouth tighten. Mo Morgan said, 'Brother, if I'd known who you were I'd have sold you Kingsley's. Come on and sit down. They think you think there's a conspiracy.'

Quite unexpectedly, the other man laughed. He said, 'I don't think I'd have bought it. No. It's all right, of course. Delighted. Let's get down to business. By the way, I thought you wouldn't mind if I brought along a second opinion. A two-man team like your own, as it were.'

'Please!' said Sir Robert. His expression had eased. As he spoke, someone tapped on the door. To the uniformed man who came in, he nodded acceptance. The uniformed man stood aside, looking behind him. He was smothering a twitch under his tarbush.

Roland Reed said, 'I'm sorry she's late. She always loses –' and stopped. He was smiling as well, for good reason. Through the door marched the orange-haired den-mother, still attired in the hat and the gauchos. She stopped level with Roland Reed's chest, and trained her gaze on his face.

'You said they'd lead me all the way from the door, and did they hell? I've been to the casino, the shops and the Gents. Next time, *you* make the bloody dinner.' She turned to Sir Robert. 'Sir Robert? Mo? And Wendy.' Her face, golden with freckles, conveyed unbounded amiability.

Roland Reed said, 'You recognized Mo and Wendy? Imagine the shock I got when I walked in and saw them. I wish we'd known who they were.'

The orange-haired woman rolled up her eyes, looked at me and Morgan again, and pulling off her water-carrier's memento, dropped neatly into a chair. She said, 'Rolly, I can't be bothered. We knew who they were.'

Rolly Reed's brown face settled in on itself, like the face of a man who has had to put up with a lot, and rather liked it. He said, 'You bloody rat,' with affection.

I couldn't imagine Sir Robert saying that to me in a thousand years. Reed had come to a secret business meeting with his reputation and millions at stake, and his stupid mistress (secretary? No.) had pulled the plug on him. Sir Robert looked as I felt. Mo Morgan looked wholly blank, until a smile such as I had never seen spread over his long beaky face. He said, 'Go on! How did you know?'

She fanned herself with the hat, grinning back at him. 'You do all you do and can't guess?'

They were smiling at one another when Sir Robert asserted himself. I was proud of him. Gazing tolerantly at the red hair, the hat and the gauchos he said, 'I don't believe, Mr Reed, I've had the pleasure.'

Roland Reed, BA, MA, LB, Finance Director and film amateur looked taken aback. He said, 'I'm so sorry. I assumed you knew each other. Sir Robert Kingsley. Miss Marguerite Curtis Geddes, Chairman and Chief Executive of the MCG Company.'

6

As an executive woman, I have never been as upset as I was that afternoon. Every normal canon of business procedure was flouted. Even Sir Robert, I could see, was quite shaken.

He must have known, I suppose, that the Chief Executive of MCG was a woman. Perhaps he also knew that she had been a professional make-up artist. It was clear, however, that he had failed to connect her in any way with the flamboyant orange-haired cooking-woman of Mr Morgan's story and mine. He had never met her before, but his breeding and experience told. He greeted her warmly and, in a friendly yet business-like manner, launched into the business of the day. It took him all of five words before she interrupted him. It took him all of three minutes to discover what he had got himself into.

It is usual, when one company proposes to take over another, for each firm to protect its position. Sir Robert, using the broader, simpler figures from Pettigrew, set out to present an impressive portrait of Kingsley's. Mr Roland Reed, undermined at every turn by his Chairperson, attempted to show that MCG was broadly based, well supported, and capable of extending both its plant and its network of up-market salons. At the end of a fraught thirty minutes, his discourse was brought to an end by his employer.

Miss Marguerite Geddes said, 'That's a load of codswallop, Rolly. Lousy debts, raw material hiccoughs, strikes in the salons – someone's working us over. We'll find out who it is and we'll mince them. No one can beat us for branded product or service, and we're not dependent on white goods like you are. Interest rates? Extra competition from Europe? What's your future?'

Sir Robert smiled. 'I venture to say, better than yours.'

'OK,' said Miss Rita Geddes. 'Put down your figures.'

By this time, Mr Reed was looking at the carpet, I was looking at Sir Robert and Mo Morgan, like an overworked snake in the Assembly of the Dead, was gazing in rapt admiration at the explosive Miss Geddes. Sir Robert said, smiling, 'At this stage of the negotiation? Before we reach that point, Miss Geddes, I think we each of us would have to feel rather more committed.'

'Well, how do we know when we're committed?' said the cooking-lady. 'Toss for it?'

There was a polite silence, during which I passed round the cakes, and Mo Morgan, getting off his piano stool, poured several more strong cups of tea. Sir Robert said, 'You mean you are unwilling to proceed further without detailed figures? I warn you, we should require the same from you.'

'You can have them,' said Miss Geddes. 'Rolly?'

Mr Roland Reed, with slight reluctance, lifted his closed briefcase and lowered it. He said, 'Whenever you like.'

Sir Robert paused. He said, 'I am really not sure. Compared with yours, mine is a very large firm with certain responsibilities. Unless I see my way clear, it would not be correct for me to reveal sensitive figures.'

'Sensitive?' said Miss Rita Geddes.

I said, 'Miss Geddes, all figures affect the market, no matter how well a firm is doing.'

She gave me a long, considering look, woman to woman. 'Oh, I know,' she said. 'The way some of your divisions have been operating, the market would go into stitches. And there's the loan you raised to buy Mr Morgan. But that's all pretty well known, surely? There's Seb Sullivan sniffing around, and Ellwood Pymm, and Danny Oppenheim and God knows who else. Even if we decide not to bite, what's the harm? Everyone knows that Kingsley's are in trouble.'

'*In trouble?*' said Sir Robert. He gazed at her, and his expression slowly softened. He said, 'And that is why you are here?'

'Absolutely,' said Miss Rita Geddes. 'Gossip says that you're failing; we're rocky; and if you can take us and strip off our assets, you could pay for Mo Morgan's photographs. But I've an eye on the long view, not the short-term. Tell me that gossip is crap, and I'll listen. I'm here on behalf of my shareholders.'

'You would make a nice sum of money,' said Sir Robert. 'You've an interest in films? You could set up your own company.'

'I've got my own company,' said Rita Geddes. 'And if you're in a terminal mess, then forget it. My backers will want to stay as they are, or find a better White Knight to depend on. So tell me. What accounts can you show me?'

There was a small silence. Outside, soft music played, and birds sang, and there was the muted and civilized sound of rich swimmers swimming. Sir Robert said, 'You brushed aside the matter of commitment, but I would remind you that I have shareholders to consider as well. I cannot make figures known unless I am assured of your interest.'

Roland Reed said, 'You are assured of our limited interest. Suppose we ask you to supply limited figures.'

'And you will do so as well?' said Sir Robert.

'Why not?' said Miss Geddes. 'What happens? Poor wee Wendy does a round trip to London?'

'I think,' said Sir Robert, 'that we may be able to collect what you want without exhausting Miss Helmann unduly. Would the day after tomorrow be too early?'

It was agreed. I had the figures at my feet, and Mr Reed's were presumably also at his fingertips. What we had decided on was a space to consider tactics. And for once, Miss Rita Geddes let it pass.

Everyone rose. Miss Geddes shook hands vigorously with us all, and pausing by the small piano, bent and dashed off a phrase close by Mo Morgan's shorts. He swung round, his prehensile fingers lifted. For a moment, I thought they were going to play a duet, then Mr Reed called from the doorway. 'Spoilsport,' said Miss Marguerite Geddes, and got up and left.

Sir Robert said, 'I think, Mo, we need a stiff drink.' There was a bar, discreetly camouflaged, in one corner. Mo Morgan cast me a brief, opaque look, and then wandered over and opened it. Sir Robert said, 'Well. That's a tricky one. I could have made a deal with Reed in a moment. The problem is that silly woman.'

'Dead true it is,' said Mo Morgan, slinging glasses before us and sitting. 'He's only the front. She's the tough one.'

'You think so?' said Sir Robert. He sipped his drink. 'My God, Mo. Do you always drink them this strong? She's a little make-up girl, that's all, by profession. Then ten years ago, she came into a fortune, raised some collateral and established the company. And a little make-up girl in mentality she still is. Did you hear she lost her way?'

'There's no secret,' said Morgan. 'She does. They ribbed her about it this morning.'

'Did they also tell you,' said Sir Robert, 'that she can't read or write? She's retarded.'

Mo Morgan said, 'It sounds more like dyslexia.'

'That's what they call it,' said the Chairman. 'Nice name. It still means she's illiterate. The poor sod with the ink in the square could manage a business better than she could. Which brings me to what happened this morning.'

My ears were buzzing. I heard him through the fumes of the alcohol Mo Morgan had poured for us all. It came to me that he hadn't liked being asked to pour it, and that he was not behaving as a loyal employee truly ought. For Executive Directors were employees, just as I was, and could be sacked. Then I remembered that Mo Morgan really couldn't be sacked, because the prosperity of Kingsley's depended on him. Mo Morgan said, 'Yes. About this morning. Reed knew who we were, but concealed it. So it wasn't an accident. We were directed to the square from the café. Johnson and Sullivan saw us lurking, and amused themselves sending us into Reed's arms. Probably Reed and his pals haunt the Jemaa every morning.'

'But why?' I said. 'Mr Reed didn't ask us any questions. Why take all that trouble and gain nothing from it?'

Mo Morgan said, 'It gave them a chance to weigh us up before the meeting, and us, if you like, a chance to underrate them. And since they were meeting us soon, it suited them to seem to be civilians. They're clever, Sir Robert. The smartest thing that woman did was to admit that they knew us all along.'

I couldn't see how. I said, 'It did nothing to help her own side. Now we know to link MCG with Johnson and Sullivan.'

Sir Robert was gazing at me without really seeing me. 'Yes. Johnson,' he said. 'The man without whom you and I wouldn't be here. I find Johnson's provocative rôle in all this a little disturbing. The more so, since I have some new facts about the gentleman. If gentleman is the word I am looking for.'

He didn't sound quite as calm as he looked. I wondered how he could have found out anything about Mr Johnson from Marrakesh, unless the Balkan lady had turned up.

What had turned up wasn't the Balkan lady, but a report from London on MCG shareholders. Most were known. Some had identities which, for one reason or another, were harder to cull from the Register. In the case of a take-over, it was usual to spend quite some effort on tracing them. I sat and heard Sir Robert tell us all that. 'And?' said Mo Morgan. But by that time, we both guessed what the score was.

'One such case,' said Sir Robert, 'has just yielded to inquiry. Under another name, and not publicly recognized, a holding amounting to ten per cent of the equity in MCG is owned by Mr Johnson Johnson. He held substantially more, but sold the rest when they went to the market. He has known Mr Roland Reed for a long time. Reed, in fact, was Johnson's personal accountant.'

There was a silence. 'And Rita Geddes?' said Mr Morgan. He had flushed.

Sir Robert raised his brows. 'Surprising though it seems, I understand there exists a long, confirmed friendship between the lady and Johnson. It dates back to the death of his wife, and there is presumably not much doubt of its nature. I am afraid,' said Sir Robert, 'that my delightful portrait is being painted by a man who wishes no good to Kingsley's, since his mistress and his money are bound up in the firm we intend to take over.'

I wondered if I should speak. I wondered if I should suggest that it was an agent of Johnson's who had caused the bomb threat in London, and achieved access to the safe and its figures. The bomb itself hadn't been meant to go off. He had been angry.

I didn't say it. Instead, I said, 'Sir Robert?'

They both looked at me. I said, 'My luggage was searched at the airport. Mr Johnson could have been there.' The royal motorcade had passed just after I did. He must have been in the Salon of Honour.

I said, 'I was carrying the company papers. The Customs took and returned them intact. But if they were read, then Johnson and Sullivan know all our figures.'

'Well, Johnson at least,' Sir Robert said. He rose, taking his glass to the bar, and after a moment, returned and collected Mr Morgan's and mine. He said, uncapping bottles, 'One of the irritating things about this sad little business is that I may have to give up that portrait. I really can't allow this two-faced blighter to walk all over our plans. Nor do I much like being made a fool of. Answer the door, will you, Wendy?'

It was an afternoon of unwanted visitors. On a wave from Sir Robert, someone ushered in Sebastian Sullivan. He was dressed as in the café, with a fringed buckskin jacket flung over his upholstered shoulders. His hair, waving all down his neck, was nearly long enough to put in plaits like Mr Morgan's. He smiled a smile straight from the Desert Song.

We knew, of course, now what he and his partner Johnson were worth. I wondered if he had heard what we were saying about them. I wondered if Johnson had sent him, and what he was going to say. I stepped back a number of paces and Morgan sat up like a whippet.

'Ah, there you are, Seb,' said Sir Robert. 'The usual tipple?' He turned to take a fresh glass. 'I was just going to tell them about you.'

Mr Morgan caught on before I did. He said baldly, 'Do I understand what I think I understand? Colonel Sullivan is working for Kingsley's?'

'I have been known to employ Black & Holroyd from time to time,' said Sir Robert, handing out tumblers. 'Not a matter that would appear on a boardroom agenda, but specialist PR consultants can help a firm now and then. Indeed you can thank Wendy, in a way, that I was reminded of them.' Seb Sullivan, grinning at me, had cast himself on the sofa.

'I thought black PR was more their line,' Mo Morgan said. 'Ah! They dug up the stuff about Johnson. And the Colonel is presumably hunting for more? In the midst of a vintage car rally?'

'Johnson and Rita,' said Colonel Sullivan, waving his drink. 'Now there's a vintage vehicle with a well-hidden love-life. And if he goes in for middle-aged red-heads, who knows what else we'll find on him, or the pair of them? There are make-up artists and make-up artists, me dears.'

Mo Morgan said, 'I can see why you don't discuss this round the Board table. Does much of it generally go on?'

'Do I detect a note of reproof?' said Sir Robert in his pleasant voice. 'The affairs of this company are above reproach, and are conducted, as you know, in the open. When, due to some sordid and criminal espionage the welfare of the firm appears threatened, I reserve the right to confront the criminals on their own ground. If you disagree, then you may take it up with me officially.'

Morgan looked at him. I said, 'But Colonel Sullivan was in the café?'

'Sticking like a brother to our Mr Johnson,' said Sullivan. 'Having spotted you, I tell you, he didn't much relish my company. In the end he turned it into a game. Bet me he could get you to follow the old witch with the sugar.'

I said, 'What did he write on the paper?'

'There might have been a few capital letters,' said Seb Sullivan. 'Maybe the film people's logo? It puzzled me too, until I rang Sir Robert to find what had happened. She knew at least to go to the Place, the old soul, and then MCG could fake up a meeting. He left a lot to chance, that bright boy, but Reed must have been watching for one of you. I trust you both kept your corporate mouths shut.'

'We used them for eating,' said Morgan. 'You didn't think to come after and warn us?'

'Would have given the game away, old dear,' said Seb Sullivan. 'Not so cut off from real life as he looks, our Mr Johnson. I've been thinking. We've got two more free days. And except that he'd know it, I'd skip the sightseeing and have a dirty good look at that yacht of his.'

'You could, tomorrow,' said Sir Robert idly. 'He's painting the royals all day. Couldn't give me a sitting.'

'Where?' said Colonel Sullivan. 'In the Palace? Or here?'

'He has a suite here,' said Sir Robert. 'I go there for my sittings. He does the rest in the Palace. How long would it take you to get to Essaouira? Two hours? Three?'

'All the time in the world to look at that boat,' said Colonel Sullivan. His eyes had stopped at my legs. He said, 'I'd need a bit of company with me. Credibility, it's all the rage in this business. What about it, Wendy, me darlin'? I'd like to know who's on that yacht.'

Mo Morgan said, 'I doubt if Wendy does. I'll go, if you want a companion.'

I was surprised. I thought they had disliked each other on sight. Seb Sullivan said, 'Not the right shape of legs, my dear fellow, and you'd blow me Kingsley cover, what's more.'

'I'm Kingsley's,' I said.

'Who cares?' said Seb Sullivan. 'What you are is classified doll. So you come. Right, Sir Robert? You'd let her play hookey tomorrow?'

'It depends what for,' said Sir Robert. He took off his jacket and threw it over a chair. His hair stuck up.

'Cross me heart, nothing chancy,' said the Desert Song. 'A spin in the buzzbox, a glance at the harbour, and straight back to the fort and the handcuffs.'

I could see Morgan's scowl, and I hesitated. Then Sir Robert said, 'I see nothing against it. The paperwork can surely be finished this evening. And if the trip brings results, all the better. Mo, would you prefer to return home to London? There is no need for you to be involved any further.'

'I thought maybe there was,' said Mo Morgan. 'No. I'll stay. Thank you.'

Sullivan left soon after that, and Sir Robert and I started to spread out the papers and work on them. Before we left London, we had made our contingency plans. The figures in my document case at the airport had catered for each likely level of discussion, although rounded, and subject to encoded updates from London. It meant that the form of our strategy might be known, but the detail, thank God, was less vulnerable.

Morgan, to Sir Robert's annoyance, stayed with us. He said very little, but the remarks he did make were quite shrewd, and caused Sir Robert to view him, I am sure, with some respect.

Morgan left first. Sir Robert might have kept me even longer except that the inner door opened and Lady Kingsley came in. She said, 'Goodness, are you still there? Your poor young lady, Bobs; she looks quite exhausted. Is she staying to dinner?'

I rose, concealing alarm. I said, 'It's very kind of you, but my mother's expecting me. And I'm not too tired. It's been very interesting.'

Sir Robert said, 'Wendy's been an absolute brick, as per usual, and she's going to have time off at the seaside tomorrow. Have you had a decent day?' He picked up and handed me papers and, taking the hint, I proceeded to pack up my briefcase.

Lady Kingsley said, 'You know the man who's painting your portrait?'

'You've met him, have you?' said Sir Robert. He looked round and found some more folders.

'I met him when he came, yes, but I didn't know him. Now I do. I've just spent the afternoon in his rooms. *What* that fellow knows about colours. And brushes, pure sable, he gave me some. And he was extremely decent about my little picture. He doesn't think it's too brown.'

'I didn't say that it was,' said Sir Robert. 'So you had him next door?'

Lady Kingsley gave a calm, wifely honk. 'Wouldn't have put it like that, but yes, he did come out on the balcony. My God, you were all talking for ages.'

'Glad you were pleasantly occupied, then,' said Sir Robert. 'Wendy? I'd better not see you out. Can you find your own way?'

I thanked him and carried my case through the suite, looking to left and to right at the door. The way to the lift appeared clear. As I pressed the button and waited, I observed a small white block on the floor by my foot. I picked it up. It was a wrapped sugar lump. But although I unwrapped the paper, there was nothing written inside it.

*

71

At sun-up next morning, a four-door three-litre '26 Sunbeam rolled up before the Hotel Golden Sahara, where a man was sweeping the steps with a palm branch. Its torpedo body was a pale powder-blue; the sidelights on its mudguards were silver, its wheels were meshed with glittering wire. The upholstery was deep buttoned leather, and the hood was let down.

At the wheel was Seb Sullivan, his arm on the ledge and his Viking hair lit by the moon and the sunrise. With difficulty, I prevented my mother from trying to climb in beside him. 'You had Mo Morgan,' I said. 'You can't have them both. It's anti-social.'

'That's the one I want, Wendy,' she said. 'Play you a tie-break.'

For two days now, Best of the Desert Song had replaced her cassette on the Equity Carrot: I had spent the night trying to wrench her mind back to business. Finally, with a sigh, she had hauled off her earphones. 'Why repeat it so often? I hear you. Kingsley's aim for a friendly take-over. Target spits. Kingsley's hire slag to bad-mouth the target, sweet-talk backers into taking fat offer. Meeting pending to clinch. You say this fine young man Sullivan is one of Kingsley's?'

'Yes,' I said. 'But Johnson isn't, and Ellwood Pymm isn't.'

'Ellwood Pymm?' she said. 'He lent you his phrase-book.'

'Yes. Well, he's a columnist. It would suit him quite well to pick up slime about Kingsley's. And that could spoil the MCG deal.'

'What could he pick up?' my mother said.

'Figures,' I said. 'That's what everyone's trying to work out. The as-is value. The actual figures.'

'So they're that bad?' she said. 'So Kingsley's have to fix this MCG deal. For if they don't persuade MCG to give in, an outside predator might just make a strong offer to Kingsley's shareholders?'

'Right,' I said. 'Taking over the company debt and Mo Morgan. Assuming, of course, that Mo Morgan still intends to keep his money and stay.'

'He's uneasy,' my mother said. 'Does he like pressed ham all that much? Or coffee? He wants to know what's in the cooking-pot.'

'They don't see eye to eye, he and Sir Robert. He doesn't like Seb or Johnson. He could make his whole team unhappy,' I said. 'I have to help Colonel Sullivan with this trip to Essaouira tomorrow. Why don't you call on Mo Morgan and mother him? I have his address.'

She took it thoughtfully in her paws. She said, 'It's illegal, boarding this painter's yacht? Remember all that pain in the Customs shed, Wendy? You let this man Seb go to prison, not you.'

'I'm just there as his cover,' I said. 'Remember, someone planted that bomb to harm Kingsley's. They can't complain if we look through their yachts.'

'They can shoot bullets,' my mother said. 'I think I should go with you. If they want a good target, they'll have it.'

She was right about that. I said, 'Anyway, you'd never fit into the Sunbeam.'

I waved to her as we drove off. 'A latch-key child at my age!' she cried after me.

7

'I thought she was supposed to be sick?' yelled Colonel Sullivan above the uproar of the 1926 engine. We had overtaken, to their vociferous delight, some Moroccan joggers on the western suburbs of Marrakesh. It wasn't yet eight, and hordes of bicycles packed the road coming inwards, while patient lines of caps and veils waited outside lanes of unopened block factories, and groups of men by the roadside drummed up tea on cloth-covered boxes. Everyone looked at us. 'Anyway,' he added, 'they let you come, and I wouldn't have betted on it.'

'I can get round her,' I said, vibrating. I saw him, Full of Eastern Promise, through my mother's glistening eyes. He had on an Afghan silver belt, and his tunic and slimline trousers were by Valentino, while his camera had a hand-made leather satchel. It wasn't a league I could enter, but I had done my best with a midriff top and thonged sandals, and my skirt was half the length of my office one. Or a quarter, maybe. The rest of the impact depended on pinned-up hair and a headscarf, and a pair of very French dark glasses. I'd paid my fees for the Image Enhancement Workshop.

Colonel Sullivan said, 'Anyone else, m'darlin', would believe every word that you spoke. As I recollect, it wasn't your mother who wanted to clamp you. Fancy him, do you?'

I said, 'I really don't know what you mean.'

'No more you don't,' he said, grinning, and changed gear with his powerful wrists. 'But I don't blame him: not with a female like Charity.'

I said, 'You sound like Ellwood Pymm. In a rut.'

He grinned again. His hair undulated in the warm breeze as we came to open country. On either side of us were almond blossom and olive trees and vines covered with matting. Lorries passed, packed with bamboo bundles, or boulders, or women, their working-veils flapping together. Sullivan said, 'If smart-ass Ellwood Pymm gets one heady whiff of what's happening to Kingsley's, Sir Robert can hang up his Guccis. You know Pymm's a tipster? He's sniffed news. He wasn't on the original Canadian rota.'

I didn't need the warning, if it was a warning. 'You were lunching with him,' I said.

'And you were lunching with Johnson,' said the Colonel. 'Field-trials: that's the name of the game.'

'You crossed to Sir Robert's side after the lunch,' I remarked.

'Nothing personally against the worthy J.J.,' said Colonel Sullivan. 'A very cool groover. But without the liquidity muscle, you might say, of Kingsley Conglomerates.'

'You didn't know Johnson was involved with MCG?' I asked. We passed flocks of goats and some kids, and chunks of thick dirty sheep and peculiar Biblical landscapes where cattle, camels and donkeys grazed together. On either side, the country was flat, with small jagged hills to the right. In mid-air, to the left, was a dazzling cloudscape.

'Not then, I didn't,' said Sullivan. 'He'd covered his tracks like a vice-king. It made us look to see if he was a vice-king. And bingo, me darlin', a harem.'

Mentally I took back from Johnson the benefit of the doubt I had given him. I said, 'A harem?' politely.

'Well, he's a sailor, isn't he?' said Colonel Sullivan. It was a fair understatement. Johnson had been professional RN in the same way that Sullivan had been professional Army. I supposed that, with men, it was like belonging to different clubs. Sullivan said, 'Anyway, isn't that why you're here? Sniff out the orgies. Help Sir Robert stitch his painter up good and proper.'

The cloud-light was irritating, like the conversation. 'Stitch him up?' I repeated.

'Come on!' said Seb Sullivan. 'What d'you think he has a yacht for? What do you think the MCG shareholders will make of that, and their red-headed nympho MD?'

He was late with the idea. It was what I had suggested myself, when I thought Dolly was Johnson's date in Morocco. Then, we were only twisting his arm over a portrait. 'And Roland Reed?' I said.

'We're working on him,' said Colonel Sullivan ghoulishly. 'Single, well-heeled, an accountant with an interest in *films*? If he isn't AC or DC, we'll surely catch him on insider trading.'

He sounded happy and confident. He hadn't a thought in his head but his job. I looked away. The haze of cloud in the sky had grown brighter. It spread into irrational patterns, and glistened. I realized that the icy glow wasn't cloud, it was mountains. Suspended over the haze, a frightening range of fierce snowy mountains rolled towards the horizon. I said, 'What's that?'

Sullivan glanced to his left. 'The High Atlas,' he said. 'The way to Taroudant and the end of the rainbow. The day after tomorrow, me darlin', and the Sunbeam'll climb like an angel. You should have seen her cleaning the hills after Azrou. But today, it's safe, sunny Essaouira.'

I said, 'There's a mountain called Toubkal.'

'A massif. You're looking at it,' Sullivan said. 'Why?' He glanced at me and back to the road. 'Ah. Mo Morgan, the microchip genius. Well, well, well. You keep going, Wendy, and Kingsley's will give you a bonus. Pile it high and sell it cheap, sweetheart.'

I didn't speak. I couldn't make him out, and the sight of the mountains had shaken me. I let him talk on, about the Sunbeam and all the other cars he had owned. His first vintage had been made in Berlin. After a while, he behaved more as I expected him to, and got his hand into my lap a couple of times; a thing I have been taught how to deal with. While he got over that, I was able to look about and size up Morocco.

There was no sand. There were no sheiks. There was nothing you could think of as a kasbah. The land was dirt brown or weedy or planted. Camels pulled wooden ploughs. Market-tents without buyers sat like capital letters in the dirt. There were windmills, and wells, and isolated red compounds full of flat roofs and narrow clay passages. There were peeling roadside arcades of village shops selling bicycle parts. There were children trudging to school, cases strapped to their backs. There were prickly pears and argan trees, with goats like cats crouched on their branches. And as we came down to the sea, there were cedars and orange orchards coming to blossom, and fields of daisies and pink and bright scarlet flowers, and the stifling smell of mimosa, and a carpet of marigolds, small and wild and raw as Rita Geddes.

We ran from the country into the bright esplanade of Essaouira, with the blue sea rolling in, and boys in T-shirts with a ball on the sand, pretending they were the Lions of Cameroon. It wasn't quite the Algarve, but it wasn't *The Desert Song* either. Sullivan braked to a halt, and I saw ahead of me the walls of a harbour, with masts and a boat on the stocks showing above it. On the landward side were the high pink walls of the older town. Parked between us and the town was a bus, from which a mixed party with cameras was descending.

Among them was Ellwood Pymm. He saw us at once, and came over. 'Why, will you look who is here!'

The hounds of the Canadian press and radio wandered after him, their faces vacant with cultural overload. They remembered the vintage car rally and Seb. They patted the Sunbeam and then, ignoring the cries of their conductor, made stolidly for the nearest source of relief and refreshment, taking us with them. Ellwood said, 'Seb, Wendy sweet baby! Why don't you come with us on the tour? The port, the fish market, the silversmiths, the spice stalls, the Portuguese artillery platforms, the cedarwood furniture!' Below the crewcut, his scalp was mahogany: his lump-like features were mottled. In one pocket of his shorts, I could see his Arab phrase-book.

Colonel Sullivan said, 'Now who could resist that, my son, except a man who's just driven all the way from Marrakesh and is medium knackered? Go on into the town. Wendy and I will relax, and have a wander, and join you.'

'Suit yourself,' said Ellwood Pymm. 'I thought you'd want to come with us to the harbour. You know, your pal Johnson has a yacht here? Not interested, are we?'

There was malice you couldn't miss in the question. Seb Sullivan said, 'Curious as the next man, but won't it be under covers? He can't be using it much.'

'You never know,' said Ellwood Pymm. 'When Cupid calls, it's nice to have somewhere to go. We could leave our visiting cards, so he'll know that we care.'

I watched the Colonel changing his mind. If Johnson's yacht was packed full of call-girls, it would do no harm to have a mass audience. On the other hand, if we let Ellwood's lot go on their own, they might scare off the prey and we'd lose it. Or her. Or them. When the Canadians moved, we walked to the harbour beside them.

It was a place Mo Morgan would have wanted to photograph. Guarded by grey, turreted forts it was crammed full of fishing boats, their names painted in Roman and Arabic. Because of the heat, everything had gone into pause. On the quay, men in seaboots and caps sat sewing or pillowed on pink and blue nets, with necklaces of floats lying around them. The unfinished boats on the stocks stood against the noon sun, their open Japanese ribs painted orange. On the water, a skiff laden with men left the ship and poled its way absently somewhere. Beyond the boats I could glimpse a few pleasure craft, jogging a bit as the waves and wind slapped them. Above them soared the two slender masts of a yacht. We walked along, and from a discreet distance, studied her.

'Ketch,' said Ellwood Pymm. 'Gaff-rigged, with a bloody big engine. Looked him up. There you are, boys and girls. That's the *Dolly*.'

I have seen yachts on TV. This one was painted gloss white. In the sun, she glistened like Toubkal. Contrary to expectations, she was not wrapped in canvas. Her cockpit with its smart awning and cushions lay invitingly open. Her decks shone unimpeded; her brass and paint glittered. On Johnson's coach roof, pin-clear to Mr Pymm's long-focus lens, a sleeping blonde lay exposing her spine to the sun, a half-full glass and a book at her side. She wore the lower half of an expensive bikini. The click of five cameras disturbed her. She turned. Eight more clicks ensued. She was elegant, tanned, and about thirty-five. She smiled without a hint of dismay and, leaning back on her elbows, called something in English. 'Jay, you're an absolute animal. Did you pay them to come?'

'In kind,' said an unemphatic bass voice I remembered. We turned. Impossibly, behind us on the wharf stood Johnson Johnson in an old shirt and creased bags, a dripping ice-cream in each non-painting hand. Behind the bifocals was nothing but resignation. He said, 'I'm so sorry. I've only got two. We weren't expecting a gang. Seb, it's just up the road. Will you bring some?'

'Ice-cream?' said my rallying colonel. It was the first time I'd seen him disconcerted. We had left Johnson in Marrakesh painting the royals. This very dawn, we had left him. Yet Johnson had got here before us.

'Unless you'd like anything else,' Johnson said, walking past us to the foot of the gangplank. 'You *are* all coming aboard? Or don't you want to?'

He stood and gazed amicably at us all. He looked the way he had in the café: his glasses impervious, his black brows meeting his hair. He had seen me there; now I was sure of it. Ellwood said, 'If you and the lady don't mind.'

'Muriel?' Johnson said. 'Do you mind?'

She got up and took the ice cream, her breasts jiggling. She stood and surveyed herself, frowning. She said, 'I don't think so. Should I?'

'Not on my account,' said Seb Sullivan lasciviously.

She smiled. 'Fine,' she said. 'Then I don't suppose Daniel will, either. Do come aboard. Lenny! Oliver!'

I suppose we had all assumed they were alone. They weren't. Lenny appeared, an elderly man in a jacket and tie, and was introduced as *Dolly*'s skipper and steward. Oliver, a charming thug with an upper-class accent, handed fourteen of us on board and helped serve us ice-cream, when Colonel Sullivan brought it. Johnson, the perfect host, took time to toss a scarf at his inamorata. 'Muriel! You're giving everyone orgasms.'

Without haste, she wrapped it over her bosom where it clung, noticeably embossed. 'Jay, I love you,' she said. Her face was healthy and heart-shaped, and she had blue eyes and dyed lashes and a large, generous mouth smeared with white lipstick. I had seen her before.

I caught Sullivan by the arm. 'That woman!' I said.

'I know,' he said. 'Not just now, angel.'

An hour later the guide from ONMT and RAM, trying hard, got his party to leave. Johnson and his girlfriend waved them off from the cockpit. Seb and I lingered, and Ellwood, slowing down, stopped on the quayside to wait for us. Seb ignored him. He said, 'Sir Robert said you were painting SM at the Palace.'

The woman Muriel was reclining, her long bare legs on the cockpit cushions. Johnson sat on the wooden edge of the cockpit, his sandshoes planted beside her. 'And so I should have been,' he said. 'Except that Muriel's husband was called to the Presence, and the painting was cancelled this morning.' He looked down, and he and the girl exchanged smiles. He said, 'Of course, you know who Muriel is?' His glasses inclined towards me.

I said, 'I saw her photograph, Mr Johnson. She's Mrs Daniel Oppenheim?'

'She's Jimmy Auld's daughter, much more important,' said Johnson. 'Muriel is a very young/old family friend, whom we've forgiven for marrying a financier. She and Danny spared me two nights from the Football Cup, but alas, they'll have to go back tomorrow. So what do you plan to do now? Test the markets?'

Colonel Sullivan, after a second's hesitation, said that he thought we would indeed tour the markets.

'Do,' said Johnson. 'Everything from a cure for the common cold to spells against evil. Though the aphrodisiacs are unreliable, they tell me. What do they tell you, Mr Pymm?'

'Ellwood, please. They tell me plenty, but I'm a believer in test trials,' said Ellwood Pymm from the quayside. 'I sure admire a guy with your track record. What's the trade like around here?'

Johnson looked at him. Then he said, 'It depends on the day of the week. I'm afraid I'm all tuckered out, but your guide would advise you.'

'Sure,' said Ellwood Pymm with dissatisfaction. 'But so far their advice has been crap. I'll maybe go on ahead?'

'You do that,' said Johnson quite amiably. We watched the other man turn and hurry after his party. The calves of his legs were red with sunburn. Johnson said, 'Now, who do you think is paying his lawyers?'

'Anyone he can get,' Colonel Sullivan said. 'Whatever you happen to be up to, I wouldn't let Ellwood Pymm know.'

'Why ever not?' Johnson said. 'You're having a rest then, from your pals? I don't blame you. Fancy finding Miss Helmann in Marrakesh.'

I said, 'My mother was ill. Sir Robert has been very kind.'

'Wonderful what twenty-four hours in the sun will effect. Look at Ellwood,' Johnson said. 'Do you really want to explore the sights with French-speaking Canada? If not, stay and have a bite with us first. Daniel's delayed; Lenny's bought far too much and it's spoiling.'

Seb Sullivan said, 'That's amazingly kind of you, now. I must say it's tempting.'

'Then do,' Johnson said. 'And when the Voice of Canada makes its way back, it can photograph Muriel and Daniel together. It would, perhaps, help to de-mist Mr Pymm's camera lenses. Now, what can Lenny bring you to drink?'

We sat in the cockpit and sipped, and I listened while Mrs Oppenheim and Johnson and Sullivan argued about the Atlas Lions, the Abiola Babes and the Pharaons of Egypt, who had been trained by a chap called John Michael Smith. Mrs Oppenheim knew him. Mrs Oppenheim knew everything about CAF, which stands for the Coupe d'Afrique de Football, for which eight African countries for fifteen days would be playing each other.

I was furious. I remembered Mo Morgan abandoning me in the Place Jemaa-el-Fna. Sullivan, who ought to be catching out Johnson, was talking at the top of his voice and demonstrating moves with his feet, while Johnson appeared to have committed to memory the entire sports edition of every Moroccan-French newspaper. '*L'ailier droit!*' he exclaimed, joining Sullivan's excited exposition. '*Vif comme l'éclair et dribbleur infatigable!*' Mrs Oppenheim kept breaking into laughter and Sullivan kicked me by accident twice. It went on through the meal, which was extremely good. Towards the end, Johnson said, 'Do you miss it, Muriel? Can't get to all the big games now.'

She had put on her bikini top and a jacket, and her style fitted in well, somehow, with Johnson's linen and silver and cushions. Her hair had a natural sweep, and where it tapered, was white as Seb's eyelashes. Oliver, in a fresh shirt, smiled at her as he poured the wine and took the dishes away, and she gave him a warm smile in return. The saloon was cool, and fitted with smooth, mellow wood, and there was an assortment of books behind latticework.

Muriel Oppenheim said, 'I do, of course. Dad doesn't get any younger. But Daniel is good. He'll up sticks and come if he can. He couldn't really afford to come to Casa just now but he just did, and brought us.' She smiled at me and Sullivan. 'I was Daniel's secretary before he persuaded me to marry him. He didn't know he was marrying a football pitch.'

I didn't know what to say. Seb Sullivan said, 'He knew a good thing when he saw it.'

She was amused. 'Loyalty, sex and good staffwork. That's what a high flyer wants from his partner. Yes, Miss Helmann? And someone to check out his spelling.'

Sullivan saved me from answering. He said suddenly, 'Makes you wonder about Miss Rita Geddes. Who provides the sex and the staffwork and the spelling? Mr Roland Reed, I suppose.'

Without Sir Robert's sanction, he was directly challenging Johnson Johnson. The Great Man, patting his pockets, failed to notice the challenge. 'Rita? She told me she'd met you. Don't ask me for any answers; Ellwood Pymm is the expert on sex. As for writing and staffwork, they all use an excellent secretary called Ella. So far as I know, she isn't a lesbian. Does anyone mind if I smoke? We'll have coffee on deck.' He had a pipe in his hand, and his glasses were milky.

Smoking is not allowed in Kingsley's boardroom. I supposed that pipes were much like my mother's Gauloises: worst when first lighted. Colonel Sullivan, after hesitating, had risen to go up on deck with the others. I asked to be excused.

Instead of leading me to the front, where I had seen others going, Mrs Oppenheim showed me to the master cabin that Johnson seemed to have given her. The washroom off it was clinical, and equipped with everything man or woman could want, neatly packaged. In all that economical space, the largest item was a medicine cabinet, surprisingly locked. I came out, and made up while she chatted. From what she said, Johnson and her husband didn't see all that much of each other.

I remembered Johnson saying that the invitation to Daniel Oppenheim's party in London hadn't been his; it had come from Muriel. At the same time, there was no doubt that Daniel Oppenheim had slept here last night: his things were all over the place. And he was coming back to share the cabin tonight. 'Without J.J.,' she said. 'It's so silly: he works so hard, and he doesn't need to. He has to go back tonight to be ready for painting tomorrow. They cancelled today.'

I said, 'But you and your husband are both staying on? It must be lovely.'

She said, 'It is, but no – we have to get back to my father tomorrow. We've taken a house in Marrakesh for the days between games. Dad has so many people to see. We did take him to Asni, and met one of your company men, Mr Morgan. He's coming to see Dad. I liked him.'

Rita Geddes had mentioned the Oppenheims, and Morgan had said nothing at all about meeting them. Maybe, like me, he thought that Sir Robert had sufficient to worry about. Maybe he didn't. Muriel Oppenheim said, rather abruptly, 'Miss Helmann?'

'Yes?' I said. I waited, fortified by my courses. How to Recognize Signals. How to Define the Purpose, Style and Goal of your Communication. I was still afraid of what she was going to ask me.

She said, 'My family and Johnson's have known each other for a long time. They're lovely people. He's given them a lot of worry, because of the kind of person he is. I hope you get on with him.'

She had let me use her mirror to tidy my hair. I pleated the bandanna round it again. Like my mother, I tan very quickly. The dark glasses were leaving pale circles. I said, 'I'm only Sir Robert's secretary, Mrs Oppenheim. I think he's a wonderful painter.'

She said, 'He's also a very good friend. Perhaps I shouldn't tell you that he's Rita's chief backer, but I expect you've guessed from what he was saying. He tells me that Kingley's are making a bid for her company?'

'I can't say,' I said. 'Mrs Oppenheim, company information is confidential.'

'Of course,' she said. 'But I wanted you to know that he'll play it perfectly straight. I'm sure you know him by now. Has he tried to pump you? Exploit his advantage?'

He hadn't, of course. He'd lied, intrigued and tried to pinch our figures instead. I remembered she'd been a secretary too. I said, 'No. Our association, of course, is purely formal. But it seemed strange that he actually came to Morocco without admitting the connection.'

'Oh?' said Muriel Oppenheim. 'I rather thought he mentioned it just now.'

'Because he knew that we knew. We very much want to help the MCG company,' I said. 'I know he doesn't want Miss Geddes to sell, but it really would be best for her and her Board if they did.'

She had very clear blue eyes. She said, 'I don't know if this has any bearing. But I know and like Charity Kingsley. And Jay has been Rita's friend for ten years without at any point becoming anything closer.'

'We heard rumours,' I said. I kept it as friendly as she did.

She said, 'They won't be the last. And if that smear doesn't stick, others will. But remember that dirty tricks, once they start, work both ways. It's up to you and the Board to protect Kingsley's.'

Loyalty, sex and good staffwork. She was of real executive calibre. *I know and like Charity Kingsley,* she had said. I wondered quite why. I wondered if Daniel Oppenheim had his weaknesses too, and she covered up for him. I thought, even if he had, she must have a wonderful life. I thought, as I'd thought all along, that the mess MCG had got themselves into wasn't surprising, however good the competent Ella might be. It was led by a rough-spoken ill-groomed illiterate, and if Rita Geddes wasn't one of the harem, then Johnson must have backed her for some other reason.

I said, 'Perhaps, when you're rich, you don't mind losing cash for the sake of a hobby. But if Mr Johnson won't let Sir Robert rescue them, the other MCG shareholders will lose even the poor returns that they're getting. I don't think that's very fair.'

'I don't know,' said Muriel Oppenheim. 'Perhaps he's heard rumours as well. But you'll know more about that than I do, and as you said, you mustn't talk about company problems. Let's go up, shall we?' And she picked up her book and her oil.

There was no one this time in the cockpit. Johnson and Sullivan were sitting on the harbour wall swinging their legs and discussing a boat, and the men asleep on the nets were now stirring. Sullivan stood, saying, 'Well, the markets ought to be open. Shall we see if the great Canadian wave was receded?'

Johnson, his pipe in his mouth, was watching Mrs Oppenheim step to the deck from the cockpit, and bestow herself on the coach roof once more. He watched her quite objectively. I wondered where the crewmen had gone. I wondered about the young crewman, Oliver.

I said, 'Right, I'm ready.' We thanked Johnson and when we left, he was back on board and swinging below, his pipe cocked between two unused fingers. Colonel Sullivan and I passed the car, and the Customs house, and made our way to the triple stone arches that lead through the walls to the town. I said, 'I didn't find anything. Mrs Oppenheim says Miss Geddes and Johnson are just friends.'

'She volunteered that?' said Sullivan. 'Why?'

I had been wondering that. 'To put us off the scent?' I said reluctantly. 'She sounded as if she believed it.'

Seb Sullivan laughed. 'Where have you been? People are never just friends. No. She didn't want Johnson's liaison with Rita Geddes made public. Why? Is *she* a mistress of Johnson's?'

'I don't think so,' I said. 'She likes Johnson, I'd say, but that's all.'

'Likes him enough to want to block Sir Robert's take-over?'

'I don't know,' I said. 'Her husband once belonged to the firm that advised Kingsley's. Perhaps he was opposed to a bid for MCG, and was overruled. Perhaps he and his wife still have some sympathy for Miss Geddes and Johnson. Sir Robert would know.' I kept cool, as my mother would have expected. It was nothing to me if Johnson had a harem, and Seb Sullivan had only invited me here for company purposes. *Preventing Job Burn-Out* was the tape my mother bought first and played most. *Maximizing Return on Time Invested* was the second.

A long rectangle opened before us, displaying arched walls, and hotels, and palm trees. There were people, but not all that many. Beyond were the porticoed courtyards of the markets, fitted with cells crammed with unpackaged goods in sacks, bowls and dishes. There were trays of crabs in the fishmarket, and aproned men wielding hoses. Mid-piazza, men sat among papers loaded with lemons and eggs, and cast handfuls of water on baskets of anonymous greenery. A barrow of mint trundled past.

The sun was still high. No one hurried too much. As we passed, I read the labels stuck on the spice stalls. *Pour la chute des cheveux. Pour la rhume. Pour l'estomac. Pour la toux.* And beyond that, in alleys lined with blue tiles and awnings, the silversmiths' shops, which didn't cure anything. Next, a street of grimy, everyday shops, selling plastic bowls and dirty cassettes and thick rolls and pastries. A street of cedarwood boxes and tables inlaid with mother of pearl. Dirt-paved lanes. Passages with carved, ornate doorways; a buzzing alley of sewing machines. Roofs with untidy storks, and windows hung with bird cages and carpets. Shutters opening, and children wandering into the street, and the sound, in all this indolence, of feet pounding down some distant street and voices shouting. A cat, backing out of an upper window, peed gracefully into the street and I stopped.

Sullivan had stopped already. The voices we heard were Canadian. Sullivan said, 'They're going towards the harbour.'

He started to hurry. I followed. My jacket stuck to my arms, and Sullivan's tunic was marked with sweat down the spine, and under the arms, and round the glistening Afghan silver belt. All the same, he ran on the balls of his feet as if made of rubber. Beyond the fish market and under the palm trees we found the whole Canadian party, face to face with a pair of disbelieving bifocals.

The Toronto Star was making the running, followed closely by Chom. The Toronto Star, who was handsome, bearded and hot, said, 'Did he come back to you?'

Johnson Johnson, his pipe in his mouth, gazed back at them all. He said, 'Who?'

The lady from Radio-TV Toronto said, 'Ellwood Pymm. Have you seen him since he left the harbour?'

'No. Why?' said Johnson. The bifocals registered that I had joined the party, with Sullivan.

The man from CFCF said, 'Because he was assaulted, that's why. A group of men started to hustle him on the Portuguese battery. He ran down the steps. We ran after, but by the time we got down, he'd disappeared. He didn't come back to you?'

'No,' said Johnson. 'I suggest someone gets hold of the police, and the rest of you start searching about from where you saw him last. Did he pick a fight in some way?'

The voices reduced themselves slightly. The Toronto Star said, 'No. Not really. Not more than usual. You're right. Let's go back to where we saw him last.'

Essaouira is not all that big. I was the one who found the Arabic phrase-book, covered with stork-shit. It lay genteelly open at the column that said:

Hi Sir!
You are Pregnant!
Congratulations!

And below the guano, the pages were spotted with blood.

8

Although the amount of blood was not large and Ellwood Pymm, to my recollection had plenty of it, it was a shock to see the soaked spots, brown already, and splashes leading off in the dust.

They petered out, and when the local police, and later someone from the Sûreté Nationale arrived, there was nothing we or the Canadians could tell them except the cause of the original quarrel which, as might have been expected, turned out to be over a woman. Ellwood Pymm, hunting for trade, had not been the most tactful of men. The outraged fathers, brothers or husbands had disappeared, perhaps to follow and knife him, but more likely to frighten him into hiding. His fellow Canadians ranged the streets in twos and threes calling 'Ell-wood!' while their ONMT host made agitated phone calls from the hotel nearest the gates.

Sullivan had settled there too, and was ordering drinks for himself and Johnson and me while I stood irresolutely, holding the unfortunate phrase-book by its cleanest corner. Mr Pymm, while far from a soul-mate, had at least once lent me the book; the police didn't want it and I felt I couldn't abandon it or him. Colonel Sullivan, when this was explained, poured the beer he had ordered and said he hoped I wouldn't mind if he didn't join me, and further that he proposed to drive back to Marrakesh before dark. There was a long pause and then Johnson, who was drinking beer also, said that if I was really keen to go back to the search, he would come along with me. But it got dark, I would remember, before seven.

Thanks for nothing. Thanks for the gentlemanly enthusiasm. I waited until Johnson had finished his drink, then he and I went off together.

Now all the shutters were open, and the sun beat down on streets crowded with men and women and animals. We walked up to the markets. I said, 'Where would you hide, if you were Mr Pymm?'

'In the Trump Tower,' said Johnson Johnson. 'Or the Barbican. Or possibly somewhere sinking or rising near Iceland. What would you do with Mr Pymm if you were a serious-minded Moroccan whose sister had just been insulted?'

'Sssst!' someone said.

'I wouldn't kill him,' I said.

'Sssst!' said someone again.

'Of course you'd kill him,' Johnson said. 'Then you'd kill your sister, then you'd kill yourself. Who's saying Sssst?'

It was a man in a striped djellabah and a strong five o'clock shadow, who had appeared, stumbling, at my side. He said, 'Ameerka!'

'British,' said Johnson.

'Ameerka here!' said the man.

'Where?' said Johnson.

'Follow!' said the man, and hurried before us.

I said, 'He means American. He means Mr Pymm.'

'You're the expert,' said Johnson. 'Send two neck foils, and the complete boxed set of questions is yours. Do you think we should be humdrum, and tell the police about this?'

'We haven't time. We'd lose him,' I said.

'So suspense writers have been saying ever since the New Testament,' Johnson said. 'What about tearing out leaves of your phrase book?'

It was, actually, a sensible idea. I dropped *'Hello!' (Alo!)* at the first corner, followed by *'Give me a kiss!' (Iteeni bawsee!)* and, as we dived into a doorway, *'Okay!' (Tayyet!)* and *'Hamburger' (Ground meat with parsley and spices cooked on skewers: very good)*. Then someone seized me by the arms, dropped a sack over my head and said, 'You scream, I kill.' In French.

I deduced, from a short obscenity behind me that the same thing had happened to Johnson whose mother, I remembered with gratitude, had also had him taught French. Then no one spoke French any more, but several people just used their hands to propel us along a confined space of some kind, and round corners, and up a flight of difficult stars, and along several other uneven floors to a place where, without warning, my feet were kicked from under me and I heard Johnson grunt and fall, also. There were other sounds, as if he had tried to get up, and they hit him.

I wondered if I were going to be killed. I wondered if they knew who Johnson was, and if the Royal Academy would hang Sir Robert's picture unfinished, and what the Moroccan royals would do (if they caught them) to the men who had ruined their portraits. I opened my eyes as the bag was pulled off my shoulders and found myself in a dim room packed with rolls of new carpets, in the grasp of two turbaned men with their faces wrapped over like women. A little way off, Johnson lay sepulchrally propped on his shoulders. His spectacles glimmered. There were columns of carpets with price tags on either side of him, but no dog at his feet. Apart from a slight flush, he looked the same as he had at his Club; and if someone had slugged him, there was no sign of it. He said, 'I forgot the damned word for "Okay".'

I didn't want jokes. I wanted Sir Robert, or Sullivan, or even my mother. It was time for what my mother would have identified as a quality response in the field of inter-personal dynamics. I addressed my captors in French. I said, 'Do you want money?'

No one answered. The two men released me. One went off down a corridor stacked with rolled carpets. The other sat on his hunkers trimming his nails with a knife eight inches long. Every time Johnson moved, the knife glittered. Then the first man came back with some cord, and lashed Johnson's wrists and his ankles. I waited for them to do the same to me and, from the expectant look on his face, so did Johnson.

They didn't. One of them placed himself behind me. The man who had fetched the cord fumbled under his robes and, surprisingly, produced a tobacco bag and a packet of papers. I wondered if he was going to offer Johnson a fill of his pipe. Instead, he rolled a cigarette, lit it, and offered it between Johnson's lips. Johnson's lips remained shut.

'Smoke!' said the man. He wrenched away Johnson's glasses, exposing an expression of mild resignation, and stabbed the cigarette forward again, without obtaining an opening. Then the man behind me made some sort of movement. Johnson looked at him, and then at the fist in front of his face. His mouth slowly relaxed. When the cigarette came forward again, he gave it a niche. It sloped from his world-weary face as in *Casablanca*. He was treating us all, I realized, to Humphrey Bogart. 'Draw!' said the man at his side.

The tip of the cigarette came to sudden life. Johnson said, 'I should prefer a pipe, if I must.'

'It is we who state preferences,' said the man. 'Be happy you are alive.' He tossed the bifocal glasses on the floor and stood on them carefully, so that the glass didn't cut up his slippers.

It still sounded like *Casablanca*, except that he wasn't acting. It was real. I didn't know what to say. 'You won't get money,' I said, 'unless you treat us well.'

They didn't bother to answer. The man behind me shifted a little. Johnson smoked. We were, I guessed, on the second floor of some carpet warehouse. Corridors on either side were stacked with rolled carpets and filled with intermittent daylight from a central well which must descend, I supposed, to the sales floor. Normally, the place would be full of tourists. Today I could hear nothing at all from below, and at first no other sounds from the corridors, which were really first-floor galleries surrounding the well. Then I heard a distant movement, and the man behind me, rising, walked towards it and called.

He spoke Arabic, and it wasn't anything that I recognized. He disappeared. A moment later, he returned walking backwards with a third man whose face was also hidden. Between them, they bore the recumbent form of Mr Ellwood Pymm, whom they dropped on the floor. His eyes were shut, but he was breathing.

I never thought that a crew-cut, pug-nosed, sun-blistered American would make me think of my mother, but Ellwood Pymm did. Ellwood Pymm, smeared with blood and lying as if recently pole-axed was the epitome of the lame ducks that swam into every house my mother ever had. My friend of the knife retired to the wall. The newcomer remained crouched by the body, his head turned to watch Johnson and me. He said, 'Mademoiselle. You recognize this gentleman, maybe?' He spoke French, but not as an Arab speaks it.

I said, 'Yes, He's Mr Ellwood Pymm. He's a guest of the National Tourist Office.'

'One realizes that,' said the man. 'One regrets. But time presses; he has been foolish, and it may be that we must take severe steps to obtain the information he has denied us. You work for Kingsley Conglomerates?'

The words came from behind a face-veil and under a turban and above a ton of fluttering clothes as worn in Mecca. I couldn't have been more surprised if a belly-dancer had walked into the boardroom. I opened my mouth. Johnson said, 'She's an Executive Secretary. She answers the telephone.' His voice was even huskier than mine, but his French was all right. I saw the cigarette was almost finished and another, already lit, was waiting.

'Of course,' said the man in Arab clothing. 'And she receives encoded fax messages at her hotel, and has a good memory for numbers. Mademoiselle, tell me you have a good memory for numbers? I hope so, or Mr Pymm will not be comfortable.' In the slit between his turban and his face-cloth and indeed all over the rest of him he was establishing Appropriate Eye Contact, Relaxed Posture, and the Comfortable Tone of Voice that Resolves Conflict. By now, I was used to being pre-empted. I said, 'I don't know what you mean!' It seemed to be my phrase for the day.

'It is simple,' said our unknown French-speaker. 'Your Sir Robert conducts business in Marrakesh. Messages reach him from London through you. Mr Pymm, being a journalist, is interested in his hotel fax machine and is capable, I should say, of interpreting what he notices there. Unfortunately, he denies this. He claims to understand none of what has been transmitted to you. We require that information from you.'

I stared at him. That was secret company information. The carpets stirred in a draught, and their price tickets dangled. I said, 'I'm not going to tell you any of that!' Johnson for some reason

91

snorted. His current cigarette had gone out: they lit him a fresh one. I said, 'In any case, Mr Pymm—'

Johnson said, 'Look, how can a girl secretary interpret numbers? If you're convinced that Pymm knows, wake him up and ask him again. You've got us now as leverage.'

This was nonsense, of course. Even if he'd intercepted them, Pymm couldn't have decoded yesterday's faxes. No one could, outside the company. But before Pymm convinced them he really knew nothing, Johnson Johnson and I could be dead. Our interrogator snapped, 'Why are you afraid the girl secretary speaks? We have no time to wake your Mr Pymm. Your friends search for you, do we not know it? Therefore I say again, mademoiselle. Reply to my questions, or Mr Pymm suffers. Will he lose a hand? Or an ear?' And the man with the knife, getting up, walked over and stood above the recumbent form of Ellwood Pymm, guest of the National Tourist Office.

I was breathing so quickly I hiccoughed. Johnson said, 'Wendy. It's bluff.' The cigarette muffled his voice, but I made him out. I've had enough practice.

The French-speaker sighed and said, 'Cut his ear off.' The knife was lifted above Ellwood Pymm. I said 'No!'

The knife stopped. The first man said, 'Ah. Then you will tell us?'

'No, she won't,' Johnson said. 'One journalist's ear against the livelihood of all Kingsley's employees, world-wide? Go on. Show us. Cut it.'

'No!' I shouted. I might have been talking to my mother.

'*Cut it!*' said Johnson. He had gone mad. I could hear it.

The man with the knife looked at the other, and the man with the curious French said gently, '*Eh bien.* You wish us to cut? Shall we cut you?'

'Only,' said Johnson, 'if you are crazy. I will say it again. If Miss Helmann possesses this information, which I doubt, it is of an importance which surpasses that of Mr Pymm's ear, or mine. She will not impart it.'

I was impressed by the extreme deliberateness with which he made this statement, as well as irritated by his bossiness, and shocked by the way he'd selected Pymm as Chief Victim. Even then, I had no chance to speak. The man who wore Arab dress said, 'Then perhaps it is not the ear with which we should concern ourselves. Mademoiselle, it is for you. Do we cut now?'

The knife glittered. The knife hung, poised, over the invisible assets of Ellwood Pymm, whom I did not especially like, whom I did not especially know, but whom I did not wish to see debarred from trade, rough or smooth, for the rest of his natural life. They were all four looking at me: three slitted pairs of eyes and Johnson's, screwed up against the smoke and more intent, somehow, than all of them.

It was Johnson who spoke, quickly and quietly, and not in English. He said, 'Wendy. Do you know German?' And when I nodded, he went on, in German as beautiful as Roland Reed's: 'They are bluffing. Force them to use the knife. If they draw blood, then I am wrong. Give them some figures at once.'

And suddenly, looking at his untouched face, listening to the cajolery in his voice, I saw I'd been duped. Ellwood Pymm had nothing to do with it. Pymm was only the hostage who got me here. It was Johnson – Johnson, backer of Marguerite Curtis Geddes who needed those figures, and before tomorrow's meeting. Johnson who hired the men. Johnson who made sure he came with me and was using Pymm, now, to convince me that I had to speak. I said, 'Mr Johnson, I think Mr Pymm is quite safe. I don't think you or anyone else would stoop to murder. And so I'm not giving you or anyone else the figures you ask for.'

'Me?' said Johnson. 'Holy Jesus, if you think I'm behind this, why did I lay a whole bloody trail with your phrase-book? If they force you to, make up the numbers.'

I stared at him, since for a moment he had sounded wholly alarmed. It still didn't convince me. He *had* laid a trail. Equally, he could have paid someone to pick up all the papers. And he needn't count on my gratitude for suggesting I dream up the numbers. I had thought of that. So had everyone else. While we spoke, a clipboard appeared in front of me. Our interlocutor said, 'You will speak English or French, if you please. Naturally, the message is known. We require interpretation of the words employed in it.

Inconsistencies will be apparent. Here is a pen. Now I will ask the questions.' He held a paper of notes in his hand.

I didn't know what to do. I took the board and the ballpoint. Beside Ellwood Pymm, the man with the knife was using its point, idly, to slit Pymm's leather jacket to shreds. Pymm, with his mouth slightly open, lay as if already dead.

If I told them what they wanted to know, MCG would know how to resist the take-over. The City would know how much we needed MCG money. Mo Morgan would realize that he was Kingsley's only prospect of long-term survival, and that without MCG he might never be paid. And anyone with the idea of bidding for Kingsley's would know that they would never have a better chance than just now. Sir Robert had thought, bringing no one but me, that he had escaped interference. Instead, I had put his whole business in jeopardy.

I watched the knife rip its way through the leather and knew that whatever I invented, it would have to be brilliant. I didn't know Johnson's numerate capabilities, but artists, while fond of money in my experience, usually let others manage it. Two of the men who might be his were hired thugs, but the third was a professional with some education, or enough, at least, to test out the answers. And considering the value of the answers, the third man wasn't, therefore, somebody's bell-boy.

My face must have changed, and my captor saw it. He said, 'You are wise. I see you are ready to speak. Then, mademoiselle, the first question is this.'

It was about the last quarter's results, and was lethal. I listened to what he was saying, but the corner of my eye was on Johnson behind him. Once the three faces were turned towards me, Johnson spat out his fag and shifted his bottom. Then, as the question rolled to its end, he suddenly jackknifed his body and with a slam of his two shackled feet, kicked the base of the carpet-stack nearest him.

Arabs go in for long, heavy carpets. They fell like limp drain-pipes, toppling the man with the knife. They crashed to the ground beside Ellwood who, roused, said, 'Holy shit!' and rolled clumsily out of the way. Dust rose and lingered in clouds, and for a moment, the carpets sprawled between the others and Johnson and me. I could do nothing for Pymm, but I owed Johnson, it seemed, another benefit. The knife had fallen: he kicked it towards me. One of the thugs appeared at my elbow.

I applied the Ten Golden Rules When You Travel. I got him in the eye with my ballpoint and the overclothed groin with my knee, and had time to slash Johnson's bonds before the other two scrambled over the carpets. I turned with the knife in my hand. The French-speaker had jumped to block the head of the stairs. The second man, his hands wide, stood before me. The one I had hit, growling, began to move on all fours towards us. Beyond the carpets, I could see Mr Pymm's terrified face.

Johnson said, 'Move!' He pulled the knife from my hand and shoved me into the gallery. It was narrow, and crowded with carpets. I stumbled, his hand on my back, and he followed at a shambling run, watching over his shoulder. As he ran, he clawed and kicked at the carpet rolls, dragging down anything that would tumble behind him. The first of our captors was hardly six feet behind him, and the other two were following fast. I didn't know if there were any more stairs. Somewhere far below, a door shuddered and opened. I thought, 'They've sent for their friends. Now they'll force me to tell, and Sir Robert will know who to blame for it.'

A voice said in English, 'It's empty.' And another voice said, 'Let's look, anyway.' The first voice was that of Seb Sullivan.

Johnson called 'Seb!' but it came out as a gasp. My lungs, as I've said, are quite good ones. I roared 'Colonel Sullivan! Help!' and behind us, the three robed figures slackened speed. Then the French-speaker strode to the gallery rail. It looked fragile. It was nothing really but a shopfitter's rail, from which carpets hung to the sales floor in layers. The man looked over, and surveyed the advancing group of our rescuers. There were eight of them. Then he called down, in French.

'Colonel Sullivan, whoever you are! The mademoiselle and your friends are our prisoners. Stay where you are. Do not leave the building for help. Do not climb the stairs. Otherwise your friends will suffer injury.'

He waited, as if he had all the time in the world, for an answer. The other two waited beside him, including the man I'd attacked.

One of his eyes was inflamed, the other glaring. And I saw why they had stopped, and why Johnson had stopped pushing me. Ahead the gallery ended. There was just a blank wall, with no way of getting past it.

Johnson still had the knife. He turned, keeping me at his back, and addressed the men. 'How can you expect to escape?'

The leader's veil twitched. He said, 'You underestimate your value, monsieur. And that of mademoiselle.'

Below, they were talking. Then someone called up. 'Who are you?'

'An impatient man,' said our French-speaking friend. 'Do you agree?'

It was Sullivan who was speaking. He shouted, 'Not on your word, you bastards. Let us hear them.'

The man turned, his hand raised. His eyes on him, Johnson obediently spoke. 'Seb? Do as he says.'

'And Wendy?' said Sullivan. 'Pymm?'

'Safe and well. Leave it to us,' Johnson said. And also said, very rapidly in my direction, 'Over the rail when I say. Done a climbing course?'

He had had a quick look at the balustrade. It was primitive, as I said: nothing more than a rail on wood uprights. From the outer side hung layers of overlapping thick carpets with price tags. Below was a drop to the floor, from which a group of pale faces peered up at us. 'OK. *Now!*' Johnson said.

They rushed us just as I jumped for the rail, and Johnson stood with the knife in one hand until I was safely over and then rolled himself over beside me. We had barely time to find hand-holds before the three men above half-plunged after us, their arms thrashing, their hands grasping our hair, our shoulders, our armpits. One of them clutched me hard by the wrist. I gasped at the pain of it, and felt him begin to drag my arm straight, while his other hand came to support me. Then Johnson leaned over, and the knife flashed, and there was blood which wasn't mine all over my arm. I almost fell, the man freed me so suddenly.

I was out of reach then, but Johnson wasn't. He swayed about with the carpet, one hand gripping, the other making a fist with his knife. A man holding a baton of wood aimed a ferocious blow at his head. Before it connected, Johnson kicked himself hurriedly off, using his weight to swing himself and the carpet to one side. There was a cracking noise from above, and he swore. Then I saw he was swearing because he had slackened his hold on the cloth and had begun to slither rapidly down, descending two trees of life and finally brushing past a sugar-pink plush mat with camels. By that time I, too, was clambering down, having realized that there are worse things than falling. Grasping the shuddering carpet, I half slid, half handed myself to the floor, where our rescuers were at last free to act without harming us. Some of them made for the stairs. The rest, including Sullivan, stood waiting anxiously below to receive us.

At one point, I looked up. For a moment, the veiled faces above continued to peer over the rail, then they vanished. I half-expected, after that, to hear the noise of battle from the stairs but there was nothing. Just the pounding of feet running upwards, and the sounds of Canadian voices mixed with French yelling and exclaiming from the gallery floor. They had found Ellwood Pymm, but the Arabs had gone.

My hands cramped, my knees bruised, my joints aching, I reached the floor and stood, unaccountably shaking. Sullivan put his arms round me. Johnson, who had fallen a comfortable six feet into cushions, remained gracefully where he was. He was talking again. 'There was another bloody way out. I thought there might be. They'll have got clean away. Well, away.'

He sounded more mellow than querulous. Someone, leaning down, took his arm and hauled him steadily upright. I saw it was the young man from the boat again, Oliver. Johnson, continuing without interruption said, 'Look. Miss Helmann. Do you want to be questioned about all this? It's fairly sensitive. Pymm will cover up, I should think, unless you want to make it all public.'

I said, 'What will Pymm say?'

Oliver had removed his hand, and Johnson remained success-fully standing. He said, 'Theft – ransom – kidnap – he'll make up some story. He's a tipster after an exclusive – he won't mention Kingsley's. Anyway, you're the one they were after.'

'Kingsley's?' Colonel Sullivan said. 'This had to do with *Kingsley's*?'

'This had to do with secret-mongering,' said Johnson Johnson somewhat breathily. 'And it may not stop there. Miss Helmann, my feeling is you ought to get out of public view quickly. Back to Marrakesh. Back to where they can't easily trace you. If you like, I'll take you now.'

Sullivan turned, his arm round me still. He smelled of after-shave like Val Dresden, and of sweat, which Val Dresden never did. He smelled safe. He said, 'I'll take her back in the Sunbeam.'

'You could,' Johnson said. Then he added, 'No. She'd be quicker with me. Take Pymm. He'll need cosseting. They gave him a hell of a time. And his bus has gone.' He looked at Oliver, who was staring at him, and said, 'All right. Come on. Let's go.'

I thought Sullivan would object, but he didn't. He held my elbow as we walked out of the door into the late afternoon sunlight, and kept his arm round me all the time we hurried back to the harbour. Behind, Johnson drifted along with the muscular Oliver, who seemed to be complaining about something: perhaps that his employer was walking out on his two guests the Oppenheims. Behind that came Ellwood Pymm, proceeding feebly between two stalwart helpers.

I found I didn't want to talk much, even to Sullivan. I told him roughly what happened. I began to feel a little proud of it, when I heard how he took it. I was only sorry that I couldn't make out who was behind it. It couldn't be Johnson, after all. Johnson had helped me escape; had stopped me having to let down Sir Robert.

'Then who?' Sullivan said.

But I didn't know.

At the harbour, the Sunbeam was waiting and Sullivan walked me towards it. 'Look. Someone else can deal with Pymm. I'll take you home.'

As usual, the car was mobbed by boys. He tossed some coins to the youth he'd left guarding it, and I saw Johnson, somewhat hazily, was doing the same further up. It had crossed my mind to wonder how he had come so quickly from Marrakesh, and how he proposed to take me back anyway. Then I saw what he was wheeling towards me. Built like a nuclear power-station, several hundredweight of custom-built Harley-Davidson motor bike. Seb said, 'Christ.'

'Spoilsport,' Johnson said, 'I do not wish to be, but this lady is in too much demand for my liking. The quicker she's elsewhere, the better. Miss Helmann, my favourite Executive Secretary, get on the pillion.'

I might have refused. I changed my mind, I think, because of Oliver's expression. Oliver said, 'You ought to be binned.' Johnson looked surprised. I hitched up my skirt, although it was almost brief enough anyway, and straddled the seat under the blue, annoyed gaze of Seb Sullivan. Then the Great Portrait Painter got into the saddle, turned the key, and gave a last, considering look round the harbour. His face was uniformly fawn, and his eyes were flat as old mud. Far down the quay, *Dolly* rocked in the water against the warm western sky. There was no sign of Muriel or her husband. Our rescuers stood on the quay, Ellwood Pymm in their midst. As I watched, they coaxed him towards the blue Sunbeam. His fine leather jacket hung about him like angel-hair pasta.

Johnson said, 'Hang on to my belt. There are absolutely no guarantees on this trip.' And with a surge that made me clutch him like a carpet, he threw the Harley-Davidson forward, away from safe, sunny Essaouira and back to the workaday menace of Marrakesh.

9

Night fell on Johnson and the Harley-Davidson and me almost immediately after we left Essaouira. One moment we were roaring through the oranges and the lemons and the mimosa, with the sun a flaming red disc in a wide rosy seascape behind us. Then the sky ahead became an interesting dull shade of violet; and it was hard to see the argan tree shadows, or the light and shade on the distant clay blocks that were buildings. For a moment more, the world behind us was pink, the warm scented air streamed past and, on the low hills, strings of camels stood like children's black cut-outs.

Then everything became dark, and a man on an old unlit bicycle wandered out of a track straight in front of us. Johnson swerved, shot off the road, scoured through a ditch of cold racing water, dashed between an unspecified number of unidentifiable trees, got back on to the road again and whined to a halt. He sat, one foot on the road and his eyes on the darkness ahead and said, 'Should we take turn about?'

It was the spirit, if not quite the voice, of the man in the lift at Kingsley Conglomerates. I wished I had gone in the Sunbeam. I thought I could hear, some way behind, the distinctive engine of the Sunbeam, being fast and properly driven by Seb Sullivan. Seb Sullivan's job, as it turned out, had been to discredit Johnson, and Rita Geddes, and Reed. Johnson's had been to cheat and lie to conceal his connection with MCG, while making waves over his portrait. Johnson had taken me to lunch at his club, and had just rescued me and Ellwood Pymm from a number of villains. The Colonel was good-looking and young and romantic and could drive really well. I said, 'It's your bike.'

There was a thoughtful silence. Two cars without lights approached, shaved and passed us. He said, 'I know. I remember buying it, and thinking it ought to go faster than a '26 Sunbeam. Silly, silly pride. You didn't take a course on the Harley-Davidson?'

'No,' I said.

'Pity,' he said; and turning the key in the ignition, resumed our erratic journey.

I hadn't noticed, until then, how he was steering. It hadn't mattered, on an empty road lit by sunshine. On a lightless road, occupied by lightless traffic, it was dangerous. We met, fairly soon, another bicycle. We shot through a village, a skein of lamps overhead, and plunged immediately into frightening darkness. The powerful light of the bike picked up, disastrously and too late, a group of camels plodding homewards with their driver. He missed the main group, but a youngster, snorting, ran zigzagging before us for half a mile. At that point, again, it seemed to me that I could hear the vintage car engine behind us. Then the beast ran aside, and the bike resumed its thundering top speed again.

The headlight picked up the blank red wall of an enclave, and then a row of booths half-lit by candles. Blackness, wind, the whipping of trees and, suddenly, a single lightbulb illuminating a cubicle filled with spare engine parts, and another lined with bottles and tins, and yet another filled with sacks of provender. The Electra Glide swooped and swirled, never quite hitting anything but never quite keeping straight. From time to time, when he skidded or slowed, I thought I heard the chug of the Sunbeam. I said, 'You don't know how to drive this thing, do you?'

For a while, he didn't reply. A dog dashed out and was nearly killed. A lorry approached, and we bounced into a ditch and back out of it. Eventually he said, 'I have a slight problem. Don't worry. Do you see something ahead?'

I thought he was testing my eyesight. Naturally, I saw something ahead. I saw a bright rectangle of flares, and a tent illuminated from within, and a number of jack-booted men wearing breeches and helmets. I said, 'Yes, of course. It's a road block. Shouldn't you be slowing down?' And then, at last, I realized what was wrong. A fawn-coloured face and eyes which, viewed at close quarters were quite ordinary and indeed rather blank. Eyes without bifocal glasses.

I said, '*You can't see where you're going!*'

'The central problem facing mankind. It's all right,' Johnson said. 'I have another pair in Marrakesh. Just tell me from time to time where the road is. I suppose we have to stop?'

For a moment, I think he actually intended to crash on. If he did, he thought better of it. Already, the police were flagging him down. He slowed. He stopped. A dark, burly man stepped to his side with a dog and said, 'Monsieur, your papers, please?' And Johnson slowly dismounted.

I got down too, because the dog was going crazy. In hot weather, I don't fancy Alsatians. Johnson didn't fancy this one either: he kept side-stepping as the dog pranced and pawed at him. The burly man said, 'Monsieur? Perhaps monsieur would accompany me to the cabin?'

There was a hut by the tent, with loud radio music coming from it. I said, 'Do you want me to come too?'

Johnson produced the hint of a smile. It was not something he did very often, and when he did, his glasses usually hid it. This time there was something about it that worried me. He said, 'There is absolutely no need for you to disturb yourself. You are totally covered by insurance.' Then, wandering off, he followed the man into the hut.

There followed a wait. Traffic arrived, was stopped, and either showed its papers or had its particulars taken down. A lorry found itself impounded. A flock of goats was allowed by. The air grew cooler and I began to think with increasing kindness of hotels and their minor facilities. I went to find myself a large bush, was restrained, and ended up with a pail in the comfort tent. I emerged, my view of Johnson much jaundiced. He had still not appeared. I returned to the bike and my viewpoint. A pale blue Sunbeam was standing at the road block. Seb Sullivan said, 'Wendy! I thought you'd be home by now! Is there anything wrong?'

'They're questioning Johnson,' I said. I didn't feel like calling him Mister. I had stopped thinking of him as Mister some time ago.

'Now, why would that be?' Sullivan said. He looked cheerful and friendly and Irish. In the yellow light, his hair turned the shade of thick honey. Beside him, Ellwood Pymm was asleep, his crew-cut lolling against the leather upholstery. I wished again that Ellwood Pymm had gone with Johnson and I'd come back with Seb, even though Pymm could never have stood all the worry.

I didn't know why they were questioning Johnson. Before I could say so, I saw the hut door was opening, and several people were leaving together. In the middle was Johnson, without his spectacles. A look of demure complaisance appeared to have become permanently attached to his features. The men round about him looked dazed. The dog, which had been in the hut too, suddenly bounded forward and began to make barking jumps at Seb Sullivan. Ellwood Pymm woke up and said, 'What?'

'It's a Moroccan dog,' Johnson said. 'Very friendly. Offer it sugar. You will excuse us, Seb, won't you? We have to get on to Marrakesh.'

He had got tanked up in some way in the hut. I could hear it in his voice. I said, 'Why don't I go back in the Sunbeam?'

'Why not?' Johnson said. He waved a hand, and made his way to the Harley. He had found his way into the saddle when the dog, leaping into Seb's car, went off its head. Ellwood Pymm's small pink mouth again opened, and Sullivan started to stride about, shouting. The officer of the patrol invited them, politely, to enter the hut. I walked across to the Harley and stopped. 'Want a lift?' Johnson said.

I said, 'They've found something in Colonel Sullivan's car.'

'What?' said Johnson. 'A pound of pork sausages?'

'I don't know,' I said; although I thought I did. 'We ought to help him.'

'You help him,' said Johnson. 'I'm going to Marrakesh.'

But he didn't immediately go. We stared at one another. Of course, he was no special friend of Seb Sullivan's. And if Sullivan was up to something, it wouldn't do Sir Robert any good if I were involved in it. I said, 'I don't like your driving.'

'You've got a point,' Johnson said. 'Want me to show you how it works? If you drive a car, you can drive this, I promise you.'

I gave this serious thought. I had never driven a Harley-Davidson but, on reflection, I thought I could do it better than he did. He showed me the accelerator, and the brakes, and how the stereo worked, and we set off for Marrakesh in a series of flashes which might have been lightning but which seemed to me to be particularly directed to the hem of my skirt.

I didn't mind. I sat in the vast bucket seat, and he sat with his hands on my shoulders, murmuring occasional directions, and frequent remarks of a vaguely irresponsible nature. Every now and then his hand would slip from its grasp and I thought he was going to sleep, until he began talking again. Then at last, the lights became much more frequent, and the traffic was thick, and I knew we were on the outskirts of Marrakesh and I would be home soon, unless I killed somebody.

Home? We had stalled at the traffic lights when he said, 'Not the hotel. Miss Helmann, where can we put you so that no one can trouble you for a day or two?'

I said, 'My mother's at the hotel. I'd have to...'

'Of course she'd have to know where you are. But it's not ten o'clock yet. Where will she be? With Mo Morgan?'

I didn't know how he knew that she and Mo Morgan were spending the evening together. I said, 'Maybe.'

'So where does he live?' Johnson said. 'Maybe that would be as good a place as any for you. I notice he doesn't advertise where he stays.'

'No, he doesn't,' I said. I knew where he was. He had told me.

The lights changed, and I restarted the engine and bounded into the centre of town. I was thinking. Johnson didn't interrupt me. After a while I said, 'He's at a small hotel near the square. He asked me to keep it secret.'

'All right. Stop,' Johnson said. I juddered to the side of the road, and shut off the engine and turned. My clothes were not only soaked, my nose was dripping with sweat. Johnson dropped his hands and sat still behind me. He said, 'You can get close and then walk, if you don't want me to know. Or I can go with you and tell Morgan what has happened. Or I can just go with you and see you to the door. Morgan may not be there. And there is some danger.'

He had put it fairly. I got off the bike, my knees trembling, and let him take my place. I let him drive me to the hotel, and wait while

I asked at the door for Mo Morgan. It just happened that Morgan was there, and heard his name, and came jumping down the steps and saw Johnson too. He said, 'Holy cow, an elopement! Angel, your mother is here, and will be furious. Come in! Come in, both of you.'

It was not what I had chosen, but it was not all that bad. I wavered into the hall and stood waiting. Morgan walked round the bike and Johnson, declaiming poetry. I heard him say eventually, 'The worthy porter will stable it. Come in and get drunk. Or no. I see the deed has been well done already.'

His sharp face full of malice, he helped Johnson dismount. I saw them both come to the doorway. I saw Mo Morgan stop. He said, 'No further, I think. What's the reason for this?' His voice was sarcastic.

I felt a small pang of conscience for Johnson. Having the upper hand of Johnson rather pleased me. I said, 'We were kidnapped at Essaouira. Colonel Sullivan freed us. Really, Mr Johnson had something to celebrate.'

Mr Morgan, Executive Director, was staring at me with narrowed, velvety eyes. 'And you? You're all right, Wendy?'

I nodded. 'I got away before they could find anything out. Mr Johnson helped me.'

'Like that?' Morgan said. He released Johnson's arm, and the Great Painter reached for a chairback and sat down.

'Been there, seen it, done it, bought the T-shirt. More or less like that,' Johnson said. 'I rather need somewhere to sleep.'

'I rather imagine you do,' said Mo Morgan. 'You can have my bed for an hour. After that, you can look out for yourself. Who kidnapped you?'

'Ellwood Pymm,' Johnson said.

He was totally smashed. Morgan got him up to his room, while I waited below in the manager's office. I must have fallen asleep. When I woke, my mother was sitting opposite in a fog of glandular scent, smoking oppressively. 'So!' she said. 'You are deflowered by three Arabs? How will you know who is the father?'

Which was where I came in. 'Well, you didn't want Johnson,' I said. 'Who mentioned Arabs?'

'Mo Morgan,' said my mother. 'He obtained the story from your Mr Johnson, he says. Mo wishes to talk to you. Not without me, he will not. I also wish something. I wish an insightful interview with your Mr Johnson.'

I quailed. Johnson Johnson and my mother had never met. They had seen each other once, in a café, before the regrettable episode of the sugar lumps. In the terrestrial globe, there were no two people who had less in common. I was half-awake, and aching and hungry. I wasn't up to my mother. I said, 'I'm going to talk to Sir Robert tomorrow, and that's enough. Let's go back to our own hotel and damn everyone.'

'Angel,' said Mr Mo Morgan, inserting his bony brown nose through the doorway. 'I have news for you. Your mother goes back to your hotel. You sign in here as Miss Smith of London, bed and breakfast, no questions asked. And no one, from this moment onwards, knows where to find you in Marrakesh except Sir Robert, your mother and me.'

'And Mr Johnson,' I said. 'Is he in favour or out?'

'A bum self-employed painter with no index-linked company pension?' said my mother, repeating herself. 'You said he and Pymm were bad news.'

'I thought he was,' I said, looking at Morgan, company director, who was shaped like a mangetout with a pigtail, and was a computer genius, none the less, who climbed Toubkal. I added, 'So did you, back on the doorstep. But he got me away from the aggro, for nothing.'

'Really nothing?' said Morgan. 'No hints, no questions, no figures?'

'No,' I said. 'He got me out. If he'd done nothing, he would have heard all the figures.'

'So would Pymm,' said my mother. 'Pymm, his rival. This is why you were rescued!' she exclaimed, coughing triumphantly. 'This criminal Johnson, his fortune depends on MCG! He blows up Kingsley's, he reads the documents, he does not wish poor Mr Pymm to learn the up-to-date figures. He wins pinkie points by appearing to rescue my Wendy. And here she is, in his clutches.'

'Brownie points,' I said automatically. Nastily, it could all be true.

'But why should Johnson Johnson bring her here?' Morgan said. 'Why not to the MCG place in the souks? He's MCG's backer. He needs those figures before tomorrow's meeting. He doesn't need me around.'

'Yes, he does,' said my mother. 'He needs to get the figures and kill both you and Wendy. This hotel will blow up. We are leaving at once. Kiss, Mr Morgan.'

'Kiss?' said Mo Morgan.

'*Kiss*,' said my mother. 'You never been on an assertiveness course? Keep it short, specific and simple. Use 'I' language. Make your offer in an attractive and affordable form. Come with us and I'll find you a room at the Sahara.'

'Doris,' Mo Morgan said. 'You're talking bullshit again. Come up and see Johnson. Whatever he's going to do, it isn't blow up the hotel. Or not tonight.'

'Tomorrow?' my mother said.

'He can blow it up if he wants to, tomorrow,' said Mo Morgan calmly. 'We'll all be away at the meeting. There's the lift.'

He called her Doris. It made me nervous. They were sparring with one another as if I wasn't there. We got my mother and himself and me into the lift and Morgan rolled a cigarette for her, as she couldn't get her arms up in the crush. Then we got her out, coughing, and he unlocked his bedroom door and ushered us in. 'Welcome,' he said, 'to the Drying-out Clinic.'

I was surprised by the size of his room, which must have been the best in the whole crummy hotel, and actually overlooked the Place Jemaa-el-Fna. Half one wall was occupied by his skiing and climbing gear. Strewn over the rest was a collection of socks and sneakers and T-shirts with obscene writing all over them. On a table by the wall was an assortment of bottles. In a corner, filled with peaceful breathing, was a studio couch occupied by a neat cigar-mould of blankets. Exuding smoke, my mother went over and looked at it. I looked at Morgan.

'Out for the count. Sit down,' he said. 'Whisky, or plonk? I've got both. And don't whisper. He ought to come to life soon. He's probably faking it now. Didn't you know what his cigarettes were?'

I stared at him. Reefers? Daughter of my mother, I had never thought about drugs. Now I did think of them, they still seemed unlikely. I said, 'They smashed his spectacles.'

'He isn't that blind,' Morgan said. 'They set him up. They got him doped. They hid dope on his yacht. They thought the road block would get rid of him finally. But it didn't.'

'Why?' I said. My mother was still leaning over the bed, and the cocoon had a brief fit of coughing.

'Because he had a sovereign pass from SM,' Morgan said. 'And he got them to ring through to the Palace. Do you think anyone would have Johnson arrested, and the portraits unfinished?'

No, they wouldn't. Any more than Sir Robert, if he could help it. I said, 'But the drugs on the yacht?'

'He expected them,' Morgan said. 'He found them after you and the Canadians left. He put them—'

I saw it all. I was outraged. '*In Sullivan's Sunbeam?*' I said. I sat up, rocking the drinks he was pouring. 'Instead of MCG being blamed, the Moroccan police are accusing *Sullivan?*'

'You like Sullivan?' said Morgan. He lifted a whisky and offered it. He had one poured for my mother already.

'He's a Kingsley man!' I said. 'It isn't right!'

'Unless Sullivan planted the drugs,' remarked Morgan.

I took the whisky. In the corner, the sleeper had embarked on another whistling cough. My mother straightened and turned. 'Is this logic?' she said. 'This bum painter packs dope in his yacht. He smokes pot when he likes, knowing no one will shop him. He has the Killer Instinct to Win. He is an expert in Just-In-Time murders. He will throw off the bedclothes and kill us.'

She turned towards Morgan, holding her hand out for the whisky. Behind her, the world's highest priced portrait painter unrolled from the blankets, made to fling them aside, and then hauled them up again to his shoulders. He said shortly, 'Interfering foreign bastard.'

Mo Morgan grinned and laid down the drinks. From a thermos before him he poured a mug of steaming black coffee and walking over, fitted it between Johnson's hands. He said, 'You would have crumpled your trousers. Stop whining and drink it.'

Johnson looked at him without love. His eyes, though less blank, were ringed like a coaster. '*Christ!*' he said.

'Or I'll ring her,' said Mo Morgan. He didn't say who.

And Johnson said something unrepeatable and took and drank the coffee while Morgan stood over him. Halfway through, the mug began to tilt and Morgan thumped him. His eyes closed, Johnson finished it. He said, his eyes still closed, 'You haven't introduced us, Mr Morgan.'

Morgan lifted the mug, pulled a sweater from one of his drawers and tossed it on to the sheets. 'Nor I have. Mr Johnson, Mrs Helmann, Wendy's mother,' he said. 'She thinks you blew up Kingsley's, copied their documents and plan to get rid of us all.'

'Bang on,' said Johnson. 'Goodbye.'

Morgan leaned over and thumped him again. I noticed the thumps were not hard, and Johnson showed no sign really of minding them. After a moment he felt for the sweater, and dragging it over his head, eased himself upwards until he was sitting more or less upright. Morgan said, 'Come on. The drugs? Yours or not?'

'Not,' Johnson said. 'Planted on *Dolly*. No idea by whom.'

Morgan poured his own drink, and then toasted me and my mother, who had slowly seated herself. 'And the papers?' he said.

'Oh, copied those,' Johnson said. 'For what they were worth. But didn't actually kill anyone. Or kidnap Pymm. Or, be it noticed, hang about in the carpet-shop until Miss Helmann came up with the figures.'

'Why?' I said.

Johnson half-opened his eyes. 'In case Pymm heard them, of course.'

'But you hope,' said my mother, 'to force her to tell you them now.'

'Of course,' said Johnson peacefully. 'You are my prisoners.' His skin was steamed up, and his eyes were like Liquorice Allsorts, and red at the edges.

My mother frowned at him, although I knew her maternal instincts were behaving like Rottweilers. She said, 'Well? You hear what he has admitted? Call the police!'

'Doris?' Mo Morgan said. 'He's so full of drugs I doubt if he could get out of that bed, even if he wanted to throttle you now, which must be a common compulsion.' He waved his whisky at me. 'Didn't you guess? Never experimented with pot? And it wasn't just pot. He should have flaked out on the spot. He certainly shouldn't have been able to bring you back to Marrakesh. They're on the look-out for you, Wendy.'

'Who?' I said. I didn't understand my new role as maiden to Johnson's flaming St George. I said, 'He needn't have smoked them. I could have come home with Seb Sullivan.'

'You could,' Mo Morgan said. 'But Napoleon here wanted to keep your address secret.'

'From Colonel Sullivan?' I asked him. He knew, as I did, that Sullivan was a Kingsley man.

'From Ellwood Pymm,' Morgan said. 'Don't you think that would be sensible?' He was looking at Johnson, whose eyes were still open.

'Pymm? He's Press. I suppose so,' I said. I remembered something so silly I didn't want to repeat it. I said, 'Who did kidnap us? Does anyone know?'

Morgan didn't reply. Johnson said, 'I'm not up to talking.' He looked, for my money, to be returning quite quickly to the status of professional prig.

'Yes, you are,' said Mo Morgan. 'Tell her what you and I decided. Who would want the figures Wendy knows? MCG: but you're their best friend and you didn't use the occasion to get them. Who else? Someone from the financial press, someone in public relations, someone representing a raiding company, with an eye to a take-over. Any one of these could have set that up directly, or could have employed some agent to do it for them. Johnson thinks the agent, for whatever boss, was Ellwood Pymm.'

I had thought Johnson was drunk when he said that. He was only out of his skull with some dope. I said, 'Why? They were going to knife him. You heard them.'

'But they didn't,' Johnson said. He had made a laborious desk of his knees, and was separating it from his head with his fists. He said, 'I pushed them as far as I could, but they didn't touch him. We had only their word that he knew the figures. We'd only their word that he'd been caught with the fax and resisted them.'

'The blood!' I said. 'He was covered with blood!'

Johnson looked up through the slits in his lids. For the first time, there was more coconut showing than liquorice. 'Did you see any gaping wounds, or even a flea-bite? It wasn't his blood. The truth was that Ellwood Pymm didn't know the new Kingsley figures: how could he? He had just staked himself out to make you admit them.'

There was a short interval filled entirely by breath. 'There's no proof,' I said. 'I mean, the blood is no absolute proof.' My mother rolled and lit a cigarette, her eyes never leaving the bed. No one spoke. I thought of Ellwood on the floor of the warehouse. I thought of his stupid cropped scalp, and his persistence, and his maniac phrase-book. It was true, it was the phrase-book that had told us where he had been. And from that spot, we had been brought to the warehouse.

Johnson said, 'You're right; the evidence is on the weak side, but there is some. I dropped the carpets towards him, and he woke and dodged them amazingly quickly. And the bully boys didn't guard him. He was awake, and unbound and their hostage, but they abandoned him to come after us. And he did nothing about it. He just waited for us to be recaptured.'

Morgan said, 'He would have to set it up. How would he know Wendy was going to Essaouira?'

I thought about that. Sullivan knew: he was taking me. But he wouldn't tell Pymm. Sir Robert knew, and had mentioned it, in an oblique way, to Lady Kingsley. My mother knew. She had ordered a five-course breakfast (extra) the previous night to be delivered (extra) by room service at dawn by the same waiters who served Ellwood Pymm. I said, 'He'd know from the hotel. He could have had all night to arrange it. And he thought, of course, Mr Johnson was safely painting.'

'Yes,' said Mo Morgan blandly. 'Amazing that, how everyone thought Mr Johnson was safely painting.' He stared at Johnson, and Johnson failed to stare back.

I said, 'But a columnist wouldn't trouble to set up all that.'

'No,' said Morgan. 'Not unless he was being paid a great deal especially to do it.'

My mother rose. I had never known her stay silent so long. She stalked to Johnson's bed, pulled up a chair, and sat down, her knees apart, her cigarette exuding smoke at her lip corner. Johnson didn't cough, but I could see it was an effort. She said, 'Then who was paying him?'

She looked like a Mardi Gras grotesque. She was wrapped, as she always was, in clashing bright colours, and her hair stuck out from under her various headscarves, and her eyes were like Old English bottles. From the moment he began to come to, Johnson had treated her with absolute indifference. Now he dropped his hands to his knees and let them dangle. He looked terrible.

'Who would want to take over Kingsley's?' he said. 'You tell me, Mr Morgan. Pymm's American. He's only attached himself to a Canadian subsidiary. When you and Miss Helmann meet Sir Robert tomorrow, it's your American competitors you ought to be studying.'

Miss Helmann. It had been Wendy, twice, in the warehouse.

'Interfering bloody Wasp, aren't you?' Morgan said. He had coloured up, which I had begun to recognize as a mark of elation. He poured three more drinks and took another coffee to Johnson. 'Are you telling us how not to be taken over?'

'Why not?' Johnson said. 'The devil you know. Whoever takes over Kingsley's might give MCG a tougher battle than you would.'

'If Pymm was really the spy of a raider,' said Morgan.

'What else? Who else?' Johnson said. He sat palming the coffee and watching not Morgan, but my mother. I couldn't understand it. My mother coughed, and tapping her cigarette into her small, grasping paw, glanced at Mo. And as if invited, Mo Morgan answered.

He said, 'The fellow who's trying to buy me.'

10

'Buy you!' Johnson exclaimed. It was the clearest thing he had managed to say since Essaouira. He said, 'Who? How could anyone buy you? I thought Kingsley's had tied you in with a funeral package? I thought they'd take you to court and strip you down to your paddock boots if you so much as re-read your contract?'

In the respectful silence that followed, my mother heaved herself to her feet and rolled placidly in between chairs, folding Mo Morgan's T-shirts and pairing his socks. She opened a drawer, tut-tutted and lifted out two Marks and Spencer shirts, heavily crumpled. She dropped them on the floor, capped all the spirit bottles and, opening the thermos, examined it and carried it over to Johnson who kindly allowed her to refill his mug. 'The direct self-surgery of capital restructuring,' she remarked. 'Going for debt, to create added value for shareholders.' Johnson lifted his eyes.

I knew what she was saying. What Mr Morgan had described was a buy-out proposal. Someone was keen to persuade him to take his original company back from King Cong and rejoin the unquoteds. Privatize it again, in other words.

And in one way, the lethargic Mr Johnson was right. This was tricky territory. Mr Morgan was stitched to Kingsley's by an extremely tight contract involving a long-term earn-out and all the usual measures. But sometimes – just sometimes – extraordinary ways could be found round that little problem. And the loss of Morgan's division would be catastrophic for Kingsley's, and twice as catastrophic if MCG also dodged us. The truly villainous element suddenly hit me. I said, 'Does Sir Robert know about this? I don't suppose that he does.' I said it standing, and coldly.

'Wendy?' my mother said. 'Management buy-outs is sensitive business. And we're talking real product, not fruit-flavoured condoms and bubble-baths. This is Mo, the cream of the microprocessor intelligentsia, building a personal juggernaut of research. He's been approached to take himself out of Kingsley's. He's playing it cool: he won't commit himself till he has his next meeting. The party who's making the offer could be behind all them carpets, and Mo did the right thing when he warned you. And what will Sir Robert get? A personal feed-back from you, Wendy, as soon as there's something to tell.'

She had prepared another broken-backed cigarette and was lighting it. It came to me that my mother and Mo Morgan had already spent the evening conducting an on-site seminar on Kingsley Conglomerates. Using three well-tried methods, I controlled my emotions. I said to Morgan, 'May I put it this way? You are privy to your company's secrets. To fail to report such an offer is a breach of your professional obligations.'

'I swear,' said Mo Morgan, fanning the smoke out of his way. 'I swear I won't tell the new figures to anyone, not even my shrink. Sweetheart, I'm not holding out on the Board. I just wanted to wait and see who the optimist was.'

I stared at him. 'You don't know?' I said.

'Nope. I don't know,' said Morgan. 'It could be General Electric, Lech Walesa or Junk Johnson here. Whichever, he or she is dealing through a third party.'

'It seems to me,' said Johnson, reviving vaguely, 'that Mr Morgan, in a way, has been rather crafty. Sir Robert will want to know who is wooing his long-term meal ticket, and if we can keep it all quiet, there's quite a good chance of finding out. Otherwise we'll have to rely on seeing who kidnaps you next.'

He was feeling momentarily better. I could see the spark, unimpeded by spectacles, in his eyes. It was not reassuring. 'In any case,' I said to Mr Morgan, 'you can't go to the Mamounia meeting tomorrow. You've an interest in MCG now.'

'Have I?' said Mr Morgan. Arm on chairback, he was twirling his pigtail, his glass-holding hand on his knee.

Johnson said, warming, 'Of course you have, don't be silly. If you really plan to buy back your outfit, then your strategy will partly depend on whether Kingsley's succeed against Rita.'

I didn't know he was capable of working that out. He added, 'Unless you're talking such megabucks that it wouldn't matter what Kingsley's short-term cash flow might be?'

'I'm not talking anything,' Mo Morgan said. 'But the sums mentioned have been fairly convincing. You mean I'm tainted?'

'Polluted,' said Johnson.

'At least he tells you,' said my mother complacently.

'Yeah,' said Mo Morgan, tilting his head. 'Notice my broken arm? Watch these Helmann girls, buddy.'

Johnson's face, as once before, had relaxed its expression. I looked from Morgan to Johnson to my mother. I realized suddenly that if my mother hadn't been there, I should probably have learned none of this. She was getting to be like my father. I said, 'You think this isn't serious?'

'Now, Wendy,' my mother said. She had packed Morgan's two shirts in her handbag and a pair of old socks with big holes in them. She said, 'Here are two babes in the world of finance. Mo needs them washing machines to support all his habits, and Mr Johnson's investing in red-heads. He'd rather like Kingsley's last quarterly totals, but he ain't whipping your soles to extract them.'

It was time to mention Company Ideals. I said to Mr Morgan, 'What about loyalty? You signed a paper. You took Kingsley's money.'

'There is that,' said Mo Morgan. 'All that caviar. All those yachts, all those dames, all those bikes. *Who* took the money?'

'Don't look at me,' Johnson said. 'I spend all my money on socks.'

I couldn't understand either of them. I wondered why Johnson's face was still relaxed, and why my mother wasn't gunning for them the way she gunned for me. I snapped, 'Well, whoever your approach is coming from, I gather he's a threat to the company secrets?'

'Could be,' said Mo Morgan.

'So who's your intermediary?' I said.

'Should I tell you all?' Morgan said. 'But you'll pass it on to Sir Robert. Or Wendy will.'

'No, she won't,' Johnson said. 'She'll keep the whole thing to herself until you've met your tempter again. Then you might find out who's behind him. Or her.'

I said, 'I'm not going to keep anything to myself. If you don't tell Sir Robert about this, then I will. Immediately.'

'Then don't tell her who the go-between is,' Johnson said to Morgan. 'Why are we having this conversation?'

'Because it affects MCG,' said my mother. 'All right. I pass. I don't wish to know who is suggesting this buy-out. No more does the painter.'

'I do,' I said. I frowned at them, thinking. Morgan must have met this unknown person in Morocco. He must have met him – or her – before yesterday, if my mother thought he – or she – could have caused today's trouble at Essaouira. It was therefore someone who had access to Essaouira. Someone who frequented the places where Morgan stayed, or went visiting. Where did Morgan stay, apart from this place and the top of the Toubkal massif?

I thought of a woman. A woman saying, *We've taken a house in Marrakesh for the days between games. We took Dad to Asni, and met one of your men, Mr Morgan. He's coming to see Dad. I liked him.*

Muriel Oppenheim. Morgan had said nothing to Sir Robert or me about meeting the Oppenheims in Morocco.

I said, 'Mr Morgan, which of them is the go-between? Mr Oppenheim? Mrs Oppenheim? Or Mr Auld, her father? Or maybe all three?' And this time, no one at all looked relaxed; even Johnson.

Then Morgan grinned and said, 'I deny all of it.'

'You can't,' said Johnson flatly. 'Or you fling Muriel and Jimmy Auld to the wolves. It can't be either of them. So is it Oppenheim?' He looked reasonably neutral, the way he'd looked when Kingsley's blew up. Reasonably neutral, except for a single, small blister of anger.

Morgan, gazing at him, had kept his pruning-slit grin. He said, 'So you didn't know. I wondered.'

'I should hardly have had him on my boat if I had,' said Johnson shortly. It came to me that perhaps Muriel's friends had not all

116

approved of her marriage. She had married her chief. Perhaps her life hadn't been as wonderful as I thought.

'But you know Oppenheim,' Morgan said. 'So whom do you think he may be acting for?'

He could have asked that before, and he hadn't. Of course, he hadn't wanted me to hear Oppenheim's name. And perhaps he really did think, before he fully realized what had happened today, that Oppenheim was acting for Johnson.

Now Johnson said, 'It would be very hard to find out anything Daniel Oppenheim didn't want you to. He's worked a long time in the City. He began life as a banker, and moved from that into insurance investment, and from there to a firm of corporate financial advisors. They looked after Kingsley's, among other things. He probably advised when Kingsley's bought you.'

'He did,' Morgan said. 'He knows all about me. Is that ethical?'

'Ethical? Since when are we talking soft values?' said my mother. 'So where does Mr Daniel Oppenheim work now?'

'Now he's left to set up a financial consultancy on his own. He's rich, he's his own man; he puts through his own deals and isn't responsible to anyone else. His client here could be anybody. Assuming, that is, that there is a major client. Do you really know?' Johnson said, looking at Mr Morgan. 'Or is he simply offering to set up a bid vehicle and go for mezzanine debt anywhere handy?'

Two babes in the world of finance.

Morgan looked at him. Then he said, 'I think there are big boys lurking somewhere. The sums involved would have to be large. Too large for most investors. Someone could end up with a good lump of equity. If so, I'd quite like to know who.'

There was a silence. Then Johnson said, 'I see. It might be someone benign, or it might not.' He paused again, and said, 'I'm sorry. I don't propose to quiz Muriel.'

'No,' said Morgan. 'Well, we shall see. Let's keep it quiet until D. Oppenheim makes his second pitch. Agreed, Wendy? No need to set King Cong digging trenches and filling sandbags quite yet. Which reminds me. Teacher, may I go to the MCG meeting tomorrow? Honestly, I won't misuse anyone's figures.'

He had a nerve. I said, 'No! You don't go to any meetings, Mr Morgan. Not until the Chairman has heard what is happening.'

Johnson was looking at Morgan as well. He said, 'I think she's right. Must you go to this meeting? I don't mind, but if you do, I'd have to warn Rita. And Miss Helmann going to tell all to Sir Robert.'

'I'm interested,' Mo Morgan said. 'Wendy and I did a lot of work on those figures. And there's another reason.'

'What?' I said sharply.

'Security,' Mo Morgan said. 'I think Johnson is right. I think someone is specifically after you. You nearly got done over in Essaouira. It might have been Oppenheim who arranged it, or it might have been Pymm. But the fact is that you need to be guarded, and I don't mean to leave it to Sullivan. Kingsley's changed the place for the MCG meeting.'

My mother knew. I could tell. 'Not the Mamounia?' I said.

'No,' said Morgan. 'The Chairman has decreed, in his wisdom, that we have a working lunch at the Toubkal in Asni. One hour's journey away.'

It sounded like a weight-watcher's recipe. Then I realized what it was. It was the hotel where Morgan had met Oppenheim.

'Appropriate, isn't it?' said Mr Morgan, printing out a small fiendish smile and distributing it among us. Johnson, who seemed to have peaked, had allowed himself to sink back among the pillows and failed to intercept it. '…So I shall take you to Asni tomorrow,' announced Mr Morgan. 'I told you, you've got a room here for the night. Miss Smith of London, bed and breakfast. Nine o'clock on the floor: nine-thirty departure. Wear a veil.'

Johnson turned his head. He looked irritated. 'What's the use of Miss Helmann wearing a veil if either Pymm or your bloody suitor is going to snatch her? They still want the new figures, even if you're valiantly withholding them.'

Mo Morgan sat back. He said, 'You haven't been listening. I, me, myself, will protect her.'

'After Miss Helmann spills the considerable beans? After Bobs Kingsley kicks you out of the meeting? Cornbollocks,' said Johnson.

Morgan's expression flattened. He said, 'No one kicks me about. What about you?'

Johnson gazed at him. He looked like an unshaven bean in a beanbag. He said, 'Miss Helmann will tell him tomorrow everything that you have just said. Won't you, Miss Helmann?'

I looked at them all. I said, 'Give me any good reason why I shouldn't.'

It was my mother who shook her head. She said, 'Fellas, you're up against all them courses. A whole seminar she went to, on Plugging the Leaks. Wendy, you stay here and sleep on it.'

It seemed a reasonable enough request. I could see they were going to argue for ever. I promised I'd sleep on it.

My mother rose to go back to the Hotel Golden Sahara. I took polite leave of Mr Morgan and Sir Robert's coked-out portrait painter having been offered, and refused, a Morgan T-shirt to sleep in. My mother picked up her bag full of washing and assured me she'd send me round a nice outfit early tomorrow. Her last words to Mr Mo Morgan were: 'You touch her, you marry her.'

'I marry her, Doris, and you stick to stud rules,' said Mr Mo Morgan. 'NFNF and no nonsense.'

It sounded obscene, but my mother merely cuffed his ear lightly. I saw her out to the lift. On the way, she raised her leg-of-pork arm and ruffled my hair, her expression amused and forgiving and loving and insupportable. 'You're a Striver, Wendy,' she said. 'You're an Achiever. You keep your eye on the gravy train, and leave all them nice men to me.'

I pushed her in, and slammed the lift doors and hammered the button.

I hate her.

I went to my room. I waited. Then walking quietly out of the hotel, I took a petit taxi to the Hotel Mamounia.

It looked just as it had before, with the twenty-four-hour clocks set to the time of Rome and London and Paris, and roses floating in the light of the wall-basins.

Charity was out, as I'd hoped, and Sir Robert was dining with friends. I said I'd wait. I passed the mirrored pool and the white leather tub chairs and the marble reliefs and the snarling gold leopard leaping on the snarling gold camel and sat in the Moorish kiosk with the fountain, and in half an hour the clerk came to tell me that Sir Robert was back, and to lead me to the suite. The Chairman welcomed me himself, and asked my permission to leave off his jacket, which he had thrown over the sofa. He helped me take off mine.

The room was restful, with pools of light from the table-lamps, and gold and marble glimmering. There were fresh flowers, too, on the coffee table and in the comfortable rooms I could see beyond. There was no one else there.

I knew him well after two years. I knew he didn't want to talk business, not at first. He would ask, when he wanted to. So, when the time came, I began with the kidnapping at Essaouira. Then he chose to stand at the window and listen quietly to all I had to say, with the curtains undrawn and his eyes on the garden below. I wished I had seen him in the cricket field, on the tennis courts. For a big, solid man he always stood and moved well. I could smell cigar smoke from his shirt and a breath of some liqueur. He looked tired.

At the end of the recital he turned. 'I'm appalled. You should never have had to go through that. And no one knows who was responsible? Only that Pymm was the agent?'

I said, 'I believe Mr Johnson's version, I think. It wasn't Rita Geddes. It might have been, through Pymm, an American predator. Or it might have been someone else, through Daniel Oppenheim.'

He didn't answer at once. When he did, his voice was very quiet. He said, 'Oppenheim? What has he to do with this?'

I felt I should stand, but I didn't. I stayed, my hands clasped together. I said, 'I've just found out. He and Mr Morgan have been meeting. He has asked Mr Morgan to consider buying himself and his team out of Kingsley's.'

'Financed how?' Sir Robert said.

'I don't know,' I answered. 'Mr Morgan doesn't yet know.'

'And Morgan has said?'

'That he wants to hear more. There is to be another meeting between him and Mr Oppenheim.'

'How do you know this?' said Sir Robert.

'From Mr Morgan. He wanted to warn me. I guessed the proposal was brought by Mr Oppenheim, because his wife mentioned they'd met.'

'And do you think Mr Morgan will try to leave?' said Sir Robert.

I had thought about it. I said, 'I don't see how he can. I don't know if he wants to. I think he's intrigued, and would like to know who's behind it. When he does, I think he'll tell you. He's odd, of course, but he means well, I think.'

'I'm sure you're right,' said Sir Robert. 'I don't suppose you could have a worse recipe for a businessman.' He had moved, his hand on my shoulder in sympathy and now, as I spoke, he walked past me and paused by the piano, looking down at the keys. He said, 'As a matter of interest, do you know Morgan's real name?'

I had never supposed it a secret. 'Mo? Moses Morgan?' I said.

Sir Robert turned. A book of his wife's occupied the chair at his side. He flung it on the floor and sat down. 'Mohammed Mirghani,' he said. 'He climbs here because he belongs here. He speaks Arabic. He hobnobs with all those eminent sheiks who come here from the Gulf. If he's going to make waves, it's not likely to be on the say-so of someone called Oppenheim.'

'So why should someone like Oppenheim bother?' I said.

He made an irritable movement. 'Because Morgan's a maverick, and might change his mind. Because he has the capacity to make a fortune for anyone who is prepared to pour money into his projects and wait for results. I thought I could do that. I can still do that.'

'If you take MCG,' I said. 'If someone else doesn't take you over first. Sir Robert, Mr Morgan will have to go home.'

'Out of my sight?' said the Chairman. In the outer part of the suite a door closed, and I jumped to my feet. He said, 'Sit down, Wendy!' as if he were angry. I sat. He said, 'Remind me. When are we to meet the Geddes woman and Reed? Over lunch at the Toubkal? Ask Mr Morgan to meet me there an hour earlier. Get him to bring you. Find out, if you will, whether he makes any move towards either of them beforehand. Then I shall have to see what I can do about Sullivan. The drugs were Johnson's, I assume?'

'He says not,' I said. 'He found them on his yacht. Mr Morgan wondered if Sullivan put them there.'

'Of course not,' said Sir Robert abstractedly. 'Not that it will make it any easier to persuade the drug squad to free him. What a pity your Mr Johnson has so many friends in high places. I really must have a talk with him some time.'

My Mr Johnson. Once he had been Sir Robert's Mr Johnson, painting Sir Robert's masterly portrait. Once, the portrait had seemed important. The door of the sitting-room opened. Sir Robert said, 'Come in, darling. We shan't be a moment. A crisis.'

'Oh dear,' Charity said. She came in, her eyes very large, and sat down, dropping her evening bag accurately on top of her book. She said, 'But I'm sure you and Miss Helmann have it in hand. No one's drinking?'

Sir Robert rose. 'What would you like?'

'Nothing,' said Lady Kingsley. 'Where's your Mr Johnson? Reception says he isn't in.'

I thought he would tell her about Essaouira. Then I realized he was afraid she might gossip. Or even take Johnson's part. 'Perhaps he's left,' Sir Robert said. 'I know the Palace hoped to see rather more of him. And I'm not sure if I want him much longer.'

She was wearing a flat-fronted crepe dress and some diamonds. She said, 'What's he done? Run off with one of your girls?' She had dined, it was clear, as well as he had.

He said, 'When did I ever mind that? Much more tiresome, he's been indiscreet. He ought not to be here.'

'I want him here,' Charity said. Her eyes, when she opened them, were enormous and grey. She said, 'Do what you usually do. Use him.'

They looked at one another, with no particular rancour. He said, 'I'd much rather you did. Get him to lend you more brushes. Wendy, I have to trust you to make sure that Mr Morgan does nothing he shouldn't. You'll bring him early tomorrow?'

I said I would. I left, passing Charity and her amused smile on the way. The Mamounia got me a taxi which took me straight to Mr Morgan's hotel, so that I was hardly aware of the leaping fires and dim lights of the square, and the secretive noise of the souks, and the distant thudding of drums for the snake-charmers, the tumblers, the dancers. Inside, I wrote a note in my room, and went to slip it under Mo Morgan's door. I had only just straightened when the same door was flung open.

Mo Morgan stood on the threshold, my note in his hand. He was wearing a pair of creased boxer shorts, and his hair fell in corkscrews to his shoulders. Mohammed Mirghani. I had no view of the bed, or of Johnson. Morgan leaned on the doorpost and looked at me. 'Well, darling, a summons? The beak's study an hour before prayers?'

If he was an Arab, he must be a Muslim. Maybe a practising Muslim. 'More or less,' I replied. He'd hardly needed to glance at the message. He'd guessed where I'd been.

I was afraid of him, just for a moment. He could have pulled me in, bawled me out, anything. Instead, his eyes ran over me once, and then levelled. He said, 'OK, it's agreed. Eight o'clock on the floor: eight-thirty departure and, Chairman's orders, no furtive cavorting with that well-known Latin-American amoeba, Reed and Rita. You wouldn't like to give a displaced man a share of your bed?'

So Johnson was still there. I stood and looked at Mo Morgan, and he didn't look as if he wanted to climb into my bed, any more than I wanted to climb into his. You touch her, you marry her. It wasn't even worth making a joke.

I shook my head slowly, and he nodded. 'Then good night, Miss Wendy Helmann,' he said. And he closed the door with a click.

I went to bed feeling sad, for no reason.

I reached the Grand Hôtel du Toubkal in Asni neither by vintage Sunbeam nor lethal Harley-Davidson but by a respectable ancient Mercedes hired by Mr Mohammed Morgan and driven by a French-speaking chauffeur who talked all the way. Asked about Mr Johnson, Morgan merely said briefly that he was, he understood, due for a painting day at the Palace with SM, two SARs and a Wali. Asked about Miss Rita Geddes and Mr Roland Reed, he added that he thought he was doing well taking me to the meeting without having to waste his time analysing attitudinal shifts. For a moment I thought he must have attended some seminars too, until I realized he was using Pymm-journalese to announce that he didn't give a damn about Rita and Rolly. For the rest of the journey we were silent.

Asni lies thirty miles south of Marrakesh on the road which climbs to the Tizi n'Test pass over the mountains. At first, prickly pear lined the way, and scattered over the foothills like litter. The motor road was narrow and broken at either edge, and we had to pull over for lorries piled with stone, and for laden donkeys and strollers. We passed carob trees, and scaled hairpin bends between cliffs and red gorges. There were clusters of red adobe buildings, and flocks of goats and heavy-tailed sheep, and fields of whiskered barley, and ditches of fiercely running reddish-brown water which furnished the occasional mill. We entered the Asni valley, which was filled with a haze of pink and white blossom. Almond trees, said the driver. Cherries. Apples. Pears. 'And look, where pine trees have been planted!' It was true. It was like England. I was disappointed, until I saw another camel, and a group of donkeys tethered asleep under a tree, and the morning haze began to give way to heat.

The sky was wide and clear with a marling of cloud, white paint brushed over blue, which, once more, turned out not to be cloud, but the High Atlas mountains which contained, nearest and best, Jebel Toubkal. Because we were sulking, nobody mentioned it.

The little market town of Asni is built at a fork, on the slope under the principal road. Isolated on the highway itself stood the hotel we were making for. I realized that Mo Morgan must know it well. It was here that he came for his climbing. We turned into the courtyard and stopped.

Arranged in bright painted rows in the car park were a powder-blue Sunbeam, a navy Bugatti, a white Auburn, a scarlet Lancia, a silver Peugeot, a blue Talbot and a primrose Jaguar. There were also a Palladium, and MG, a Bentley and several others I could name from my session with Sullivan. The Vintages were here for the last of their rest break. In the sun, under the dazzling Disneyland peaks, they looked like a collection of prime Corgi Matchboxes.

It produced life, at last, in Mo Morgan. 'By God!' he exclaimed, and jumped from the car. The driver also got out, and the two of them walked up and down, stroking bonnets.

I descended at leisure, thinking of carpets. Tomorrow, the vintage car rally resumed its route south, presumably making do without Colonel Sullivan, now languishing in jail on a drugs charge. I looked at the empty Sunbeam, now no doubt the charge of co-driver Gerry. Its paint glittered, its wheels and lamps and radiator blazed in the sun.

Beside it, neatly parked on its stand, was a Harley-Davidson Electra Glide with dog-scratches on it. I stopped. I said, 'I can't *believe...*'

Mo Morgan stopped too, and sighed, and came back to me. The problems of Kingsley's visibly descended again on his shoulders. He said, 'You think Johnson would actually present himself here? You still think he's some formula dickhead?'

The driver tramped off. I said, 'He stayed all night? What did you talk about?'

He was unforthcoming, for Morgan. 'Blue paint and micro-technology. We didn't mention you once.' I stared at him, where he stood in the fresh breeze and the brilliant sun with his hatchet face and his pigtail and his distressed jeans and his relieved Marks and Spencer shirt which must have been delivered to him, washed and ironed at dawn and stinking of Gauloises. Behind him, the Atlas mountains towered into the sky, and rose bushes budded, and boys with trays of sparkling rocks converged on him as on Elizabeth Taylor. He spared them a smile and some dirhams.

He would. He was one of them. He said, 'He lent the bike to the Ritas. Shouldn't we hurry inside? Or we'll get six on the bottom for dawdling.'

He didn't like me any more, even though my family took in his washing.

11

You could put the Grand Hôtel du Toubkal into the front hall of the Hotel Mamounia, and in some ways it would do the Hotel Mamounia quite a lot of good. The central eating-place, dominated by a whacking great fireplace, was empty, but the garden terrace beyond was crammed with damp-haired vintage vehicle owners relaxing under red and yellow umbrellas, and talking largely in English. I could hear two American voices. From the rolled towels lying about, I deduced the owners had all found the pool. They were on holiday.

One degree away from the really dizzily wealthy, these (according to Sullivan) were largely nutters who were happiest when spending all their considerable petty dosh on building and rebuilding their cars, and then competing against one another in places traditionally endowed with decent watering-holes. There were grander species of the breed in existence but this bash had suited Seb, it was clear; he had enrolled for Morocco some time ago. Because of Johnson, he wasn't enjoying it.

As the thought came into my mind I observed, seated under a willow, Mr Roland Reed and Miss Rita Geddes, drinking coffee. The willow was weeping. Miss Geddes was wearing stretch pants and a poncho: also her water-carrier's hat and her pink cartwheel spectacles. Reed, as before, was dressed in neat holiday togs. So was I. We were the only two I would have trusted. We left them alone, and made our way instead to the private dining-room, for Mo Morgan's special chat with the Chairman.

Sir Robert, in silk scarf and cashmere, welcomed us briskly and impartially. 'Ah, Mo. Good of you to join us. Good of you to bring

Miss Helmann along.' He had come without Charity. He added, 'Perhaps, Wendy, you could see if the restaurant could manage two coffees?' In boardroom matters, he was always punctilious. Executive Secretaries do not get to hear Executive Directors being burned by their Chairman.

I went off and had the coffees sent in, and overcome by uncertainty, ordered one for myself, alone among the dim exotica of the public room, which offered divans heaped with wool cushions below Moorish lanterns and stucco work, and walls hung with pictures and hunting-weapons. A number of stuffed heads inspected me.

The staff made as if they'd known me for years. Since we stepped in the door, they had greeted Mo Morgan like a cousin. How long could he stay? Was he climbing again? Had he seen the Voitures de Collection? Ah, Mr Mirghani should buy himself a car such as that!

I drank my coffee, and watched the sunlit terrace outside the windows, and the drying drivers with their wives and/or girlfriends and helpers. The tables were now set for lunch. The drivers seemed to come in all sizes: a pair of jolly, tough women; several effective-looking chaps like Seb and Gerry, and some older men with pretty companions. The Americans were of different ages: a middle-aged man and a youngish mechanic. Their sunburn was as recent as Pymm's, and I put them down as North Sea Oil exiles. There were Frenchmen the colour of chocolate. Lolling beside them was a brown and burly young fellow in swimshorts. Gerry Owen, of Black & Holroyd, PR consultants, last seen asleep in Johnson's club dining-room.

Far from mourning his partner, the Sunbeam co-driver was chatting up talent, and the talent was responding with squeals of shocked laughter. The glances people gave him were tolerant. Because of Sullivan, Gerry was out of the rally. Because of Johnson, of course, to be accurate.

The sun was high now, and the terrace dazzled with light. On the left, beyond steps and lanterns and flowerbeds I could see the way to the pool and the changing-rooms. On the right, still seated under the willow tree were the Chief Executive of MCG in her tarty clothes with her soigné accountant. Behind them, the distant snows of the mountains looked cold behind a row of red urns, a children's swing and some cages. Studying these, I could detect budgerigars calling to each other, and a tangle of small, active monkeys, and a solitary den with a short, powerful beast with big tusks. It made an interesting group. Now and then Mr Reed turned and fed a monkey a peanut butter biscuit, but didn't offer one to Miss Rita Geddes, who was laying off about something.

I supposed argument was a substitute for writing, spelling and business comprehension. I could see a wet towel on a chair beside them: Mr Reed's crinkled brown hair was still fuzzy. They had come early and swum; or he had. I couldn't think the gaudy Miss G. got her feet wet. The Ritas knew their way around. Johnson Johnson knew his way around. I remembered Mr Pymm quoting him in praise of this place and its rye. I couldn't see anyone drinking it.

Later, I should have to take the MCGs up to the meeting. The Ritas, Mo Morgan had called them. But not yet. Not until Mr Morgan came down.

I didn't have to wait long. His distressed and braceleted figure appeared, intact so far as I could tell, escorted by two new members of the owner's family, to whom he introduced me. Recalling all I wanted to recall of Ellwood Pymm, I said, '*Assalamou AlaiKom*,' and was repaid by pleased surprise and an immediate service of Scotch, commanded by Morgan.

Morgan said, 'It means Hi. You told me. I remember.'

'You ought to know,' I remarked. It came out sourly.

The drinks arrived, and he paid for them without speaking. Then he said, 'Yeah. Your high-performance, family model, unleaded Arab. So who told you – Sir Robert? Then here's another piece of shattering news. *Assalamou AlaiKom* doesn't mean *Hi*! It means, in its own foreign way, *Peace be upon you*. So peace be upon you, dear Wendy.'

He drank, but I didn't. I began to say, 'You might have told me,' and pulled myself together in time. He was, heaven help us, a Company Director. I said, 'I'm sorry, Mr Morgan. I know you're upset about me. Can you tell me anything about what happened upstairs?'

'Were you listening for the chainsaw?' said Mr Morgan. 'Well, I'll maybe find the internal injuries in the shower, but as of this moment, Sir Robert is coming on with all the sensitive charm of Mr Nice Guy. After his first reaction, I quote, of disappointment and horror, he has come to a better understanding of my conduct. He accepts that I received an unwanted approach, of which I hardly understood the significance. Had I been more experienced, I should have reported the matter immediately. I now understand that I am morally and legally bound to this company. Happily, and I am still quoting, he sets store by my clear intention to stay. I have made the right decision. With the resources of this great firm behind me, mine will be a scientific career of international significance. With Sir Robert's good help, I can expect to be buried a K.'

I gazed at him. He had a new rubber band in his pigtail. I blurted, 'That's crap.' I heard myself, and goose pimples came out all over my arms.

'I resent that,' said Mr Mohammed Mirghani. He tipped back half his whisky and rapped the glass down. He looked much more like himself. Also, he seemed to have come out of his sulks.

I said, 'Of course, I mean, Sir Robert didn't say all of that?'

'Cross my loof. Followed by a single snap of the jaws. If I'm discovered at it again, he would find it hard to stop the Directors from taking immediate action.'

'What action?' I said. That, at least, sounded like Sir Robert. I was glad.

'Hard to make out,' he said. 'My vee-tuft toothbrush would go, and a few other concessions. He had a few quarried words to say, too, about Mr Daniel Oppenheim. Doesn't want me to meet him again.'

'I'm glad to hear it,' I said. I had almost recovered from my embarrassment.

'But I want to,' said Mr Mo Morgan. 'Shake hands and say goodbye, both with our caps on. Told Sir Robert as much. He wasn't pleased.'

I sat up. 'Mr Morgan, one meeting was bad enough. If you and Mr Oppenheim are seen together again, it will start rumours. You mustn't go. It's unfair to the company.'

'All right,' said Mr Morgan. 'Keep your hair on, if not necessarily anything else. I've had all that explained to me, darling. Operating

129

to Agreed Quality Standard and Committed to Zero Defects. Good as gold, and that's saying something. Shouldn't we be going up?'

I'd even forgotten the meeting. I stood and said, 'We?' I couldn't believe he was going.

'All debt has its price, sweetheart. Kingsley Conglomerates have to be nice if they want me. I came to bum my way into this meeting, and Sir Robert can't stop me, so long as I behave myself. We all know that MCG will have had a tip-off by now from pal Johnson. They'll know I've had a buy-out approach. I don't mind letting them see that it didn't work. Sir Robert quite accepted the point when I mentioned it. Same applies to my future behaviour. Any hint of my resignation, of course, and my vee-tuft toothbrush will be smashed, and very likely my matched double set of vee teeth.'

I said, 'You're not being asked to go home.'

'No,' said Morgan. 'Hard luck, Wendy. The premise is that I'd dash straight into Harrods, turn east and bump my head on the carpets. I like Morocco. I shall simply hang about here and there while you watch me.'

'Me?' I said. I found I had fallen back on non-verbal signals.

'Who else? Company watch-bitch,' he said. 'Sullivan's in clink on a heroin charge and when he gets out, if ever, is going to spend all his time getting even with Johnson. Or do you think Charity could be coaxed to keep an eye on me? I bet Bobs has tried to persuade her already.'

'You don't ride horses,' I said.

'No,' he said. 'But Bobs sure got her eventing with Johnson.'

If Sir Robert had planned that, he must be regretting it. Johnson had ended up within earshot of Sullivan. But still, Sir Robert hadn't tried to ban Johnson from Charity's balcony. Maybe he recognized that he couldn't. I said, 'Did Sir Robert mention the dope in the Sunbeam?'

Morgan grinned. 'He doesn't think it was as funny as we might. He's trying, of course, to spring the Colonel from jail, eager to dig up more dirt on MCG. He also says Johnson wasn't telling the truth. The heroin was not planted on *Dolly* by Sullivan, so it must be Johnson's personal cargo. Sullivan believes so as well. I don't think,' Morgan said, 'that I'd like to be present at Mr Johnson's next painting session, if there is one. I think Mr Johnson should take the money and run at any speed in excess of that of a Sunbeam.'

I thought some more. While in Morocco, Kingsley's had to keep the lowest of profiles. As Sir Robert had himself said, they couldn't confront Johnson with anything formally. I wondered if Johnson did use his yacht to shift heroin. Last night, he'd been high as a kite on something powerful. I wondered what else Morgan knew. I said, 'I'm told he has quite a harem – Mr Johnson.'

Mo Morgan got to his feet. 'It doesn't include me, if you're asking. But I still shouldn't advise you to try for it. Our friend's more than a match for Bobs Kingsley. Come on. The terrace. You collect Reed; I bags Rita.'

He was sore. I suppose it was natural. I followed him out to the terrace and stopped, because things had changed under the willow tree.

Leaning over the Ritas was Gerry Owen, and he was addressing himself to Miss Geddes. His remarks were so soft I couldn't hear them, and none of the ralliers had bothered to watch him. Rita Geddes stared at him through her spectacles, but her beringed fingers were scaling the table. Her tall accountant rose to his feet, his face flinty. He was well enough built, but older than Gerry. Rally-driving develops the shoulders. Above and below Gerry's swim-shorts, muscles rolled and dimpled.

Beside me, Mo Morgan gave an inquiring cough and walked nearer. Gerry Owen paid no attention. Staring smiling into their faces, he lifted first Mr Reed's drink and then his companion's and poured them carefully over the ground. Then stretching forward, he lifted the amazing water-carrier's hat and clapped it on his own head. With its steeple crown and its cords and its fringe, it looked as mad as it had done on Miss Geddes. Without it, her orange hair climbed slowly erect like a parrot's.

For a moment, her hand stayed round the jar it had closed on. Then she pushed it away, and pulled off the pink glasses. Her unmasked eyes regarded him coldly, while her mouth made a small printed line. She said, 'Piss off. You're disturbing the monkeys.'

'My God, it's Scotch,' Gerry said. The voice was officer class, like Seb Sullivan's. He lifted the hat from his head and turning the rim in his fingers, began systematically to rip off the chenille tasselled fringe, grinning at her. When Reed snatched, he swayed back on his toes, out of reach. He said, 'All in fun. Don't get excited. I just want to ask one or two questions. Such as, where's the other high-rolling chum, the ship's painter? I want a word with him about Colonel Sullivan. You're not surprised, I suppose, about that? You know, I'm sure, what's happened to Colonel Sullivan?'

Mo Morgan moved up to the table. He said, 'Mate, he was a big man the last time I saw him. You the pal he sends to fight his corner with women?'

'I'm the pal who acts for him when he's in jail,' said Gerry Owen. 'Did I leave you out of the discussion? I do apologize. I thought you were one of the waiters. I see you have the ship's hooker with you. Maybe she knows where friend Johnson is.'

He took a languid step, and with a cruel movement, rammed the wrecked hat on my head. His fingers, clawing down, broke away my good necklace and tore my midriff top nearly in two. I could feel the heat from his suntan.

Mo Morgan pulled me sharply away and stepped between us, his hands hanging loose, Western style. Everyone had seen too many films, including Gerry Owen. He smiled. 'Don't get excited,' he said. He strolled back to the table and turned, forcing beads off my necklace. He wasn't praying. I took off the hat with one hand. It was ruined.

Roland Reed was still standing. He said, 'That's enough. Wendy, call for the manager.'

'Yes, do,' said Gerry Owen. 'Do call for the manager. I'm rather drunk. I'll be sent to sleep it off with my friends. But won't everyone be so interested to know why you're here? And exactly why Seb was shopped, to cover your rich yachting pal and his habit? It would fascinate so many people back home. So where is your dear old friend Johnson?'

I should have realized. He knew he couldn't be touched. He knew neither company could afford the publicity. Mo Morgan moved. He moved quite quickly, and I saw Owen's fierce muscles harden. But all Morgan did was pick the peanut butter jar from the table and hold it out helpfully. 'Don't stop,' he said. 'Bend the forks. Smash the dishes. That should lose Black Holroyd the whole Kingsley contract.'

'Contract?' said Owen in affected amazement. He had turned his gaze back to Miss Geddes.

'Your big PR deal with Sir Robert, you stupid wee nyaff,' said that lady. 'Did you think we didn't know? Did you think we couldn't connect you with Kingsley's? You should have called Sullivan, son, before you began roughing up his boss's new cash cow. Mind, if that's roughing-up, I've seen worse in a back green in Helensburgh.'

If she had been a man, he would have hit her. What she actually said passed in steam over his head. Gerry Owen whispered, 'Well, now: do let's improve on it, darling!' He shot out both arms and, taking grip, gave a sudden, hard twist to the table. The heavy board tilted, sending plates, glasses, cutlery crashing and threatening them with its weight. Roland Reed seized his wrists, braking the movement. Rita's eyes flicked towards Morgan. And Morgan, with a flamboyant gesture raised the jar in his hand and, from quite an adequate height, upended it over Gerry's head like a baptism. Gerry gasped. He wrenched his arms free, but too late. Peanut butter, adroitly assisted, descended his trunk in seductive, dense dollops. Miss Geddes watched. Then she leaned back in her seat and knocked open the latch of the monkey cage.

I remember screaming. By then, all the nearer diners had turned. I saw waiters' faces made blank. A dog began barking and birds pecking for crumbs suddenly flew up the tiled walls of the hotel and soared over its roofs. Morgan fell back, pulling me with him. Colonel Sullivan's co-driver, half-blinded, swung vicious punches with one hand while he wiped the mess on his face with a forearm. His swearing was basic. Then the monkeys streamed from the cage.

They swirled around us, because we were nearest. They jumped on the table, upending everything that hadn't fallen, and demolished the biscuits. Then they noticed the other food-laden tables. People leaped from their seats and backed shouting. Wine toppled; crockery smashed to the ground. Lithe as dancers, the monkeys swung on the tablecloths. They chased among plants and picked up the red pots and threw them. They gambolled along the low walls, and ran up palm trees and sat on the roof quarrelling over handfuls of food. But most of them stayed with Gerry Owen.

The firstcomers went for his hair, licking, munching and scouring through it with vigorous fingers. Then they clawed the stuff from his shoulders and cheeks, poking into his ears and trying for more up his nostrils. He staggered about with monkeys clinging to his waistband and slobbering into his chest, and when he tried to fling them off, they bit him. He had red marks all over him. And all around, their immediate fright over, his companions were shrieking with laughter.

I think even Mo Morgan was sorry for him by then. He said, 'Rita…'

And Rita Geddes, sitting at her wrecked table with a monkey eating a peach on one shoulder said, 'Well? What's holding him? Can he not take a jump in the pool?' And then, softening, 'Oh well. Come on,' said Miss Geddes. 'Let's round them up, the chummy wee bastards.'

Maybe Gerry heard her dismiss him so lightly. Maybe he wanted to pay everyone out. Maybe he just lost his head. But he turned as she spoke and made for our table, or so it seemed. Except that he passed it. He blundered instead to the cages, and shaking off the last of the monkeys, opened the latch of a different cage.

The beast inside was not a monkey. For a moment it stood watching the door, its red eyes puzzled, its muzzle dripping under the tusks. Then it snorted, and shouldered open the bars, and hurled itself out like a thick, stinking cannon-ball.

Owen had let free the boar.

The laughter stopped. Gerry stood, between contempt and defiance, and let it pass him. Roland Reed, moving incredibly fast, seized and swung up a table and ran forward, carrying it like a shield. Morgan did the same with one hand and snatched a chair with the other, waving it as he ran forward.

The boar pounded forward and halted. Its saliva hung under its snout.

Behind, in a confusion of screaming and shouting, the waiters were rushing the ralliers indoors. The last to go were the two women drivers and the Americans, who had to be persuaded to leave. I didn't follow them. I felt what was happening was Kingsley's and my responsibility. Morgan said over his shoulder, 'Get back, Wendy.'

I didn't. I picked up a chair, as Rita was doing. Men were running forward with jackets and sticks. Rita said, 'Anyone know if pigs swim?'

I saw why Morgan liked her. I remembered something my mother once told me. I said, 'Not very far; they're too fat. They end up cutting their throats with their trotters.'

Facts of life can sometimes strike you as funny. With the boar glaring before us, Morgan snorted and Reed squeaked and Rita's face split into a grin. Then she said, 'Oh, sod it. The silly brute's going for Tonto.'

She meant Gerry. And it was true. Having passed its liberator in the rush, the boar had been cast into doubt by the chairs we were brandishing. It jerked up its head, breathed threateningly. It turned as if to go back.

The only person between it and freedom was Gerry, who didn't have a chair or a table, but had only wanted Johnson's present address and revenge. Roland Reed and Morgan flung their chairs at the same moment, and Gerry caught one. The other landed in front of the boar, which turned, noisily. Then Rita raised her voice in friendly encouragement. Rita shouted, 'Come on!' to Mr Owen. She added, 'Come on, are ye deaf or just daft? *Chase the stupid beast into the water!*'

Gerry glared at her. The boar turned from side to side. And losing patience at last, the Chairman and Chief Executive of the MCG company slammed down her chair, jumped in front of the boar and said, 'All right, buster. Here I am. Get me!'

Beside me, Roland Reed screamed 'Rita!' with real fear in his voice. He began running, with Morgan beside him. They had no hope of catching up. A simple make-up mutt with no brain, Sir Robert had thought her. And a non-swimmer, of course, I assumed. We should have taken more note of her friends. Her legs carried her over the terrace like pistons, and down the steps, and across the path to the pool, the boar wheezing hot at her heels.

She paused, once, at the edge, to drag her poncho over her bra and discard it. Then she dived like a small, compact swallow, and the boar followed her into the water.

Perhaps prime fattened pigs cut their throats when they swim, but feral boars don't. She knew it, of course. She struck across the water like a bluebottle fazed by a fly-spray, and the boar wallowed after her. We saw them as we rushed to the edge. Morgan, seizing anything he could lay hands on, began wildly pelting the beast. Reed, flinging himself to the end of the pool, plunged in, arms driving, and made for the resolute streak that was Rita. For a moment, it seemed as if Rita, Rolly and boar would all meet in the middle. And then something flashed in the air, and the boar squealed, and a fountain of blood rose and sank, staining the water like claret. Rita and Rolly looked up. We all, in our various ways, stared and turned.

Sir Robert Kingsley stood on the balcony immediately above us, his hands gripping the rail, his face scarlet. 'Get out!' he said. 'You silly fools, they don't die as quickly as that. Get out while you can!'

And Rita and Reed, splashing, hauled themselves out, just as the boar began to froth and thresh, with Sir Robert's boar-spear in its body.

12

The critical meeting between Kingsley Conglomerates and MCG plc took place, a little late, in the small dining-room immediately afterwards.

By then Gerry Owen, uneasily disdainful, had been haled off by the management for what promised to be a long, cold interview in the office, followed by a heated exchange with his fellow ralliers which ended with his sullen retreat to his room.

A similar fate was expertly avoided by Miss Rita Geddes who, bundled into a robe, announced herself a certified idiot, and disarmingly offered to pay compensation up to any sum the hotel cared to calculate for having let out their poor bloody monkeys. The hotel, already brainwashed by Morgan, accepted a very large cheque and forgave her.

Through it all, I sat in a corner and trembled. I didn't expect to be noticed, but Sir Robert himself found me and sat down. He said, 'Wendy? That silly young man, on top of yesterday. Are you all right? Would you like to go back to Marrakesh?'

Of course, he knew I wouldn't leave, but it was nice that he cared. Until he put his hand lightly on mine, and then felt for and held out his handkerchief, I hadn't known I'd been crying. I hadn't known he knew about pig-sticking, and he laughed off insistent efforts to thank him. He'd pulled the spear from the wall of the restaurant. He said it reeked of cous-cous.

The hotel had left a buffet lunch in the room set aside for our meeting. We helped ourselves and sat down with our briefcases. Sir Robert, still in his immaculate cashmere, was flanked by me in my ruined resort wear, and Mr Morgan in the wreck of his laundry. The monkeys had burst his rubber band and picked out his pigtail, and he hadn't had time to replait it.

Opposite, in pink towelling robes and bare feet sat the Accountant of the MCG Company and his Chairman, their hair like shredded wheat. On either side of Rita Geddes's positive nose, the spectacles glittered like melamine saucers. Walking into the room, a Career Clothing Consultant would have despaired.

'So,' said Sir Robert. 'Let us put the last hour aside, and talk about something of mutual benefit to our companies.'

What followed, naturally, was double-talk.

MCG batted first, with the intermediate-level figures we'd agreed on. My notebook out, I scribbled as Reed first read them out, and then passed round some supplementary papers. Placing them on the table, MCG didn't run very much risk. They were international, certainly, but small compared with Kingsley Conglomerates.

Of course, they kept something back. We didn't get anything like the facts we'd expect at the next stage. We didn't get the past trading performance, or the debt situation, or the discounted cash-flow to an optimum ten-year horizon. And, of course, they'd have done a lot more homework than that. Their managers, like ours, would have sweated over their SWOT analysis: strengths and weaknesses, opportunities and threats. They would have examined the size of their market, and totted up their debts and their assets.

The time would come for all that. All they were doing at present was indicating their own view of their value. They gave us as much as they had promised, and I knew it bore out what Sir Robert expected.

The tricky point was how far Kingsley's could go along the same road, and the answer was, not very far. To begin with, our figures were much more complex, dealing with different divisions with different expectations. But the other factor was secrecy. If the deal should break down, MCG could freely take what they knew to a firm whose goodwill they wanted, and that firm might quite easily transfer its predatory attention to us. The figures Pettigrew had sent were therefore guarded and weighted. Yet they had to conform, at least broadly, with the figures Johnson had seen at the airport. A lot of hard work had, indeed, gone into making them roughly compatible. MCG consequently should have been satisfied. But clearly, they weren't.

Roland Reed queried almost every figure Sir Robert produced. Increasing in number, his civil interventions began to take on the style of an inquisition. We hadn't expected it. At the same time, we had no right to resent it. We, after all, were the suitors. The top management of MCG had once already indicated their lack of interest in our offer. If they were here at all, it was either because they were playing for time, or because they wished to be convinced that Kingsley's were equipped for secure and successful future trading.

Sir Robert, attempting to move away from raw figures, was gently compliant when checked but you could see, if you knew him, the slightest trace of heat in his broad cheeks. He was concerned to explain the international importance of Kingsley's, the excellence of its products and management and the benefits it had to confer on all associated with it. He then set out to show the potential areas of synergy.

He put it all in his own words, which being Chairman he could do, but he really gave a text-book presentation. He dealt with the integration of planning and marketing; with the sharing of management skills; with improved physical distribution (PDM); and better material requirements planning (MRP). He made a point of referring to tax benefits and a glancing reference to what I recognized as performance tables and a two-by-two matrix of product/market divisions. And he said it all in a way that was formal but comfortable, using sensible words and putting in the merest trace of humour now and then. He was perfect.

During all this Mo Morgan was silent and so, too, was Rita Geddes. She rose from time to time, as the rest of us did, and put her empty plate to one side, and collected another. Once, when the head waiter tapped on the door with a question, she got up and called just as Sir Robert was sending him off. 'Oh, you!' she said. 'Listen! I don't know your name, and I hope it isn't a trade secret or anything, but come in and tell me what's that I could taste in the galantine? Jimmy, it was ten-out-of-ten brilliant. Fennel. I knew there was fennel. But there's another thing, son...'

And as the rest of us waited, our discussion suspended, she and the waiter bent over the table, talking vigorously. Eventually, smiling, she straightened and led the man like a friend to the door. He was smiling as well. Sir Robert wasn't. He said, 'Forgive me. I was making a point.'

'No, it's me. I'm really sorry,' said Miss Rita Geddes cheerfully, sitting down with a heaped platter of something. 'But I never like losing a recipe. You were talking about extra cash generation for the divestiture of under-performing or unwanted assets?'

'Was I?' said Sir Robert after a moment. 'I don't really think so.'

'Oh well. We've all lost the thread, and it's my fault,' said Miss Rita Geddes. 'On you go. We're enjoying it.'

After that, of course, it was more difficult for him, even though Mr Reed interrupted less and less and Mo Morgan never uttered a word, apart from a slight sound during the talk about fennel. But Sir Robert, as you'd expect, had no trouble keeping his head or his style, dividing his glances equally between the two of them although his argument, of course, was directed at Reed. He knew very well when it was time to draw his case to a close, which he did with a smile. He said, 'Am I convincing you with every word, Mr Reed, or is there something I've omitted? Whatever it is, I think we've now gone over the territory, and it remains to see whether we have reached common ground. Can Miss Helmann help you, Miss Geddes?'

'No, no. I'll be Mother,' said his opposite number, turning with the coffee pot in her hand. Unpainted, her face looked freckled and healthy, and all her movements, it occurred to me, were surprisingly deft. She came round, pouring. 'And while we're at it, your mother's well, Wendy? Just a ploy to get you here, very sensible. You bring her to see me. Johnson says she's the best news since Golda Meir. So what made you buy Mr Morgan's business, Sir Robert, seeing that you hadn't the cash or the prospects to back it with?'

The stream of coffee continued to flow and she never even looked up, although Roland Reed did. I saw Sir Robert's foot shift under the table. Rather little had been said about Mo Morgan's division. Nothing at all had been said about Mo Morgan being buried a K.

Sir Robert said, 'I'm sorry. Perhaps I said rather less than I should about Mr Morgan's work since it is so highly technical. Perhaps, first, he would allow me to give you a summary, and then he may wish to talk to you himself. Do you know anything about electronics?'

'I've got a washing machine,' said Rita Geddes. It was a depressing reply. It reduced the status of Mr Mo Morgan to the sort of handyman he'd been in our house, and I didn't like it. I intervened for him.

I said, 'It's really valuable business, electronics, Miss Geddes. It offers world-class opportunities in every field. Electronics supply the armour that gives modern military systems their new winning edge.'

I had read it somewhere. Or really, my mother had read it somewhere and quoted it to me. There was a short patient silence and then Mo Morgan said, 'Well, it beats selling budget-priced tights to the grocery trade. What do you want to know about it, Miss Geddes? If it's the business angle, Sir Robert's better at it than me.'

It turned out to be the business angle. We had been warned by a previous encounter, and we should have taken note. Mr Reed merely laid the bricks. Rita walked over them. She did it quite briefly. She said, sitting down with her coffee, 'I just wanted to know why you bought him. I know why he needed to sell. Technology's dear. Needs extraordinary cash resources to reach viability. Private, he'd be selling his patents and getting his royalties, but how far would that help him towards new development? Zilch. So he sells and you buy all his problems. Long-term development eating up cash. As-now expenditure needed to defend and exploit patents. And globally, the high-tech sector in crisis: the John Does and Japanese got it buttoned up. No returns from Mr Morgan for how many years? Yet you buy him.'

'You haven't heard of the European market?' Sir Robert said mildly. He would never lose his aplomb. Only I could see his foot tapping.

'You need cash now,' said Rita Geddes. 'Hence us. And you do need us, or you'd never be trying so hard. Know the cost of a hostile bid in this game? Of course you do. Three point four per cent of the expenses if you win: and that's how many millions? And the City doesn't like EPS dilution one bit. You'd be given three to four years to restore it – could you make it? I wonder. And if you fail, you're a sitting duck for a predator.'

'So are you,' Sir Robert said.

'Not if we burn the crops,' said Rita Geddes. 'Scorched earth tactics, they call it. Sell off all the stuff that someone like you might have stripped, and use the money to keep a core business that random raiders wouldn't quite kill for. If we allowed you to buy, what guarantee do we have that you wouldn't be taken over tomorrow?'

'No one could afford us,' said Sir Robert.

'Bullshit,' said Miss Geddes. 'But do you know what I'd do? I'd consider your offer if you agreed to one clause. A form of capital restructuring that gave me first right of refusal to any new raiding company.'

Sir Robert's foot stopped. The silence was so absolute that I could hear the men's voices outside, and the sound of tables and chairs being righted, and paving swept. Then Sir Robert said, 'But, Miss Geddes, you are talking of the options open to two companies who agree to become allies in a strategic joint venture. We are Kingsley Conglomerates. You are an excellent but small single company in need of help.'

'Then I think,' said Rita Geddes, 'that maybe we can find help elsewhere.'

Sir Robert smiled. He said, 'We have hardly begun to discuss the issues. Why don't I call for more coffee, and we can really talk about what we've been saying?'

Rita Geddes got up. She didn't even glance at her accountant and Roland Reed, a strange look on his face, gazed at his hands and didn't attempt to look at her. She said, 'We have talked. I have listened. Sir Robert, I wouldn't touch you even with the pole you stick pigs with. I did enjoy the galantine. Goodbye.'

She was actually walking to the door. Sir Robert sprang to his feet. Mr Reed, an apologetic look on his face, rose also. Morgan remained where he was and so, uncertainly, did I. Sir Robert said, 'Do I understand that, without even the courtesy of a discussion, you have turned down my offer before you have heard it?'

142

Miss Marguerite Geddes turned. Her hair had dried in a mess. Her bathrobe drooped. Her face, shining with health, held some vestigial streaks of mascara and rouge. She said, 'You're the firm in trouble. You're the Chairman who fucked it. I don't like anything at all of your package, and neither will a single one of my shareholders. The answer is no. You probably saved our skins today, and thank you, but no.'

'Wendy?' said Sir Robert. He wasn't looking at me.

'Yes?' I said. I got up.

'And Mr Morgan. Leave us,' said Sir Robert. 'Never mind your things. Leave us, and shut the door behind you.'

I obeyed without thinking. I realized, outside the door, that Morgan had taken longer to yield to his Chairman. When he walked through the door to join me, his expression was not just thoughtful, it was stunned. I grasped his arm. 'It's all right. Come downstairs. He does this.'

'Does he?' said Morgan. He followed me down the steps and into the silent public rooms. The drivers of the Voitures de Collection had dispersed and so had most of the cars, departed back to Marrakesh to prepare for their start in the morning. We sat, as before, in the comfortable dusk of the central room with its hunting weapons, one of which was no longer there. Morgan said, 'The chauffeur's outside. We could go.'

I didn't answer him, because he couldn't be serious. I said, 'You kept your word. Sir Robert appreciates loyalty. Mr Morgan, he will do everything he has promised.'

He didn't answer. He closed his eyes. Looking at him, his narrow ringleted head sunk in the embroidered wool cushions, his eyes shut, I saw he was actually sleeping. A director of Kingsley's. I sat as erect as I could, and waited for the footsteps descending the stairs.

When they came, I knew from the very sound it was bad news. First emerged Roland Reed, his bathrobe elegant, his expression oddly apologetic as he made for some wing of the ground floor and, presumably, his proper clothes. Miss Rita Geddes came next, her red head flaming, her strong feet grasping their way down the steps. She not only saw me, she came over and looked at Mo

143

Morgan. 'That's a really nice fellow,' she said. 'You tell him. Here. I brought down your dispatch-case.' And smiling warmly, she pushed the case under my chair before passing through the same doorway as Reed.

Last of all came Sir Robert Kingsley. I thought I'd missed him. Then I realized that, of course, he had stayed to vacate the room formally. He walked downstairs, his bearing easy, his expression sardonic. 'Dear Wendy,' he said. 'The riff-raff have prevailed. Have they gone?'

It was easy to tell whom he meant. 'Yes, Sir Robert,' I said. 'What happened?'

'Nothing cataclysmic,' he said. 'We are not to assume our seats beside the present management of the MCG company, and I must say that personally, I feel nothing but gratitude. There is nothing more to be said. Is Mr Morgan capable of bearing you home?'

'His driver is,' I said. 'Sir Robert? I'm so terribly sorry.'

'Why?' he said. 'It might have been good for business but, my dear, I don't think I could have borne it. Don't be concerned. It's of no possible import. Go home. Don't trouble your head. Enjoy yourself.' He knew that I couldn't: he was just being kind. But I stood, smiling, and watched as he strolled out of the hotel and got into his car.

Then Mo Morgan unaccountably woke, and reached under my chair, and drew out my briefcase. This he laid on his knees and unlocked with keys from my handbag. Then he flung back the lid and sat looking. Inside, the spindles on my recording machine were still slowly turning. Morgan switched them off and took out the tape. Then, and only then, he released the climbing-grip he had used to keep me from fighting him.

I snatched my wrists back and rubbed them, still ejaculating. I said, 'What d'you think you are doing? That's mine! How did you know that was there?'

He closed the case on the machine and looked up. He still held the cassette in one hand. He said, 'Legacy of my forebears. We've exceptional hearing.'

I believed him. I remembered something as well. The case had arrived from my mother that morning. Along, of course, with Mo Morgan's washing. I didn't speak. He went on talking.

'You taped it all, like a good secretary, and probably no one else knows that you did. You don't want me to hear it?'

I took my time, answering. My wrists were sore, and I was furious. It probably didn't matter whether he heard the play-back or not: in fact, it might reassure him. Dismissing his staff from a difficult meeting was a card Sir Robert occasionally played. It left him alone, without apparent defences, and sometimes the other side fell for it. He liked the drama, as well. Eventually I said, 'I can't stop you. But you've no right to do this.'

He said, 'I might disagree with you there.' We had both risen. He had the case in one hand, and had slipped the cassette into his back trouser pocket. There wasn't much room.

I said, 'Where are you going to play it? Here? In the car with the driver?'

'No, Wendy,' he said. A surge of powerful noise from outside the hotel told that the Harley-Davidson was being revved up. It escalated into a roar which increased in volume and then started to fade. The Ritas, the triumphant Ritas had removed themselves finally.

Morgan said, 'I'll keep it private. But wherever we go, I think we should hear it together.' Towards the end, his voice faded, and I saw he was gazing beyond me. I turned.

Tramping busily towards us was the feminine half of the Ritas. The dyes of her poncho had run, and her stretch pants had shrunk and she had no hat and, as yet, no new paint on her face, but she looked as friendly as ever, and perfectly helpful. She came to a halt and examined Mo Morgan. 'Ah, you've got the tape,' she said, viewing his buttock. 'That's nice. You'll want to hear it of course. Mo, I've sent Rolly off on the Harley and unless you give me a lift, I'll need to walk all the way back to Marrakesh. Can you drive?'

'Yes,' said Mr Morgan slowly.

'Good, because I've paid off your driver. No need for an audience. And I got a rubber band off a box. Here it is, so wind up your hair: it's a guddle. You'd do better with bicycle clips. Are you for speaking to me again? If not, bend your mind to it quickly and see if you can. And come on.' She had turned and was walking out of the hotel, waving a hand at the desk. We found ourselves walking beside her. I realized it and stopped.

'You haven't asked me, Miss Geddes,' I said. 'I wouldn't go with you anywhere.'

'Rita,' she corrected. 'Then I'll just have to hike. I've the legs for it.' She didn't look worried. She said, 'By the way, the take-over plan isn't off, it's just become sort of radical. You really ought to know what Sir Robert was saying. Because I'm not dead convinced that he'll tell you.'

'But then you don't know him,' I said.

She looked at me with her sandy lashes. Her face without paint was as vivid in its own gaudy way as with. She said, 'I know. Not the way you do, but still. Take a chance. Listen to me. Hear the tape. Go straight back and tell Sir Robert everything. I won't stop you, or Rolly, or Johnson. Mo might.'

Morgan suddenly said, 'All right, I'll buy it. You've refused to sell, but Kingsley's still want your company, yes? So they're planning a hostile take-over bid, right? A bid to capture MCG and get rid of its management, you?'

'Right,' said Rita Geddes.

'Which means you're still the enemy?'

'Depends what you both call an enemy. It's getting late,' Miss Geddes said. 'Come on, Mo. Take me or leave me?'

It wasn't late: it was mid-afternoon. She was the enemy. I didn't want to take her with us. Morgan walked to the car that brought us and stood, one hand on the bonnet. He turned. He said, 'OK. We'll risk it. I drive, and you and Wendy sit in the back, and at the first sign of trouble I hit you with this boar-spear I have. Incidentally, he did save your life.'

'I know,' said Rita Geddes. 'Thank God. There, at least, we know where we stand.'

'Then why are you fighting him?' I said. I didn't want to get into the car. I didn't know what to do, but I had to trust Mr Morgan.

Miss Geddes looked at me. I tried not to think of her as Rita. She said, 'Hell, I don't know. I don't like being made to do something I don't want to do by somebody bigger. I was brought up all wrong.' And getting a resigned nod from Morgan, she got into the car.

We both followed, and Morgan checked over the various controls and got started. As we drove off from Asni, a solitary monkey hurled a rock at us from the hotel roof. It hit the post between our two open windows and filled our laps with glittering pieces of genuine amethyst. The monkey seemed pleased.

We joined the road to Marrakesh, turning right out of the forecourt. After a while, Miss Geddes lifted the tape recorder out of my case and sat silently nursing it. I wondered why she was putting off time. Then she said, 'All right. Give me the cassette,' and took it from Morgan.

I was at her elbow, but she didn't need me to help. She slid the cassette into place, rewound it to the beginning, and then wound it fast-forward to the moment when Morgan and I left the meeting. There she stopped it again.

A moment passed. Morgan said, 'What is it?' He was driving less than well, with a frown on his face that wasn't usually there.

Miss Geddes said, 'I know what's in the tape; I was there. I just wanted to warn you. There were bad scenes: real shit-and-fan category. So I'm not doing this for a laugh, or to get back at someone, or anything. It's just a thing you must hear; and I'm sorry.'

Morgan said, 'We should play it later, maybe?' I saw their eyes meet in the mirror.

'No dice,' said Rita Geddes. 'It can't be helped, Mo. It can't bloody be helped.' And she pressed the button and set the tape going.

13

The recording we heard, above the sounds of the car engine and of our own breathing was very clear. The briefcase had been under my seat: it was unlikely that Sir Robert would have remembered it, even had he known I was taping. His was the first voice I heard, after the click as the door shut behind Morgan and me. It was, to begin with, a little crisp but quite pleasant. He said, 'I am sorry to ask you to stay, when you clearly feel there is nothing to gain from it. But there is one matter I must insist on discussing, whatever you and I feel about the words we have just exchanged. Would you oblige me by coming back and sitting down?'

The tape ran silently. Rita Geddes said, 'If it concerns Wendy and Mo, I don't mind staying.'

'It does,' said Sir Robert. 'Miss Geddes.' The tape emitted sounds of chairs moving. In front of me, Mo Morgan gave no sign he was listening. The tape continued with a sharp, stuttering sound, as if a coin had been dropped on the table. I looked at it quickly. Sir Robert resumed, still speaking crisply and pleasantly. He said, 'Do you know what that is? It's a listening device. I found it here, in this room. Did you arrange to have it installed?'

'Hardly,' said Roland Reed. 'We have reasonably good memories, Sir Robert.'

'I will take your word for it,' Sir Robert said. 'It is of no material interest, as I found it before the meeting began. I use a scanner, as I expect you both do, as a matter of course. I would have mentioned it before, except that it opens a wider matter, the matter of business ethics. As you know,' Sir Robert said, 'there exists, as there should, a recognized code of ethical practice. Where it is breached, it is difficult for two companies to continue doing business together. Where it is seriously breached, it is a matter for the courts. On the other hand, an individual case of malpractice or personal misconduct might not be the fault of the employing company. It might indeed be grateful to have the offence drawn to its notice. We, Kingsley's and MCG, have not been free of this blight during our recent exchanges.'

'You suspect Wendy and Mo,' said Rita's voice. It was, as ever, helpful.

'On the contrary,' Sir Robert said. 'I have asked them to leave because I think they are in danger of becoming the innocent victims of other people. The bug in this room is not the first example of espionage in our dealings with one another. You say you are not responsible for this: neither, patently, am I. It is worth, I think, devoting a moment to think who might be so interested in the affairs of our two companies.'

'I'm sorry,' said Roland Reed. 'I don't see the need. If there are internal or external problems of spying or sabotage, we should expect to deal with them ourselves. And you and we no longer have meetings to safeguard.'

'Perhaps not with each other,' said the Chairman. 'But what future meetings with others may not be endangered? And here is a chance to exchange notes. Today, for example. Is there anyone we know who has been in Asni before, and could have suborned a member of staff – it would require as much – to put this in place? Mr Johnson, I believe, but we know he will receive a full oral report from yourselves. Mr Oppenheim, I am told; but he is a friend of Mr Johnson and the same may apply. What about Mr Pymm? He is a journalist with an interest in financial and international affairs: does he also undertake private investigative commissions? Mr Johnson had his suspicions at Essaouira.'

'Sir Robert,' said Rita Geddes, 'if you want to know who's behind Mr Pymm, you're going to have to find it out for yourself. I wouldn't tell you if I could. Anything else?'

'I'm sorry,' said Sir Robert, 'that you feel like that. You might remember that the valiant Miss Helmann was kidnapped, it seems, for the information she possessed and which she still possesses. To find the spy would at least ensure her safety.'

'Send her home,' Rita said. 'She'll be safe in a week, the rate your figures change. We really have to be going.'

'Then,' said Sir Robert, 'let us move immediately from the question of outside espionage to something closer to the matter of ethics we were speaking about.'

He paused only, it seemed, to draw breath, but both Reed and Miss Geddes spoke together. Reed won. He said, 'On the other hand, Sir Robert, let us not. Mudraking is not of great interest to either of us. Is this your only reason for keeping us?'

'No,' said Sir Robert. From that single soft word, I knew he was about to bring out his cannon. I found I was shivering with a kind of fearful excitement. I knew, from the changing sounds of the tape that he had risen, as he often did at such a point, and had walked a little distance away. His voice was still clear, though fainter. I could see him at the end of the table, a wrist perhaps laid on a chairback. In the same gentle way he repeated, 'No. I should have preferred to place my reasoned explanation before you, but you force me to be blunt. You have told me you don't wish to become part of my firm. You are not convinced by the data with which I have provided you. You have finished by saying, as if it ended the matter, that MCG do not intend to sell to Kingsley Conglomerates.

'I am not sorry. I rather expected it. But of course, that is only the preliminary. You may not yourselves wish to sell, but very shortly you will find that your shareholders are eager to do so. I and my Board will take pleasure in submitting to them by mail a statement of the true position of the company in which their money is invested, and the personal qualities of its Board and some of its preferential shareholders. I felt I should properly inform you of this before you departed. I felt you should have an opportunity, both of you, to make some comment. Perhaps you wish to make none.'

Roland Reed answered. He said, 'This is linked to your sermon on ethics, I gather?'

'Does that amaze you?' said Sir Robert. 'Considering what is now known, for example, of your Mr Johnson? Mr Johnson was, I understand, a major source of finance behind your unquoted firm. As it progressed to the market, he diminished his shareholding so that you, Miss Geddes, and you, Mr Reed should, with others move towards major control. This you have done. He did, however, keep a considerable interest, although none of it in his own name. He obtained a commission to paint me, therefore, in the full knowledge that a dialogue was taking place between MCG and my firm, but said nothing of it. It is, of course, quite apparent why.'

Roland Reed said, 'Johnson paints tycoons all over the world. Do you think they ask to see his portfolio?'

'Perhaps they should,' said Sir Robert. 'Few people have quite such privileged access to boardrooms as he has. Through his proximity to me, he obtained unlawful sight, on his own admission, of secret company documents in Miss Helmann's possession. He has also applauded, I gather, the misguided attempt by Mr Oppenheim to seduce our Mr Morgan. Perhaps he abetted it. The loss of Mr Morgan would, of course, affect the negotiation between MCG and my firm. Mr Johnson may even have instigated an explosion at my London office, which enabled sensitive papers to be located and read...'

'Did he?' said Mo Morgan's actual voice from the front of the car. Rita stopped the tape. 'No,' she said. 'Or that's what he said. Wendy heard him. No hand in the explosion, the killing, the kidnapping, but a lot of busybody stuff about papers. Did he ask you to give some thought, Mo, to the Kingsley figures produced at the meeting?'

The car rumbled on, passing lorries and donkeys and children. Morgan said, 'During the night in my room. Yes, he did.'

'I thought he might. Can we go on?' said Rita. And she pressed the button, as if everything necessary had been said.

'And then,' said Sir Robert's voice, in its own extinct context, untouched by what we were saying. 'And then there is Mr Johnson's other, proved crime: that of perverting royal Moroccan justice by stowing a consignment of dangerous drugs where Colonel Sullivan would be blamed. That can be proved and, now there remains no need for secrecy, I shall see that it is. I have also to assume, and shall tell the Sûreté, that the drugs came from Mr Johnson's own stock in the yacht *Dolly*. That he is, in fact, a drug-trafficker.'

'That is not true,' said Roland Reed to Sir Robert. In the car, Morgan didn't speak, and neither did I.

'No?' said Sir Robert's voice on the tape. 'I understand that it has been proved that drugs of that exact nature have been stored aboard within the last thirty-six hours. Forensic science is very precise in these matters.'

'He doesn't deny it,' said Reed. 'They were on his yacht. But he didn't put them there.'

'I am sure he says so,' said Sir Robert. 'I am sure you believe him when he tells you that he is not a drug-user. I gather there are those in Essaouira and Marrakesh last night who might disagree. I shall always regret that I was stupid enough to be deceived by this man. For his rescue of my unfortunate Miss Helmann at Essaouira I am, of course, grateful, although one can remember better and more intelligent secretaries. The rest of his activities I should indeed prefer to have been spared. What must concern you,' said the even, resonant voice, 'is that Mr Johnson has, although he has not hitherto proclaimed it, the strongest possible link with the MCG company. That he is and has always been your strongest backer, your ally and your personal, I shall not say intimate friend. Do you think your shareholders will see this as the mark of a responsible management?'

'Bullshit,' said the unemotional voice of Rita Geddes. 'The drugs charge won't stick. *Dolly* was swept when she arrived. Your precious Sullivan's had no more than a fright – routine police work will cancel the charges. The rest is fantasy. Nothing connects J.J. to the bomb in your office. It was more likely to be Pymm, or even your freelancing Sullivan. Tell my shareholders that, and you'll bore them to death or worse, they'll all want to sit for their pictures.'

'And Mr Johnson's own confession?' said Sir Robert.

Rita Geddes sounded no more disturbed than before. 'He got hold of some figures. You paid Seb Sullivan to do the same if he could. You expose J.J., and we expose Seb and Gerry. Today's scene would make a great story.'

There was a brief silence. Then again, the tape recorded the sound of Sir Robert's tread as he returned to his place and sat down. His voice, rebuking now, said, 'And you are prepared to drag Mr Johnson through all that, rather than allow me a quiet take-over? Well, perhaps you are right. But what about yourself, Miss Geddes?'

The tape ran silently for a moment. I tore my eyes away from the spools. In front, Morgan was driving mechanically, his chin on his chest. Beside me, Rita Geddes didn't seem to be listening at all. Her eyes, seeing or unseeing, were on the landscape outside, and her face showed an expression I'd rather not have caught. Her voice said from the machine, 'You mean the time I took up professional bonking? That was just a young girl's cry for attention.' Her voice, on the tape, was flatly caustic. Beside me, her face didn't change.

'I mean,' said Sir Robert, 'the kind of life indicated by these photographs. Where was that taken, for example? Ah, Madeira, I think I was told. And another. And another, over the shoulder, I do believe, of a particularly notorious photographer. We have more. We even have some of your Mr Johnson.'

There was a space. Then Reed's voice said, 'How particularly nasty. Who took these? Sullivan, I suppose.'

'He was at Essaouira,' said Sir Robert's voice placidly. 'The half-naked lady, I gather, is Mrs Daniel Oppenheim. The yacht, as can be seen, is the *Dolly*. And there, of course, is the latest.'

There was another brief silence. Then Roland Reed's voice said, 'And how do you justify that?'

'You don't find it attractive?' said Sir Robert.

Reed said, 'Johnson helped Wendy escape from Essaouira. Without him, brave as she was, she might have been forced to speak; to damage you and your firm. And this is their reward?'

'She has quite passable legs,' Sir Robert said. 'On a machine of that power, her arms embracing your drug-sodden friend Mr Johnson, I thought she looked almost fetching. Repressed, of course, and eager for sexual favours, but not normally promiscuous. One must blame Mr Johnson, not Wendy.'

The tape went quiet. I thought Miss Geddes had switched it off, and then realized that it was the silence in the meeting-room that I was hearing. Roland Reed said, without haste, 'I find what you have said to be singularly offensive. As to your threat, I cannot believe you expect either of us to entertain it for a moment.'

'Threat?' Sir Robert said. 'It's not a threat, my dear fellow, it's a promise. If you force me to do so, I'll publish. I'll send copies of these and every other photograph, every other gossip item I can find to news agencies on both continents and to all your shareholders. You and your Board will be forced to resign, and your investors will be thankful to welcome us. So what is your answer?'

Mo Morgan said, 'Turn it off.'

Rita Geddes was looking at me.

Morgan said, again, with passion, 'Turn it off.'

'Will I?' said Rita Geddes.

I said, 'No.' I wanted it over. I'd rather suffer it now, and not in instalments. I watched her press the button again, and the tape resumed, with her own voice making its answer. It sounded forthright, and Scottish, and grim.

She said, 'I don't know how you ever ran a company, and you such a poor judge of people. My answer is, of course, go ahead: publish. We have more friends than you think, and I'd pay a bigger price than my privacy to see you and your company off. You've shown us we're right to give you the boot. You've shown us that Kingsley's is garbage.'

'I see,' said Sir Robert. 'Mr Reed, I know you comprehend what I have said.'

'You think Rita doesn't?' Reed said. 'And I understand now why you sent these two decent people away. There is, I think, nothing more to discuss. I trust we shall not meet again.'

The tape gave back the screech of two chairs. Sir Robert said, 'And that is your final conclusion? You will forgive me for saying that I think you have been unwise to the point of real folly. It is your unfortunate shareholders who will suffer.'

'I think,' said Rita Geddes, 'that they will prefer our folly to your ethics, Sir Robert. Goodbye.'

The door opened and shut. There was no conversation, but I thought I heard Roland Reed cursing under his breath. Listening hard, you could hear feet treading lightly on carpet: running even. The sound of one pair receded. The other went on. The tape was jerking in rhythm. The feet stopped. The voice of Rita Geddes said, as it had said by my chair in real life, *That's a really nice fellow. You tell him. Here. You forgot your dispatch-case.*

Sitting beside me, the same Rita Geddes didn't speak. As prosaically as she had turned it on, she switched off the tape, returned the machine to its case and sat back, her rings all interlaced, saying nothing. I looked out of the window. I thought if she touched me, I'd slap her. But she kept as still as if she were sleeping.

After a long time, Morgan said, 'The fucking bastard.'

She didn't reply. Then she said, 'He can throw a boar-spear.'

'It doesn't make any difference,' Mo Morgan said.

She looked at him through the mirror, and waited until his eyes turned to hers. She said, 'Then you haven't seen real villainy, Mo. It stinks. I can smell it. So could Johnson, as far back as London. Robert Kingsley is nothing.'

And then the tears started to come, but I stopped them.

Lured by a lump of sugar, Morgan and I had been to the Ritas' house in Marrakesh once before. It looked the same now, in late afternoon sunlight, except that the door in the wall was ajar. Across the patio, leaning against one of the pillars was the Harley-Davidson. Reed had arrived; we were expected; but there was no one about. Rita herself didn't call up as Rolly had done. She simply led the way past the fountain towards a different door and ran up a flight of tiled stairs, while we followed her.

The only discussion we'd had, after hearing the tape, had been about where to go. They wouldn't let me return to the Golden Sahara or to Morgan's hotel. I didn't want to face my mother anyway. I didn't care where I went, but I listened to what Morgan said. I found I was tired. Morgan parked in the Place Jemaa-el-Fna, which was full of late afternoon tourists. Two water-carriers stood in our way as we began to cross the square, and Morgan automatically searched in his pockets. He dropped the coins in their cups without speaking. None of us wanted to speak.

Another time, I suppose, I would have joined an umbrella party and gone to witness the snake-charmer, the sword-swallower, the acrobats and the story-teller; the man with the monkeys; the man who sold potions to cure coughs, or love. I walked across the most exciting square in Morocco and saw nothing, because of the voices speaking inside my head. I followed Rita Geddes and Morgan up the tiled stairs in the same way.

At the top stood Roland Reed. His expression eased, when he saw Morgan and me. But his eyes were mainly on Rita, and seemed to be passing a warning. Then he said, 'We have company, but Johnson thought you should all come in anyway.' He opened the door of a sitting-room. Standing inside, still wearing his Palace clothes, was Johnson Johnson. Beside him was Sir Robert's wife Charity.

She was kitted out for riding, in jodhpurs and shirt, a kerchief tied round her elegant neck, her well-cut greying hair ruffled. Her large, light eyes turned to us were unsurprised. Perhaps she thought we dressed like this regularly. She said, 'I know Miss Helmann, of course, and Mr Morgan. You must be Miss Geddes.'

'Rita – Lady Kingsley,' said Johnson. The last time I'd seen him he'd been propped up in Morgan's old sweater, drying out from something other than water. I hardly remembered it now. He was a voice, like a voice on a tape, played in the presence of actual catastrophe. If Sir Robert thought the way he did, what was I to Charity Kingsley?

'I wanted to meet you all,' said Lady Kingsley. 'I captured Mr Johnson at the Palace and made him bring me back and show me the film clips. You have extraordinary talent, all of you.' It was her usual, rather grotesque social manner. She seemed to be sincere.

'We've spent the rest of the afternoon in the kitchen,' Johnson said. 'Raiding Rita's refrigerator and gossiping with all the boys and the grips. Lady Kingsley didn't know about Miss Helmann's bad time at Essaouira. I told her we thought it safer if Miss H. went to ground for a bit. She's sworn not to tell where she is.'

As he spoke, Charity wandered over the room and seated herself in one of the armchairs. 'He's been trying, politely, to get me to leave ever since. Come in,' she said. 'I shan't tell Sir Robert where you are, if you really insist. Miss Geddes is the wonderful cook?'

I hesitated still in the doorway. Morgan walked in and sat down facing Lady Kingsley. He said, 'She's not a bad swimmer either.'

I saw Rita, beside me, look at him. Then she took me by the arm and marching in, planted us both on a sofa. Roland Reed came and stood behind us. Johnson said sharply, 'Has something else happened?' Then, when she didn't immediately answer, he added, 'Lady Kingsley doesn't perhaps know that you've been discussing business with Sir Robert at Asni. Rolly's only told me the outcome.'

'How boring,' said Charity. 'And why are you showing the whites of your eyes? Bobs has been especially tycoonish?'

'He has decided to launch a hostile take-over bid, Lady Kingsley,' said Roland Reed. 'I think J.J. has only been trying to spare you embarrassment.'

'It would be a pleasure,' said Lady Kingsley, 'to be embarrassed by Mr Johnson. Or J.J., is that what they call you? Or is it Miss Helmann and Mr Morgan who are embarrassed? Isn't this what is called fraternizing with the enemy?'

'I suppose it is,' Johnson said. 'But we are delighted you're here, and we shan't breathe a word to Sir Robert. What happened, Rolly?'

Roland Reed had perched on the back of our sofa. 'Sullivan's side-kick Gerry turned up and had a go at us for jailing his partner. Rita saw him off.'

'How?' said Johnson. It had been his fault, I remembered, that Sullivan had been put away.

Reed said, 'She let the monkeys out on him. Only he went off his rocker and unlocked the boar. Nasty scenario. Then Rita lured it into the pool and Sir Robert disposed of it with a boar-spear. Saved Rita and me. Accurate throwing.'

'All that cricket,' said Charity vaguely. She was looking at Rita. 'Let the *monkeys*…'

'Fucking stupid,' said Rita. 'Cost me a fortune.' She returned the look in the same exploratory way. She said, 'You're into horse-racing; you know what we're saying. You get dirty tricks, honest traders in business. We're not swapping firm's secrets with Kingsley's, but they help when a screwball attacks us. You think that's right and good, but it's not. You let each other get killed, or the tabloids will think you're defecting.'

'And you're not,' said Lady Kingsley. She was looking at Mr Morgan.

There was a silence. Johnson said, 'For what it is worth, I think that Kingsley's possess in Mr Morgan and Miss Helmann two valuable and honourable employees who would never abandon their firm or its Chair unless driven to it. But you don't need to believe me.'

'No, I don't,' she said. 'Bobs was furious when it turned out you were the opposition. Are you going to finish his portrait?'

'It's finished,' he said. 'Or will be tomorrow. He telephoned this afternoon to arrange a final sitting. I plan to add the horns and the tail.'

She had turned her whole attention to him. She said, 'It's interesting. Whatever's happening, you don't let it into your painting. I think it's a generous portrait. Will you paint my picture one day?'

'Will you want it painted?' he said.

She stood up. She said, 'Why ever not? May I come another time? I'd like to see Mr Morgan's mountain photographs.'

Morgan said, 'I may be off taking more.'

'You'll probably want to, after the Oppenheim party,' Charity said. 'Or maybe you love endless talk about football. Robert and I aren't going. I must be off; I'm late for my ride. Goodbye. Goodbye, Wendy.'

Wendy.

Johnson left to see her out. Morgan got to his feet. He was flushed. He said, 'Johnson had no bloody right—'

'Wait,' said Rita Geddes. 'Tell him when he comes back. How is he, Rolly?'

'As you see,' said Roland Reed. 'Or rather, you don't. Under all that, I suspect, notably uptight. Here he is.'

Now that I looked at him, Johnson didn't look uptight, only faintly unhealthy. His fresh pair of bifocals hid any other aftereffects of last night. His hair was unnaturally tidy. Rita said, 'You've upset Mo, telling Lady K. about his Oppenheim party.'

'I know. I'm sorry. I don't know what came over me,' said Johnson. 'But before—'

'Well, I bloody know what came over you,' Mo Morgan said. He was still standing up. I rose slowly too. I didn't know what they were talking about.

Johnson said, 'Well, you think you do. Listen, sit down for a moment. I must hear first what has happened. Rolly, how did Rita get on?'

'Fabulous,' said Roland Reed. He came round the sofa, pressed me back into my seat and sat himself on the arm. 'Like an essay from Global Perspectives.'

'What the hell's Global Perspectives?' said Morgan. Finding himself isolated, he sat himself slowly down in his chair.

'Great publication,' Johnson said. 'Adopts a global stance to examine the mega-dimensions of current issues from a new standpoint. Rita's dyslectic; couldn't read; can't find her way about. With the coloured glasses she's practically Einstein. Rolly writes out the stuff, and she reads it off when she wants to. The rest is up to her own fertile mind.'

And that was true. Reed could never have prompted all of that performance. Johnson said, 'And the figures?'

Across my head, I felt Reed and Miss Geddes look at one another. Unexpectedly, it was Morgan who spoke. He said, 'They were roughly the ones Wendy brought, provided by Pettigrew and then merged with later updates. Nobody would expect them to be other than broadly favourable.'

'But?' said Johnson. From where he was sitting, he could see both me and Morgan. He had peeled off his expensive jacket and tie and had settled back, his shirt neck hauled open. He said, 'It's up to you whether you tell me. It's a hostile bid now, which does make a difference.'

Morgan looked at me. Once, I would have stopped him. Now, I didn't know what to do. He said, 'It's my funeral. Wendy's free, if she wants, to tell Sir Robert all that I'm saying, just as Charity will tell him I'm going to this meeting with Oppenheim. The—'

'Are you sure Charity will tell him?' Johnson said.

I said, 'What meeting?' at the same moment.

'You think she won't?' Morgan said. 'Is that why you told her? You're mad.'

'So you'd rather not talk about figures?' Johnson said. Nobody answered my question.

'I couldn't anyway,' Morgan said after a pause. 'But you asked me to think about them, and I have. The initial figures from Pettigrew were far too favourable.'

'They would be weighted,' I said. It didn't seem too disloyal to say that.

'I know what my division costs,' said Mo Morgan. 'I don't think any good accountant would allow them to be weighted so far, unless he were heavily overruled.'

'Or given the wrong figures to work with in the first instance,' Johnson said. 'Wendy, do you really hate pipes?' He had his in one hand.

I said, 'Sir Robert doesn't allow them. No. I don't mind.'

'Yes, but I do,' said Rita, getting up and taking the pipe from his fingers. She sat down again, leaving Johnson staring at her empty-handed. He looked resigned, rather than cross.

Reed, on the arm of the sofa, glanced at him briefly. 'Tell your tubes to be grateful. It would be bloody silly to risk it. Mr Morgan, if it's any help, we'd already spotted the likely cosmetic work. We did think it extreme. What we didn't know was whether it was created for us, or your own Board. Then, if the books were being cooked, who was cooking them?'

'I don't know,' said Morgan. 'And I shouldn't tell you if I did.'

'But you'll perhaps look into it?' Johnson said. 'It does affect your financing as well.'

Morgan was silent. Beside me, Rita shifted. She said, 'Don't wrap everything up. Morgan thinks we're setting him up for his meeting with Oppenheim, and of course we are, in a way. Mo? You know a lot more about King Cong and Co than you did. Oppenheim will push you towards a management buy-out, which means you would try to leave Kingsley's. Maybe that's a good thing, maybe not. It's not for us to tell you. But it's worth a good bloody think.'

And then I realized what they were talking about. I said, 'You're seeing Oppenheim *today*? You're going to the next buy-out meeting after all?'

'I meant to, all along,' Morgan said. 'I'm sorry, Wendy. I didn't see why you should be worried. But he'd set it up for this evening, and I accepted.'

'For when?' I said.

'In an hour,' Johnson said. Morgan must have told him that, during the companiable, coked-out night they'd spent together. And Johnson had told Lady Kingsley.

In a single day, I had lost my hold on the entire orderly world of the seminars. But I was sure of one thing. I said, 'Mr Morgan. You're still a director of Kingsley's. You're still responsible to the Board. You can't do this without reporting it.'

'Then come with me,' said Mo Morgan. 'And report it, if you want to.'

'Will she be safe?' Rita said quickly. She looked at Johnson. 'There was a bug at Asni. Pymm, I suppose. Kingsley pulled it out before the meeting began. By now, whoever planted it will know it didn't operate, and they may come again hunting for Wendy.'

'Pymm's been with her mother all day,' Johnson said. 'I'm told they had an incredible schedule. Rita, really—?'

'No,' said Miss Geddes. 'Have a drink and shut up.'

I was watching a grown-up man asking to be allowed to smoke his own pipe. I was watching him ask Rita Geddes. Neither of them showed the least rancour, and Reed was grinning. They were like brother and sister. They were the way I imagined students to be. I said, 'My mother and *Mr Pymm*?'

'She's quite safe,' said Johnson. 'He saw her back to her hotel a short time ago. And if it was Pymm's Asni bug, he'd imagine he'd got all the dope he wanted, forgive me, on tape. Now, of course, he'll know better.'

I said, 'My mother doesn't know anything that Pymm would find...' and stopped.

'Wendy,' said Mr Morgan. He knew and I knew that my mother was the original bug.

Johnson struggled up and went across to the drinks tray where he stood, looking unhappy. He said, 'So we need, I'm afraid, to take a few precautions. Mr Morgan is quite all right: he's the gold at the end of the rainbow and no one's going to touch him. Wendy and her mother are different. If they think Kingsley's can protect them, then of course that's all right. If they want to leave it to us, that's all right, too. Wendy's not a director; she's not going to tell us anything we don't know already, and since the meetings are over, she has no more work, presumably, to do for Sir Robert. In fact, what did he tell you to do?' Johnson asked me.

No one, clearly, had informed him of all that had happened in Asni. I supposed they would, as soon as they got a chance. They would play him the tape from the lunchroom. As if I'd said it aloud,

Rita said, 'By the way, there's your case. It's locked, and the key's in your bag. Don't forget it. You don't want to leave anything.'

I looked at it, and remembered at last what Sir Robert had actually said, in the big room at the Hotel Toubkal. I said, 'He told me to go home. I want to go home.'

Morgan said, 'You'd still need protection in London, and you'd have to ask Kingsley's to do it. That's OK, I'm sure. The other way is to stay here with us. What are you doing?'

He snapped the question at Johnson. Johnson said, 'Rita, Rolly and the rest are going back to Ouarzazate. I have my last session with Sir Robert tomorrow. Then I'll see. The royals, thank heaven, are flexible.'

'Jay?' said Roland Reed. I could hear Morgan hiss. I thought, too, of Sir Robert's voice on the tape, reciting his wrongs. The concealment of Johnson's MCG holding; the subversion of Morgan, the spying, the drugs.

Johnson looked at Reed, bottle in hand. 'Oh, shut up,' he said, as Rita had done. He poured a large drink and carried it back. It was just mineral water.

Morgan said, 'But Reed is right. You need to watch out. You're on Sullivan's particular hit list. You didn't see the way Gerry acted today. You ought to go with the rest to Ouarzazate. Or get back to London.'

'After I've finished the portrait,' said Johnson. 'Anyway, the Colonel's in jug. Look. First things first. Morgan and Wendy and I go to Daniel Oppenheim's party, and Mo has his fateful interview and decides whom he's going to rat on and how. Then we call on Wendy's mother, come back here—'

'We?' said Roland Reed. 'Where do you come into this?'

'I've got an invitation,' said Johnson, looking surprised. 'From Muriel Oppenheim and her husband and, of course, her father, the great Jimmy Auld. So has Mo. Party's really for Jimmy. He got a nice little medal at Casa, and is fitting in the odd hooley for pals. Africa Cup, here we come.'

His glasses flashed. For a moment, crazily, I saw that he and Morgan were actually enchanted by the idea of going to the Oppenheims' house, and meeting Muriel's famous football coach father, and discussing the Africa Cup the way they had done on the yacht. With all that was happening, they longed to talk football. I made a statement. I said, 'I can't go dressed like this. And I don't have time to get anything else.'

I was not unsupported. I could see the resistance in Rita's eyes, and Roland Reed stayed silent. Johnson contemplated them both. Then he turned to me and said, 'Have you glanced at Mo recently? But the great thing about film outfits is that they travel with wardrobes. Rita, could someone Kwikfit them up?'

'What as?' said Mo Morgan suspiciously. Like Johnson, he had begun to revive.

'Spoiled for choice,' Johnson said. 'A pterodactyl, a ground sloth, or any two legs of a dinosaur. Rita'll do all your make-up. Won't you, Troon?'

She threw a cushion at him, and he fielded it. She had flushed with what seemed to be relief, even pleasure. In due course I dressed and when Rita came, I let her do my make-up to show I felt better. I thought I knew what to expect, but I didn't. At the end, she said, 'You don't really need me; you make a better job of your face than most people. Listen, don't feel you have to carry it all. Let the men take the strain. They'll see you right, and your mother.'

She had talked of my mother before. She hadn't mentioned Sir Robert. I said, 'Are your parents alive?'

She took the towels away and laid her hands on my shoulders. 'Oh, no. They went a long time ago. I have a bitch of an auntie in Troon. Keeps me right. Keeps me wrong. Don't know what I'll do when she dies.'

'No,' I said.

14

Let the men take the strain, the Geddes woman had said. Advice that would bring out the street militants on any professional business course I'd ever taken, or listened to. I thought of my mother's cassettes piled up back at the hotel. *How to use the Triple-Tick System for Making Problem-Free Travel Arrangements. How to Avoid the One Secretarial Mistake That Could Destroy Your Career.* I sat in the yellow taxi taking Johnson and Morgan and me to the Oppenheim party, and I let them take the strain.

I thought they might be good at it. Dressing, I had already listened to Johnson delivering a lecture to Morgan as he changed in the next room. There was no doubt which was which. Johnson and Sir Robert might have been to the same school. Johnson said, 'May I bore you with a circumstance you will have thought of already? An Oppenheim-aided buy-out of you and your microchips would hit Sir Bobs and help, I have to say, to keep Rita out of his clutches. At this moment, you may like the idea as much as I do, but there are several possible glitches. One, Oppenheim might be fronting for a crook with BO. Two, King Cong won't unbundle you lightly, and he's got Muriel's picture.'

'And yours,' Morgan said. 'And Wendy's.'

'I don't mind if Wendy doesn't,' Johnson said. 'And lastly, there's a strong possibility, I should say, that someone will come and sing you a sweet song to the effect that, if only you agree to stay on at Kingsley's—'

'I'll be buried a K,' Morgan said.

There was a pause. Then Johnson's voice, wholly fascinated, said, 'Did someone say that?'

'Sir Robert,' Morgan said. He began laughing at the same moment as Johnson. When I met them outside, he was looking cheered-up and almost respectable in a check shirt outside a pair of fresh pants and a pair of Mafia dark glasses. He said, 'Wendy. My God, how did you ever give birth to your mother? Turn round.' And as I did so he added, 'Just had my first naval briefing. Always look at the print under the small print. That's really pretty fetching.'

'I'm fetched,' said Johnson surveying me. He put a calm, steering hand on my back. 'Come on. Into the circus.' And they kept up the joshing, in between talking football, all the way to the Oppenheims'.

Thirty years before, when African Cup games began, Jimmy Auld had been flown out to coach in Morocco: a married man with a toddler. He was a widower now, and the same toddler was thirty-five, and married to Daniel Oppenheim the investment advisor, and had been photographed semi-nude in several postures on Johnson's yacht *Dolly*.

None of us could have avoided that thought, driving into the sweeping courtyard before the Oppenheims' rented pad in the French quarter. Even Johnson broke off as we crawled through the crowds in the driveway. The mansion was large, and the ground full of flowering bushes and people and palm trees. Mixed up with the guests on the lawns were quite a lot of Desert Song extras on horseback, and groups of tinkling women, and people with drums. Everybody, including the folk-performers, had come to show how much they loved Jimmy.

We climbed the steps and were welcomed by Muriel inside the large marble hallway. Tanned and expensively unadorned in a silk toga dress, she kissed Johnson and shook hands with Morgan whom, of course, she'd met climbing in Asni, and greeted me with the same friendly warmth she'd shown on the yacht at Essaouira. Her gaze had lingered a fraction on Johnson. She knew about the cannabis, I suddenly thought. Then she cried, 'Father! Danny! Look who's arrived!'

In size, Daniel Oppenheim fitted my recollection of the pyjamas I'd seen on his bunk. He was above average height; a well-fed man with fine, dark hair and a trace of a jowl. His eyes were strikingly brown, and his mouth took its shape from a double set of prominent, very white teeth. He said, 'J.J.? We drank all your brandy, did Lenny tell you? And I'm not at all penitent. Nothing here as grand as a yacht except Jimmy. He's longing to see you. And Mo Morgan, the intrepid inventor and climber, of course. Welcome, welcome. And—?'

'Miss Wendy Helmann of Kingsley's,' said Morgan. 'Mrs Oppenheim knows her; she was on *Dolly* yesterday. I hoped you wouldn't mind if I brought her. She's on holiday in Marrakesh with her mother.'

'She's *Mrs Helmann's* daughter?' said Daniel Oppenheim. A familiar cry which, nevertheless, still makes me shiver. He continued with hardly a pause. 'Your mother came quite early, Miss Helmann. I think she's over there, with the Canadians.'

He must have been surprised by the effect of his words. Morgan whipped his head round, Johnson's spectacles flashed and I took one violent step forward. I was pulled up by four fingers and a thumb on my arm, taking the blood-numbing grip that starts gangrene. 'No, you don't,' said a bright, nasal voice. 'Not before you've given wee Jimmy Auld a good cuddle. Where've you been hiding this one, you two?'

Holding me was a short, broad-chested man with a shock of corrugated grey hair over a raspberry nose. His eyes, round as snooker balls, shifted from Johnson to Morgan. He said, 'J.J.? See the legs on that fellow! He climbs.'

'I've seen them,' Johnson said. 'Hello, Jimmy, you dirty old man. Come on, let her go; she'll need massage. What makes you think he can climb?'

Jimmy Auld released me, pinched me painlessly and feinted at Johnson with a small, speckled fist. He said, 'And you look your usual. Only painter I know who goes about like a doggie chew-toy. I know he's a climber, my boy, because I saw him at Asni, and he's in with the tigers. Alan, Roger, Dykie, the lot. Nearly as crazy as you. Climbed Anrehemer east face a week ago. You infect him?'

'We've only just met,' Johnson said. 'Getting my pigtail delivered tomorrow. What the hell are the Green Eagles up to? You saw the second goal there?'

I was forgotten. Twenty people converged on our group from which Mr Daniel Oppenheim had discreetly melted, leaving Jimmy Auld and Johnson in the middle, with Mo Morgan in a light trance beside them. The names of the Enugu Rangers and the Harambee Stars came and went.

Muriel Oppenheim said, 'I do apologise. That's Dad all over. It's just like Jay to start him off, but he does love it. Look, are you all right? I mean, you look perfectly edible, but I heard horrible things happened after you left us on *Dolly*.'

'I'm all right,' I said. 'I owe the way I look to Miss Geddes. There wasn't time to go back to my hotel.'

Muriel Oppenheim smiled. 'I recognized Rita's invisible touch. If she did that, she's adopted you, and you're lucky. Only never, never say a word against Jay. He's God. You'll have realized.'

I said, 'You mean they *are* more than friends?'

For a moment her eyes widened, then she smiled again. She said, 'Oh, my dear, no. He is just God. Unattainable to everybody. On the other hand, there are lots of extremely attainable people right here. Come and meet them.'

She was nice. She was exactly the proper wife for someone like Daniel Oppenheim. She had filled the room with all the right people; the kind who needed to be referred to merely by initials. The President and Secretary-General of FIFA. The President of CSSA. The top officials of CAF and the chiefs of APOTM. The Canadian Ambassador, the French and British Consuls General, the Deputy Ambassador of the Low Countries and the President of the Jewish Community of Africa. We were down to the National Tea and Sugar Office when the sound of many Canadian voices near at hand told me I was getting near my private goal. And there, handsome and bearded, was the Toronto Star, accompanied by CHOM, the lady from Radio-TV Toronto and the man from CFCF along with all the other familiar faces from Essaouira. And Mr Ellwood Pymm. And my mother.

My mother said, 'And this, I think, is Wendy my daughter. That, of course, is not your dress. What have you done to receive such a dress with Mr Morgan in Asni?' She had encased the dome of her torso in an assortment of brightly coloured and glittering wraps, above which her brisk hair and strong, dark features emerged like a thief from a jar. Over her arm was a shopping bag.

Mr Ellwood Pymm, in a white linen suit and bow tie, shook my hand with both of his and said, 'Is she something, this lady your mother? You know what we've seen today?'

'*La perle noire, le champion du monde de kwik-boxing,*' said my mother. Her cassettes had left her accent intact. 'The dress?'

'A loan from a woman friend,' I said. 'Where else did you go?'

'The Hassan II Tennis Trophy,' said my mother. 'It was passable. Lecture at the Faculty of Letters on Think Europe. I was critical. A swimming contest. The 200 metres *dos* was reasonably competed for. The tournament of *mini-basket*—'

'What?' I said. The Canadians were standing in a silly circle, grinning at her. Muriel Oppenheim had slipped away.

'*De petits basketteurs,*' said my mother. 'You need a revision course on the Sony? And *la projection du film Annie Hall.* Ellwood says he's exhausted. Is this New World vigour?'

'Isn't that something?' said Ellwood Pymm proudly. He didn't look as if he could kidnap himself and force me to hand out Kingsley figures at knife-point. He looked like a footman from Toad of Toad Hall. By natural association, I was reminded of all the Matchbox cars, and of Gerry and Sullivan, and I was thankful that the Matchboxes and Gerry were at Asni and Sullivan was in jail. Pymm said, 'Wendy angel, you know what I owe you, and all the boys and girls here who raised the alarm at Essaouira. And Johnson. You and Johnson an item? You don't plan to come home at night, you should tell your mother.'

I had told my mother. I fixed her with one eye and said, 'No, we are not an item.'

'An item of what?' said Mo Morgan, crashing into our Canadian circle. He looked round. 'Hello, Doris. What's in the bag?'

'Your socks,' said my mother, delving in and bringing out a ball of wool, three pins and a toe. She stared at Morgan's feet, and Morgan stepped rapidly backwards. 'You trying to indicate you don't need socks?' said my mother. 'And inside your shoes at this moment are butterfly nets? All I ask is to try them on before I am turning the heel. Come with me.'

She turned and rolled off between the pillars and the flowering bushes in tubs and the whitecoated servants with drinks trays. I didn't know where she was going. I excused myself and followed, aware that Morgan was dragging behind. He said, 'Sssst!'

It was like the time with Johnson Johnson in Essaouira. I almost looked around to see if the American-Arab phrase-book was lying about. I said, 'I can't stop her. Go away if you want to.'

Morgan said, 'No. I have to go to Mr Oppenheim's room for this meeting. You said you wanted to come.'

I stopped. We were both employees of Kingsley Conglomerates. I ought to want to. Ahead, my mother pushed open a door, turned, and beckoned. As we arrived we heard her saying, 'Well, now, I do beg your pardon. We was just looking for somewhere to try on some socks.'

She had found Mr Oppenheim's study.

It took a little sorting out. In the event, my mother left her socks and allowed herself to be escorted back to the party by Mr Oppenheim while Morgan and I sat down and waited. My mother, in her incomprehensible way had evidently accepted that Mr Oppenheim had invited Morgan and me to his own little special party of three.

Mr Oppenheim, when he returned, was not at all sure he had invited me to anything, and was visibly put out when told that it didn't greatly matter whether or not Mr Morgan was seduced privately here or in Kingsley's boardroom, as Sir Robert knew all about the attempt.

'Through you, Mr Morgan?' asked Muriel Oppenheim's husband. His face, when only part of it was smiling, was symmetrically folded and formidable. I was surprised that he had to ask: I thought his shipmate Johnson would have told him. Then I thought back to the naval briefing, and it occurred to me that Johnson had perhaps changed his mind about a management buy-out being a good thing. And that the Aulds, after all, were his friends, not Mr Oppenheim. I thought I would do the decent thing.

'I guessed. I told Sir Robert,' I said. 'These things have to be above-board, Mr Oppenheim.'

'Of course,' he said, his brown eyes on Morgan. 'And have you come to tell me, then, that you are no longer interested?'

Mr Mohammed Mirghani sat with his tough, bony fingers relaxed on the arms of his chair and said, 'I came because I thought you might have more you wanted to say to me. And I found I had some things I wanted to ask. As they say, without prejudice.'

'I see,' said Daniel Oppenheim slowly. He rose, and crossing to a table, began lifting decanters and asking silent questions. He said, handing me a cowardly sherry, 'Sir Robert is not the most patient of men. I am sorry if he received the news badly.'

'Not to the extent of throwing me on the street, Mr Oppenheim,' Morgan said. 'Any wish of mine to leave Kingsley's would be powerfully blocked. I wondered, in that case, if it were worth my while attempting it.'

I sat and drank my sherry while Mr Oppenheim explained why it was worth his attempting it, both in terms of technical viability and financial and social rewards at least the equivalent of being buried a K. His voice was deep and peculiarly attractive. And as he spoke, it became clear that there were indeed advantages in Morgan retrieving the company that had been his before he joined forces with Kingsley's. At Kingsley's at present, as I knew, he was neither happy nor secure.

I supposed Morgan wouldn't be sitting here even pretending to listen if he hadn't suspected Sir Robert's candour with figures. Or if he hadn't heard that childish, ill-judged and nasty attempt to put pressure on Rita and Rolly. Except for my tape, Morgan would never have known of it. Nor should I.

In the event, of course, Morgan was doing more than pretending to hear Mr Oppenheim's case. As it drew to a close, he asked questions. He was neither a financier nor an accountant, but they were sensible. The briefing hadn't been wasted. To me, it seemed that he received frank answers, with which he might well be satisfied. Only on one subject did Mr Oppenheim refuse to be drawn. However much pressed, he wouldn't outline his plans for raising finance for the buy-out. It would be spread, he said, over many sources. Mr Morgan had no need to fear over-dependency. He had no need to fear loss of sovereignty. But, naturally, until a final agreement was signed, it would hardly be ethical for Mr Oppenheim to reveal which companies, which institutions had this kind of money to offer.

Again, it seemed reasonable; but Morgan received this reply, and the others, with all the enthusiasm of a totem pole. In his dark narrow face his mouth opened and closed, short as the slit in a whistle. At the end, Mr Daniel Oppenheim said, 'I think I have told you all I can. Mr Morgan, it is for you to make the decision.'

And Mo Morgan said, 'I wish it were.'

Daniel Oppenheim frowned. He said, 'You are concerned with the strength of Sir Robert's position. It is against my own interests to say so, but you know, of course, that if Sir Robert proves to be in any way an undesirable Chairman he may be removed, and the company may continue with another, perhaps more compliant?'

'I know that,' said Morgan. 'But meanwhile, Sir Robert is Chairman.'

There was a silence. 'And so?' said Oppenheim.

'And so he has photographs of your wife sunbathing on *Dolly*,' Morgan said.

For a moment, the other man sat quite still. Then he said, 'And others?'

'Of Miss Geddes. Of Miss Helmann here, riding pillion with Mr Johnson. They are unfortunate, that is all. They could add fuel to rumour.'

'But these individuals have nothing to do with your buy-out?' Oppenheim said.

'No. The threat was made to smooth the way for Kingsley's to take over Miss Geddes. But photographs of that kind have many uses.'

'I see,' said Oppenheim slowly. 'Who took them?'

'Of your wife? Sullivan, I believe,' Morgan said. 'Colonel Sullivan, of Black & Holroyd.'

Oppenheim's hands were loose on the desk before him. He said, 'This threat was made in connection with Sir Robert's attempt to take over MCG? What was their response to it?'

Morgan said, 'Miss Geddes told them to publish.'

Oppenheim said, 'So, because Mr Johnson is involved with MCG, my wife's picture may be made public in any case? Even if that were not so, I am not the man, Mr Morgan, to be impressed by that sort of blackmail. What you make of Sir Robert is your own affair. I can only say that if, on reflection, you will throw in your lot with me, I shall receive you gladly, no matter what may come—'

He broke off. Without warning, the door to the study had opened. 'I was most unwilling to believe this,' said Sir Robert Kingsley from the threshold, 'but I see, Oppenheim, that it is true. May I ask to have noted my disappointment, my anger, and my intention to take this breach of City practice to its furthest possible limit?'

He came in and slammed the door, and walked to the desk. Oppenheim made to speak. Sir Robert said, 'No. If you please. I should like to make my point first. This man, Mohammed Morgan, with whom you are holding this meeting in secret, is a director of my company, has signed a contract, has accepted a substantial sum of money in return for his position. In coming here, he shows himself foolish. In inviting him here, you expose yourself to everything I and my friends can do to discredit you, and your business, and your practices. Be sure of that.'

I had seldom seen him so angry. His voice was soft, as it had been in the boardroom in London, disputing with Johnson. But this time I felt it cost him to keep the fury banked down: he was flushed with it. Coming in, he hadn't even spared Morgan a glance. I saw, because I was looking for it, the flicker when his gaze passed over me. He hadn't expected to see me. He didn't know yet what I knew about Asni. He couldn't be sure which side I was on. He ignored me.

Daniel Oppenheim rose to his feet. 'I hope you do,' he said. 'Fabricate a report against me, Robert, and you'll have time to regret it. Blackmail is a serious offence.'

Sir Robert looked from Morgan to me. Morgan said, 'We've talked to Miss Geddes. We know what happened at Asni.'

'You think you know, perhaps,' said Sir Robert. He was partly prepared for that, too, although his colour increased a fraction. His eyes came at last fully to mine. He said, 'I had to protect you.'

I had hoped, at first, that he might have had that in mind. But only at first. I said, 'By using that photograph?'

'It was a threat, that was all.'

'You didn't intend either to use the pictures of Muriel on *Dolly*?' said Daniel Oppenheim.

Sir Robert turned from me. He said, 'Oh, wait a moment. Are you seriously comparing young Miss Helmann with what we know of the private life of your wife? Half-naked on *Dolly,* who would be interested? It is the other pictures I should use.'

'What?' said Oppenheim. His face had changed.

'Look,' said Sir Robert, and flung a plastic folder on the desk.

What it contained, I couldn't see. Only Oppenheim sat, and taking out the glossy package of photographs, shuffled them through one by one. At the end he placed them face down on his desk and lifting his hands, held them apart as if they were wet, or contaminated. He said, 'If you made these public, I think I should kill you.'

'You are welcome to try,' said Sir Robert. 'Do I gather you feel no need now to pursue your illicit courting of Mr Morgan?'

Oppenheim turned his head speechlessly. Morgan looked at his face and said, 'Mr Oppenheim, you don't need to say anything.' He got up, and I found I was standing as well. Morgan said, 'I don't think, Sir Robert, I've ever seen a dirtier way of halting a deal. If it matters, I came to hear Mr Oppenheim out, without expecting or meaning to leave you. I've changed my mind about that. If I could, I'd ditch you tomorrow.'

'My God,' said Robert Kingsley. 'Are you still in napkins, or what? I may be nothing to you; you may be nothing to me, but what does it matter? You have a talent, and nothing. I can provide you with equipment, premises, buyers and more money to play with than you'll find anywhere else in the world. What more do you want? What more do you expect? Men like Oppenheim will come, ten a penny, because they want the use of your brains; but it's Kingsley money that will let you realize your potential. That of you and your team.'

Morgan stared at him. He said, 'You think *I* have nothing? I don't even know how to talk to you. Mr Oppenheim—' He looked at the desk. Oppenheim sat without moving. Morgan said simply, 'I'm sorry. We're going.'

I had dreaded meeting Sir Robert again. I had been frantic with anger and misery. But for that display of the brutality he had shown at Asni, I might have been uncertain of my own feelings still. As it was, I said, 'Wait. Sir Robert, I wish to give a month's notice.'

He smiled. 'Indeed,' he said. 'I suppose it shouldn't come as a total surprise. Your resignation is accepted, of course. You will make immediate arrangements, if you please, to vacate the holiday room you and your mother are currently occupying at the company's expense. And I don't believe you will be required to work out your notice. You will not, I am sure, expect a reference.'

'She'll get one from me,' said Mo Morgan. He gripped my hand and began to stride to the door, but Sir Robert reached it before us. He pulled it open and walked out, letting it crash and shudder behind him. Morgan caught it and, still holding the doorknob, turned round. Outside, I caught sight of Pymm in the crowd, with my mother.

Daniel Oppenheim had lowered his palms. The pile of pictures still lay there reversed: now his fingers closed upon it convulsively. Clutching the photos, he looked up and spoke, quite politely. 'I am sorry, too. If you don't mind, I shall join you all later.' So we left him alone, and walked back to the party.

My mother stood waiting, as at an invisible bus stop. She said, 'Are you starting a cold? People are beginning to leave. You're meant to leave, or their dinners get cold.'

I said, 'I've resigned.'

She stared at me, her eyes set like hazelnut whirls. It was the way she probably looked at my father. He had never resigned. He had never even got the hang of getting methodically sacked. His way was to start up his own spanking new business, and go on his beam ends when it did. My mother knew me better than that. All the same, I could see the text in her head before it got printed out. References... Pensions... Redundancy money. And by the way, what about our room at the Golden Sahara Hotel?

She didn't get to say any of it because Morgan spoke first. He said, 'She did the right thing. And she's got a new job. Helping me.'

'She can't cook?' said my mother. I knew from the tentative way she spoke that she was interested.

'Jeez!' said Ellwood Pymm. I'd forgotten he was there. He said, 'You resigned too, Mr Morgan?'

'Unfortunately, no,' said Mo Morgan. 'But I can choose what staff I please, and I need a personal assistant. If Sir Robert doesn't like it, I'll pay her salary out of the rivers of gold I've been promised.'

'He sure came out of that room looking like thunder,' said Mr Pymm. 'Would I be right in guessing at an ideological clash? Some kinds of Englishmen, they've got no respect for other men's colours and creeds. You a practising Muslim, Mr Morgan?'

Mo Morgan, thinking his own thoughts, looked taken aback. He said, 'Brother, we're at a drinks party.'

'I wouldn't think that you were,' said Ellwood Pymm. 'Any more than Mr Oppenheim can be Orthodox, with Muriel there as his wife. But to some Englishmen, a foreigner's always a foreigner. You want to look at how much better we do things in the New World. I could take you to a party or two back in London where you'd hear things that would open your eyes.'

'Oh, there you are,' Johnson said. 'Mo, Jimmy wants to have another look at your legs. The public figures have gone, and there's a move afoot to transfer the whole detritus to the Place for a special knees-up folklore performance in honour of Auld. Pymm, your Canadian pals have sent out a raccoon call for your company. Mrs Helmann—'

'She's resigned,' said my mother, staring at him over a plateau of ethnic emigrant garments. 'Sir Robert was here. Wendy's resigned.'

'What happened?' said Johnson. He looked busy. Perhaps he was.

I said, 'I thought you said my mother'd be safe. She's been with Mr Pymm the whole day, and now we've no hotel. And you told Lady Kingsley where we were. Sir Robert knew just where to come. He walked right in on Mr Morgan. If you want to know what happened, ask Mr Oppenheim.'

'That's why I came,' Johnson said. 'Message from Muriel: the party's moving outside. And really, I'm sorry about Sir Robert getting into a spat, but I don't think it was Charity's fault. Ask her. She came after all: there she is, talking to Oliver.'

Oliver. I saw him now, for the first time: the large young man from Johnson's yacht. Johnson said, 'He's been with your mother all day as well, but I don't think she noticed him.'

'Yes, I did,' said my mother. 'Thought he fancied me.'

Johnson's mouth moved. 'So I think you'll be safe,' he said. 'If, that is, you'd like to join the party. Horse-drawn carriages waiting outside, service free. All the drivers have nephews coached somewhere by Jimmy. I'll go and tell Oppenheim.'

I watched him walk to the study door and tap on it. I thought of Oppenheim sitting alone, looking at all those photographs. I realized we had to go with the party, because we didn't have anywhere else to go. I set off for the door, walking slowly because I didn't want to catch up with Muriel, and also because my mother had collected five different people who wanted to talk to her. Then we stood on the steps by the carriages, which was where Johnson eventually found us. He had brought Oppenheim with him and would have launched my mother into a vehicle except that she suddenly vanished.

I gave myself five minutes to panic. She reappeared in rather less, preceded by a large ball of wool which bounded publicly down the Oppenheims' steps, there to be cheered to a landing and pounced on by many dribbling feet. Professional and amateur, Jimmy Auld's guests clotted into a jumping, elbow-swinging, hollering crowd that moved off with the ball down the drive, on to the grass and then back again to the steps, by which time it was a collection of yarn.

Mo Morgan, I noticed, had been in there with the team: he passed us once, giving the thumbs-up sign to my mother. She stared back at him violently. She knits very good socks, as well as cooking and baking and ironing shirts and fixing up courses to get me appointments from which I resign.

176

15

I read an article once. It said, *The Most Difficult Transition of All: From £1 to £2 Million Turnover.*

It isn't.

That was the evening I gave up what I had worked for. That was the evening I sat in the lee of my mother on a bench behind two trotting horses and watched the sun go down twice and maybe for ever in Johnson's spectacles opposite.

Nobody spoke. The wheels jolted over the potholes on the way to the Place Jemaa-el-Fna, and the horses' hooves kept the same steady beat as the braces of horses before us pulling the coaches of Jimmy Auld and his footballing cronies, and the line of horses behind bringing Daniel Oppenheim and his much-photographed wife. Bringing Lady Kingsley without her eminent spear-throwing husband; and Ellwood Pymm, who organized charades to do with kidnapping and knives; and Mo Morgan who, having ratted in vain, had offered me a share in his highly uncertain future. Bringing Johnson's high-class thug Oliver, whom I remembered hovering over the svelte topless Muriel on *Dolly,* and who might – who just might – feature in those later, shocking pictures shown to her husband. Unless, of course, the man in those pictures was Johnson. Sitting with him in that barouche I should have told him what happened, but I wasn't going to. Morgan could do it.

A cheerful throng escorted us every step of the way. Boys somersaulted and cartwheeled beside us. Folk-dancers scampered on bare feet and leaped, their djellabahs flying. Singers rode beside us in pairs on Motobecane Vespas, ululating above the buzz of the motor. And although the main body of horsemen had galloped ahead to prepare the display they had promised us, the occasional rider appeared, and upset the carriage horses by firing his rifle.

The first time it happened, I saw Johnson glance at my mother. I couldn't be bothered to turn. I didn't even peer at the riders to see if I recognized Sullivan's vicious friend Gerry Owen. Men got shot; rooms got blown up; people were blackmailed and threatened. I didn't care. I didn't work for Kingsley's any more. My mother said, 'You lost your nerve?'

She wasn't speaking to me: she was speaking to the twin setting suns which were Johnson. He showed no particular desire to respond. Scents of lemon and orange and garlic whipped past our noses. Every building was pink; lamps glimmered; the Koutoubia minaret was abruptly outlined in light bulbs. Johnson said, 'Yes. I think you should both go straight to Rita's.'

'Nix,' said my mother, groping inside her bag. 'Wendy? You did all them courses on self-defence? You got your hatpin?'

My hatpin was at Rita's with my modest holiday clothes. I shook my head, and was handed a long battered skewer with a scuffed crochet ball on the end. 'Are you a coach potato?' asked my mother. 'You take that, and do what you have to.'

It isn't my fault my mother is crazy. I wished we really were going to Rita's. I had given up calling her Geddes.

Johnson murmured, 'Go easy.'

'My name's Doris,' my mother said. 'You think you know better than I do?'

He never really smiled. He said, 'No, Doris. I don't.' I thought the next thing we knew, he'd be fixing her pipes or her wiring. At least one thing was for sure. He wouldn't be moved to paint her flaming portrait.

We arrived in the square, and dismounted, and piled with the rest into the forecourt of one of the cafés that lined it. Jimmy Auld was absorbed by a robed crowd of men who kept kissing him on either cheek. Johnson hefted my mother into a seat while I looked about me and patted the horses, which were fitted with blue plastic eyeshades, and answered to Françoise and Bijou. As soon as the café seat by my mother was filled, I went and found another one, by itself, with a view. I looked for Mo Morgan and saw him with three men with big jaws, whom I suspected must be some of his climbing friends. I saw Oppenheim arrive with his wife, who had flung a cashmere shawl over her toga. In the rosy light she seemed to be smiling, although Oppenheim beside her was expressionless. I thought she saw me, but she didn't come over. Ellwood Pymm, who did, said, 'Well, is it my lucky day! You don't mind, baby? After all those close shaves we had together?'

He had brought his own chair. I couldn't stop him sitting down. He couldn't do anything to me surrounded by people. I looked about but didn't see Johnson, or Oliver. Oppenheim took his seat, in the end, beside his father-in-law among the front tables edging the Place. I saw Muriel moving about, talking and smiling. Eventually she sat down with some couple. Pymm said, 'Your mother reads Arab newspapers?'

I was about to say no, and then remembered where he was staying. I said, 'Sometimes.' I kept my voice low, because he did.

'Naturally, she's sympathetic. And Mo there, why not. And you're a nice girl: you do what your mother says, and I like it. But as I was saying to Mo, Arabs ain't natural businessmen. You want a contract, you want it legal, in words your lawyer and my lawyer understand. I say, don't get round a table with Arabs. You tell that to your mother. And J.J., whatever commission he's getting up there at the Palace. And you wise up old Danny boy there.'

'Mr Oppenheim?' I said. I had no idea where Johnson stood racially, but if anyone was the opposite of an Arab, it was Daniel Oppenheim.

Pymm shrugged. 'You never seen him with those Arab princes? And listen, you pass all that on to Mo. Mo wants to have fun and get rich, all he has to do is stay where he is.'

I said, 'But he doesn't get on with Sir Robert.'

Mr Pymm smiled, his pug nose expanding. He looked like a door-to-door fruit bat. 'Some things get sorted out,' said Mr Pymm. 'My gut feeling is that some things get sorted out if you wait long enough. You doing anything later tonight?'

I had wakened up. I stared at him. I said, 'Yes. Having my dinner standing up with my mother.'

'Hey, baby!' said Ellwood Pymm. His voice conveyed hurt. 'I didn't mean her. Your mom's a real proper lady. But say, what about after dinner? There we are, in the same big hotel. I don't want for you to be lonely. It can be lonely, being out of a job. Friends are useful.'

I used the skewer. He took his hand off my thigh with a gasp just as Charity Kingsley settled herself in a chair on my other side. She was still wearing her jodhpurs, and maybe even her spurs. Pymm hesitated, then got up and walked away. Lady Kingsley said, 'Those poor bloody horses. You look very nice.'

'Thank you,' I said. 'I've resigned.'

'Good,' she said.

She wasn't getting away with that. Not now, she wasn't. I said, 'Sir Robert came. You told him where Mr Morgan would be. You said you weren't coming to the Oppenheim party.'

'I know. I didn't mean to bother,' she said. 'And then some friends at the stables persuaded me. Actually, I didn't tell him: I don't know how he found out. If you're sorry, I'm sorry. Are you in need of a job?'

'I've got one,' I said. 'With Mr Morgan.'

For a moment her surprise showed; then she laughed. She said, 'Oh, dear.'

'What do you mean, oh dear?' I asked. They were serving drinks. I saw Morgan had got up in response to a wave from Jimmy Auld, and had gone to the front to join him and Oppenheim. A table arrived, and a plate of pastries and two full glasses of whisky. Lady Kingsley took one, so I took the other. She smelled faintly of horse.

She said, 'Just that I think you're rather splendid. Look. We ought to watch. Isn't Jimmy Auld marvellous?'

'I thought you didn't like football?' I said.

I could see her profile, as she trained her large, light eyes on the arena. She had no make-up on, and I had a suspicion she wore glasses for reading. She was bestowing critical attention on the lines of black caps and swaying white djellabahs before us, and the rows of bright, fleshy feminine faces topped with coins and gauzes and flowers and looped with beads big as onions. The women were singing already, holding hands and stamping their feet to a welter of sound arising from drums and percussion and tubes and fiddles and a man wearing a brass cap and chiming himself monotonously with a stick. Lady Kingsley said, shouting a little, 'Football? My dear, I think it's ludicrous, but I adore Jimmy Auld. Mr Johnson, don't you adore Jimmy Auld?'

I didn't know where Johnson had come from. He placed a chair plumb in front of us and, sitting, shouted amicably back, 'Legendary,' Johnson said. 'Nicest tackle I know. May I blanket some of the sound for you?'

My mother appeared to have brightened him up. I could see her where he had left her, a coloured bolster surrounded by people, her mouth opening and shutting. She had got one elbow on the table, which was equivalent to a performance by Houdini. Her presumed guardian angel Oliver was not to be seen, even doting on Muriel; but I saw Pymm, and he was nowhere near her.

Johnson wasn't looking about him at all, but was good at refilling our glasses and talking. The lines of singers were replaced by clapping men and dancing girls in glistening kaftans. There was some slapstick with drums, and some juggling. There was another dance, done by men dressed as women. We applauded, and everyone drank and ate and chattered and Johnson, receiving permission, took out and loaded his pipe and smoked it peacefully. I remembered he wasn't supposed to, and realized he was skiving from Rita.

At some point Morgan noticed us sitting behind him and turned and grinned. He had pinned his pigtail on top of his head with a twist of frilled braid and a cherry. I wondered if he had had a chance to tell Johnson that the great Oppenheim–Morgan buy-out was off, and exactly why. For a while the two of them held a drawling conversation about something I didn't understand, although Jimmy Auld turned round now and then and threw in a remark or a bellow of laughter, and once Oppenheim turned and gave a measured view of his well-cared-for teeth. Then Johnson said, 'Look. The horses are coming.'

By then, the light had almost gone. The space before us flickered with acetylene lights from the stalls and the open-air cooking places. Hot charcoal winked in the dark, and yellow filaments beaded far buildings. The glare of light from our café threw our shadows over the tables and on to the ground of the Place.

Now the story-tellers, the snake-charmers and the acrobats had given way to a solid phalanx of sturdy, quarrelsome men mounted on tasselled horses and brandishing rifles. The Fantasia was imminent. The Fantasia which reproduces a tribal cavalry charge with all its speed, its swerves, its manoeuvres, as can be seen at the Hotel Golden Sahara, outside the front door on Mondays and Thursdays.

The horses were excited already, rearing and prancing, and their booted riders, robed and turbaned in white, would have ridden straight over a Desert Song audience without even noticing. Lady Kingsley said, 'Now, this is going to be something.'

Johnson agreed. His pipe had gone out, but he looked none the worse for having smoked it. A waiter, threading softly among us, placed a candle on Morgan's table and then on ours and lit them both, protecting them from the wind with his palm. He had moved away when Johnson touched his pipe and called something to him. His French was quite idiomatic: I wasn't even sure what he said until the man returned, smiling, and handed over his matchbox. He waited, answering politely, while Johnson relit his pipe and made friendly small-talk. The flame pulsed and Johnson, puffing gently, lidded the bowl with the box.

It took all that time for me to realize that the waiter's voice was familiar, and to remember where I had heard it before. I paid no attention to the body of men now massed into a horde at the end of the square. I didn't hear any command, or even the distant rumble of hooves as there began, deceptively slowly, the series of large ragged movements that would climax at top speed before us. I just said to Johnson, '*It's the carpet man!*'

I suppose I screamed it. Lady Kingsley jumped. Morgan turned round, half-rising. The waiter took a step back. Johnson dropped the matchbox and killed the candleflame with a sweep of one hand, shoving me low with the other. He was calling to Morgan, who began, all too slowly, to reach for the flame on his table. His and ours were the only two candles alight. Then I was down from my chair on one knee, and gasping as Johnson half-landed on top of me. Something clattered and flashed. I saw the waiter's sandalled foot turn, and then stop as its ankle was seized. The foot kicked, and Johnson rolled back to go with the blow, but still holding. The waiter twisted to scoop up the thing that had fallen.

I still had the skewer with the crochet ball handy. I chose the leg the waiter was standing on, and drove the thing up to the neck in his calf. He cried out twice, the second time because Johnson had got better leverage and jerked him right off his balance. He began to fall, bumping against tables whose occupants, thinking us drunk, were only mildly distracted. Johnson rose to seize him, to cries of disapproval from all those whose view he was blocking, as the Desert Song at full pelt swept towards us.

By now, you couldn't ignore it. The riders, howling, thundered over the square. The heat and smell of the cavalry charge hit us. The delirious explosion of scores of rifles wrapped us in smoke, pungent with the stench of cordite and onions and horse-dung. The white-clad army skidded to a glorious halt at our feet, and went on shouting and firing its rifles. Johnson, reaching out for the waiter, threw a rapid glance over his shoulder. The waiter tugged, the rifles fired, and Daniel Oppenheim gave a scream and crashed forward over the table.

'And sucks to you,' said Johnson viciously, and tumbled flat as the waiter dragged free and set off between tables, running. Johnson got up and, swearing, began to race after him. Against him came the horrified rush of Jimmy Auld's friends who had just witnessed his son-in-law being shot. I saw Johnson thrust through them, answering nothing. He passed Muriel, who was standing quite still, her face ghastly.

I scrambled up, and found Charity Kingsley beside me. She said, 'I don't know what all that was about, but shouldn't we help?'

I said, 'Mr Oppenheim!'

'Plenty of people helping him, if he needs it,' she said; and, taking my arm, began to rush after Johnson.

It was hard to make any progress. All the cooks and waiters had run out to see what had happened, and guests were standing clutching each other, or crouching in groups under tables, or climbing on tables to see better. A number had fled to the café for shelter.

The waiter had a clear start, and was better motivated than almost anyone. He darted across the main forecourt followed by Johnson, employing an erratic outflanking technique. We followed.

I found myself breathless from sheer fright and anxiety, but Lady Kingsley galloped ahead, wielding her shoulders and elbows like truncheons. I saw, now, what the waiter was making for. In the most obscure corner of the forecourt was a service gate, beyond which was the Place Jemaa and a typhoon of spectators and horsemen. And beyond the present traumatized crowds was the labyrinthine web of the souks.

Our quarry was almost there, when I saw that his bobbing black head had ceased bobbing. Behind, Johnson put on speed. Realizing it, the other man began to run forward. Lady Kingsley and I, battling through the last of the crowds, had a sudden view of the gate, and the waiter and Johnson, and perceived why our villain had paused. Solidly blocking the gate was my mother.

I heard Johnson shout, telling her to let the man through. Certainly, he had no other chance, outside pole-vaulting. Instead she stood where she was, a pillarbox with a fag in its mouth, with her arms folded as near as she could get them. I thought the fellow would hit her, but no. He just took out a knife, laid it against the side of her neck, and backed her through the gate, using one of her arms as a tiller. Behind, driverless at the moment, was the line of horse-drawn barouches we had come in.

That was where Lady Kingsley and I caught up with Johnson, standing still at the gate. He was murmuring something. Lady Kingsley said, 'I don't think I'd follow, if I were you.' She pushed past.

'But you aren't,' Johnson said. He had begun to move, a hand in his pocket. 'Wendy, it's all right, she's safe so long as we stay with her. Charity, you can drive one of these things?'

'Of course,' she said. 'I'd take the third lot. They look better goers.' She paused. She said, 'He can't do much damage while driving.'

'Do not,' said Johnson, 'worry your elegant head about that.' His accent was the same as Sir Robert's, but his style suddenly wasn't. Running, I saw Charity look at him quickly, as if he were a horse that had surprised her. Then no one spoke, for our waiter hadn't made for the barouches at all. Instead, he stopped by a Super Bleu bike with a sidecar. He heaved my mother inside, vaulted on to the bike and shot out into the Place, engine roaring.

We had got to the horse-carts by then. 'Right,' Johnson said; and taking hold, shot me into the seat of the third, before swinging up on the box beside Charity. She had the reins collected already. He said, 'Let it rip, lady. If our villain can't get through the Place, I reckon he'll try for the souks. Tell you what to do when we get there.' The horses trampled and fussed, and then suddenly began to move off together. The wheels picked up speed. The cart jolted. Watchful as a traffic controller, Johnson sat scanning the crowds. But the rest of his attention, I saw, was concentrated ahead, on the bike and my mother.

My biggest burden in life is my mother. I had never seen her scared. Now she must be. If anyone scared her, I wanted it to be me, and not a French-speaking spy from Essaouira. I wondered if he knew, whoever he was, that Sir Robert's own wife was behind him. I rather hoped that he didn't.

Charity Kingsley knew how to handle her horses. She clucked and shouted and wheedled, and their ears started to stiffen. She coaxed them to move into the noisy, dark square after the even noisier bike. In spite of the throng in between us, we could follow the sound of it plainly, and see my mother's kerchiefed head and broad back, and the knife-arm laid lovingly near it.

Her captor steered with the other hand until it was clear that the crowd was too thick to be passed. Then he leaned to the right and, pulling away, set off fast back the way he had come. If the Place had been empty, we could have cut him off, but it wasn't. Charity Kingsley had to follow his arc, or run people under the horses. Johnson didn't question what she was doing. Only after a bit, he said, 'Closer, Charity.'

She said, 'You'd risk Wendy as well?'

And he replied, 'I shan't risk anything I don't have to. Do it.'

She was a powerful lady, and older even than Johnson, but she simply stretched her hand for the whip, and then used it. We raced through vacant patches of darkness, fringed with the lights of stalls which, tonight, had no customers. It wasn't far, now, to the neck of the principal lane to the souks, and the man ahead was making straight for it. I thought of the packed open markets, and the badger-tunnels of workshops that connected them. I said, 'We'll get stuck, and we'll lose him.'

'No, we shan't,' Johnson said. 'He may even get stuck before we do.' His voice from the box was calm and rather precise. He added in the same tone, 'Rolly, he's going for exit three. Look at the map. What's happening?'

And, from the air high before me, the voice of Roland Reed answered. 'They've gone. Boarders repelled. We're all right. What about you?'

'Oppenheim copped it,' said Johnson. 'Our man's got Mrs Helmann in a passenger Vespa and we're in a brougham. Where will he take us to jam us?'

'Souk Attarine,' said the voice. 'Or I would. There should be someone around where you are.'

'That would be nice,' Johnson said.

I stared at his back. Lady Kingsley, her horses dropped to a maddening trot within the busier confines of the souk spoke without taking her eyes off them. 'What's going on, Mr Johnson?'

'Later,' he said. Ahead, the Motobecane had been forced to drop its headlong speed also. The intermittent lights of the trading stalls gleamed on the driver's white sleeve and my mother's shoulder and arm. I couldn't see even her profile. A laden donkey appeared, plodding across the path of the bike which veered, upturning one of its panniers. For a moment the way was blocked by gesticulating people and faggots of watercress, and I saw the waiter look round as we bore down on him. Then he was through and off, and a moment later, had disappeared down a right turning.

He was out of sight for only a moment. Quicker than might have seemed possible, the way before us was cleared: the donkey was held hard to one side by men with smiling faces, and our horses raced past, their hooves squelching on greenery. Then we took the same turning, and found ourselves crossing a space strung with lights and heaped with red and blue kitchenware. The bike had already gone through: the bowls and jugs and basins were still spinning and rolling and bouncing under our wheels. No one ran alongside, or stopped us. I thought, but couldn't believe it, that I heard someone cheering. A voice said, 'Jay, I have them in view. We're not alone.' It sounded, this time, like Oliver; and he was neither smiling nor cheering.

'I was afraid not,' said Johnson.

We plunged into the opposite lane and found ourselves this time in near darkness. From caverns on either side fire glared from brazier and furnace where smiths hammered and bent molten metal. Old men looked up as they sat at their burnishing, the dull kettles and pots all about them. Light gleamed green through mint tea and brilliant orange from a bent iron bar and glittered red on the bike, stationary in the lane far ahead of us.

Beyond it, a man was washing a car with a hose, and in no hurry to let anyone pass. We could hear the argument above the rumble of our wheels and the clatter of the eight steady hooves. It was not until the machine was set directly at him that the man leaped out of the way, wielding the hose like a weapon and sending a wavering stream after the bike. We passed, again, without trouble. Johnson said, 'He's had three chances to get out and run. Why isn't he taking them?'

Lady Kingsley said, 'If he did, you would lose him.'

'That,' said Johnson, 'is the least of it. Do you know the spice market?'

She said, 'Is that where he's going? Ah. He can get through to the carpet souk, and we can't.'

'Yes.' Johnson said. 'So that's where you stay, when we get there. I'll call Oliver in to take care of you.'

She said, 'Why waste Oliver's time? We still have the horses.' I saw him look at her. She said, 'I assume you know how to ride?'

'After a fashion,' he said. There had been a slight pause. Then he said, 'But Wendy?'

'I'll take her,' said Lady Kingsley. 'Tell me when, and I'll unshackle them both.'

I didn't say anything. There was nothing I could say. They were taking these risks for my mother, and I couldn't do less. Ahead, I could see, the lanes we were following were about to debouch into a place much more open and brightly lit. Yet again, the progress of the bike ahead had been hampered; first by a group playing cards at a lamplit, inconvenient table, and then by two men bearing a long metal rod which by no means could be angled to let the bike pass.

That time, we nearly caught up with them, and it was bad; for the waiter's hand rose from behind my mother's back, and the knife was still there. I said, '*No!*' and Lady Kingsley had begun to draw on the reins when Johnson took her wrists and held them. He said, 'No. He won't hurt her.'

Charity Kingsley paused. Then she said, 'Of course. He's only keeping the woman to get you to follow. Is that our market ahead?'

The dark lane had come to an end in a dazzle of brilliance. A large uncovered square lined with stalls lay ahead, busy with people. Below the dusty trees in its centre, the ground was heaped with merchandise and knots of vehement vendors. The Motobecane, slowed to a crawl, was threading through it. Johnson said, 'All right. Yes. Unbuckle them now, if you want to. Rolly, we're leaving the wheels in the spice market, and about to try to ride into the souks. Where is everyone?'

The transmitter crackled, and spoke. The voice this time was neither Rolly's nor Oliver's. It said, 'I don't know where everyone is, but I know where Mr Reed is, the poor soul, because someone's just broken into his van and disabled his microphone. Are you in trouble, J.J.? May I help you, now?'

'Who is that?' said Charity Kingsley.

I knew, and so did Johnson. He said, 'Seb? How was the slammer? I've got Lady Kingsley beside me.' He sounded calm; even amiable.

Seb Sullivan's voice said, 'Why else do you think I would bother? Tell her there's not the least need to worry. If you get her into a mess, Gerry and I will take care of it.'

His voice in turn sounded earnest, with the merest trace of derision. He was Sir Robert's employee. He had a score to settle with Johnson, but he wasn't going to antagonize Lady Kingsley. I could hear myself panting.

The air was sickly with powerful odours. I inhaled musk and cinnamon and the smells of dung fires and frying fat. Among the crowds in the square and the souks I could see no familiar and powerful shoulders. Among the hanging corpses of foxes and bats and the walls pinned with mystical papers, there appeared no flash of silver or glint of more ominous metal. Johnson's eyes, like mine, were examining every inch of the square, but he made no effort to explain to Lady Kingsley. He murmured into his mike. 'Please don't trouble. We think we can manage.'

'I'm sure you can,' said Sullivan's voice. 'Don't be offended, me darlin'. I'm not here as your nursemaid. You could call me a neutral observer.'

'He's on the roof, Jay,' said the voice which must be Oliver's. The last word was torn off. Someone had either got to him, or had killed the transmitter.

The barouche had stopped, and Lady Kingsley jumped down and ran to the horses. Johnson said, 'No. Stay. This is dangerous.'

'No doubt,' said Charity Kingsley. 'But you've got that girl's mother into it, and I'm not going to leave her. And a horse isn't bad in a tight spot.'

He vaulted down as if he would stop her. The barouche suddenly staggered. He swore, and reaching up, pulled me out of the vehicle. He said 'You don't need to come.'

I said, 'Yes, I do.'

His hands, his painting hands gripped my waist and he stood still for a moment. Then he said, 'Yes. You do. All right. Charity?'

She was on the freed horse already, without saddle and stirrups and nothing but the girth to hold on to. She leaned down, and between them, they propelled me up and into her arms. Her big hands, full of rein, settled me in front of her body and the leathers filled my lap as she shortened them. She said. 'All right?' to me, and then repeated it over her shoulder to Johnson. She was already moving off when silently he swept up the festooned reins of the second horse and mounting from the barouche, flung himself on its saddleless back.

He did know how to ride. I saw Lady Kingsley glance, once, to confirm it. Then we were scampering over the square and into the mouth of the souk which had swallowed my mother, and where Sullivan invisibly waited, with a score to settle with Johnson, and maybe with me.

16

We had been quick, but not as quick, obviously, as the vanishing bike and sidecar. I thought we might just manage to track them through Oliver. It hadn't struck me that if Oliver didn't help us to find them, then Sullivan would.

We had entered the broad, meandering souk that above all the rest, catered to tourists. Between sundown and supper they followed their gowned and elegant guides under the optimistic sequin-strewn rugs of the entrance and into an endless bazaar, paved and roofed and lined with brilliant slots that were shops. The tourists were buying gauzes and djellabahs and lingering before mitred rows of sewn velvet slippers, or tables flashing with jugs and boxes and basins of over-bright brass. The actual and varied subjects of SM the King of Morocco, robed and veiled, turbaned and capped, swirled round the shops and the tourists in pursuit of their own personal buying and selling, and made way for donkeys, and hand-barrows groaning with cress, or beans, or bananas; or men with a rug on one shoulder. On either side, now and then, there would be the entrance to a narrower souk, floored with crumbling tiles and lined with other, more anonymous caverns.

I said, 'How can we know where they've gone?'

And Charity said, 'Where the sidecar can go. This souk. Nothing narrower.'

We pushed on as fast as we could. We passed camel harness and saddles, and our unhappy mount jibbed, so that Charity had to grab me. Both the barouche horses were nervous. They were used to the road and wheeled traffic, not the sight and smell of hundreds of people pressing around them. I couldn't see how

190

Johnson was faring. We passed wooden honeycombs packed full of sewing silks, and I thought how much my mother would like them. Would have liked them. Would like them.

We had to assume she was ahead. Perched high as we were, we could see from one bend to the next, and if there was a bike threading the crowds, we would spot it. We would never hear it in the general din from the crowd and our hooves. It was hot near the roof. Bunting brushed by our faces, and head-carried parcels nudged at our elbows and begging women picked at Charity's jodhpurs and my tattered dress. The Wardrobe's tattered dress.

Lady Kingsley had no dirhams to give, but no one seemed to mind. They even responded, in a leisurely way, to her County voice calling *Balek! Balek! Attention!* We pressed on round a bend, and still the souk unreeled ahead, and still there was no sign of a scooter and sidecar, or of Oliver, or of Sullivan.

I wondered what Sir Robert's wife thought of Sullivan, and if she believed that he was only here to take care of her. Sullivan hoped that she did, that was sure. He didn't know, as I did, that she had heard what had happened at Asni. She must know, or guess, that Gerry not only blamed us for Colonel Sullivan's jailing: he was looking for Johnson. I said, 'I hope Colonel Sullivan won't do anything stupid. Or Mr Owen.'

I couldn't see her face. She just said, 'Not while I'm here.'

I had wondered.

I thought that was the end of the subject. It wasn't. She added, 'Not that that will help Mr Johnson. I gather it's Pymm's man, there ahead with your mother. One of the party who shot Daniel Oppenheim and has presumably brought us here to get rid of Mr Johnson. Your mother will be all right, I'm sure.'

Pymm had spent all day in the company of my mother. All day today. I looked at Johnson, posting in a desultory fashion behind us. He looked uncommonly alert, but not apprehensive. I said, 'Ellwood Pymm wants to get rid of Mr Johnson? Why? How do you know?'

And Lady Kingsley said, 'The waiter tried to stab him back at the café, and failed. He hasn't a gun. Johnson thinks that's why he's leading us after him. He's got to get hold of a weapon.'

The souks were full of weapons. Every other shop was filled with jewelled daggers and swords and knives with plastic handles. I saw that you could do little with these when driving a Motobecane Super Bleu. You needed something with bullets.

The souk, still covered, had widened now. We were moving more quickly, and you could tell from the dry smell of wool that the carpet stockhouses were near. Then suddenly they appeared in the distance, heavy carpets hanging in layers, or lying spread on the ground, or being displayed, upheld by two corners, to groups of spectators or buyers. They reminded me of various things I preferred not to remember. They blocked the passage before us as effectively as a stage curtain. Among the people and machines brought to a halt was a rider on a blue motor scooter with a passenger in a sidecar.

My mother couldn't turn round, but her captor did. I saw the blur of the distant, sallow face turning, and then the agitation with which the driver thudded forward the wheel of his bike on the carpet, shouting angrily. Because of the damage rather than any mood of compliance, they let him scrape past, and closed ranks again almost immediately. Johnson, beside us, swore under his breath, and Charity looked at him. She said, 'He'll make sure we catch up.'

'Bang to rights,' Johnson said. 'D'you think I could jump that?'

The carpet, still on display, stretched before us. Lady Kingsley looked at him. She said, 'I can't, not with Wendy. What's the trouble?'

'He's got a rifle,' said Johnson; and set his horse at the barrier.

It was a carriage horse, and he hadn't a saddle, so that it was an ungainly business, and got him wreathed in the process with bunting. But he did it, and we heard the mare's hooves clatter distractedly on the other side, and then seem to recover and set off. 'Well done, the Navy,' said Charity Kingsley, and rode forward. After some moments of commanding argument, she forced the carpet away and pushed her horse past in pursuit.

By then, we could no longer see Sir Robert's portrait painter, although we could hear the hooves of his horse. We followed the sound out of the souk and into another, and then along a busy lane that led to a space lined with buildings and roofed with a series of fringes made up of eye-blinding wool hanks slung on rods. The ground was surprisingly vacant of people, and those who were there stood like spectators, smiling as we dashed past. *Trying not to make a film…*

I lost the thought, because suddenly we were in a network of dark lanes lined only by fences, and waste ground, and occasional sheds. We had left the busy traffic of the souks, and I could hear neither the horse nor the bike with its sidecar. Lady Kingsley drew our mount to a halt, just as a hand laid itself on my knee. Johnson said, 'Get down, both of you. There's a ditch and a fence to the left. Lie there, and don't move. He's ahead, and waiting.'

Lady Kingsley didn't try to say anything. She handed me down, and Johnson caught me competently and helped me to the side. He was breathing quite hard. My knees were shaking. Lady Kingsley, dismounted, gave him her bundle of reins. She said, 'Have you seen Sullivan?'

You couldn't see his face; only the glint of his silly spectacles. He said, 'No, but I'm sure he's seen you. That isn't the problem.'

'We have a problem?' she said. Her voice drawled more than his. She wasn't here because of my mother. She was here because she was the only one who could protect him from Sullivan.

'Nothing that dynamite wouldn't solve. Someone's left a lorry where no one can shift it. This is where the show-down is going to be. Music. Action. Popcorn.'

'And the gallant Oliver?' she said.

'Probably back in the spice market,' said Johnson. 'Unless he's got a flying carpet, that is. However. We have Right on our Side.'

'Oh, good,' said Lady Kingsley. 'How can I help?'

'By tying up the horse and lying there in the ditch alongside Wendy,' Johnson said.

'And not going for the police?'

'And not going for the police. You are my favourite Charity, Charity,' he remarked; and vanished abruptly. He hadn't mentioned my mother, who was alone with a man with a rifle. Or that somewhere else in the same darkness was Sullivan, possibly waiting to pick off the survivor. Or that, if we had any friends, they had long since been outstripped by the hooves and the wheels.

I looked about. Below me was dirt and patched grass. The lane in which we lay ran straight ahead for some distance, then curved. It seemed to be lined by an ancient wood fence, just discernible in the glow of some light from beyond. I saw that Johnson had walked to the bend and was standing there in the shadow. He had his horse with him. I wondered about the source of the light. It could have come from the scooter, or the lorry's two headlamps, trained back the way we had come. If Johnson moved, he would step into a spotlight. And the man who shot would shoot from darkness.

I wanted to see round the bend. When I moved, Lady Kingsley grasped my arm, but I pulled away, and when she held out, I hit her arm, hard, and dragged myself free. Even then, she scrambled after me, as if she thought I was going to do something stupid. I wasn't. I just wanted to see what Johnson would do. To see what I could do for my mother.

Perhaps he heard us both rustling behind him, but he didn't look round. Only, rather suddenly, he slapped the horse on the rump and, as it jerked and took some steps sideways, he picked up a stone and threw it hard. Then it snorted and began to trot forward, and he began to move too, jogging along the edge of the fence in its shadow.

I didn't try to stand, or to follow. I crawled to the ditch where he had been and watched the galvanized shape of the horse, and the twin headlights blazing before it, and the minor dodging shape of darkness and light which was Johnson, running hard to the light, and away from me. I felt the thump as Lady Kingsley came unspeaking to join me. Then there was a flare of light from under the headlights, and a crack of sound, and a scream, and the horse started to stumble.

I could see the man who shot it. I could see the motor scooter between the front wheels of the lorry, and the driver perched there with his rifle. I could see the huddled shape in the sidecar, but not whether my mother was dead. I wanted to dash out into the road, but bike and lorry were a long way away, and a decoy horse wouldn't work twice. I saw the rifle blaze another couple of times, each time pointing at a different spot by the fencing, but couldn't see whether Johnson had been hit or not. I wondered if he was trying to get to the sidecar, and what he could possibly do. I wondered where Sullivan was, and how long he would wait for Pymm's friend to do his beastly work for him. I saw the rifle barrel glint again as the marksman swung it round, trying to follow Johnson's quiet movements. It barked; and then there were two other reports, much deeper and quite close together from somewhere to the left.

With the first, the man with the rifle suddenly jerked, and began to heel over. With the second, I heard the thud and ring of metal from somewhere behind him. I was hardly aware, then, that Charity Kingsley was forcing me into the deepest part of the ditch underneath her. I kept my eyes on the man with the rifle because he was tumbling stiffly over the sidecar, his hands clawing at the hopeless, emigrant unchic of my mother's outer garments.

He hadn't touched the ground when he became a silhouette. Everything became a silhouette. Instead of car, motor bike, human beings there were two black cardboard figures and the black cardboard struts of a bike, outlined against a dazzle of brightest vermilion.

With a roar, the lorry burst into flames; and in explosion after booming explosion, lorry, bicycle and all living souls in or near them were turned to molten metal and grease there before us.

The blast hit the fence where I lay with Sir Robert's wife. I suppose the worst passed over us, and the red-hot metal and flaming fabric fell short, but we seemed to lie half-buried there for a long time, choked with dirt and pummelled by fragments of debris. Then my hearing returned, and I felt, in a little, the weight that was Charity Kingsley lift from my back, and her hands began to clear the dust from my face, and carefully brush off my shoulders and arms, looking for injury. I let her do it. I knew she was more likely to be hurt than I was, but I couldn't speak to her. I knew now what I had seen, and what it meant, and I crouched in all that heat, and shivered and shivered. And then my stomach rose into my throat, and I began vomiting.

She held my head, and then wiped my eyes and my mouth with her handkerchief, and rocked me in her arms without speaking. She had daughters and stepdaughters, I remembered. She looked after them. Sir Robert never had time.

I could hear people running. From the souks, from the cabins inside the fence, they came to see what had happened. I could hear a car, turning in from a lane where it must have been standing. Through my closed eyes, I could see its lights glowing red, and I opened my eyes and looked up, because it was near; and saw my shadow thrown black by the far greater light burning behind me. Charity knelt by my side, her eyes pale as water in her blotched face, and one arm clotted with blood. Before me stood a pair of hide boots.

Wearing them was Colonel Sebastian Sullivan. He soared above me, with his immense shoulders and his athletic frame and his rippling, honey-combed hair all outlined by the light. Full of Eastern Promise, he was: the Romantic East my mother in her wistful, caustic, sentimental and outrageous soul had hankered after. He said, his face calm, his voice solicitous, 'May I offer you ladies a lift? It's just too bad, of course, but you know what they say. If you can't stand the heat, you should get out of Morocco.'

Charity Kingsley stood up. She said, 'I am glad you are here. Are you responsible for what has just happened?'

He looked consoling, deprecating, conciliatory. 'My dear Lady Kingsley, I didn't shoot up the truck.'

'Can you prove it?' said Lady Kingsley.

'Of course I can,' said Colonel Sullivan. 'Would you like me to turn in my firearms? Ballistics will find the bullets that exploded the truck and killed the thug with Wendy's poor mother. Don't feel sorry for him. He or his friends shot Daniel Oppenheim. The police won't regret that he's dead.' He paused. 'It's a rough, crude country, Lady Kingsley. You should never have come. I'm sure Sir Robert would be happier if you were safely at home. May I give you a lift?'

'I would rather travel by donkey,' said Charity. 'And Wendy will go home with me.'

'Oh?' said Sullivan, with the warmest interest. 'I thought she'd resigned.'

I supposed his car had been hired: it wasn't the Sunbeam. He slid behind the wheel and drove off, waving elaborately. Before that, I'd begun retching again, and some women came along, and helped Charity. Someone spread a carpet, and we sat on the grass while kind people brought water to drink, and cloths to wipe our hands and faces, and cotton to wrap round Charity's arm and the other places where we were bleeding. A police car arrived. I said, 'What do we say?'

A half-familiar voice said, 'You mustn't say anything. Wendy? Lady Kingsley? Are you all right?'

But for the words, it might have been the Colonel again, kneeling beside us with his mellow, acceptable accent. It was Oliver. Oliver from Johnson's yacht *Dolly*, who had protected neither Johnson nor my mother. For the first time, my thoughts went to Johnson, and how he had died; and from there, to Rita and Oliver. I said, 'I'm sorry.'

Lady Kingsley was looking up at Oliver too. She said, 'We must tell the police something.'

He said, 'No. Please. Will you trust me? Wendy, listen. Your mother's alive.'

Nothing would obey me, my nose, my mouth, my throat. I didn't turn round to the glare. I said, '*Look at it.*'

'She wasn't there,' Oliver said. 'She's safe. Wendy, she's safe, but we don't want the police to know the whole story. You must say you took a ride through the souks for the fun of it, and lost your way, and the lorry suddenly blew when – when J.J. tried to get past it.'

'But *he* isn't safe,' I said. 'He went with it.'

'You saw him,' said Oliver. His voice had flattened.

'No,' said Lady Kingsley. 'We saw him run towards it. The other man fired several times. Then there were two different shots, from a revolver perhaps.'

'Jay's,' Oliver said.

'He had one?' said Lady Kingsley. She paused. She said, 'The first hit the driver, and the second started the fire.'

The police were coming over. I didn't care who heard. I said, 'So he killed my mother.'

'No,' Oliver said. 'I told you. She wasn't there. That was why he risked shooting at last. Pymm's men took her into the souks while you were unshackling the horses. They switched her driver, and wrapped all her shawls round a dummy. I saw them. We've got your mother. She's safe. She should be at Rita's by now. I'll take you there. I just have to… to look.'

It was Lady Kingsley who jumped to her feet. She said, 'Oh, go. Go. Please go. We shouldn't have kept you.'

We told the police what we'd been told to say, and they accepted it, once they knew who we were and where to find us. They wanted to fetch us an ambulance, but we said that Oliver would take us to where we were staying. We didn't even know his second name. When we were free, I went towards the smouldering wreckage with Charity.

I didn't look at it, although Lady Kingsley stood for a while, before she turned away. Somewhere in that glowing mound were the driver and Johnson, but not my mother. My mother, that huge, strange, ill-defined shape in my life was still in existence, more mysterious than she had ever been. What I had lost was a new acquaintance who was liked, I now knew, by many people. I followed Sir Robert's wife back across the scorched grass to the blackened remains of the fence. The stretch by the fire had been consumed. Nearer to where we had been, a postern gate hung in charcoal effigy, and I thought I heard voices beyond it.

Voices.

We would have gone through, but Oliver saw our shadows and came back quickly to stop us. He said, his voice a little unnatural, 'No, we can't get out here. Look, why don't you ask the police to take you to Rita's? She'll know by now you're both safe. I've got things to collect, then I'll come.'

I made to speak, but Lady Kingsley took my hand firmly and stopped me. She said only, '…Yes?'

And he said, 'Thank God, yes. But *no* to everyone else, except Rita.'

So the police took me when I paid this, my third visit to Rita's. They drove in the gates and rang the doorbell while Charity Kingsley and I stood there, pale and grimy, with blankets round our tattered shoulders. Rita was the first to rush headlong out of the house, with Reed just behind her. She stopped for just a moment. Then she came pelting down the steps and took Charity's hands, and then turning to me, put her arms round me and hugged me. Then one of the officers spoke to her in French, which she didn't know; and still holding me, she turned towards Rolly.

I knew what the policeman was going to say, and I had to let him say it. I saw the effect of every word on Reed's face, and then its reflection on Rita's. At the end, he translated clearly for her. The officer had finished with some delicacy. 'My commiserations, mademoiselle. One can hold out small hope, except for confirmation when daylight allows. One may say only that such things are quick.'

In the pause that followed, Rita was silent. Her eyes were rimmed with red like a drunkard's, but they were dry. Queerly, before we arrived, she had filled in the time decorating her face like teenagers once did. It was all patterned in tiger stripes and little whorls, and her red hair was done in elaborate spikes. Reed looked at her once, and then began, admirably, to say the right things, walking to the gate with the officer; seeing him off with excessive formality. I held Rita's arm and said, 'No.'

She looked from me to Lady Kingsley, but didn't move. The police car reversed, turned and drove off. Reed came back. I said, 'That's the story Oliver told us to spread. He isn't missing.'

Rita lifted her arm out of mine. Reed, his hands at his sides, stood beside her, looking at us.

'He's alive,' said Charity Kingsley. 'Oliver found him. He was in the explosion. We haven't seen him, but we heard him speak. He doesn't want it known that he survived.'

'Thrawn,' said Rita. I didn't know what she meant.

Rolly Reed put a finger on her shoulder, which came no further up than his elbow. He said, 'So you don't know quite how he is. What is Oliver doing?'

'Waiting, I think,' said Lady Kingsley. 'When the coast is clear, he'll bring him here. Should you warn a doctor?'

Reed said, 'We have one, for the crew. Oliver knows how to reach him. I think we ought to go in.'

It was good advice. In spite of the heat, I had begun to shiver again. When I turned to go up the steps I found two other people standing there. One was the middle-aged steward called Lenny, whom I'd last seen on *Dolly* at Essaouira. Beside him, even more unexpectedly, was the narrow, mangetout face of Mo Morgan. Morgan said, 'Wendy? You'd like to go up to your mother?'

It embarrassed them, that they'd forgotten my mother. Rita suddenly began to bustle about; taking Lady Kingsley indoors to be tended; giving orders. We all moved up the steps after her. Morgan touched my blanket. 'Maybe you should get looked after first. You'll give your mother a fair old fright when she sees you.'

'She gave me one,' I said. She was resting, he said, in a bedroom. He took me there, and then went away. I should have asked him how he came to be there, and the man from the yacht. I should have asked about Mr Reed, but I didn't. I opened the door of my mother's room, and she was sitting facing me, bulbous, bow-fronted, draped in some vast spread of cloth from the Wardrobe Department which was already out the price of one wrecked cocktail dress for the Oppenheim party.

She wasn't smoking. She looked me up and down with screwed eyes just the same. Her fierce hair was rammed full of hairgrips and her eyes were stamped with brown beer rings, and her nose was obscene. On her brow was a swollen bruise the size of a penny.

Only a short time ago, I had lain in a ditch and thought I had lost her. No more harangues. No more arguments. No more mortification.

I said, 'What the hell were you doing? With Pymm? At that gate? You deserved to be blown up. You did. You did.'

She said, 'Oh, Christ God,' and stared at the floor as if someone had thrown up all over it. Her hands were more or less on her knees. As I looked, she rocked herself once, and then stopped.

I was crying with anger and bafflement. I have never understood her.

I understood her.

I said, 'No,' and got down on my knees by her chair. I said, 'I think it's all right. Not for the waiter. But Johnson was further away.'

She looked at me. I said, 'Oliver is bringing him here. No one knows it's all right except us. If it is. It is, I think.' I put up my hand and touched the swelling. It was shiny and hard. I said, 'You should have sent for the bloody course first. How to nick murderers.' Then I burst out crying into her lap, and she hugged me as far as her arms would go round, until she needed to get a hand free for her

Gauloises. We didn't actually get talking even then, but I sat on the floor, hiccoughing occasionally, while she trembled smoke from the side of her mouth and patted me with a hand like a small boxing mitt. It was sort of comforting.

We went downstairs ten minutes later, because Rita tapped to ask if we'd like a wee cup of tea, and my mother, flinging open the door, prodded her shoulder and said Rita was to leave all the food and tea-making to her, and go off and do what needed doing. Wendy would help, she announced, once she'd got all the muck off.

They had known each other for about five minutes. Up to that night, my mother had regarded Miss Marguerite Geddes, Managing Director and business illiterate as a personal threat to the stability of the yen. On the other hand, up to that moment, she thought she had caused the death of Rita's friend Johnson. When I washed and went down, in an expendable top and pants from the Wardrobe, my mother was away in the kitchen and Rita and Lenny were making up beds, while Roland Reed was answering the telephone, which rang all the time.

Since the police knew we were here, everyone did. Everyone knew that the wife and secretary of Sir Robert Kingsley of Kingsley Conglomerates had escaped serious injury as a result of an explosion in the Medina of Marrakesh. And that, tragically, the gifted English Academician Johnson Johnson was one of those known to be missing. To everyone, Reed said the same thing. *Apprehension shared by all Mr Johnson's colleagues and friends. Gallantry of the two ladies, who wished to stay as long as some hope might remain.*

The London news agencies had been in touch. The Mamounia phoned to communicate its genuine concern. A secretary rang from the Palace, expressing deep shock, and asking to be kept informed. The bell in the gate began to ring, and a heavy from the film crew was found, to stand inside and send off reporters. Jimmy Auld phoned, and Mo Morgan objected, at last, when Reed put down the phone without changing his story.

He said, 'If the man's alive, why can't you say so to his friends? Look at the distress you'll be causing. It'll be all over the papers tomorrow. And what if he requires burn treatment or surgery?'

'If he does, he'll get whatever he needs,' Roland Reed said. 'I don't know why he's asked for this any more than you do, but you may be sure that he has. Oliver wouldn't stage this alone. We all have to be patient.'

You could tell, now, that Rita's financial director was not a young man, despite all his elegance; and on the side of his face, his skin showed blue and red like my mother's. He had been working the film van transmitter when he had been surprised and attacked. There had been a brief, highly skilled attempt to enter the house, foiled by the sophistication of the Ritas' defences. Morgan, joining them on a hunch, had not even been needed. They didn't know whose hirelings had been used. Only Sullivan, insolent and secure, had identified himself over the radio to me and to Lady Kingsley and to Johnson. He had no fear of reprisals. He had only to wait, and others would shoulder the blame.

The phone rang, and was answered, as I realized it had to be, in case the call was from Oliver. My mother came in with a tray bearing strong tea and plates of sweet things she had mixed and taken out of the oven and defied us to refuse. Rita returned, and so did Charity Kingsley, her face raw, her bandaged arm and shoulders invisible inside a man's tailored dressing-gown. My mother brought her a cup and a table and two cushions to keep her back off the chair, and then returned to wedge herself beside my former employer's rich country wife and embark on a merciless inquisition about horses.

My mother knew nothing about horses. There wasn't a course, although she might want to create one. Three Sure-Fire Ways To Get A Horse Killed. How to Strategically Analyse Your Opportunity Environment and Learn to Split More Than Infinitives. I saw Lady Kingsley relax, and answer, and deliver a smile that seemed surprisingly genuine. In the middle Roland Reed, who had gone to take some further calls returned to say, 'Lady Kingsley? That's Sir Robert on the line. He wants to speak to you.'

They looked at one another. Reed didn't repeat what he had said to Mo Morgan, but his expression said it all for him. Johnson is missing. Not dead. Not alive. But missing. His expression came as near to an appeal as I'd seen it.

And Lady Kingsley said, 'Perhaps you would like to tell him about Johnson yourself. Then I should like to have a word.'

They both spoke on the phone to Sir Robert. Rolly Reed's talk was brief. By the time Lady Kingsley returned to the parlour we had all finished tea, and my mother had got a pack of cards from somewhere and Mo Morgan and she were playing gin rummy for matches, as she'd left her purse and his toe in the café. Everyone candidly looked up as Sir Robert's wife walked back in and sat down. She looked rather hot. It was Rita who said, 'Is he keen for you to go on back to the Mamounia?'

And Lady Kingsley said, 'We discussed it. But he would prefer, really, that I got a flight and went home.'

'Is he going home?' Morgan said, snapping cards at my mother. He had just won a game from her, which meant he was cheating. He didn't look like a man who would bother with ballcocks, or even a man who would give a damn for Daniel Oppenheim's marriage. He was, I remembered painfully, my latest employer.

Lady Kingsley said, 'London? Robert's not going there, or not yet. He has a meeting tomorrow, he says, longish journey. He had planned to leave after the portrait, but now he thinks he may set off first thing.'

'Where?' said Roland Reed.

She didn't seem to notice the brusqueness. 'South of Marrakesh, he didn't say where. The vintage cars are going to cross the High Atlas tomorrow, and he could ride along with them, he says.'

Everyone in the room became silent. Then, 'Really?' Mo Morgan said. 'With Gerry and Sullivan? Who's he going to meet?'

'He didn't say,' said Lady Kingsley. 'But I suppose, whoever it is, they must be quite important.'

It was then that we heard the sound of a car carefully entering the yard, and of someone getting out and locking the gates, and of quick, furtive footsteps returning. And Rita rose, and Lenny, and Reed, and when they walked to the door no one stopped them; for, in whatever condition, the last of our circle had come.

17

There followed an interval I didn't enjoy.

My mother put down the cards, and Morgan got up. So did I. Lady Kingsley stayed where she was, her eyes on the door. The window was darkened, but beyond it I could hear Oliver's voice, and then Rita's, suddenly halted. Through the silence that followed you could hear a dog barking, and Arab music from a distant radio, and a girl and a man, or maybe several men, laughing somewhere together. Then the same cautious footsteps resumed their advance, and were joined by others, presumably belonging to Reed and Lenny. The escort party transferred itself indoors and could be heard heavily climbing the staircase. Then the door opened.

Large and well-developed and dirty, Oliver Thornton stood on the threshold and gazed in turn at Lady Kingsley, and my mother, and me, and gave us each a flicker of recognition and sympathy. To Mo Morgan he said, 'I have something really important to ask you. Laugh quietly.' And he moved to one side.

Behind him, leaning on the doorpost, his hands in his pockets, was Johnson. He had no spectacles on, and the shirt and trousers he was wearing weren't his. Inside them, from his hair to his shoes, he was green.

My mother's chins descended a rung. Lady Kingsley's lips parted. Mo Morgan's pigtailed head raised itself, and his teaspoon mouth turned up and his adam's apple blipped so that he coughed. He sat down. His eyes were full of water. 'The dye yard?' he said. 'The pigeon pellets? The turkey droppings? The camel-pats and tubs and tubs and tubs of nice, wet, coloured liquid? Oh, you superior bastard, what have you done?'

'*Le Maroc en Fête,*' said Johnson, surveying himself in a profoundly leisurely way. '*La Blague du Jour. Service Après Vente Assuré,* plus *La Taxe Sur La Valeur Ajoutée.*'

'Today's joke, all right,' said Roland Reed, appearing behind, and taking an arm of the apparition. 'There was a dye-yard at the back of the fence. He dived in and escaped most of the blast. Come on, Jay. No one can understand you. He always talks French when he's pissed.'

There were two vacant chairs beside Morgan. The accountant pushed Johnson carefully into the middle one, and sat down beside him. Lenny hovered. Lady Kingsley perched herself again by the bulk of my mother. Rita, failing to seize Oliver's attention, blew her nose, buffeted it, and went and sat with a thud beside Rolly. She said, 'OK, but *why* is he pissed?'

'Half,' said Oliver. 'Only half. Wants to talk to us.'

'If I get a chance,' Johnson said. He had given up French. 'We went to the doc on the way. He says it's all right. The green'll fade.'

'*Hooker's Green,*' said Mo Morgan ecstatically. 'Green Peace. Green Fingers. Green Giant. The Pillock of Hercules. What is there to talk about? We've been knifed, hammered, shot at, and told to tell lies to our buddies. Nothing we need to know, is there?' He had been angry all evening, and now he was furious. He added, 'What's the French for Hooker's Green? You don't even know that, you bastard.'

'Yes, I do,' Johnson said drowsily, and treated him to a short, clear translation. Charity honked, but Morgan's odd face had pain in it.

'If you ask me,' said my mother's loud, firm, foreign voice, 'Mr Johnson's quite right. Time for a TAM. Team Action Management, Wendy. Action plans, budget, long-range corporate plans, strategy, purpose and objectives. Nine coffees. Right?'

Johnson's eyes were half-shut. 'Eight coffees and a very large whisky,' he said. 'Doris, I love you more than Morgan does. Charity, you'll have to forgive us.'

His eyes had opened. My mother, pursued by Lenny, made a Dalek-type exit and began clanking cups, leaving Lady Kingsley beside me. She didn't take the hint. She said, 'No. Either you trust me, or you don't.'

There was a silence. Then Johnson said, 'Rita?'

'Men!' said the dyslectic head of the MCG company. 'Of course we bloody trust her, but she's married, isn't she? To Sir Robert, isn't she? What right have you to meddle with that? Lady Kingsley, he's going to speak about Sir Robert. Do you want to hear?'

Charity Kingsley was pale. She sat, her hands on the arms of her chair and said, 'I'd be a damned poor wife if I didn't. Don't think, because I mend Robert's fences, that I won't add my shout on his side. And if, in the end, you want to keep me here, I shan't make it difficult.'

'They may have to,' said Rita. 'This is serious.'

'Is it?' said Morgan. 'May I say I'm bloody glad to hear it?'

'You may,' said Johnson. 'You may also take this meeting if you want to. In fact, I wish you would. Doris, I said whisky and I meant it. I'm sorry.'

She had brought nine cups on a tray that looked like a roll-on ramp held up by hawsers. She stood, her jaw swerved to one side, her eyes on Oliver. Then without a word she set about dishing out coffees while Lenny went and poured whisky into a tumbler. He was a small, soft-footed man with muscles like wire. He put no water in the whisky at all. Johnson took it in a green hand, drank, and set the glass down on the card table with a crack. Because of the green you couldn't tell how drunk he was. He said, 'Well, Mo?'

'Not at all,' said Mo Morgan. He had picked up the pack of cards and was doing long, elaborate flips with them. 'The Chair is yours. I'm sure you know what to do with it. Item, Minutes of the last meeting – but we didn't have one, did we? You've been poncing about entirely on your little own. Item, Apologies. Oh dear, Mr Oppenheim couldn't be here.' He was angry, all right.

Johnson said, 'Simmer down. Let's get started. Two of you know exactly what's happening, two have a good idea and the rest of you have to be told, for your own safety and, indeed for ours.'

'Ours?' said Lady Kingsley.

Johnson glanced at her. He said, 'Accept for the moment that the yacht is my base, and Lenny and Oliver help me on her. Accept, too, perhaps that Rita and Rolly are old friends. When I need help with radio transmitters, like today, then I get it.'

'Accept, too, that today you were armed?' said Lady Kingsley.

'Are you sorry?' said Johnson.

I thought of the explosion, the flames, and blackened cinders where the man with the rifle had been. Lady Kingsley said, 'We should be grateful, perhaps. But I should like, yes, to know more. Business espionage seems a more violent affair than I imagined.'

She didn't know, then, why the London bomb was set off. No one told her. Roland Reed intervened. He had a split lip. 'There's a lot of it about, Lady Kingsley. Bugs are fixed; people are wired; electronic mail tapped; couriers intercepted. Key technicians are bribed or blackmailed or discredited. Everyone's caught out some time.'

'Rolly's C3 defence speech, slow handclap Rolly,' said Johnson. 'She knows, we all bloody know it isn't common for gangs of bully boys to be found trampling all over the pavements hammering chosen representatives of Upper Management as well as each other. For one thing, it gets into the papers. So obviously we're not in your ordinary rat race, although business strategy has something to do with it. Why did we come here?' He looked like a good course instructor, except that they don't come in green.

'Because of us,' Rita said, participating dutifully. The streaks had come off round her nose. 'Kingsley Conglomerates proposed to take us over.'

'And wanted to begin with a little private wooing,' Johnson said. 'I *do* remember. I got Sir Robert all annoyed and set the whole game up in Marrakesh, sorry Wendy. When Rita refused to be taken, the going got rough and then extremely rough: courtesy Gerry, who went the whole hog; and courtesy pretty pictures of extremely pretty Wendy of which I want copies. The obvious reason for the take-over attempt was that Kingsley's couldn't afford Morgan short-term without Rita's outlets. The other reason was that Sir Robert was planning to sell someone Kingsley Conglomerates, and the someone wouldn't take them without Rita.'

He was looking straight at Charity. And Charity said, 'That is news to me.'

Rita said, 'We're fairly sure of it. We gave Sir Robert a test question at Asni. Of course we refused his take-over. We don't want unknown masters.'

'Never mind that,' said my mother. 'Bolt-on Goodies, this is what we are talking of. Rita—' She broke off. 'What makes you call yourself Rita? Marguerite, that is a nice name. And you like your hair that way?'

'You don't bother,' said Rita. She just looked interested.

'I am a smallest-room girl,' said my mother.

'Back-room,' I said. 'What about Rita?'

My mother put down her cup, a movement of an inch and a half. 'She is a nice girl, and has a nice company, and is important. But A Company's Competitive Edge Depends Upon People. Whoever takes over Kingsley Conglomerates, they will need Mr Morgan much more than they will need the MCG.'

'Doris,' said Johnson. It sounded wistful.

'Yes?' said my mother. 'You want a pipe? You've had too much whisky. Rita agrees.'

'Doris,' said Johnson again. 'Belt up, will you? Having said that, you're right. Business Deal Number One, Kingsley's want to take over Rita. Business Deal Number Two, person or persons unknown want to take over Kingsley's. Business Deal Number Three, Morgan is being privately courted to buy himself out of Kingsley's at the cost of astronomical debt which may or may not commit him to another master altogether. A series of moves with which the City is perfectly competent to deal in the normal way, and which in the normal way would be a matter for careful and mannerly negotiation. But.'

He stopped. I thought he had run out of steam, or he had heard something we hadn't. I looked round. Charity's face, except for her eyes, was artificial as plastic. Rita was biting her nails. Roland Reed was doing something to his split lip with a clean handkerchief. Morgan had stopped flipping the cards and was sitting outstaring Johnson, his ferrety chin on his chest. I could see his underlids and the whites of his eyes, and the cherry still on top of his head.

My mother stabbed a Gauloise into her mouth, lit it, and drew on it so fiercely it nearly came down her nose. She said, 'You're not one for responsibility, no?' She was speaking to Morgan.

He turned his head. His dark skin looked a shade hectic. He said, 'Sod it, why pick on me? It's not my fault if Sullivan's into mass murder; I didn't appoint him. I'd no part in the muck-raking. I don't want to spend my working life de-programming hitmen.

I'd have considered Oppenheim's offer, if he hadn't been forced to withdraw it. Is that irresponsible? Or more so than your family painter here, who's been two-timing us from the beginning?'

'As a secret backer of Rita?' said Lady Kingsley. No one answered her.

Johnson drew an irregular breath and compressed it, looking at Morgan. He said, 'If you know that, you also know why.' The compression burst. He said, 'Until quite recently, I thought you really didn't know what the stakes were. But, you stupid sodding prima donna, you did.'

He had insulted Morgan before, and been given back as good as he gave. This time, it wasn't like that. It was savage.

Morgan said, 'Do you have a cassette player?'

'For the Asni tape? No, I don't,' Johnson said.

'Not the Asni tape,' Morgan said. 'Oh no, not at all. That only rubbished Sir Robert and Wendy. No. You remember – of course you do – that Wendy's mother spent the whole of today with Ellwood Pymm at your suggestion? You twigged that Pymm needed insider facts for *his* bosses. So you let her string him along, feeding him figures and hinting that he might find Wendy helpful. Sir Robert's tactics, in fact. And Mrs Helmann, because she is a nice, intelligent woman, performed like a hero. And because she wasn't born yesterday, she listened to Pymm when he asked her, as a favour, to get into the room where Oppenheim was going to talk to Mo Morgan, and plant a tape-recorder there. And afterwards, to retrieve it and give him the tape.'

I looked at my mother. Everyone did. She was staring at Johnson: black brows, black eyes, the smoke from the Gauloise screwing her eyes and drifting into the thornbush of her hair. I knew she'd done it. I knew how she'd done it. The shopping bag with the sock in it had been in Oppenheim's room all the time he was speaking to Mo and me. She had recorded all that happened, including all Sir Robert said, bursting in with the photographs. She had recorded Oppenheim's surrender, and Morgan's bitter statement of intent.

Johnson said, 'She told you she'd done this?'

'I wonder why she didn't tell you?' Morgan said. 'Yes, she told me before we left Auld's house. She also gave me the cassette. I still have it.'

209

Johnson's eyes stayed on him. Then they moved to my mother. He said, 'So Pymm's men wanted you anyway? They wanted the tape?'

'And have I not given it to Mr Pymm as he wished?' said my mother. 'With the warm Texas handshake? Not realizing in my state of elderly faff I have handed him the wrong one? There's always tapes in my shopper; I keep them for Wendy. They'll be turning my bag over now, and your toe, Mo, I'm sorry. I know the very cassette I gave Mr Pymm. *Overcoming the Anxiety of Change,* it was called. He must have played it pretty damn quick.'

'Doris?' Johnson said. I still couldn't see his expression under the green. 'I love you to die. So the real recording is here?'

'But what's the point? You haven't a player,' said Morgan.

'For that, I have,' Johnson said.

Morgan smiled. It wasn't a smile I'd seen before, and I didn't like it. He said, 'Well, now. Why don't you bring it out and we can all hear it?'

There was a pause, but it didn't last long. Johnson said, 'I would gather you've played it. All right. So be it. It's open-kimono time, folks. Rita? There's a machine somewhere about?'

Oliver said, 'There are nine people here.'

'Three more to make a jury,' Morgan said.

'Six more to make a rugby side. Don't be a berk,' Johnson said. 'A pig-ignorant twit, but not a berk.'

Morgan's angry smile only widened. 'Oh, look. We've sobered you,' he said. 'What a pity.'

'Adds to the thrills,' Johnson said. 'Lenny? I need fifteen minutes.'

Fifteen minutes proved to be the same amount of whisky with as much water again. Then the tape machine was brought in, and the tape from Auld's party was played.

Only Oppenheim, Morgan and I knew the conversation it began with, and the same three people and Sir Robert knew how that interview ended. The photographs were produced; Sir Robert strode out, and Morgan and I spoke, and then left the room also. The tape ran silent, and Johnson touched it off. He said, 'Wendy. Did you see the pictures of Muriel?'

I said, 'We saw the sunbathing ones on your yacht.'

'But the others?' he said. 'The ones that shook Oppenheim so badly?' He looked directly at me and not at Morgan, whose face had produced one of his small split-pea smiles.

I said, 'No. Were you in them?'

'No, as it happens,' Johnson said. 'Not even Muriel was in them, I rather fancy. I don't especially want to explain, but I rather suspect that I'll have to. Yes, Mo?'

The split-pea smile widened. 'You haven't finished the tape,' Morgan said.

'I was sure you would remind me,' said Johnson. He looked down at the tape. Something about him reminded me of Rita in the car coming from Asni, and her hesitation before she switched on. He looked at Lady Kingsley, and at me and my mother. He said, 'After Wendy left, Oppenheim had another visitor. The meeting was secret, and of course no one was aware it was being recorded. I don't suppose even Mrs Helmann knew, when she took out the tape, that she had two meetings on it, not one. The mercy is that she gave the tape to Morgan and not as she promised to Pymm, or the attacks we all suffered tonight would have had a different ending. I'll play it for you. Then you will have to make up your own minds what to do about it.'

Wherever a device has been planted, I suppose there is a tape, and a group of people somewhere, hearing it for the first time as we were; with lively curiosity, with a raw excitement quite outside the formal processes of boardrooms. We listened, all nine of us; and I watched Roland Reed watch Johnson, and Oliver look at Rita, and Lenny scowl at them all. Whether or not they had heard the tape, they had an idea what was on it. And we, Charity, Morgan, my mother and I were to be the jury of four.

Johnson switched on, and we heard the door close behind Morgan and me, and then a long silence filled with the sounds a man makes at his desk, moving papers and writing and opening and shutting drawers. Then there came a tap at the door, and Oppenheim's voice said, 'Oh.' It sounded dull. Then he said, 'Yes. Well, come in.'

The door shut. 'What is it?' said someone. 'What happened? There isn't much time.'

The voice was Johnson's own.

Oppenheim said, 'I don't know how to tell you what happened. Well, I've blown it, if you want the quick news. I had Morgan ready to fall, and Kingsley somehow got news of our meeting. He's just been here. He said if I didn't let Morgan alone, he would publish some pictures. I've told him I'll let Morgan alone. End of mission. End of bloody mission.'

'What were the pictures?' said Johnson. After a while he said, 'Danny? What were they? I'm accountable. I'll have to explain this.'

And Oppenheim said, 'What do you think? What's the only thing that would force me into letting everyone down? They were of Muriel. Muriel. My wife. With... more than one man.'

There was a little silence. Then the tape said, 'Show me,' in Johnson's voice. It was very quiet.

Oppenheim said, 'What do you take me for?'

'They may not be genuine,' Johnson said. 'That's all I meant.'

Oppenheim seemed to swallow. Then he said, 'I know my wife's body. And I know the men. Be glad you were spared this with Judith.'

There was another pause. Johnson's voice said, 'Of course. I'm sorry. Look, I'm helluva sorry, but think. Are you saying what I think you are saying? If so, do you really want to pay such a price to protect her? Is she worth human lives?'

Oppenheim said, 'She's my wife.'

'Now? Still?' said Johnson's voice. 'You'll show her these, or not show her these, and continue as if nothing happened?'

Oppenheim's voice sounded distracted. He said, 'That's my affair. Hers and mine.'

'It isn't your affair,' Johnson said. 'If you don't act, Morgan will stay at Kingsley's and we shall be very unwelcome in many joyful places. And I like my job.'

'Do you?' Oppenheim said. 'Maybe you liked your job once; maybe you needed it. But that was a long time ago. Why don't you take it easy? Why don't you stick to painting and cruising? I'll report back and say that I've blown it. Who cares what the little shit does?'

'A large number of villains: that's the trouble. Oh, come on, Danny,' said Johnson's voice. 'Either the pictures are fake, or Muriel isn't worth lawyer's fees. Morgan is ready to walk: the great Cong is an idiot nobody. I can nurse him, but it needs financial credibility. I can't suddenly drown him in junk bonds.'

Oppenheim said, 'You really mean he doesn't know what he's doing?'

'I think,' Johnson said, 'that he thinks he's working on washing machines.'

'Christ!' said Oppenheim's voice. 'Then pretend you're into consumer durables, and just set about levering him out. You don't need me.'

'Dammit!' said Johnson's voice.

'You don't,' insisted Oppenheim. Then, after a pause, 'She's my wife.'

No one spoke. Then Johnson's voice said, 'She's Jimmy Auld's daughter. That is all you ever need to know about Muriel. Do what you like.' His voice was the way it was now, level and metallic and bitter. A moment later we heard footsteps cross the room, and the door slammed. A moment later, there came the sound of my mother's voice, inquiring after her knitting.

Johnson shut the tape off, and looked at Morgan. He said, 'Ask.'

Morgan said, 'Who do you work for?'

'A British department,' Johnson said.

'You and Oppenheim were told to get me out of Kingsley's?'

'Obviously,' Johnson said.

'Because I make brilliant washing machines?'

'You know what you make, and what it can be used for,' Johnson said.

'What does he make?' said Charity Kingsley.

Johnson turned to her. He said, 'He creates microchip programs. He makes fault-tolerant prototype systems for domestic machinery. He does research. He devises experimental machines using advanced alternative architecture. Before he fell out with the blue-collar berks attached to the officially recognized labs, he was blowing their minds with new procedures in molecular electronics. Unfortunately, what's good for the kitchen can be equally good in the war zone. Adapted, extended, all his stuff has high-performance military potential. He knows this. He has fooled himself that he can handle it. He has been lolling back, enjoying the dogfight.'

'We all have our hobbies,' said Morgan. His face was press-creased down the middle.

'As a bone?' Johnson said.

'I refer you,' Morgan said, 'to your very own quota-quickie. If they want me, they're not going to hurt me. Anyway, if I was into the big stuff, why didn't I keep my own company?'

'I've told you,' said Johnson. 'You quarrelled with the authorities. You told the science and engineering boys to go home and stuff it. You were mesmerized by your own precious research; you demanded carte blanche to do it; you didn't care where it was leading; you couldn't get any more loans for the equipment you needed.'

'I could have gone to the States,' Morgan said. 'Or to Japan. Or to Germany.'

'Bully for you,' Johnson said. 'So you did know what you were making. Did Sir Robert, when he came to acquire you?'

'No!' said Lady Kingsley.

Johnson looked at her. He said, 'How do you know?'

She didn't mean to glance at me, I think, but she did. She said, 'I know him rather well. He's proud of his country.'

'I'm not suggesting otherwise, Charity,' Johnson said.

She pursued it. 'You may not even be right. About what Mr Morgan was making.'

'Washing-machine parts,' said Mo Morgan softly.

'When and if,' Johnson said, 'you and I, Mo, ever get back to England, I shall take you to a large factory, and I shall show you an exact replica of your washing-machine parts, together with a number of other parts which you will recognize as designed in your workshop. Put together, they don't make a washing machine. They make the launching system for a nuclear missile.'

'But they cancelled the project,' said Morgan. 'OK, I know what can be done with these things. So what? Everything's potentially lethal. You could make a bomb out of Lego.'

'And that's your damned answer?' Johnson said. 'Because of you, two men are dead, and several others and a woman were in serious danger. And that's not including what I owe you, thank you very much. You think Sir Robert is a charming, extrovert capitalist of only moderate intelligence? Oppenheim a dangerous and ambitious opportunist? Pymm a silly, vicious man who has seen too many private-eye movies? So do I. But the big Daddy in this scene is Morgan, an intellectual slob with the boredom threshold of a brain-damaged hen.' He had forgotten Charity's presence. Or perhaps he hadn't.

'Dear, dear,' said Morgan easily. He had turned a deep red. 'This from a man who runs a whole upper-class lifestyle on the proceeds of back-to-back spying, painting and secret investments? Who the hell do you think you are to criticize me?'

'The man who wrote the handbook on slagging,' Johnson said. 'Listen to me. You're killing people.'

'I'm a *designer*!' said Morgan.

'Hard luck,' Johnson said. And a long silence fell.

It was my mother who broke it. She said, 'You know what I'd do? I'd tell those hicks at the laboratories to apologize.'

Johnson looked at her. He said, 'Doris? Were you listening? What the hell do you think I've been doing?'

I gazed at them both. When I looked at Morgan he was staring too, but in a different way. I didn't know why I was sorry for him and not for Johnson, who had saved my mother, and whose self-righteous story had two whopping holes in it. I said, 'You told Mr Oppenheim that Mr Morgan didn't know what he was making. And you as good as told him to go public and declare his wife is a tart.'

Johnson's eyes left those of Morgan with what seemed to be reluctance. Then he said, 'Of course I told him. I knew he couldn't. Muriel worships her husband, and would never, ever, in a million years do anything that would harm him.'

'But the photographs?' my mother said after a while. Her voice, for her, was moderate.

'They didn't exist,' Johnson said. He didn't say it immediately. It was as if two dialogues were taking place, one audible and one not.

Lady Kingsley spoke without moving. She said, 'My husband saw them.'

Johnson looked at her; and I remembered that he had wanted her to leave, and began to guess perhaps why. He said, 'He pretended to see them.'

She said slowly, 'Pretended? Why should he pretend?'

He had lifted his glass, and found it empty. Replacing it, he left it sealed with his palm. He said, 'Because the whole scene was a pretence. Oppenheim knew he was coming. You didn't tell Sir Robert about Morgan's meeting. I trusted you not to, and you didn't. No one could have told him but Oppenheim. And as I've said, the pictures couldn't have been real. Couldn't. Not with Muriel. So the entire quarrel was staged, so that Morgan would report it. Staged by partners who wanted to appear to be enemies. Oppenheim never really intended that Morgan should leave Kingsley Conglomerates. Quite the opposite.'

He removed his palm and interlaced his green fingers. Lenny watched him. Johnson said, 'My guess is that Oppenheim has found a buyer for Kingsley Conglomerates, and provided Morgan will stay, and provided another predator doesn't step in before him, both he and Sir Robert are about to become very rich men.'

Everyone was looking at him. It was my mother who said, '*Oppenheim?* Daniel Oppenheim is alive?'

Johnson looked as if he might have shrugged, but didn't want to. 'He was wearing the same kind of proofed vest that I was. I didn't know until Oliver told me. That's why I am officially missing.'

It was Morgan, of course, who pursued it. 'Wait a minute. Oppenheim was your partner and double-crossed you? For Sir Robert?'

'For someone rather bigger than Sir Robert,' Johnson said. Between sentences, the pauses were longer. 'In fact, I don't fancy Sir Robert will last very long after the take-over. Your very particular skills are about to transfer themselves to an unknown if wealthy consortium. It's my job to find out its identity. I'll find it easier if Oppenheim thinks I'm dead. I'd also find it easier if you felt like co-operating. But of course, you haven't, up till now.'

His own people, now, had fallen silent. Rita and Rolly were mute, and Oliver waited uneasily. My mother sat watching them all. Lady Kingsley said, 'I think you under-estimate Robert. Perhaps he thinks the firm needs new capital, and Oppenheim is the best person to help him. Perhaps he sees Mr Morgan simply as a maker of brilliant components for domestic machinery. Is anyone interested in what else he can do? Surely, most governments are reducing their arms?'

My mother got up and began collecting coffee cups. 'A lot of people don't recognize governments,' she said. 'The man who pays

Mr Pymm, who is he? He wants to control Kingsley's, and I do not think it is because of their washing machines. And who, behind the screen of smoke, are Mr Oppenheim's bosses likely to be? I suspect arms manufacturers or dealers, or those who buy from them. Sir Robert may know nothing of this. You are a good wife, and you think so. I say he wants to know nothing, which is to say he has a very good suspicion but will not admit it. He is a young man at heart. A nice boyfriend, your Sir Robert would be.'

She had stopped beside Morgan. She said, 'You listen to what they are telling you. You make a good microchip, the world will beat a path to your door with live mines in it. I say no more. You are mad, but not stupid.'

'A minority opinion,' said Mo Morgan. From red, he had turned a paler colour. He said, 'So what is teacher going to do? Make a team of the trusties and lock up the rest?'

Johnson was looking at Charity. He said, 'If it would make it easier.'

She seemed to know what he meant. She said, 'I'm sorry. But of course, I couldn't agree not to tell Robert. I've done as much as I can.'

'I know,' Johnson said. 'I know what you've been doing. I wish I deserved it. If you'll let us, we'll send you somewhere safe for a day or two. Sir Robert will be told you're with friends.' He turned his head a little more. 'Mo?'

'What are you asking? Can you trust me? No, you can't,' Morgan said. 'How bloody condescending can you get?'

'You'd be surprised,' Johnson said. 'Now you've heard what is happening, will you let me organize you out of King Cong?'

'No,' said Morgan.

'No. All right,' said Johnson. 'If I bring you proof that King Cong is about to be taken over, and by someone who will twist your bloody pigtail out of your skull, will you let me organize you out of King Cong?'

'I might,' said Mo Morgan.

'That's what I thought,' Johnson said. 'So for God's sake don't commit yourself till I've done it. And hand over the tape, there's a sport.'

'Why?' said Morgan.

217

'Because,' said Johnson, 'Ellwood Pymm wanted to hear it, and I think that he should. Good and early. Before the rally sets off. When does it set off?'

'Early. About nine,' Oliver said. 'It's a horrendous trip, and they need daylight to do it in. Pymm could catch them up, though. If, that is, he thought Oppenheim was going as well.'

'Of course he's going,' Johnson said. 'We're all bloody going. Rita and Rolly with the convoys, trundling down to Ouarzazate and forming the radio link. Oliver and myself on the Harley. Morgan by morning plane to Ouarzazate once Mr Pymm has been motivated. Doris, would you extend your dissembling performance with Ellwood if I were to ask you nicely?'

'You mean give him the tape?' asked my mother. She liked to edit her theses.

'With four sure-fire apologies that make him feel like a company favourite,' Johnson said. 'You meant him to have it. You muddled them up by mistake. You'll never sleep again if he doesn't forgive you. Then leave for the airport, nine-fifteen at the latest.'

'Why?' said my mother.

'Because you and Wendy are going to London,' Johnson said. 'Aren't you?'

She didn't even consult me. She said, 'If you and Mo ain't going to protect us. We thought we had an offer. We thought we'd accepted it. We want to go to Ouarzazate.'

Johnson said, after a moment, 'You had an offer. You nearly let it go past the expiry date, that's all. All right. Amendment. You present yourselves at the airport as if you were going to London. You tell Ellwood Pymm you are going to London. In fact, you fly to Ouarzazate with Morgan. Mo? This is all for your crappy benefit. Will you go along with it?'

'For the moment,' said Morgan. His eyes were tiny, like currants.

'Well, don't hurt yourself. Oliver, wake me at six with a map, and we'll do a little serious plotting. Are there enough beds for this lot?' He wasn't speaking French; he was just speaking very quickly indeed.

'Now, there's a problem,' Rita said. 'You could come with me and count them, and then we'll see how many pillows and blankets we've got. I reckon you've got about three minutes left. Come on. Get up.'

She was on her feet at his shoulder. So were Lenny and Oliver. 'Boil an egg,' Johnson said, getting up by degrees. 'Boil a *green* egg. Rolly? the MTBFs are getting a teeny bit close.'

Mean Time Between Failures. He knew a lot of jargon. It isn't jargon. It's the necessary vocabulary of global business relations. He was almost at the door when Roland Reed answered. 'They always were. What the hell do you want? Job satisfaction?'

The green face considered him, and the green hand made the smallest and rudest of gestures before our portrait painter turned and plodded out, Lenny and Oliver with him. The door shut. Lady Kingsley said, 'What is wrong?'

Rita Geddes turned and sat down again. She said, 'Burns.'

'No,' said Lady Kingsley. 'Basically wrong.'

It was Roland Reed who answered. 'He's immunocompromised. Full of chemicals that take exception to other chemicals. Hence the whisky, not morphine this evening. Otherwise he's the same as you or me.'

She said, 'I was not being critical.'

Morgan said, 'That's your privilege, lady. By the way, I've got the rest of my climbing photographs. Want to see them, anyone? I shouldn't mind a professional contract.'

Reed said, 'You could probably get one. I'll give you the name of someone to write to. Would you like a dictionary, by another way? Blackmail is when you use the truth to hurt someone. White lies are when you hide the truth to avoid ditto. I'm going to bed.'

'I've put you in the bath,' Rita said. 'I'll wake you at five.'

'No. I do that,' said my mother. 'And at five-thirty, I make all the breakfasts. You show Lady Kingsley where to sleep. Mr Reed, you go to your bath. Mo? You are guilty; stop trying to pin faults on everyone else. Where does this character Mo spend the night?'

In the end, he slept on the floor of our room, while I shared the bed with my mother. That is, I laid a hand on her lower foothills and she tucked it under her arm, and squeezed it, and let it lie there. We hadn't shared the same room for ten years.

I have no idea whether Mo Morgan slept. I know I did.

18

I was wakened by the rain drumming in the dark outside the open windows. I should have heard nothing else if I hadn't decided to hunt for a bathroom, always assuming there was one without Roland Reed sleeping inside it. My mother continued to wheeze as I slipped out of the bed, and if Morgan stirred, he didn't say anything. I found what I wanted and coming back, stopped to listen in the dark passage.

The house wasn't quite silent. There were nine people restlessly asleep in the rooms round about me, maybe more. Rita had left a fire in the kitchen: I could hear it crackling. I could also hear, far off, the low ringing of a telephone and someone answering. I realized that I had heard the same sound several times through my sleep. America as well as London wanted to know who was dead in Marrakesh.

The answering voice was a woman's. I didn't want to meet anyone. I had started to walk away when I was stopped by the sound of a car coming to rest outside the walls in the rain. There was a rustle of movement from the kitchen. A door opened, and I heard the squeak of naked feet hurrying down the steps in the rain. With infinite quietness, the car rolled away. I moved along the passage in the darkness and I opened, fractionally, the door that led to the living-room, letting in a crack of dim light. Then I stood back and watched.

It was not Rita but Oliver Thornton who returned, backing into the room, his hair soaked, his daytime jacket slung over bare shoulders and trousers. The man he ushered in, without speaking, was tall. The Burberry he wore was of English make, and the cut of his thick grey hair was also somehow English. The only non-English thing about him were the dark glasses he wore. I had never seen him before.

Then Oliver shut the door and said, 'We have him, sir. It's all right.'

The man paused. With deliberation, he put down the briefcase he was carrying, threw off his Burberry and finally took off his glasses and, folding them into a pocket, sat down, without invitation, in the most comfortable divan in the room. 'I should hope so,' he said. 'Or really, my Oliver, your career would have come to a halt. Tell Rita, if she will stop listening behind the door, that I should like some strong tea and some of her scones, and her presence while you both tell me precisely what has happened.'

For a moment, I thought he had spotted me; then I realized he had been listening to some continuing sound in the kitchen. He spoke like the head of a company. You can never mistake it. And Rita, coming in with her hair flat and her face clean and a dressing-robe over what was probably nothing, replied in a subdued voice I had never heard from her before. She said, 'Do you want him wakened?'

'And earn your hatred for life? Of course not,' said the man, getting up and smiling down at her. He put his hands on her shoulders and kissed her. 'One from Frances, and one from Joanna. Go and get the tea, my dear. I rather need it. And you have a long report, I think, to give me, both of you.'

She went. The man watched her and then sat, the smile fading. He said, 'He is thought to be dead. Presumably he suffered some damage. What capacity can we rely on? A quarter? A half? Or enough to be useful?'

They were talking of Johnson. I have heard coffee-percolators being discussed with more solicitude. Oliver said, 'Enough to be perfectly useful. You couldn't stop him, in any case.'

'Oh? Why?' said the man. Rita had come in with a tray. 'Chagrin over Oppenheim? I take it he's sure about Oppenheim?'

'Oh yes,' said Rita. 'I wouldn't like to be Oppenheim. I'd even less like to be Colonel Sullivan.'

'An ex-SAS colonel amusing himself with a black PR firm? Is that in J.J.'s league?'

'I think he has the idea that all former mercenaries come into his league,' Rita said. 'I wouldn't know why. There's the tea. Lady Kingsley is sleeping two doors away.'

'And who else?' he said. He picked up the cup she had poured.

She ran through the names of everyone in the house. Lenny and Reed he clearly expected. 'And Morgan?' he repeated after her. 'He came here? I'm interested. But of course, he knew what he was designing?'

'He knew,' Oliver said. 'J.J. jumped on him this evening and gave him a shellacking. He'll recover.'

'I trust he will,' the man said. 'Whether he recovers or not, he'll have to be taken out of Kingsley's. That silly man Robert. I presume that he's deceiving himself that he is being wooed for his charm?'

'More or less,' Oliver said. 'You'd need to get J.J.'s extremely biased opinion.'

'I want yours,' said the man. 'In a moment. And who else have we to consider? The girl, of course, and her mother. A pity they had to become mixed up in it. I take it they go home tomorrow, with Charity Kingsley. Now tell me the lot.'

Standing outside the door, I listened to the events of the last days being related by Oliver Thornton who was more, I had already realized, than a crewman of *Dolly*. I knew by now, too, that the man who had arrived must be Johnson's controller, and that he had come, fast and privately, when the first reports of Johnson's death had reached London. I don't remember now at what stage of the report I realized that Mo Morgan was standing in the passage behind me.

I nearly made a sound; then he put his hand on my shoulder and stopped me. His eyes, like mine, were on the slit of light and the little we could see of the room and the three people in it. He had kept his shirt and shorts on, and his hair was half loose and half plaited. In the event, we stood together and listened as the narrative came to a close.

By the end, the man had finished his tea and was lying back, eyes lightly closed, hands together. Without opening his eyes he said, 'You've put it very clearly. And Jay is right, of course. Flush out Pymm, flush out Oppenheim and let Morgan see what is going on. He'll want to get out of Kingsley's, and Sir Robert will have to be nobbled and made to unbundle him quietly. If that doesn't work, we go public, admit what Morgan is doing and rely on small-print procedures to bail him out of Kingsley's, set him up in some sanitized unit, and give him reins of a kind that won't throttle him.'

Roland Reed seemed to consider it. He said, 'Perhaps that would be the best thing that could happen.'

The man opened his eyes. He said, 'If I'd thought it the best thing, I shouldn't have sent Jay in the first place. Morgan's work is wholly sensitive. It can affect issues he couldn't even imagine. I do not want it made public. I do want to discover the names of the two organizations employing Pymm and Oppenheim. If we're right, the moment Morgan publicly walks, they'll lose interest in Kingsley's and, from what you tell me, Kingsley's will go down the drain. I want to know who they are before that.'

'And MCG?' Rita said.

'Ah, yes,' the man said. 'I think I ought to have been told about MCG and Kingsley's, don't you? A little something I have to take up with our verdant and mutual friend. Oliver?'

'Sir?'

'Open that door, will you?' said the man.

There was no time to get away. The door before us crashed back and light exposed us where we stood, Morgan in his shirt and me in the Wardrobe's idea of a robe. I don't know how he knew we were there. Rita said, 'It's Wendy and Mo. You should talk to them.'

She had come over to stand beside us. She looked the way she had at the hotel in Asni, after the boar. She stood in the middle, holding each of us close by the arm. The man had risen. He said, 'I suppose I should. At any rate, I'm not going to eat them. Come in. I can't blame you for listening. Saves time. Miss Helmann? Mr Morgan?'

'Who the hell are you?' Morgan said.

It was Oliver, collecting himself, who shut the door and coming forward, got us seats. He said to Morgan, 'This is—'

'Bernard Emerson,' said the man. 'A friend of Johnson's. We're both rather keen, as you will have gathered, to keep you inside the family, but I've no idea how to persuade you. In fact, I don't think I shall. You can play, or observe, or go home with certain restrictions, like Lady Kingsley. Miss Helmann the same.'

Morgan said, 'Johnson does what you tell him? What are you going to tell him?'

The man spoke perfectly calmly. 'He proposed a course of action. It seems sensible. If you wish to proceed, I shan't stop you. Presumably you've weighed up the dangers.'

Morgan said, 'You would let him do it?'

'Reed says I couldn't stop him,' Emerson said.

'Because of Sullivan?' Morgan said. He was looking at Rita. Rita's face, looking back, was impassive.

Emerson said, 'There are scores to settle, I gather. But surely that isn't all. Do you really think Sullivan works for Sir Robert? Or even Oppenheim?'

Roland Reed's wits worked faster than Rita's or mine. He said, 'You mean he works for Oppenheim's principal? That is why J.J. wants him?'

'No,' Emerson said. 'That is why I don't want him to die before he has answered some questions. Do you understand me?'

'Yes,' said Reed.

'Oliver?'

'You want me to say this to J.J.?' Oliver said.

'Save your breath. He knows,' Emerson said. He was sitting forward again and, elbows on knees, had laced his hands in front of his chin. He said, 'I have two things to say. Morgan, you owe nothing to me, but it matters a lot to Sir Robert that you forget any plans to leave Kingsley's. Will you let him think, for a bit, that you're staying?'

'I might,' Morgan said. 'It might be true. A sanitized unit isn't the hell of a lure.'

'That's true,' Emerson said. 'The best you can say is that you wouldn't be killing your friends. The second matter is this. You told Johnson you thought the Kingsley books had been laundered?'

'We discussed that. Yes,' Morgan said.

The man looked from Morgan to me. He said, 'If you're staying, and I gather you very gallantly are, it would be a great help to have some idea of real figures. If there are raiders about, it would deter them.'

He was right. It wouldn't be letting Kingsley's down, only Sir Robert. I said, 'Mr Morgan and I know roughly what they should be.' The papers were here, in my case.

Bernard Emerson said, 'I have to go. How quickly could you work them over and write them down? Could you give them to Lenny for me? Would you trust me with them?'

It was Morgan who agreed, and I let him. I supposed, climbing mountains, he was used to weighing up briefings from experts. It didn't stop me from feeling frightened. Soon after, Emerson rose, and Reed rang someone and had a car brought round with a driver. I didn't know where he was going.

I went back to bed an hour later, and found my mother awake. She said, 'What is it? Is it bad news?'

'No, I don't think so,' I said. 'Our plans are sort of the same, but official.'

'Official?' repeated my mother.

'Yeah,' said Mo from the floor. 'She means we *all* get buried a K.'

The following morning, everyone who knew Johnson and was capable of reading a newspaper was aware that he was missing believed killed while on a painting commission in Marrakesh. Anyone who knew Jimmy Auld might have found, among the small print, a reference to a minor shooting accident involving his son-in-law Daniel Oppenheim. I didn't see the papers: I was asleep.

I slept so late, I missed Lady Kingsley going away, and Lenny leaving with my revised papers, and the first of the convoys of film people departing with Rita and Rolly for Ouarzazate.

Because his door and mine were wide open, I didn't fail to hear Oliver waking Johnson, after the injection they weren't supposed to have given him. Johnson's voice couldn't have been quieter, but I heard every bitten-off syllable.

Oliver said, 'Will you give me a chance? I was told to do it. Sir Bernard was here.'

This time, he had punched the mute button. 'Was?' said Johnson eventually.

'For an hour. He wouldn't disturb you. Wanted to know the agenda, and agreed it. Your folks will know you're OK: he's having them moved out of circulation for a day or two. He says keep the lid on it all if you can, remember you're dead, and he'll see you after the Resurrection which means Easter, so get a move on.'

'He'll see me where?'

'I didn't ask him.'

'Shit,' said Johnson. It was what he had said when Kingsley's office blew up. I dragged on the last of my borrowed garments and opened the door.

They were standing just inside Johnson's bedroom. Johnson had got hold of bifocals from somewhere but not yet a razor, and had slept in his borrowed shirt, which was now blotched with dye. I was getting used to his skin being green. Then he saw me, and turned a fraction to exclude me. He said, 'All right, that's enough of all that. Who's still here?'

'Wendy and her mother and Morgan. Look, there are the maps, and I've got all the gen on the rally. The vintages have to get over the mountains, and end up by nightfall in Taroudant. There are two passes over the High Atlas, the Test and the Tichka. It isn't a race: they only have to get their cars over, but the Tichka pays maximum points, so they're all trying that. Seven thousand four hundred feet, vertical ravines, hairpin bends, and snow at the top. The idea is that they cross the mountains this morning, rest and lunch at Ouarzazate, and then do the second leg under better conditions to the Sous, where they spend the night at the Gazelle d'Or outside Taroudant. Sir Robert goes with them, so his meeting could be in Ouarzazate or Taroudant. Taroudant seems more likely.'

'In which case why choose the Tichka?' Johnson said. Except when he forgot, he had returned to his more pleasant voice.

'Because he hasn't mentioned a meeting to anybody except Lady Kingsley,' Oliver said. 'He has to take the Tichka if he's sticking to Sullivan. It makes it look like an excursion with friends. He maybe wants Sullivan's protection against Pymm. Or maybe he's picking up Oppenheim. The col is open: the film Range-Rovers should make it all right. Rolly has started: he's already radioed back. The Rally sets off in an hour. I've sent someone to find out how Sir Robert is travelling.'

He had spread the map on the bed and Johnson had avoided bending by kneeling to study it. I wondered how he was going to manage the Harley. I turned, and came face to face with my mother equipped with her tray on a halter. She wasn't wearing bunny ears or a puff. Her hair was wrapped in strong patterned cloths that shadowed the great black and blue bump on her brow. Smoke from her cigarette erupted over an assortment of breakfast dishes, shaving equipment, medical equipment, and a bowl full of greasy pink fluid.

'Paint stripper,' said my mother, indicating it. 'Mixed by Mo. Dab with cotton wool. Do not pour over your ricicles, I am to tell you, or you will regret it. Are you still in paid employment?'

'So far as I know,' Johnson said, getting up. Oliver took the tray.

'Mo thought so,' said my mother. 'But who knows? Like any other, spying must be a business. Downsizings, give-ups and rollbacks of senior payscales and privileges. Sir Robert Kingsley is in the sitting-room. Does anyone wish to give him a golden hello?'

She is a devil. Oliver's nostrils flew open but Johnson produced a rare smile in green. He said, 'Come to woo Morgan?'

'Morgan is with him, that is true. They are agreed it is a pity you blew up, and without a chance to finish the picture. I came away because I seemed to embarrass him. Wendy? You could go down and embarrass him more?'

'I think you are both doing very well where you are,' Johnson said. 'Let's leave Morgan to play out his hand. Did you hear what line he was taking?'

'The one you wanted,' said my mother. 'Sir Robert hopes Morgan will devote all his great talents to Kingsley's, and Mo has said that he will. I think he probably means it, but never mind. There is news. Oppenheim flies to Agadir for a check-up, though his hurt is not serious. The papers report that his wife, reassured, has flown with her father to Casablanca for the final games in the Cup. Sir Robert leaves this house to go straight to the Rally. He will travel by the pass Tizi n' Tichka, in an extra maintenance vehicle. In the Sunbeam, he would hold back Tom and Jerry.'

'Gerry and Sullivan,' Johnson said. 'Doris? Did you like Rita?'

I thought I had misheard. It was nothing to do with what we were saying. My mother took it quite seriously. She said, 'As a daughter. You deserve none of these friends. Now Wendy and I are going to Pymm with the tape. Morgan is driving us.'

'Is it still a good idea?' Johnson said. 'I was fairly tight when I suggested it.'

'Why not?' my mother said. 'I have dealt with many Pymms. My kill ratio for Pymms is quite exceptional.'

'Yes. Well. It should be all right. He doesn't know we connect him with the waiter and the rest of what happened last night. The tape will reassure him that no one has separated Morgan from Kingsley's as yet. He can't lay traps for Wendy if he thinks she's off to London. And he ought with any luck to settle down now, and concentrate on leading us to his rivals. So I'll see you in Ouarzazate.'

She agreed, smiling. I think at the time she actually meant to fly safely to Ouarzazate, but I could never be sure. I was sure that Morgan had told her everything that had happened last night. I found Rita had left me some clothes, and some make-up, and presently we heard Sir Robert drive away and Morgan came through to collect us and talk briefly to Johnson, who had dissolved himself back to an off shade of beige. I was glad not to have to see Sir Robert. I didn't know if I could have defended him as Charity had. But then, she was his wife.

Morgan drove us first to his hotel, where he picked up sacks of climbing equipment and his cameras, and then to the Hotel Golden Sahara, where my mother packed, and I got into my own jeans and shirt and paid for all the room service and breakfasts that Sir Robert would no longer take care of. I had no trouble. Mr Morgan had stood me the money.

I had trouble looking after my mother, who was roving round the marble floors and the brass tables and the potted exotica looking for Ellwood Pymm. I had him paged. For a terrible fifteen minutes, we thought we had missed him; then the lift doors opened and he limped across the expanse of the foyer to where we sat with our cases. He wore a safari suit with long socks and deck shoes, and his general manner was cautious. I went forward and said, 'Mr Pymm? I'm sorry. I was hasty. Wasn't it terrible? Mr Johnson? Mr Oppenheim? My poor mother?'

He was so surprised and relieved he went scarlet. He grasped me and walked me across to my mother. 'You're all right? My God, when I heard... Where were you staying last night?'

'We sat with Miss Geddes,' I said. 'It was terrible. We're catching the plane back to London right away. My mother wanted to speak to you first.'

Behind me, I could hear her breathing. She thinks she is the only one who can fib. I stepped aside.

Ellwood's eyes went from me to my mother. A lot of his skin had come off, and what was left behind was shiny and red and frayed round the edges. His crew-cut had risen nearly to midshipman level. He said, 'Doris?'

My mother sat, her knees apart, her fag in her mouth. She said, 'You got one of my tapes.'

Mr Pymm sat down beside her. 'You gave me a business tape,' he said. His voice was tentative.

'Well, I need it,' said my mother. 'That's the next bit of the course we was doing. I must have handed it out by mistake.'

Pymm waited. Then he said, 'I'll go and get it. Did you… Have you still got the other one, then?'

'Mr Oppenheim's recording? You still want it?' said my mother, surprised. She forked her cigarette out of her mouth and wheezing, bent to rummage in one of her baskets. She came up with a cassette.

Mr Pymm made a grab, but she held on to it. She said, 'That's a real nice one: *How Expectations Go Up and Down in the Other Man's Head.* You want to try it?'

'Not just now, Doris,' he said. 'You haven't got…'

'*Emotions in the Workplace?*' she said. '*Sex: The Key to Success and the Trap-Door to Failure?* They've got that on video. Now see, this is yours. Them villains that kidnapped you wanted it. You know they're in Marrakesh?'

'I heard,' said My Pymm. He looked awed.

'Well, you be glad I made a mistake and gave you the wrong one. They were nasty men, those. They'd have killed you.'

He took it carefully from her. He said, 'Doris, if you'd come to harm through that tape, I'd have killed myself. You've done the right thing. You've done a real American thing, protecting the little investors. Now I'll go right up for your tape, and you'll have it. When's your plane?'

'We'll be all right,' said my mother. 'You go on up. We'll pass the time somehow.'

He bought us two Cockburns Aged Tawnies and we drank them while he went off to his room with the tape. When he came back, bringing ours, he kissed us both and offered to buy us two more, but my mother said we had to get to the airport. He hugged us both again, and said to be sure to look out for poor Oppenheim, who was catching a flight to Agadir. A helluva end, he said, to a really nice party.

He watched the taxi out of sight, and we wasted a lot of time taking a sweep back to the Ritas' because the last person we wanted to meet at the airport was Daniel Oppenheim. The problem being that we were supposed to be flying to London, and were actually travelling a hundred and thirty miles in the opposite direction.

When we got back to Johnson and Oliver, we received a mixed welcome. Oliver said, 'You might have gone to the airport and made some inquiries. We had a man waiting for you.'

'To stop us from flying?' said Morgan. His temper at the moment was short.

'To keep you out of Oppenheim's way, at the very least. As it happened, Oppenheim wasn't going where he said he was going in any case.'

'Where was he going?' inquired my mother.

'Supposedly to Agadir, but actually to Ouarzazate. You would have been on the same plane. That's why our man—'

'So it's just as well we came back. We need wheels,' Morgan said. Crossing the courtyard, we had seen Oliver's saddlebags already strapped on the Harley, presumably full of loan items for Johnson. Being dead, he had nothing. He couldn't even draw money. There had also been a Land-Rover, loaded with film kit.

Johnson said, 'Take the next plane.' As well as beige, he had returned to middle-management brevity.

'There isn't one to Ouarzazate for three days. We need wheels.'

Much later, I was to realize that Johnson had known that. Much later, I was to realize what the duty of the man at the airport had actually been, and that if we had gone, we should have found ourselves sooner or later back in London. As it was, Oliver glanced at Johnson and then said, 'All right. I'll see to it.' He went to the door. 'Tell him all that happened with Pymm.'

Johnson listened, but not very closely. He had expected my mother to deal with the tape business, and she had. He wandered to the window and stood, looking out, as she talked to him. Then he suddenly swore, and turning, bounded over the room. Morgan sprang up and followed him.

By then we, too, had heard the roar of the Harley-Davidson, silently wheeled out of the gate and now roused to life outside the patio by a helmeted and familiar figure. We saw it, both of us, from the window. Without waiting for Johnson, Oliver was taking the rally trail over the Tichka.

The door opened and Morgan came in, breathing quickly. For inspiration and help, my mother often looks to the apt phrase from business. 'Vertical disaggregation,' she suggested. 'A rising chasm of inequality between insiders and outsiders. Are all these fellows fighting with or against each other?'

Morgan walked to the window without speaking. Oliver had gone. Outside, Johnson was chucking stuff out of the Land-Rover and a driver was trying to stop him. Morgan said, 'Want my guess? They're a team, but no one can direct that particular bastard but Emerson. And not even Emerson, sometimes. All right. Do you want to get left behind, or are you going to help me load our stuff into the Land-Rover before Johnson drives off without us?'

19

With Mo Morgan at the wheel, we set off to cross the High Atlas and save the world for mankind in an acid silence, broken by the clack of my mother's spare knitting-needles initiating a toe. Because the front of a Land-Rover accommodates three, we had heaved her in beside Morgan. Johnson and I bounced about in the back wearing anoraks. Mine was my own; Johnson had peeled the other off the stranded film driver and sat warmly recessed in its hood, his dark glasses perceptibly misting. He looked like Paddington Bear. Every now and then Mo inspected him through the mirror and grinned spitefully. Outside it was pelting.

By that time, the polite shouting-match was over. Johnson being no longer in mint condition and moreover dead, my mother thought it perfectly sensible that Oliver should have sprinted off to track Sir Robert's moves unescorted. Morgan agreed, adding that the Helmann girls (as he put it) had run enough risks, and it was no more than reasonable that he should take them to Ouarzazate, witnessing on the way anything that Johnson thought should impress him. And since Johnson was dead, Morgan volunteered to do the driving.

Johnson's intention to drive off on his own was accordingly dissected, demonstrated to be unsound, and dropped by majority vote. That is, once my mother was inside the vehicle, there was absolutely no way he could fork her out again single-handed.

In fact, he emerged from his sulks fairly quickly, if he was ever in them: he presumably had a lot to think about. It was my employer Mo Morgan who kept up the needling, for reasons my mother claimed to understand and even tolerate. He was feeling defensive and guilty. His eccentricities had been exploited; his pride was touched; his feelings ruffled; his relationships all ungummed without previous notice. He said, 'So it's real High Noon time, bud? Ain't that just kicky? All them mountains jus' crawlin' with natives.'

'High Noon?' said my mother with interest. Without the benefit of her tray, her ball of wool ran about her feet like a puppy, frequently jumping between the clutch and Morgan's lap. We had, by then, emerged from Marrakesh into the rolling plain full of palm groves that lies to the south, punctuated by olive groves and almond and apricot orchards, drenched with rain and floating in mist that sometimes lifted to show distant layers of amorphous grey mountains.

Morgan said, 'Well, Pymm's got a red skin, but he can't be ahead of us, can he? But the Sunbeam is, with Gerry and Sullivan. And the rest of the rally, with Kingsley. And Oliver on his bike.'

Johnson said, 'He's a cowboy.'

Morgan flashed a look in the driving-mirror. 'You don't say? And we're cowboys as well? What about Rita and Rolly?'

'They've orders to get to Ouarzazate,' Johnson said. He had returned to sounding placid. 'There should be a transmitter van on this side of the col, and another in place very soon just beyond it. Oliver will check both, find Sir Robert's car and the Sunbeam, and tell us all where they are going. There are very few hostelries where Oppenheim and Sir Robert could meet.'

'If they meet,' Morgan said. 'You have to prove it. You have to prove whom they're meeting. How do you propose to do that?'

'Whoopee cushions,' Johnson said. 'And Mr Pymm and his friends. Pymm's been interested in Oppenheim for a while: that's why he wanted a bug in his study. If we know Oppenheim switched to fly to Ouarzazate, then you may be sure it's no secret from Pymm. It's the shortest of hops: twenty minutes. He daren't get on the same flight, but he's sent someone Oppenheim wouldn't recognize.'

'Who? How do you know?' Morgan said. We were still in the plain, but the rain had stopped. You could see the hills better now, and they were a pale grimy red, the colour of the earth round about us. Behind them, I thought I could see floating shapes, covered with snow.

'It wasn't terribly difficult,' Johnson said. 'Oppenheim booked for the flight, and so did Pymm's clever thug who speaks – did you spot? – Canadian French. The carpet-bugger at Essaouira who interrogated us about Kingsley's. Our much-loved friend the café waiter at Marrakesh.'

'His name is Chahid,' said my mother. 'There is a very old car.'

I wondered how she knew that the name of the third man was Chahid, and then was ashamed to have forgotten the sidecar ride to the souks, and the bruise. Morgan had remembered. His face was grim, but he didn't say anything. He was peering where my mother's needle was pointing.

My mother was right. Between the road and a wide pebbly river bed pouring with thick ochre water stood a scarlet Lancia I remembered from Asni, its bonnet up and two anxious figures leaning under it, wearing impeccable boilersuits over their cashmeres.

Morgan instinctively slowed. 'Keep going,' Johnson said briskly. And in the same tone of voice, 'Oliver? Let us keep this conversation polite. I'm in the Land-Rover behind you. Tell someone the Lancia's stuck at the river by the Ait-Ourir bridge. Where is everybody?'

I recognized the walkie-talkie in his fist from the chase through the souks. There was a crackle. Then Oliver's voice said, 'Who's driving?' It sounded aggressive.

'Morgan,' Johnson said. 'The two Helmann ladies are here. Let's get on with it.' We waited. My mother drew up yarn from her ball and it hopped up and tight-skated ostentatiously round the gear lever. Morgan swore.

'Right,' said the voice of Oliver. From aggressive, it had become merely grim. 'The good news is that Oppenheim has landed at Ouarzazate, was met by a car, and is travelling north. Pymm's chap also landed, hired a car and is following. They've passed the hotel at Tifoultout. So either they take the route to Taroudant when they come to it, or the rendezvous is on the road we are on. The junction's only sixteen miles out, and Rita's left someone to watch it. Your drawings, I'm told, were spot-on, and the fax chap at Ouarzazate thinks you should take up portrait-painting.'

'And the bad news?' Johnson said. The road had become distinctly steeper and instead of a plain, the horizon was bounded

234

by caked red ridges sliced and moulded by wet, and patched with emerald barley. The lower slopes were candy-coloured with flowers. Moisture hung in the air.

Oliver said, 'The col is open, but the road is horrendous. Rita got over the pass fifteen minutes ago, but it needed chains. The radio vans are in position, and so are the check-points for the rally, but none of the vintages is within two hours of the crest. Jay, the snows are coming down with the rain. They've had a collapse in one village already, and the road is smothered in water and mud. I don't know if the old cars will get over, or you. I think you should leave it to me.'

Johnson said, 'Where is the Sunbeam? And Kingsley?'

There was a torrid pause. Then Oliver said, 'The Sunbeam is into the hairpins after Touama, going well, and high on brotherly love: he's stopped three times to give help to buddies. So he's slow but not all that slow: he's made no effort to hang back and wait for Sir Robert. Kingsley is in a support jeep at the tail end of the rally, and being equally helpful and considerate. He's passed the hotel at Ait-Ourir, and the Ourika and Imguer turn-offs, so the rendezvous isn't there. His car has a dun hood, and painted with SECOURS in yellow. If it's stopped, you may have to pass it.'

'OK. Warn me if you can. What's it like south of the col?'

'Better,' said Oliver. 'Oppenheim will be making reasonable time. If he's turning off west to Taroudant, he's nothing to worry about.'

'And if he isn't? If he's coming north on this road, where's the meeting?' Johnson said.

And Oliver said, 'I don't bloody know, and I'm not sure if I can find out. If Kingsley keeps coming south, there's only Taddert ahead, and the vertical bends to the col. And if it's over the col, he may not even make it; the road may be swamped by that time. Jay, this is lethal.'

'You amaze me,' said Johnson; and cut Oliver off.

No one spoke as we climbed. About us now were vistas of red hills of varying sizes, some with walled and fortified villages made of hill-coloured vermilion clay. They plastered the inclines in long, smooth rectangles, defining ridges and perpetrating sudden verticals of tower or mosque. It came to me that some of these buildings were kasbahs – crow's nests, robber fortresses – with Ramon Navarro in them, and black satin sheets, and my mother was being whipped straight past them.

I saw she wasn't watching her knitting, but her fingers zapped through her needles, and her sock continued to grow like a print-out. We drove alongside the dark netted green of a royal game forest from which, impetuously, something bolted as we approached. Morgan braked. It was a boar. I waited for Johnson to speak, but he didn't. Soon, we came to the first of the infinite succession of loops by which the road to Ouarzazate climbs up to the snowline. The large behind of a navy Bugatti loomed ahead of us, and we began to pass beautiful cars.

On our way to look for the *Dolly*, Sullivan had treated me to a monologue about vintage cars, beginning with the first he had ever rebuilt and proceeding with a list of all he and his fellow officers had ever owned or aspired to. I had received further exposure at Asni. I concluded that vintage car ralliers were like Seb and Gerry, a mixture of macho competitive handymen and dedicated collectors with their own brand of drop-dead chic humour. In between driving up mountains, they navigated with buckets over their heads to their co-drivers' orders. On the High Atlas before us were a dozen nutters and a few million pounds' worth of vehicles, plus Sir Robert Kingsley on his way to a quiet business meeting with someone.

The metalled carriageway of the Tichka, engineered by the French, is less than two lanes in width, joined by a jagged fringe of potholed tarmac to a broken hard shoulder. From Marrakesh, the distance is seventy miles to the crest, of which the last twenty-mile stretch contains frequent blind and precipitous turns of 180 degrees, alternating in sequences of two or three clusters of S bends. No one had mentioned this to me when we set out.

To begin with, the climb seemed merely difficult because of the traffic. The bends were not unduly steep, and allowed Morgan to weave his way among the vans, the lorries, the cars in varying degrees of repair and the twice-daily CTM bus service, none of which had been deterred by the weather and all of which, as they passed up and down, gave passionate attention if not very much room to the labouring vintages. Once, we had to crawl behind a sad Ford HE

236

14/40 two-seater on the end of a tow-rope until safely flagged past, and once we met a girl with a herd of red plushy cows which took a long time to pass, allowing Morgan to exercise his libido as well as his Arabic. Then he had to shut up his window because Oliver's voice spoke to us again. It sounded tentative.

'J.J.? Oppenheim's passed the Taroudant junction. He's coming north on P 31, your road. Time to the col, about an hour and three-quarters. If he doesn't divert, Oppenheim will get to the top about the same time as Sir Robert. There's nothing there. A Berber hamlet. A lot of snow. A bunch of tourist stalls selling fossils and amethyst. They're going to meet at Taddert, or south of the col.'

I looked at the map in Johnson's hand. Taddert was five and a half thousand feet up, and fourteen miles short of the col on our side. And a lot of zig-zags away. 'In a tent?' Johnson said.

'I don't see how,' said Oliver, clearly in the grip of anxiety.

'No. Neither do I. Keep trying,' said Johnson, and lurched to one side, swearing, as Morgan avoided running over a bullock.

That proved to be the start of a livestock problem. The carriage-ways of the High Atlas are put to excellent use by hill-farming and amenable Berbers in robes and shorty green wellies who drive sheep, goats, cows, mules and donkeys along the water canals at the verge and occasionally straight over the road, in the process of descending from road-bend to road-bend as on a convenient ladder. We had two fairly abrupt halts, followed by a close encounter with a long vehicle coming round a bend like a lariat. After that, Johnson took to saying, 'The camber on the next one is wrong.' And once, 'There's a passing-place just ahead, but the shoulder tends to be broken.' I remembered that the film company were based at Ouarzazate, and he must have driven there on other visits. I thought Morgan looked a bit worn, and was thankful to see that the two of them had taken to talking. They weren't joshing, but they were talking all right.

We passed, to its patent annoyance, a noisy Riley and then a rumbling Alvis whose camshaft drive met with the disapproval of both Morgan and Johnson. A sign, looming up on our right, said COL TIZI-N-TICHKA: OUVERT, and added something about chains on our tyres. There was an argument about that, which I didn't listen to. My mother apparently did. At the next decent passing-place, she said, 'Stop!'

It was a nice spot, if we had wanted the scenery. Below the road, a slate-blue river had made its appearance, heavily populated by Berber women washing cress or scrubbing brilliant garments, undisturbed by a horizon full of roaring machinery. Dots on the slopes rising behind them were children with bundles of fuel and fodder. On the riverbank, the leafless grey branches of walnut trees flapped with cerise and green silks; and ragged patches of clothes were spread over carpets of tulips. Kettles steamed above small brush-wood fires and when Morgan switched off the engine, you could hear women's chatter and laughter.

Far from mentioning chains, my mother merely wished to get down from the Rover. After the briefest bachelor hesitancy, Morgan and Johnson hoisted her out of the passenger seat. I didn't help. I knew she had a bladder the size of a football, and whatever it was, it wasn't what they were thinking. In the event, she merely heel-toddled straight down the hillside, carrying one of Morgan's aluminium canteens, and climbed it again ten minutes later with a bundle under one arm and the canteen full of unhygienic mint tea. The women who pushed her uphill remained for a moment, giggling and nudging each other, and then went back, their robes full of Gauloises.

'Doris?' said Morgan. 'You have a cassette on how to speak Berber?'

'You live in London, you communicate,' said my mother, pouring liquid into tin mugs from Morgan's unshackled haversack. 'Mint tea is better than whisky. Five bends up, there has been a bad avalanche: watch out for boulders. And hear this: them high buildings are kasbahs.'

She hadn't missed them. I looked at the bundle she had laid carefully down and wondered if she had fixed herself harem pants and a rug. Then I realized that what she had brought was Berber clothing, half-dry and authentic. Morgan said, 'Doris: if we get out of this, I'm going to build you a kasbah.'

'In Ealing?' said my mother.

'In Ealing,' he said, handing her his empty mug and seizing the wheel. He didn't roar into the climb because there was a line of donkeys before us, all with filled double-panniers, and a bus approaching. The driver shouted something as he passed, and Morgan waved as he crawled. A loaded donkey travels at five miles an hour. We were still behind them when we got to the avalanche, before which was a short line of traffic, including the Bugatti, a Chrysler and what Morgan said was a Darl' Mat Peugeot with smoke or steam coming from under its silver bonnet. They had stopped because the road was full of robed men tugging at boulders and sweeping up stones which might inconvenience little hooves. Above was the scar where the boulders had fallen, and beyond it an older gash containing the remains of two handsome villas, one with a tiled roof whose front edge drooped like an envelope over nothing.

Morgan, who had used the wait to go visiting, lifted himself back into the Land-Rover with the gossip. 'Happened last year, the old landslide. Seventy million dirhams' worth of holiday house built by Saudis and battered out of the way by the mountain. They say we'll have to watch for slides from now on; mud on the road and holes in the tarmac. The Ford's terminally out: big end gone. The Frazer-Nash has had a chain failure but the Alvis is oke: shifted a nut from somewhere else to the camshaft drive.'

'It was,' Johnson said.

'Yes, it was. The Sunbeam, you'll be sorry to hear, is still in good nick and swallowing S bends. If I interpret that rightly, Tom and Jerry have got marching orders: they've no quarrel with me, they aren't worried about Wendy or Doris, and they're clearly not hanging about to nurse Kingsley or Oppenheim. Kingsley's service jeep is still ahead, going well and handing out swigs of whisky and sparking plugs from a tinny like caramels. The Bentley's changed a couple of wheels and that's radiator hose trouble in the Peugeot. Also, someone in front went short of lock at one of the hairpins and needs to patch up their steering linkage. There's a Berber market over the hill with spare parts. Well, bits of wire and metal and rubber. I reckon they're going to have one or two clients. That's my news. And that's Oliver.'

The radio crackled. The procession in front of us started to move, the car wheels scrabbling in mounds of red mud. The Chrysler went into the lead, and Morgan passed the Bugatti and the Peugeot and sat behind it, slithering up round the bend past which the downcoming traffic had halted. The mud thinned beyond, and the road looped up and round the next turning. Far across the valley, a waterfall hung like a strip of grey satin. Oliver's voice said, 'Are you all right? There's been a fall where you're heading.'

'We knew,' Johnson said. 'Doris had a tip from the Berbers. Who's in the lead?'

'The Sunbeam,' said Oliver. 'Nearly up to the radio van and within twenty minutes of the summit. Tail-end Charlie's the Lancia: had to change its head gasket. I'm going to move up off the road: a Harley passing six times is getting obvious.'

Johnson whisked off his glasses. I didn't know why, but it obviously made him feel better. He said, 'You bloody fool: I told you—'

'They haven't seen me,' said Oliver. 'I'm just taking precautions.'

'The man who fixes my word-processor,' said my mother. 'He talks exactly so. Tell him to stay off the road.'

Johnson told him. He had some trouble, because we had arrived at all the blind bends, and our torsos were switching like metronomes. Then we fell on our backs, because on the next bend thirty large speckled goats were discovered crossing the road in the charge of an eight-year-old child and a mongrel. We recovered. We slewed round long, slow arabesque curves, and slewed back over others. Morgan said, 'Oh, hooray, there's the Lancia.'

There weren't very many places where you could pass, but the Lancia's driver soon did, waving cheerfully as he went by. Having passed, he maintained a decorous pace. Indeed, he dropped speed. Red and elegant, he occupied the whole road before us.

A shining Lancia is a handsome sight, and it annoyed me to hear Morgan cursing it. Then my mother said, 'Why does he linger? His gasket is weakening?'

'I don't know,' Morgan said. 'But if he gets any slower, we're going to slide backwards.' I could see the dials. I could see how the temperature was rising. And if the gradient got any steeper, I could see the Lancia relapsing back into us. She must have realized it as well. At the next bend she crawled halfway round, viewed the highway ahead, and signalled flamboyantly for us to pass her.

Morgan was a good driver. From a standing start, he gave the Land-Rover as much power as would provide grip and steering and set it at the bend outside the Lancia. He was halfway round when he met the oncoming truck full of half-ripe tomatoes. Because it was coming down, it was using part of the hard shoulder as well as the centre, spraying loose stones and small rocks as it came. We had the flexibility, the tyres and the presence of mind, but what really mattered was how wide the hard shoulder was. As the truck driver slammed on his brakes, Morgan swerved round his outer side with a snarl of his engine. For a moment we rocked on the brink, gravel flying, wheels whining and spinning. And then we were round and past, and crossing the road to hug the inner side of the next U bend while the truck blared its furious horn, and the Lancia dropped demurely behind us. I said, 'The Americans! These were the Americans!'

'They sure were,' Morgan said. 'And one of the John Does was Pymm.'

'*Pymm?*' I said.

'Of course,' Johnson said. 'That's why they broke down by the river. They shed a passenger and took Pymm aboard. Folks, we've found Ellwood Pymm's contacts.'

'Great,' said Morgan. 'Now explain why they tried to get rid of me?'

'Because they didn't recognize you,' said my mother. Her needles ran along, fast and soothing as sleeper wheels. 'You they have hardly seen. But they observe me and Wendy, who have lied about our departure to London. They do not wish me and Wendy to see what they are up to. They are up to something, for sure. There is the radio van. We are not far from the summit. With Pymm behind you, I do not recommend that you stop.'

Now and then, I felt she had a grasp of the situation. This time, however, my mother and the High Atlas stood face to face. Now the mountains about us were deep with snow and the air was cool and fresh and thin, making us breathe quickly. There were ovals of snow at the roadside, valanced like sea-shore sand with patterns of thawing, but as we got higher they spread, and the red and yellow snow-posts stood sunk in them. There was a barrier ready to drop, if the road became impassable.

This morning, Rita had driven through snow. Now the passage of cars had half melted it, making it easier and also more difficult. We veered round sickening bends, braking abruptly for oncoming traffic and accelerating sharply when pushy drivers behind bounded forward. We slid through slush and lurched into potholes, but we kept going. We didn't stop at the radio van, although we saw faces watching us pass. Near the top were the efficient fawn block-houses, labelled GENDARMERIE ROYALE, and beyond that, the checkpoint trestles with their freezing officials bundled in anoraks, and a white-topped police car with cheerful men in red-banded caps and grey uniforms and two or three Vintages, cars and owners steaming together.

It was a temptation to halt, but we didn't. His hair undone, his face rather set, Morgan drove to the top of the col Tizi n' Tichka, seven thousand four hundred feet high, and slid over the crest. My mother said, 'Born of a corkscrew, I knew it. Open your mouth.'

She put chocolate into it, and fed me and tried to feed Johnson, who was crouched over his crackling transmitter. When he shook his head, she turned back to Mo. She said, 'The Lancia will stop at the checkpoint. You take your time.' And Morgan, his face widening, smiled.

She knew, I suppose, that our road would be worse going down. Around us, also, the mountains seemed different. The lower slopes weren't red any more, but ochre dusted with grit, and all the hamlets, the shacks, the terraces were the same colour crusted with snow, with jade water rushing between. The road looped and coiled and wound far below us, and behind the blotched, crumpled cups of the valleys the snowy mountains rose, rank upon rank. For the second time Johnson called Oliver, and for the second time, he didn't answer.

The third time of asking he did, and duly shrivelled, rushed to excuse himself. 'Christ, I'm sorry, but I'm bloody dying. I had to take off my helmet: big deal, don't have kittens, I'm off the road. I'm up above you; I can see you. The Sunbeam and Kingsley have both passed the radio van and the summit and are on their way downhill ahead of you. Oppenheim has passed the south radio van on his way to the summit, and so has Chahid, still tailing him. The gap between Oppenheim and Sir Robert is closing, but I don't know where the hell they're expecting to stop.'

242

'They may not try,' Johnson said. 'Pymm is in the red Lancia, travelling south with the worst of intentions. He's had a swipe already at us, and will do the same, I assume, to anyone he thinks Kingsley is courting. God knows what will happen if and when he finds Oppenheim and Sir Robert are buddies.'

'Is that a note of hope?' Morgan said.

'That,' said Johnson, 'would be an overstatement. Oliver, can you climb any higher? I'd really like to know if Kingsley has stopped or turned off.'

'I'll try,' Oliver said.

Johnson put his hand on Morgan's shoulder and Morgan slowed. My mother laid down her knitting. Morgan said, 'I'll have to keep some momentum.' We'd seen a car have to back down already, to take a run at a bend.

Johnson said, 'I know. I want to keep within Oliver's cheapo binocs as long as it's possible.' I wondered what he was afraid of, apart from a landslide, or a crack in the road, or a perfectly legitimate crash. I thought of a number of things he might be afraid of, because I was. Oliver's voice came abruptly again.

'It's conclusive, I think. Kingsley hasn't shown up at the next checkpoint after the summit. And Oppenheim passed that checkpoint and vanished. They've met, J.J.'

'Or crashed. Or stopped for a pee, or a picnic. Or Chahid has wiped them both out. Let's be crazy,' Johnson said, 'and suppose we are right. Where are they meeting? Rumour says there's a Berber market somewhere about. What about that? Can you see one?'

'No,' said Oliver's voice. 'At least, maybe. There's a dip over there, and a road of sorts with some mules walking along it.'

'Wide enough for a car?'

'I should think so. Dirt surface. But where could they meet in a market?' He broke off. 'Hey!'

'Hey,' repeated Johnson with patience. 'What?'

'The Lancia!' Oliver said. 'The Lancia's coming behind you. It's pulled out to pass!'

'It can't,' said Morgan. My mother stopped knitting. Morgan said, 'It can't. We're on a blind corner. *Christ Jesus!*'

In a flash of red, the Lancia drew alongside on the left, and I prepared for the squeal of metal, the bump that would slam us into the core of the hill. But the cars roared side by side without touching, and then the other car pulled past at top speed, still on the wrong side, full into the bend. Morgan was pumping the brake, slackening speed as much as he dared; trying to keep steering power for anything. His knuckles were white on the wheel.

There was no crash. The Land-Rover, answering painfully to the accelerator, brought us round a bend that was free of traffic and empty, but for the tail of the Lancia vanishing down and round the next bend. Oliver said in a shrill voice, 'You saw that?'

Johnson said. 'How the hell did he know how to pass? Oliver?'

'I don't know. He's two bends down and fairly gunning it. No, he isn't. He's slowed. Jay, do you hear me? The Lancia's stopped on the hard shoulder. He's unloaded something... someone. He's unloaded Pymm, and gone on without him. Pymm is making for something. Chahid's car! I can see Chahid's car! Chahid's car is standing on the verge just below where the Lancia stopped. But it's empty.'

He was still speaking when Johnson broke in. He said, 'Oliver, Chahid's on the hill. He must have signalled the Lancia. *Oliver, look out for Chahid! Chahid! He's there, and he knows you.*'

Oliver didn't reply. Instead of his voice, there came a number of thuds, a clang, a shout, and the sound of the Harley-Davidson's engine revving and roaring. Then I realized that I was hearing it myself, and not just through a transmitter, and that it was coming from the fold of the hill just above us. Looking up, Morgan braked with all his strength, regardless of the consequences. No one spoke.

The Harley-Davidson, so smart at Essaouira, came bouncing down the high ground above us in a spray of mud and tumbling rubble. It shot over the road, Oliver's boot trailing sparks, and bounding over the verge, continued screaming and slithering through the scree to the road loop below us. It flashed across between cars, and slid over the verge and veered down the next slope the way goats did, descending from bend to bend of the road until they reached valley bottom.

Except that Oliver didn't reach valley bottom. Seven hundred pounds of Harley-Davidson skewed, slid and trembled and finally heeled over flat on the scree, throwing Oliver like a dummy far below it. It rumbled on with its own weight for a while until it came to lodge in the end at a bush, its two tyres, torn by bullets, pointing upwards. There was a pause, during which I heard Johnson's voice speaking clearly in French like a CAF commentator. Then the Harley exploded.

20

The Land-Rover slewed to a halt. Morgan jumped down and ran to the back. Johnson, still transmitting, had swung Morgan's climbing-boots from their satchel and, one-handed, was rapidly loosening the laces. Morgan tore them from him. 'They wouldn't fit you,' he said. 'And you're dead. And you couldn't bloody do it now, anyway.'

He picked up Johnson's discarded shoes and flung them into my lap, then set about exchanging his own for his boots. He said, 'Drive this down but don't take any bloody risks: there'll be others nearer than we are. If he can be moved, I'll bring him down to you.' He had rope over one shoulder, and a stick, and a ground-sheet. The next moment, he had walked to the edge of the road and stepped over, and Johnson sat in his socks, looking after him. Then he switched on his radio, and began talking quickly again.

I stood up, until I could see where Morgan had gone. I had never seen a man surfing on boulders. Plunging down between roads, plastered with snow, the mountain slope was an avalanche waiting to happen. Morgan planed on it. He rode it like a man skiing on rock, in a skimming cloud of sharp grit and slush, a racing carpet of stones underneath him. He looked intent, precarious, wire-taut as a spider. 'Your Mr Thornton,' said my mother, 'is lucky.'

'Yes,' said Johnson; and slid out of the Land-Rover. He was wearing his shoes again. A moment later, Morgan's door opened and shut and Johnson was starting the engine. He said, 'It's called riding the scree. Atlas scree is the worst in the world. He'll be with Oliver in something like three minutes.'

'He knows the risks,' said my mother. 'Delegation, Mr Johnson.' Johnson didn't reply. He was busy doing what Morgan had told him not to do.

It took us fifteen minutes of near-suicidal driving to reach the road nearest to the slope where the bike was. Halfway there, the radio sprang to life and I took it. It said, 'Ambulance on its way. The car you describe has not passed the col or either van: it is still in your vicinity. If it appears, it will be followed and stopped. Support is coming from Ouarzazate. What is the news?'

And at Johnson's request, I replied. 'We don't know. When we do, we'll tell you.'

We found five cars already there at the bottom, including the official Vintage Support Vehicle and a gendarmerie van from the col. Above us, the Harley still smouldered but the young fellow, they said, had been taken in by the Berbers, and the support's auxiliary medic was with him.

Across the road, we could see the hamlet they spoke of. It straddled the stream and rose up the opposite hill in tiers of clay houses with flat rush-woven roofs and ladders of exterior steps. Hens and children and adults wandered up and down the steep snow-streaked lanes, their heads turned to watch us. Among them was Morgan, striding over. We heard him say, 'It's OK. They seem to think that they'll manage. He's alive, and there's help on the way. Nasty fall. Take care yourselves. And thank you.'

The waiting cars loaded, and began to disperse. 'True?' said Johnson. In the cold and the snow, his hood and dark glasses looked natural.

'True. He'll make it. Berber magic.'

'They climbed up to help you?'

'Hassan did. I know him. He was a guide when he was young, and his son is a skier. Listen, I didn't mean it. I'm sorry.'

'No. I ought to know better by this time. He's over there?'

'That's the house. There's an ambulance on the way. From Ouarzazate, they can fly Oliver anywhere. Doris, do you want to be carried or pushed?'

'On that news,' said my mother, 'I can fly.'

The house he pointed out seemed little more than a mud compound, built to one side of the river. Walking towards it, I felt numb. My mother said nothing, and Johnson, who had returned briefly to the Land-Rover to radio, was questioning Morgan. I couldn't hear what they were saying.

I had spent more time listening to Oliver's voice than I had in his company. I knew nothing about him. I wondered what I was going to see, arriving at the low house; stepping over the rushing stream at the door into the throbbing darkness of the chamber inside. Morgan took my elbow and steered me round a vast, recessed grinding-stone, turning and shuddering with the force of water beneath it. A cone full of grain hung above it. Beyond was daylight, and a yard full of litter and curious children, and a cow, and the door of a bath-house. Further than that was another door, and a clutter of low-walled rectangles, roofed or latticed or open that constituted the living quarters, the kitchen, the storehouses, the place for the hens.

Oliver lay unconscious in Hassan's bedroom, on a low mattress covered with rugs. His face was pale under its tan, and covered with bruises, and his limbs were splinted with skis. The young medic explained the splints he had put in, and the jag he had given, and prepared another in case it was needed. Then he left to join his support truck and travel back to where they were supposed to be. Only then did our host, the Berber Hassan appear in the doorway.

He was a tall man, with the full lips and smooth olive face I was beginning to recognize among hillmen. His chin was ringed with grey bristle and he walked with a limp. My mother said, 'I wish to greet him in Berber.' Her own bruise was quite lurid, like a caste mark.

'He would appreciate that,' said Mo Morgan. 'But he speaks pretty good English. And French and German, as a matter of fact. Runs a mean hut, and stands no nonsense. What do you think?'

This to Hassan, who bowed to my mother and me, and then entered. He said, 'The hospital will X-ray him. The lungs are not pierced. The pelvis, I do not know. This is your friend?' He looked at Johnson.

'Bontine Graham,' Johnson introduced himself politely. Morgan looked at him. Johnson continued, 'Without you, the boy would have died. Has he spoken?'

'Only one word. He said *Chahid* as we lifted him. A name? The name of the one whose bullets ruined his tyres?'

'This is known?' Johnson said. Dropping to the floor, he took Oliver's wrist and felt for the pulse.

'To us in this room. When the fire took hold, as Mr Morgan has reminded me, there was nothing to see. Who is this Chahid?'

'An enemy,' Johnson said. He tapped Oliver's hand and sat back. 'We think he is not far away. Is there a market?'

'A local one. You would soon notice a Westerner.'

'Perhaps,' Johnson said. 'It might be worth trying.'

He and Morgan and Hassan stayed by the bed, watching it and talking in low voices, while my mother reacted as was her custom, picking up Oliver's wet things and folding them into his jacket, and taking charge of his keys and his radio and his papers and his very smashed watch, and taking a quick look at the way the bandages were. She fished out two dry hankies of her own and put them by the syringe, and finally laid a palm like a muffin on his brow.

He didn't stir. I left the room before she did, and found myself pulled along by children and girls who didn't speak English or German or French, but wanted to know if I was hungry or thirsty, and show me their sitting-room, which had thick-carpeted window sills, and a recess full of tattered school books covered in flour, and a TV draped in gold cloth also covered with flour, as was the single lightbulb. I was still there when the ambulance began to come down the blue winding road. I found my mother by the fire in the kitchen, hunkered down on the floor beside another old woman in black. She had taken her teeth out as a gesture of courtesy. An oil-can hung from the ceiling, and they batted it sloshing between them, making inarticulate conversation and goat cheese. They were both smiling blackly and coughing. Then I told her, and she see-sawed up to her feet, put her teeth back, and came with me to look for the others.

They had begun grinding again when Oliver, still unconscious, was carried out of the house. The woven cone dribbled barley on to the stone and the white flour poured out from the sides. The noise it made was like the chuff of a steam train. The ambulance driver, speaking French, said, 'I have also to take the two ladies.'

Morgan had gone to fetch Johnson. My mother doesn't speak French. I said to her, 'You'll have to get in. They want you to go with him.'

She glared at me. 'Go on,' I said. 'The Implications of Being a Woman. Creating a Trust Climate where Two-Way Communication Thrives. Go and tell Rita what's going on. Bloody delegation, remember?'

I had heaved her into the van when Hassan appeared and said, in his excellent English, 'But, mademoiselle, they wish you to go as well.'

'I thought so!' cried my mother from the recesses of the ambulance.

'No,' I said. 'I'm Mr Morgan's Executive Secretary. Where is Mr Morgan?'

He appeared at that moment, looking harassed. He had put on his anorak, and his pigtail was all done up again. He said, 'I can't find...'

'Mr Bontine Graham,' said Hassan, 'has gone.'

'Where?' Morgan said. 'The effing bastard. To the market?'

'He asked about the market,' said Hassan. 'He asked about the sources of power. I told him the excess of mud is due to the laying of cables; especially telephone cables.'

'Telephone cables!' said Morgan.

'To the kasbah,' explained Hassan peacefully. 'The approach lies through the market; the fortress occupies the rise of the hill just behind. Once a ruin, and now restored at a cost of many millions of dirhams by the new owner. He is an Arab. He is an Arab not of Morocco.'

'And J. – Mr Graham's gone there,' Morgan stated. The ambulance driver had started his engine.

'He wished to see it. You are to wait for him here. The ladies are to go to his friends at Ouarzazate.'

'I'm staying,' I said. I didn't want to. I didn't want to know about Arabs. I had found the way to Omar Sharif and Peter O'Toole and Ramon Navarro at last, and I was petrified.

My mother said, 'Wendy?'

Morgan said, 'Wendy. Get into the damned thing and go. For God's sake what do you want? Overtime?'

I felt myself flushing. I shouted at him. 'You needed Oliver. You've got to have somebody. Anyway, what are you worried about? You're the blasted cream of the microprocessor intelligentsia, and no one can touch you.'

He didn't even answer: he gazed at my mother. My mother said, 'Wendy, you just got the big picture perspective. You're a trailblazer. You trail it. I'm proud.' I still couldn't tell whether she was serious. Then she lifted her paw, and the driver let in the clutch, and the ambulance drove off to the south with a splash. The last thing I saw was her bruise. She must have had a headache since yesterday.

Morgan said, 'OK. Come on, Oliver,' and made for the jeep.

Because no one could touch him, Morgan drove to the Berber market quite openly, and parked the Rover, and joined the crowds with me at his side. His intention, I knew, was to find Pymm and Chahid and keep them out of Johnson's way. His further intention, I suspected, was to do something quite nasty to Chahid. We didn't discuss it.

On the face of it, we were reasonably safe. If Pymm and Chahid were about, they had no reason to jump out and slug us. Johnson was dead, Oliver had just had an accident, and my mother, who had failed to go to London, had now been removed from the scene. Morgan said, 'She's the one Pymm must be suspicious of, not you. Stick to me, and all you'll get is hay fever. That must be the road up to the kasbah.'

I could see it, a narrow band of slush rising behind the massed roofs of corrugated iron and canvas that covered the stalls, the mats, the mud of the market. If Johnson was up there, there was no sign of him. On the other hand, he might not have arrived yet.

Entering the market, you could see what a good place it could be to hide in. As Hassan had said, there were very few Europeans, although I did see a pair of fine tailored tracksuits turning over an array of spare parts and spanners. The Bugatti had come for some shopping. The rest were all Arabs and Berbers, with the occasional Black face among them. I noticed for the first time how tall and well-grown some of them were: silent figures standing bowed within a tent weighing grain, or presiding over a table of dusty cassettes which perhaps discussed familiar questions (Mid-Career Plateau or Launching-Pad?) or perhaps offered no more than the mournful Arab music the owner was playing, broken into by a gabble of French.

Because of the weather, a lot of the stalls were enclosed. We walked between them, peering at beans and coffee, washing-powder and bowls, carpets and baskets and wrought-iron, tinny jewellery and hanks of rough turquoises. It was like the Marrakesh souks in a small way: tribal market and tourist centre in one. Morgan bought pastries and we devoured them as we went. We found a story-teller and a man charming snakes, but not Ellwood Pymm or his agile, numerate and ruthless friend Chahid. We passed a vat of hot fat flanked by doughnuts: some uncooked, some crisp and coloured. I said, 'I saw a film once. The fire-eater blew into the frying-fat, and the hero escaped.'

'That's the trouble,' said Mo Morgan. 'All the clichés have got used already. Like the chase in the souks.'

'What?' I said. A boy with a fibre suitcase offered us a choice of cheap watches.

'You hadn't rehearsed it,' said Morgan, 'but the crowd had. I'm told they demanded extra pay when it was over. Look, we've been this way before. Let's go back to the cassettes.'

'Why?' I said. 'Want to buy one?'

'Maybe,' Morgan said. 'How's your French?'

My French is quite good. Good enough to pick up the chatter you could hear from the stall, mixed up with the wails of the music. The moment we got close, it stopped. We lingered a moment, turning over the cassettes while the well-built Berber at the stall watched us as if we meant to steal them. Mo bought one, and we walked on, the music receding. The voice didn't restart. I said, 'He was taking a radio message. It said, *They are here, both of them.*'

'They said it in Arabic too,' Morgan said. 'There are others. Try not to seem to be looking. We'll do this, and get back to the middle.'

We had come to the abattoir. On the rough wood benches beside it, choppers thudded and banged and sliced through soft meat and brittle poultry. Sheeps' heads lay by sad heaps of wool, each chopped-off spine sticking up, a pale cylinder in the red welter.

A man stood, stuffing sausages. Grey and shining, they whipped in his fingers like eels. He was tall, as the others had been. Tall and muscular.

Their industry was the more remarkable because the number of shoppers had dwindled. The trampled ways between stalls had become easily passable. The noise of laughter and bidding had lessened. Even the bamboo pipe of the snake-charmer was fading. The only customers who had remained in their places were the captive ones in the barbers' row of mud cubicles, each with its one chair and zinc bowl of water. All the clients were men. They sat wrapped in cloth, submitting to the comb or the razor: to being trimmed, shaved or apparently scalped. Most were elderly. One had a crew-cut.

It was Pymm. He turned his pug-nosed, frothing face in that moment, and saw me and Morgan, and reacted with an expression of shock that trembled towards a diligent smile. He got up, the soapy towel still round his neck. The barber in the next cubicle also rose. Approaching us, Pymm opened his mouth. Morgan stepped forward. The barber from the next cubicle began to stroll in our direction. He had an open razor in one hand. At the last moment Pymm turned and saw him. Pymm gasped. The barber said to Ellwood Pymm, 'You will come with me.'

A hand closed over my mouth. 'And you will come with me,' said another man softly behind me. I struggled. Morgan, intent on Pymm, didn't turn. The man behind me pinioned my arms and, tripping me neatly off-balance, whipped me back out of sight of the others. 'It's all right,' said the same voice reassuringly. 'Mo's in no danger. But Pymm is bloody going to involve him, and I'm not sure if you'd be as lucky. Turn round, Wendy.'

The hands fell away. I turned. Over Johnson's nice lockknit jersey he now wore a rather natty djellabah, clean but creased from my mother's knitting-bag. We were in a space between empty stalls, and I could hear Pymm's voice raised in protest. Johnson said, 'I've got some gear for you, too, but do you mind if we see what is happening?' He spoke as if it were a video show. Holding me, he moved cautiously forward.

They had got Pymm by then: the barber and at least one other helper. The towel had been twisted tight round his neck, and above it his half-lathered face had become scarlet. He was calling, 'Morgan, Morgan! You know me! Any size cheque that you like! Help me, Morgan!'

Talisman in the microchip world, the name Morgan was unknown to Pymm's captors. It merely indicated that Pymm had a friend and an ally: someone who equally, therefore, merited lifting. The large man, with no trouble whatever, restrained Ellwood Pymm. It took three others to get hold of Morgan, and all the time he was looking for me. Then, satisfied that I had gone, he abruptly stopped struggling.

'It is good,' said the man who had first spoken. 'And now, we shall go to the kasbah.'

I turned. Inside Johnson's hood, I caught a single black gleam. Then he said, 'No, I'm not going to help him. Neither are you. So, are you on? I'm after Chahid, and it might be tricky. You can come, or go back to Hassan.'

I said, 'Only Chahid? Not Sir Robert and Oppenheim?'

'Oh, they're in the kasbah,' said Johnson. 'But I don't need to see them. Morgan will.'

That was why he hadn't stopped Mo being captured. Johnson wanted him captured, so that he could learn for himself what Oppenheim and Sir Robert were up to. I thought he was mental. I said, 'According to Hassan, the kasbah's owned by an Arab. A pan-Arab. Not a Moroccan.'

'Surprising, isn't it?' Johnson remarked. We were retreating silently between empty stalls. 'You could imagine Ellwood Pymm pimping for anybody, but I didn't connect Daniel with Arabs. I should have. He's subtle, although he can't fathom a mystical idiot like Morgan. And of course, these are not your usual investors. They've no links with the al-Baraka or the al-Rajh or the IDB: we checked these all out at the start. Daniel's Arabs are very quiet fellows, pissing-rich and broad thinkers. The kind who want bangs for their bucks.'

Two babes in the world of finance, my mother had said. Now I knew she was joking. I said, 'You've got your chief browned off with you, anyway. You didn't tell him the MCG were being hunted by Kingsley's.'

I had followed a train of thought of my own. He must have followed it too, for after slowing, he began walking again. He said, 'You met Sir Bernard, all right. I sometimes do a thing for a friend, and he flips. If I'd let Rita go down, he'd have killed me. Here's the mule. So, Wendy, what about it?'

There were a lot of mules. He laid an arm on one of them, and it tried to bite him. I said, 'Of course, I ought to be on my way to Ouarzazate.'

'That was the plan,' Johnson said. 'But if you want to see goalmouth action, I'm easy. Or you can say No without feeling guilty. I know you can. I saw the cassette.'

He really did seem unconcerned which I chose. I chose to go, which of course he had counted on. At the time, I just got dressed in the loose robes and veils he had brought me, and he gave me my orders. They were lucid and pleasant. He was in so many ways like Sir Robert. Then I splashed up the steep snowy road to the kasbah beside Johnson's mule, which Johnson was riding in an indolent and leisurely manner. Its panniers were filled with goat cheeses.

Only once, as we went, did we hear wheels behind us and found ourselves sprayed by a battered Land-Rover full of men, its back tarpaulin-laced for privacy. It vanished ahead between gushes of brown snow.

'Pymm and Morgan,' Johnson said. 'On-Time Delivery. I should think Pymm's in over-drive now, trying to fathom whom he's got to face, and whether he can claim he's here to write up kasbahs for Canada. That dirty trick with the Lancia will take some explaining. And if he gets connected with Chahid, he's had it.'

'Where will the Arabs put them?' I asked. I was dripping. Whatever happened, I kept getting annoyed with him.

He knew it, of course. I could tell from the way he sat and considered, while his shoe absently tapped the mule's shoulder. 'Depends on the kasbah,' he said. 'The Caids used to chain their prisoners together and drop them into some hole dug for storage. Sometimes they ran to your genuine dungeons. Latterly it got pretty civilized. Choice of poisoned tea or a cage on a camel. The Glaoui, who held the Tizi n' Telouet pass until practically yesterday—'

I said, 'Will they hurt them?'

'—had a marvellous kasbah: Saadian plasterwork, Lyons brocades, tiles and carpets and painted yew ceilings. Girls. And boys. And crimson silk palanquins. They won't hurt Mo,' Johnson said. 'And they can't really prick Pymm. He'll just become a crew-cut balloon with a piece of string round his minuscule hooter.' He wasn't really listening to what he was saying, but he wasn't speaking French either. I thought he was thinking.

We reached the kasbah quite soon. Its red sundried bricks were of the stuff of the hillside and hardly seen at a distance. Close to, the knifed patterns showed in blocks and bands of geometrical ornament. Once, like all of them, it had probably been a small town within fortified walls, with its citadel. Now only the fortress remained, with a high wall and a pair of solid gates giving on to its courtyard. To one side were gardens and orchards, watered by the stream which ran on down through the village; full of snow-water now, but in summer probably shrunk to a trickle. As in the village, it fed an arm into the house through a grille. Behind the fort was a double-leafed service door. There Johnson dismounted. Then the mule with its panniers was led off, and I was told to tie it up in the trees and stay with it.

I wish now that I had. I knew Johnson was following Chahid: that Pymm had remained waiting below while the other man came to spy on the kasbah. Chahid could have found no way into the fortress. But he could have watched by the gates and, if Johnson's guess was correct, he could have seen Sir Robert and then Oppenheim enter. Perhaps he had even witnessed the lord of the kasbah arriving. The wheel-marks of more than one set of broad and powerful tyres had preceded us up the hill, and disappeared through the gates of the building.

But if Chahid had done all that, he had not returned to Pymm with his tale. So Johnson was stalking him; moving unremarkably uphill in his gown, his gaze vaguely bent to the ground. It came to me that Chahid was wearing city clothes, city shoes, and was now on foot. Once past the churned mud at the gates, his footprints must have been quite distinctive. It was hard to imagine what he could be doing, high on the hill behind the kasbah.

He was coming down when Johnson saw him. I saw Johnson stop, and then slip into the trees to one side. I was hidden already.

Not in waiter's clothes, not in the robes of Essaouira, the man was still recognizable from his carriage, his Westernized stride. As he walked, he swung a carrier bag in one hand, and had a camera hung on his shoulder. He could have been a Canadian tourist.

Johnson called him, in a whisper. 'Chahid!'

The man stopped and looked. He was frowning.

'Chahid!'

He thought it was Pymm. He glanced round once, then moved swiftly and quietly to the trees. Then I heard him give a gasp.

I suppose he found himself facing a revolver. I heard Johnson speak, but not quite all he said. He spoke in French, to be best understood, and I heard the name Essaouira, and my mother's name, and then the name of Oliver. I think he asked him to confirm that he was paid by Pymm, but I didn't hear the reply. There was one cry, abruptly ended, and then a thud. Then Johnson said, 'If you have finished lurking, you might as well come out and help me.'

His voice was colder than it was breathless. I walked reluctantly up, and found him with twine in his hands. The man Chahid lay on his face on the ground. After a moment, I saw he was breathing. Johnson said, 'Since we can't invoke police help at the moment, I am proposing to tie him to the grille over there. I can drag him, if you think it's too much for you.'

I didn't know why he felt contempt for me. I helped him carry the man, and we gagged his mouth, and tied his feet and his arms, and secured the rope to the grille. He lay quite safely to one side of the water. Then Johnson said, 'Thank you. Now the rest of the programme, if you're still willing.' He was drawing long breaths, from the thin air and the effort. So was I, from thin air and sick terror.

I had never broken into private premises before, but Johnson had. We returned down the hill. Johnson untied the mule, rang the service-door bell of the fort, and was admitted to the back yard, while I followed him. Then he produced the goat cheeses.

All the talk was in French. Hassan had told him what to say and whom to expect: there was a pretty girl, and a cook and a man who might have been a hired butler. Johnson disappeared into the kitchens with his cheeses and took his time coming out. There was a lot of laughter. By then I was hidden, and they had forgotten me. Johnson led out his mule, jingling dirhams, and the double gates were shut and locked fast behind him. Everyone re-entered the house.

I thought he would come back immediately, but I was shivering with cold before I heard his low whistle. He slipped through the gate when I unlocked it, and had already gone by the time I had locked it again. I found him levering open a window. He did it like a practised criminal, his hood thrown back, his glasses again on his nose. I said, 'The alarm?'

'Switched it off from inside. Hassan knew where it was. Are you ready? Could you do with a hoist?'

I shook my head. He had said nothing of burns, ever. I let him get himself through the window, and then followed.

I had been five days in Morocco. I hadn't met a sheik or a film star. But I had found my way into a kasbah, along with a guerrilla in bifocal spectacles.

21

We were in the laundry. The weekly wash, it was apparent, was not being pummelled by stones in a river. I could see boxer shorts going round in the tumbler in a room lined with pulsating machinery. There were beds of small cashmere socks, and corridors of ironed shirts airing on hangers. All the pockets were embroidered with B. Johnson crossed the room, listened, and opened a door, and I crept out behind him. A savoury smell filled the passage outside, and I could hear distant loud voices arguing in French and Arabic, and the clatter of dishes. It was two o'clock, and everyone was eating but us. We began to explore.

The kasbah was, in itself, the Arabian palace everyone dreams of. It possessed secretive courtyards with fountains, and irregular passages, and stairs which abruptly led up or down to sequences of uneven rooms with cedarwood doors and millefiori doorknobs. We found a drawing-room sixty feet long, and a lot of scented bedrooms and dressing-rooms, all of them empty, and a wing we didn't go into, because we could hear women's voices.

I was glad my mother wasn't there because in other respects, she might have felt disillusioned. This kasbah was furnished from Turin and Milan in steel and lacquer and glass and contained a quantity of fitted carpets, some of them with mould peeping out of the corners. It was not without ethnic concessions: tiled floors, some wall hangings and a number of brass and wrought-iron lanterns. But the pictures had been bought by an agent, and the ornaments by an interior decorator: probably the same who had created all the crowned and plumed and canopied beds. They were a bit the way I imagined them, and one of them had black satin sheets. It also had mirrors and other things. Johnson said, 'You're too young for all that. Seen enough?'

We hadn't found Morgan or Pymm. They weren't in the dungeons, because these were full of wine racks. We didn't spend much time looking anyway, for what Johnson wanted was the business room of the lord of the kasbah.

'Mr B.,' I proposed.

I was feeling high. There were really very few people about. We had had two narrow escapes, after which Johnson had rammed my bright clothes in a corner, saying I was less of a liability in my own jeans and a shirt, which would only get me sexually assaulted, and he would see what he could do about it later. He didn't mean it, but I was getting to understand him. I wondered what it would be like to work for Johnson.

We had come to a broad, well-lit passage with the floor done in marble, and concealed spotlights on tables with flowers. There were several large double doors. Johnson said, 'What about this?' and carefully opened the first. Then he shut it quickly and quietly and hauled me fast round a corner.

I had seen what he had seen: a commodious thick-walled room which, from its equipment, might have belonged to the Chairman of Kingsley Conglomerates. In the central position stood a single magnificent desk and great chair, backed by a pristine lacquer screen. Before it, and near to one wall a walnut conference table was furnished with blotters, paper, ashtrays and tumblers for six, its chairs neatly drawn up around it. A young man in Western clothes had just placed a crocodile case on the desk and was moving towards a far door. He disappeared through it. Something about him made me think of Val Dresden. After a moment, he emerged into our passage by a second door further along and, turning away, made his way down some steps and up others. He tapped on a door.

We were near enough then to hear the murmur of polite conversation inside, and the resonance, equally civilized, that comes with the use of bone china and crystal and silver. The young man announced something deferentially, listened, nodded and, retreating, shut the door and, walking even further away, disappeared.

I didn't know the voice that had answered him, but I recognized two of the others.

So had Johnson. 'Sir Robert and Oppenheim,' he said. 'Lunching in private with the lord of the kasbah, and thereby settling the main point at issue. I wonder. What do you think? Fruit, cheese, coffee, ablutions… We've got a clear half an hour till the meeting. Come on. Let's see what else we can turn up.' And drawing me with him, he opened the door that the secretary had come from.

The room inside was empty of people. There were two big modern desks and a VDU secretarial work-unit of the kind Trish had at Kingsley Conglomerates. There were telephones with three lines on each, and one answer-phone. There was a photocopier and a stationery cabinet and a transit box. The PA's desk was like mine, only more expensive, with a pile of messages held down by a clip and the files and papers he'd been working on. The door to his chief's room was beside it. The third table was leather-topped and immaculate, and all its drawers had locks. Along the walls were handsome filing cabinets, and each of the two principal desks had a dealing screen. Both were active. One showed market prices. The other was running a message in Arabic.

'A man of heavy interests, Mr B.,' Johnson said. 'A desk for his PA: a working spot for his travelling executive. Not a place where he'll keep permanent records, but while he's here, it should tell us quite a lot about him. First the case in his room. Then the drawers. And what do I hear?'

What he heard was the chirp of a fax machine, intimating it was sending a message. Presently it came groaning out, a curling scroll covered with figures. We went and looked at it.

'There is a God,' Johnson said with real reverence. 'Oh, Hallelujah.' And sitting down at a desk, he began to scribble a message.

Johnson picked all the locks and restored them. I spent most of the time at the door, listening for the footfall that the noise of the fax might conceal from us. In the end, it was a telephone call that alarmed us. Instead of being received by the answerphone, it rang live to one of the handsets with the insistent toots that meant internal paging. Someone wanted the PA, and pronto.

If the PA had been less sharp-eared, less scared of his boss, we'd have made it. As it was, I heard his running feet bounding down the steps at the end of the passage. I shut the door and said, 'He's coming back.'

Johnson was near the inner door. I couldn't leave without being seen, but he could. I felt the draught of his robe as he made for it, whirling briefly to check out the room. It looked undisturbed. He was a demon for detail. Then he said, 'See you later,' and left.

The door nearest to me was flung open. Coming in with a bound, the young man who looked like Val Dresden snatched up the phone and spoke into it. For a moment, I thought I might manage to dodge him. But as he talked, he looked up and caught sight of me.

He said, *'Alors… Alors…'* and dropped the phone. I was making a dash for the door when he tripped me and carrying me to the ground, fell on top of me. I thought he was more alarmed than vindictive. He said 'What are you doing?' and put his knee on my stomach. Before I could answer, he reached up and pressed on a buzzer, and two men with eighteen-inch biceps came in and took me away. I had seen them in the market when they got hold of Pymm. In fact they took me to Pymm. He was with Morgan, locked in a lavatory.

If you convert a kasbah, I suppose bathrooms are the only places left with small windows and locks. This was a very palatial one, with everything done in gold down to the toilet hinges. It had high and low paper, and all the towels and the bathrobes had B on them. Ellwood Pymm sat on the toilet, and Mo Morgan sat on the bidet. It was a really bad moment, until I saw they were both fully dressed and there was nowhere else for them to sit, except the Jacuzzi. Then I was battered aside by Ellwood Pymm making his way to the door and yelling at the two men who were closing it. 'Let us out! This gentleman is Mohammed Mirghani! Tell your employer! Your employer will give you big money!'

The man said, *'Sivahell! Imshi!'* and shut the door in his face. You could tell that Pymm understood, even without his American phrase-book.

Long before then, I was in Morgan's peak-climbing hug, and Morgan was saying, 'Aw Christ, are you all right, Wendy? Oliver?' Over his shoulder I saw Ellwood Pymm's distracted red face. He walked slowly round and sat himself again on the toilet. Then Morgan stood me off and said, 'Did they hurt you?'

I said, 'Not when Bontine's around. What are you doing here?'

I didn't have to underline it. His black eyes glittered and he produced a smile like a double-barbed arrowhead. He said, 'Oh, maintaining brand share. They think I'm a buddy of Ellwood's.'

He said it with no particular stress, and Ellwood didn't react when he said it. During their joint lavatorial session, Morgan clearly hadn't even touched on the topics of spying and incitement to murder. Morgan's knuckles were skinned, but not, I would gather, on the candlewick nose and puffed eye of friend Ellwood. Yet I had seen Morgan's fury at Oliver's bedside.

So Morgan had thought up a scheme. Morgan, I would guess, was setting up a tripwire for both Pymm and Chahid. I didn't know what to say. I said, 'Well, why not explain it to someone? They're all having lunch in the kasbah.'

'You know who's here?' said Ellwood sharply. 'He won't tell me. No one'll tell me. I am an American. Excuse me all to hell, but no one kidnaps an American.'

Morgan looked at him. 'Ellwood,' he said. 'Everyone kidnaps Americans. There's a merit scale of award, and a gold watch if their mother speaks English. Will you quit screeching? When the bosses do come, you'll probably wish that they hadn't.'

'They don't understand,' said Ellwood Pymm. 'All Morgan has to do is to explain who he is and they'll spring us. Here's a nice girl, you don't want to scare her. Her mother wants her safely back in the parlour. Mo here, his folks will be worrying. We all want the hell out. If it takes a yell, then it's worth one in my book.'

I wondered what a yell was in his book. The same as *Hi!*, I should imagine. Morgan said, 'They're a bunch of robbers, Ellwood, out for all the ransom money they can get. The whole process will take months. Spring us? Forget it.'

Then I saw what he was after. There was a silence. Pymm got up from the seat and walked the few steps he could and then back again, flipping the bathmat agitatedly out of his way. He leaped on a pipe and tried to see out of the window; failed, and jumped down again, his hand on the cistern. The toilet instantly flushed, and he squealed, snatching his hand back. He said, 'Don't you know who's up there?'

'Arabs,' said Morgan.

I never thought much of Ellwood Pymm, but I almost felt sorry for him then, as his need to get free fought with five days of determined self-interest. Then he said, 'I guess you don't know what's going on. I don't know who the Chief Monkey is, but I can sure tell you who he's entertaining. And that's Sir Robert Kingsley of your firm, Mr Morgan, and also Mr Daniel Oppenheim, who is meant to be in medical care in Agadir. Now do you see what I mean?'

'I think so,' said Mo. He looked thoughtful. 'But if that's so, Ellwood, why did they capture you? And how did you know, in the first place?'

There was a long hesitation. 'I'm a columnist,' said Mr Pymm. He glanced again at the window.

Morgan said, 'Bollocks. They wouldn't panic over a columnist. Unless it's serious? Unless you were really tracking down figures? Ellwood, did you stage that kidnapping in Essaouira? I must say I had my doubts when I heard of it.'

'No one got hurt,' Ellwood said. 'Come on. Shout through the door. They'll be so upset you've been harmed, they'll do anything.'

'And the bug at Asni?' Morgan said. 'Of course, you wanted to know if MCG would agree to a takeover. Ellwood, you've been naughty.'

'Everyone does it,' said Pymm.

'And persuading Wendy's mother to leave her recorder in Oppenheim's room? You were really serious, Ellwood. Who were you going to report it all to?'

'Just my paper. She didn't mind. Did you hear the tape?' said Pymm, suddenly casual.

'Oh, yes,' said Mo. 'I know we're talking war fodder.'

There was a silence. Then Pymm said, 'Then you know we're thinking in telephone numbers. Money you've never dreamed of. Get me out of here, and it's yours.'

'I don't know,' Morgan said. 'If you arranged the self-kidnapping at Essaouira, then Chahid is your man?'

I saw the name strike home. Up till then, he had felt reasonably secure. Up till then he was a columnist, or a magnate, with an alibi or a bribe as a shield. Then he said, 'Who? Never heard of him.'

'I think he'll say differently,' Morgan said. 'He threatened Wendy and Johnson at Essaouira. He helped the man who shot Oppenheim and he tried to knife Johnson himself. He assaulted Wendy's mother, and lured Johnson to where he could kill him. On the hill just now, he smashed up Oliver, Johnson's young crewman.'

'That's a goddamned lie,' said Ellwood Pymm. He sat on the seat, and looked as if he wanted to use it. 'I've never heard of this man. Why the hell should he want to kill Oliver? The poor guy fell. I was told.'

'With bullets in his tyres. We have the bullets. We have Oliver's testimony. We know why Chahid did it. Oliver was watching him. He saw Chahid park his car. He saw you leave the Lancia and walk towards it. Why did you try to kill us in the Lancia?' Morgan asked.

'I didn't!' said Ellwood.

'You damned well did. Because you saw Mrs Helmann, and didn't notice that I was driving? Why did you join Chahid's car if you didn't know him?' said Morgan.

'I didn't!' said Ellwood.

'Then how did you come to the market? And why? And where is Chahid now?'

I could have told him. Pymm said, 'How should I know? What does it matter? I tell you what matters. Getting out of his bloody shit-house but fast.'

'Ellwood,' Morgan said. 'If you get out of here, you'll meet the guy who wanted you captured. If you learn the identity of the guy who wanted you captured, you'll never leave the kasbah alive. We shall. He needs us. But you won't. So calm down. Give them time to consider it all. And in any case, if I can put in a good word for you, I won't.'

I really was sorry for Pymm. His nose had started to bleed by itself. He might have found something witty to say, but just at that moment the door rattled, and a key turned, and two men came in, looked about, and took possession of both my arms. *'Marche!'* one of them said. And I did.

The big room with the conference table looked quite different with six people sitting round it, the glasses of water half full, the papers at odds and the chairs at different angles. I saw Sir Robert at once, in a pale hot-weather suit that was wrong for the snow, and his hair gummed down flat, and the bantering lines nowhere visible. Oppenheim sat beside him, solid, handsome, the white ribs of his teeth firmly shrouded, his shoulder and arm in a sling. The PA sat near the top. The other three I didn't know, but I looked at the man at the end, who wore western dress exquisitely tailored, and viewed me through the undisturbed smoke of his cigarette. He said, addressing Sir Robert in French, *'This* is your mistress?'

Once, it would have been the end of the world. Once it would have been an anguish, at the very least, not to be bathed and made up and dressed in a way that matched my chairman's importance. Now my hair was uncombed and tangled, my shirt creased, my jeans filthy from the mud of the grille, and to see Sir Robert's cheeks flush did my heart good.

He had flushed because of the gibe, but my presence hadn't astounded him, or startled Oppenheim. I said, 'You knew I was here!'

It was far more awkward for Sir Robert than it was for me. He said, 'We heard there was a young woman. It didn't seem possible… You were going to London. What were you doing with Pymm?' Something made his voice very sharp.

'Pymm?' I said. 'I wasn't with Pymm, I was with Mr Morgan. Remember? I'm his Executive Assistant.'

Daniel Oppenheim was staring at Sir Robert. The Arab at the head of the table laid down his cigarette and exhaled delicately. Sir Robert said, 'Morgan is here? Where is he?'

'Locked up with Pymm,' I said. 'The men thought they were partners. They captured Morgan as well.'

Oppenheim swore. The man at the head of the table sat slowly erect. He said, 'Morgan? The man we are speaking of? He is here?'

'He and I were in the market,' I said.

'But,' said the man, 'you were found in the kasbah. Why were you in the kasbah?'

'Looking for Mr Morgan,' I said. 'And I found him. He is angry.'

'I expect he is,' said Mr B. very softly. He had large dark eyes, well-trimmed hair and a fine moustache. His olive skin was perfectly smooth but he was older, I thought, than at first he seemed. He said, 'Well, gentlemen, what is your recommendation? This Mirghani, you say, is a genius. He must have an idea of his worth. Why not confide in him, and trust his good judgement?'

'And Mr Pymm?' one of the other men said.

The lord of the kasbah glanced at him. He said, 'Of course, we wish him no harm. He will be released. First, as a civility, he will perhaps tell us the names of his employers. We wish no other favour. As for Mr Morgan, Omar will take our apologies. Clothe him if necessary. Give him whatever he wants, and ask him, of his kindness, to join us.'

The secretary left. Whatever he offered, I could imagine the answer he got. Morgan was at the door in three minutes, his pigtail springing. He crossed to where I stood in the middle, and put one hand on my shoulder, and proceeded to examine the men round the table. Last of all, he gazed at Sir Robert and Oppenheim. 'Well, well,' he said. 'After all that drama at Auld's. How's your wife, Mr Oppenheim? Working up a few other snaps for your album?'

Oppenheim rose slowly to his feet. He looked mildly haggard. He said, 'I understand. You think it strange to find us together. I thought I'd never speak to Robert again. But we've talked, and he's persuaded me that you ought to stay with the firm. It means raising finance. Hence this meeting.'

'All this is true,' said the man at the head of the table. He also rose. 'Mr Morgan, I trust you will forgive me. My men are fools. We suffer, you understand, from the paparazzi. Learning that one was about, they restrained both him and one they thought his companion. I cannot hope to make amends. But perhaps you will indulge me to the extent of taking this chair by my side. What may I bring you?'

'A self-drive car would be nice,' Morgan said, shoving his hands in his pockets. 'Wendy and I would like to leave, and while I'm not fogging up over Pymm, there's no doubt he'd feel safer with an independent appraisal.'

Mr B. sank into his seat, and directed his case to Sir Robert. Sir Robert took up the running. 'Don't be an ass, old boy. All you've ever wanted is freedom and money, and now you can have what you like. Send off Pymm and the girl by all means, close the doors, and let's get down to some wonderful planning.' His tone, while urgent, held a trace of genuine excitement. It was quite odd, really.

'My God, that's wacky,' said Morgan. And when Mr B. cast him a look, he translated immediately, 'No.'

'Why?' said Oppenheim, reseating himself. His hair didn't stick up, and he didn't play with pens, or visibly wish he were somewhere else. He said, 'Is it because of Muriel? The photographs? I blamed Sir Robert as you do, until I saw why he'd done it. I had to tell myself my marriage couldn't have lasted. I agreed to join him, and why? Because the most important thing for us all is your work. Isn't that so? Can there be any question now of leaving Sir Robert?'

'No, there can't,' Morgan said. 'I'm sure as hell leaving him, the moment I crack how to do it.'

I didn't stop him saying it. If I could have, I probably would. Then Sir Robert said, 'Well, you can't. Don't be a fool, Morgan. You know you're on to a hot deal.'

Morgan didn't speak. Neither did the three Arabs. It was Oppenheim, thoughtfully tapping a lip, who withdrew his hand, slapped the table and said, 'I think we have to talk about this. Morgan, I want to ask you a question. Is it the management of your firm that disturbs you?'

'Among other things,' Morgan said.

'Specifically,' said Oppenheim, 'the quality of its leadership?'

'That specifically,' Morgan said. He knew what he was saying. He was looking straight at Sir Robert.

Oppenheim, on the other hand, had turned to the head of the table. Mr B., in his Savile Row suit, and his fine Charvet shirt accepted his cue in a leisurely way. He said, 'Perhaps, then, we should reconsider our Board. Would that alter your view, Mr Morgan?'

He didn't even look at the present Chairman of Kingsley Conglomerates, whose Board he appeared to think that he owned. Sir Robert was, however, staring at him. Sir Robert said, 'I beg your pardon!'

Mr B. paid no attention. 'Would it?' he repeated.

Sir Robert stood up. The Arabs lifted their eyes very slightly, to keep him in focus. Oppenheim folded his arms. Sir Robert said, 'You are speaking of a public limited company. The suggestion you have made to Mr Morgan is not only insulting, it is quite invalid. I hold the position of Chairman. If Mr Morgan remains, as he must, he will continue to serve under me.'

Ignoring him, Mr B. addressed himself for the third time to Morgan. 'Would it?' he said.

Sir Robert remained standing. He said, 'Did you hear, sir, what I said? I really cannot entertain this line of discussion. Morgan? You will kindly forget what you have heard. I am, and will remain Chief Executive. Whether you dislike me or not, I am offering you everything you will ever need for your work. That, I take it, is all that really concerns you.' Contemptuous, confident, his eyes were not on Morgan, but on Oppenheim.

Robert Kingsley had a fighting spirit, when crossed, that was the best thing about him. I knew the shabbiness, now, that it could lead him to. I knew how it dominated, that streak of iron self-interest, even when we were alone together, and closest. Sometimes, towards dawn, I used to sense that he was bored: that his stay had outrun his patience and interfered with the most important thing in his life – the royal right to do what he pleased. I had thought, in my naïveté, that in time I could change that.

But Oppenheim, here and now, was not in awe of anyone. He looked up, his arms still crossed, the thick signet ring of his marriage still gleaming on his third finger. He said, 'I'm afraid you're wrong, Robert. Under the terms of this loan, the lender would have a seat on your Board, and a significant share of the equity. You couldn't raise such sums otherwise.'

Sir Robert, resuming his seat, heard him out with excessive patience. He said, 'A certain transfer of shares was agreed. To oust the resident Board, your friends would require substantially more power than that.'

Oppenheim's opulent face didn't change. He said, 'But Robert, they have it.'

My chairman, my former chairman raised his eyebrows. He permitted his eyes to wander without haste round the table. He said nothing aloud, but the figure calmly smoking at its head became very still.

Oppenheim said, 'It's your one great weakness, Robert. You don't trouble to assess the opposition. They have the power, through nominee holdings. Added to the block they now have, it gives these gentlemen what I have just correctly described: a significant share of the equity. If they wish to remove you, they can.'

22

'How curious,' said Sir Robert. His sardonic smile was still in place. 'You seem to think that, without my knowledge, shares could have been purchased by these gentlemen anonymously? Indeed, you imply you knew such a thing had happened, and didn't report it to me? That all seems fairly extraordinary.'

'It happened,' said Daniel Oppenheim.

'But you didn't inform me?'

'I thought I had,' Oppenheim said. 'But then, our meetings were brief.'

'To me,' said Sir Robert, 'they seemed comprehensive enough. Perhaps I might refresh your memory. You told me you had been paid to extract Morgan from Kingsley's. I have just taken part in a farce to free you from that obligation. You claimed you had found a source of funds for the company, but that this would depend on retaining Morgan, and the quick asset-stripping of MCG. Steps to both ends were taken. The present meeting was then arranged. The rift between Morgan and myself was to be healed, and the final steps taken towards a secure future for Kingsley Conglomerates.'

'It will be secure,' Oppenheim said.

'But under different leadership. My relationship with Morgan has been destroyed so that Morgan will stay, while I leave. Shares have been bought, so that when these so-called gentlemen conclude this arrangement, they will have effective control of the company. In a long business life,' said Sir Robert, 'I have never experienced such blatant deception. It will not, of course, succeed. You and your associates will face the full weight of public condemnation. I shall see to that personally.'

'I doubt it,' said Daniel Oppenheim. 'You would own up to blackmail? The attempt to blacken my wife will not be widely approved of.'

Sir Robert searched his face, frowning. 'Those pictures were blank. You provided me with them yourself. Your wife is absolutely blameless, as you very well know.'

'But can you prove it? I doubt it,' said Oppenheim. 'Whereas I have absolute proof of that entire interview between you and me in Auld's house. It was taken from Mr Pymm's pocket. Apparently he had it recorded.'

The Arabs remained motionless, but beside me, Morgan suddenly spoke. 'If the pictures of Mrs Oppenheim don't exist, they can't be produced as items of blackmail.'

'But I can describe them,' Oppenheim said. 'And play the tape. It is fairly explicit. Really, it doesn't sound like the farce Sir Robert called it.'

'And would you play the second half of the tape?' Morgan said. 'The bit that makes it clear that your original partner was Johnson?'

The large, dark eyes of Oppenheim appeared to focus, at speed, on Morgan's pupils. 'You've heard the tape? How?'

'Magic,' said Morgan.

Sir Robert, half-aloud, spoke his thoughts slowly. 'Johnson and Oppenheim? No. MCG was the firm Johnson was backing. He failed to tell me his interest.'

Morgan said, 'He failed to tell you a lot of things. He was Oppenheim's chum in the original scheme to uncork me from Kingsley's. The pantomime at Auld's house was for Johnson's benefit. Oppenheim had switched sides for money. He didn't want Johnson to know, so he invented the excuse of your blackmail to drop out. Johnson, on the other hand, stuck to his remit and went on trying to winkle me out of the company. That's why he was picked off at Marrakesh.'

'He wasn't alone,' said Daniel Oppenheim. 'I also suffered through Mr Pymm's immediate circle. But of course, Morgan is right. If our late portrait painter had survived, Kingsley's would have lost MCG and then Morgan. That, however, is not the immediate point. Robert, you really cannot make threats. The Board of Kingsley's will change. And the change will cause hardly a tremor, why should it? No factories are going to close. You make an admirable product, but high-tech consumer durables have little political mileage. Who, Robert, will care about washing machines?'

I opened my mouth. Morgan kicked me.

Sir Robert said, 'We are not talking of washing machines. It is not for his work on washing machines that Morgan is being sought after.'

'But it is!' Oppenheim said. 'He has always said so. You have always insisted on it.'

Morgan said, 'You've forgotten the rest of the tape. *Is she worth human lives?* When he said that, Johnson wasn't talking of high-tech consumer durables, was he? *Who cares,* you said – thank you – *what the little shit does?* And *A large number of villains* is what Johnson replied. Washing machines, would you say? It was Johnson who led you to think I didn't know what I was designing. I knew. We all knew. Sir Robert's just as good as confessed it.'

'But no one is recording this conversation,' Oppenheim said. 'And I have the tape from Auld's house in my pocket.'

'Well, one of the tapes,' Morgan said. 'I'm glad to say we made plenty of copies.' He waited to let it sink in. Then he said, 'So the City *would* be interested, wouldn't they? And the Department of Trade? And the MOD, I shouldn't wonder.'

'Not in me,' said Sir Robert suddenly. 'I have nothing to do with all this. I didn't know what Morgan was making. And I didn't agree to a major change in the equity. It was Oppenheim who bought those shares secretly.'

'You mean the nominee holdings?' Oppenheim said. 'But you know, I did send you the papers. A good while ago. Quite some time ago. Didn't you see them? I sent them to your office. And someone signed for them.'

It seemed to me that every face in the room turned to me: Sir Robert's and Morgan's, Oppenheim's and the impassive face of Mr B. with his two moustached executives. I said, 'I didn't see them. They didn't come. They couldn't have come to the office.'

'Your mistress is also your secretary? Does she have shares?' asked the lord of the kasbah. His voice was emotionless also.

Sir Robert said, 'Of course she doesn't. And she isn't my mistress. My God, she's just one of several perfectly nice little occasional girls who...' He came to a halt, his face sulky. 'If she says she hasn't seen it, she hasn't.'

'Now you mention it, I think I remember,' said Oppenheim. 'The little lady is right: she was vacationing. I gave the share details to your Mr Dresden.'

Val.

I wondered what he had done with them. I remembered all those depleted filing cabinets. I believe that, thinking myself back to my career, to my office, to last week, I even told myself that this would scupper Val, and the PA's job would be mine. Then I saw Sir Robert's face.

There was a silence. Morgan unexpectedly slipped his arm into mine. Oppenheim was smiling. The Arab at the head of the table had raised his black brows. Oppenheim said, 'And I'm sure he will be ready to testify. But would you want it? Sullivan tells me there are photographs with a little more substance to them than Muriel's.'

Morgan pressed my arm, but it was actually a moment before I understood what had been said.

Val. Val coming smiling out of Sir Robert's suite that morning. *Slept in the office last night. Don't go rushing in, sweetie: he's shaving...* Charity's determined individualism and her care for his girls, and for me. Her pity for me. And looking at Sir Robert I remembered that he enjoyed risk and variety. For him there was nothing unnatural about his choice of casual partners, just as he had seen nothing wrong in teaming foreign finance with superb weaponry.

He ignored the reference to Val. He said, '*Sullivan* tells you? Sullivan is working for me.'

'He isn't even working for me,' Oppenheim said. 'Don't you know he was one of the Onyx company? He could have retired ten times over on what he's made in the past as a mercenary. He prefers to drive beautiful cars, and freelance for our very good friend here.'

I thought of Sullivan, and his powerful wrists. I thought of that ride on the Harley, and was thankful I chose as I did. I said, 'So he put the heroin in Johnson's yacht?'

'I am tempted to say yes,' said Oppenheim. 'But in fact, it was a stray idea of mine. Robert? Shall we look at the final position of Kingsley's? The company has to have Morgan. It has less need, sadly, for you. We are inviting you to resign from the Chair. You will not be the poorer, and your activities need not reach the public domain. Such as the fact, for example, that you took steps to sell out your company – and Morgan – without referral to your shareholders or Board.'

'That won't wash,' said Sir Robert. 'One hint of what Morgan designs, and the Defence Departments would jump in to prevent him from working for you.'

'It could be done,' Oppenheim said, 'without touching upon exactly what Morgan does. With everything to gain, he'd hardly force us to be explicit.'

'Then I shall announce it,' said Sir Robert. 'From what you say, I have nothing to lose. The day I leave Kingsley's, I shall tell the world exactly what Morgan is good at.'

'Given the chance,' said the man at the head of the table. He was sitting back, a lit cigarette over his fingers. He watched it, then raised his eyes slowly. 'On the other hand, Sir Robert, your retirement would bring untold compensations. Does business play such a large part in your life? It would appear otherwise.'

Given the chance. I thought of Sullivan's large, golden form, his blue eyes with their ring of white lashes. I gazed at Sir Robert and willed him to play safe and give in. He sat as if ruminating: vanity and disbelief and dismay struggling together. The offer of wealth, I knew, would weigh nothing against the blow to his ego. He drew breath, and was saved from replying.

The door behind opened. The PA stood until acknowleged, and then glided up to the head of the table. There was a fax in his hand. His master read it, nodded dismissal and passed it to his two colleagues. Then taking it with him he rose and walked to the ornate single desk where, reseating himself, he picked up the phone and addressed it. When he put it down, he remained in his chair, and made no effort to return to the table. He said, 'I have left the meeting, gentlemen, because the meeting is over.'

'What?' said Oppenheim. I saw the two Arabs look at one another. At the desk, the lord of the kasbah laid down his cigarette and picked up the fax in short fingers. Then he addressed us.

'We in the East, gentlemen, have a great respect for western methods of business. We read your manuals, we study your journals and papers, we meet you over the conference table. Yet always you surprise us. Sir Robert?'

At the table Sir Robert sat, one hand in his pocket, and said, 'I am listening.'

'Sir Robert, you gave me certain figures indicating the approximate value of Kingsley Conglomerates. They are worthless. Here are the correct ones. They show that without us, the company of itself cannot survive, far less mount the hostile bid you were planning. I am disappointed.' He picked up the cigarette and drew on it slowly.

'You are mistaken,' said Sir Robert. 'If it matters.'

'Am I? What about this?' said the man in the turban.

The figures he reeled off were familiar: they represented half my night's work. At the end he looked up. He said, 'You say, "If it matters." Perhaps it does not. It is further evidence, however, of bad faith, of questionable competence.' He turned to another part of the table. 'Mr Oppenheim?'

For the first time, Daniel Oppenheim looked guarded. He said, 'Yes?'

'Mr Oppenheim, you came to me with a proposal. You engaged my time and attention, and that of my executives. You brought me here to conclude it. You were not aware that these figures were false?'

Oppenheim's hands were spread on the table. He said, 'I had every reason to believe they were true. They came from Sir Robert. The safe in London yielded a set for comparison, and I got others through Johnson.'

'Before he knew you were leaving him? Or perhaps, even then, did he suspect?' the man said. 'Mr Oppenheim, you have not been the most adept of agents. Even your amateur rival Mr Pymm is still alive, and has had you attacked with impunity. It might have been better for you if his marksman's aim had been accurate. I do not enjoy wasting money and time.'

I felt sick. What he said was criminally threatening. Oppenheim's face had become blank. Beside me, Morgan suddenly slid his arm down mine and took my hand, hard.

'My dear sir,' Oppenheim said, 'you have wasted neither. You will pay no high price for the company. And your income will more than repay your outlay.'

'My income from Morgan,' said Mr B. repressively. He looked at Morgan and then said something short and violent-sounding in Arabic. Morgan replied. The Arab turned towards the table and Oppenheim. He said, 'It seems that even there, your calculations have gone amiss. The man is an Arab who does not wish to work for his fellow-countrymen.'

'Without me, he can't leave,' Oppenheim said. He held his bandaged arm as if it was paining him.

'It seems he can,' said the Arab with continuing calmness. He studied the fax, his cigarette held between two fingers. 'According to this, the British Government are about to remove Mr Morgan and his team from Kingsley Conglomerates.'

'I don't believe it,' said Oppenheim.

'That there has been a leak? That is apparent. I am hardly concerned with the source. I am only concerned that, at this ultimate stage, my investment has come to nothing. It means, of course, that Kingsley's are ruined. There would be no question now, Mr Oppenheim, of our using your services. And Mr Morgan, I suspect, is threatened with an unhappier future than any of us. A suspicious government, Mr Morgan, can be more restrictive than a private and generous employer. You would have been wiser and richer, all of you, to have settled for what you were offered. As it is...'

He nodded briskly. The two Arabs at the table rose. Sir Robert made to do likewise, and was discouraged by a hand gently pressed on his shoulder. Oppenheim remained where he was. I stood, my hand crushed in Morgan's. At the beginning, he had flashed me a look, but I had no answer to give him. None of this was part of any plan that I knew of.

'As it is,' said Mr B., 'none of you can now bring me profit, and all of you could be an embarrassment – Mr Morgan, of course, in particular. In the present nadir of your fortunes, you may find it a positive comfort to relinquish all responsibility for the future. Omar!'

The secretary had only to run from his own room next door. Beneath the Arab's grasp, Sir Robert tried to start up. Oppenheim's strapped chest heaved and he gave a whistling cough. Morgan, so close to me, began to move, and then stopped.

Omar failed to answer the summons because it didn't reach him, broken as it was into a whisper. Round Mr B.'s chest, a creased djellabah arm prevented him from moving. And below Mr B.'s hair, a business-like revolver was pressed hard at his temple. I knew how he felt.

'I read about this in a book,' Johnson said. 'Tell them to do what I say, or I shoot. Naughty bits first. And remember, Morgan knows Arabic.'

The pinioned Arab, his eyes slewed, looked at the screen behind, and then at his captor. He didn't waste effort. 'Who are you?'

'The late Johnson,' said Johnson. 'Go on, tell them.' He seemed the way I had left him, but with his hood back and his bifocals bland as a sneeze-counter. He waited until the Arab started to speak, and then, rummaging one-handed through the desk, brought out a small, handsome gun, which he tossed to Morgan. Morgan's face was inflated with happiness. 'Oh, my God,' he said. Oppenheim and Sir Robert stayed where they were, stiff as waxworks.

'Right,' said Johnson, and prodded his captive. 'Tell your colleagues to face the wall and lift up their arms. Morgan, search them.'

The two Arabs hesitated and did what they were told. Morgan, patting them, came up with another revolver.

'Give it to Kingsley. Can you use it?'

'Yes,' said Sir Robert. He had risen. 'You pretended to die.'

'Of course; it was a lot of damned trouble. Daniel—'

'You're alive,' Oppenheim said. 'Great God, J.J...' There were actually tears in his eyes. He said, 'When he picked up the phone... I know him... He was phoning for help. There'll be eight men outside these two doors. Give me the gun. I'll distract them. Take the others and run.'

'It won't wash, Daniel,' Johnson said. 'As has been said. Were those your boxer shorts? Never mind. Whatever you're going to say, you can say to someone else, preferably when hanging up by your thumbs in the Channel Tunnel. Go and stand with the rest by the wall. Wendy, get down under the table. Morgan, will you cover the door to Omar's room? Kingsley, the one to the corridor. And now,' – in French, to the man in his grasp – 'call Omar again. Loudly. And only his name.'

The lord of the kasbah had a face to save, too. He called Omar's name. He had begun, rapidly, to say something else in Arabic when Morgan's gun fired, and he gasped. The wound was in his arm, and superficial. But at the sound of the shot, the door to the passage and the door to the office both burst open.

There were four guards at each, as Oppenheim had predicted. Hovering behind, in the office, was Omar. They saw the revolvers, and their chief in Johnson's grasp, and they began to spread, their hands to their sides. It was Mr B., one hand clutching his arm, who shouted at them to stop and Morgan who repeated, in Arabic, the instruction to throw down their guns, or they would have no employer.

For a moment they hesitated; but another hiss from their lord made them do it. The weapons clattered. Morgan, his eyes watchful, went to collect them. Johnson prodded the man in his grasp. 'Tell them to line up with the others, moving slowly.' His gaze, too, was running over the room. Crouched on the floor, I saw the feet treading heavily, and then beyond them, a movement much swifter.

Johnson must have seen it as well. I heard his gun fire, and a moment later, a slight figure dropped to one knee in the doorway. The secretary. The Val Dresden of the establishment. I peered up at Johnson. He had turned the gun back to his captive and the man gasped as the muzzle touched his skin. 'Anyone else?'

No one spoke. Johnson said, 'I am going to give you orders in French. After that, Mr Mirghani will repeat them in Arabic. I want you to listen carefully. The gunfire will have been heard. When we leave here, you are hoping for help from your colleagues. There will be none. They are leaving the kasbah. What I am about to tell you will enable you too to escape with your lives. Do you hear me?'

My eyes on Johnson, I got up slowly from under the table. His face revealed bifocals and nothing. Morgan was watching him as intently as if he were lip-reading. Sir Robert stood erect as a soldier, gun in hand, eyes on the uneven line of silent prisoners. Oppenheim had crossed to the young man who was moaning and holding his ankle. Johnson said, 'Leave him,' and he straightened.

'Right,' said Johnson. 'Last instruction coming up. There is a bomb due to go off in thirty minutes. There is just enough time for you to leave: I will tell you how to do it. There are horses and cars. Take the staff and the women. If you behave, your master will follow.'

No one believed him. Morgan pursed his short lips. Johnson said, 'Don't translate, my dear man, if you want to be buried a dork.' Morgan shot a glance at him, and started to speak.

'It isn't true?' said Sir Robert. 'You wouldn't risk it.'

'I wouldn't, but Pymm bloody would,' Johnson said. 'Wendy, go and unlock the little brute. The key's outside the door. Don't be afraid, he'll be too keen to get out to harm anyone. Come back here. If you can't get him, come back without him. There's half an hour's margin. Morgan...'

Half an hour, he had said. That was all I thought of as I rushed back to Pymm's bathroom. I rushed because I had an idea that Johnson wasn't inventing. I was inclined to believe in that bomb. Pymm had been desperate to get out.

He was still desperate. I could hear his cries, and the blows on the door. When I answered, he broke off immediately. 'Wendy? Is there a man with some keys? Wendy? Tell the man I'll make him rich? I'll make you rich, Wendy. And Morgan.'

I said, 'I didn't know you were wealthy?'

'Oh, Christ God, yes! Yes! Yes! Wendy, do you have the keys, honey? You can have it all, Wendy.'

I thought of something suddenly. I said, 'I don't want your filthy money. In any case, how could you be rich?'

'I've got money!' he said. 'From the people I work for! Big people, Wendy!'

'The people who paid you to do all this?' I said. 'Who are they, Ellwood?'

'I can't tell you,' he said.

'Then I can't let you out. I've got the key in my hand, Ellwood, but I won't let you out till you tell me.'

'Holy shit!' screamed Ellwood Pymm. 'Chahid's planted a bomb!'

'That's all right,' I said. 'Everyone's left. Tell me the names of the people who pay you, and I'll unlock the door.'

I was yelling by then. I was pretty frightened myself. I would have let him out in the next second, but he began shouting names, and I had to wait and listen and memorize them. He had just finished when there was a bang like the end of the world, and everything in the passage jumped and clattered, and the wall I was leaning on shook, and the lights went out and people in the distance began screaming and screaming.

There had been a bomb all right. But it hadn't had a margin of anything. It had gone off right now.

23

I had hardly turned the key in the lock when Pymm wrenched back the door and began blundering out. He had no idea where to run. I took him by the arm, and began to drag him back the way I had come.

The screaming came from the women's wing, and was only partly because Morgan had dashed in to rescue them. They came out, hauling black cloth over the Ungaro, the Jean Muir, the Bill Blass, and warbling like muezzin. There were some children with them. Morgan pushed them before him towards the front of the kasbah, yelling over his shoulder. 'Learn to Delegate Interesting Tasks' was, I think what he was saying. Towing Pymm by the elbow, I followed him.

If we had had any doubts about the way out, we need only have followed the servants. They raced before us, up and down stairs and over courtyards while solid vibrations ran under our soles, and vases toppled and crashed. As soon as we caught up with the backrunners, Morgan thrust the women among them and darted off sideways, yelling to me to follow. I looked at Pymm, running beside me. I could see the whites of his eyes. I said, 'Listen. Chahid.'

I didn't expect him to care, but he did. He stopped dead. 'Oh, my God, Chahid,' he said. 'He doesn't know that I'm here. He'll set off another. He has set off another. Hear that? Oh, Holy shit, Holy Mother, I don't want to die.'

I heard what he had heard, a rumbling crash from the back of the building. I said, 'He can't have set off another. Ellwood, he's tied to a grille by the conduit. You've got to go back and free him.'

'He is?' said Pymm. His face filled with relief and he kissed me. 'Wendy baby, I love you.' Then he scampered off after the others.

Morgan yelled 'Wendy!'

I pelted after him. He had come out of the office, and his arms were full of files and boxes. 'It's all right,' I said. 'That was Pymm leaving Chahid to perish.'

'Another Pymm Number One Cock-up,' said Mo. 'Johnson told the gendarmerie where Chahid was left. He'll survive to be sentenced.'

'The gendarmerie?' I said. I took some of his files and set off running again at his side. Several further shocks ran through the building and a crack appeared in one wall.

'Uh, uh,' said Morgan, and taking my hand, began to pull me along very much faster. 'Yes, the police. What d'you think Johnson was doing, all that time he had in the office? Phoned and faxed everyone, including his bookmaker. Courtyard's full of fleeing Arabs and incoming policemen and cowboys.'

Suddenly, the only thing that interested me about the courtyard was getting there. Smoke had begun to fill the passage behind us. I could hear masonry falling. I couldn't hear anyone else running anywhere any more. They had all got out except us. I said, 'It's an earthquake!' I shrieked it.

'No, it isn't,' said Morgan irritably. 'It's Johnson, playing silly buggers with bombs. He reburied Chahid's, so that it blew up the stream and the hillside. That's the hillside falling down on the kasbah, and the kasbah's nice pisé bricks beginning to pisé into the water, and all the water preparing to electrocute us, if we don't get out pretty damn quick. This is all your bloody doing!' he roared.

'I know,' said Johnson, appearing at the end of the passage. Something like Pymm's relief showed for a second behind the glasses. He was dressed like us again, in his lockknit collared jersey with his gun in his pocket. Then he said, 'Is that why you're crawling? Drop the files.'

'Drop the files,' commanded another voice at the same moment. 'And put up your hands. All of you.' Behind him was Oppenheim, with a gun in his good hand.

Johnson turned round rather slowly, and they faced one another. Then Johnson said, 'It's no good. Even if you save the papers, that set of jackals won't take you back. It's all been for nothing.'

Oppenheim's fine hair was a mess, and his strapped chest rose and fell painfully, but his manner fell short of the apologetic. He said, 'Don't let it trouble you. Whose bomb was that? Pymm's?'

'Adjusted by me. The back of the fort is collapsing as the river comes through. Why did you detonate the one in London? For fun? Or did Sullivan do it to cover the shooting?'

'Muriel thinks you paint very well,' Oppenheim said. 'If you like that kind of thing. Never made a pass at her, have you? And all the chances you had. Kick the files towards me.'

'If you really want them,' said Johnson. 'But I shouldn't hurt yourself bending. Wendy and I have been through them all already.'

'In the office,' I said. 'While you were lunching.'

'Shit!' said Morgan. He stood on my foot, getting in front of me. Behind us somewhere, I could hear running water. There was another rumbling thud, and plaster fell from the ceiling. Lamps swayed.

'But it doesn't really matter,' said Johnson. 'Because we faxed all the interesting pages to Whitehall.'

Oppenheim stared at us for a moment. Then he said to Johnson, 'Open the transit box.'

I knew what the black box was for, and so did Morgan. It carried all the company's disks. All the archives. All the information Mr B. had brought with him. I shouted at the same time as Morgan, but Johnson had already bent over the carton. He put his hands round it. But instead of slipping the catch, the threw it, hard, against the wall beside Oppenheim.

It exploded as it was preset to do, had Johnson opened the lid. Oppenheim swung up his gun. Johnson jumped, and Morgan flung himself forward. They seized Daniel Oppenheim and wrenched the weapon from his hand just as the passage crumbled and caved in behind us. Johnson hurled me running into the clear, and for a second, I saw his eyes lock with Morgan's. Then the two men bent and, grabbing Oppenheim by either arm, dragged him to safety through the dust and the spray to the entrance, and down the steps to the screaming bedlam full of jeeps and cars, vans and horses and crowds of shouting people that was the courtyard.

For a moment I looked up, and where the hillside had been was a child's slide of red sludge, ending in a wall of black smoke. The front of the kasbah was intact. Behind, at the highest part of the fort were chimneys and mounds of melting red mud, pouring with water. Small explosions shook the buildings every few moments, and there were flashes of red in the smoke. The sound of rushing water had deepened. On the far side of the courtyard, stretch limousines with darkened windows were drawing off smoothly, and open lorries crowded with people were starting their engines. Men in uniform moved about briskly, blowing whistles and shoving folk into vehicles. Morgan said, 'The market?'

'Evacuated long ago. And the village,' said Johnson. He bent over Oppenheim, who lay awkwardly in the mud, one hand to his side, which was bleeding.

Oppenheim said, 'What now?'

Johnson took off his glasses. Underneath was a rather bleak face like a schoolmaster's. He said, 'Hospital, I imagine. Someone might murder you there, but it won't be me. In fact, you haven't much hope, have you, of eluding the jackals? Or Bernard – he's in Marrakesh somewhere, by the way.'

Oppenheim continued to lie and gaze upwards, not really seeing us; still mentally running over the options. Johnson said, 'But if you come near me again, I shall probably kill you.'

Then Oppenheim looked at him. 'With your handbag?' he said. 'I'm not even your man: Sullivan is. Wendy will tell you. And Sullivan is quite safe, on his way to the Gazelle d'Or beside Taroudant. He killed the safe-breaker. He was told to kill you if Pymm's man didn't do it. It was his partner's gun that exploded the lorry. It was his radio message that warned the kasbah to watch out for Pymm and get rid of him. Do you suppose Pymm has survived? I truly hope not.'

Morgan spoke, looking at Johnson. 'Perhaps you should leave Oppenheim here.'

'Perhaps he should,' Oppenheim said. 'Any nice wussy would.'

I thought Morgan would hit him. But Johnson had already risen and left us. I saw him rap on an ambulance door and have a word with a driver. A couple of people ran to him, and he spoke to them briefly. Then I got to him and said, 'Pymm's told me who he's working for. Whom. You ought to know.'

'Yes,' said Johnson. 'Yes. Well done. Wait. Blackie?' One of the men who had spoken to him ran up. I had seen him before. 'Paper. I'll need an envelope. OK. Go on.' And he put on his glasses.

I dictated, while the ground shuddered under our feet. I thought Johnson's eyebrows went up, but he didn't otherwise comment. What he scribbled down seemed to have nothing to do with the names I was giving him. At the end the envelope arrived, rather damp. He shoved the paper inside, sealed it and wrote something on the outside. 'Sooner than soonest,' he said.

The man Blackie said, 'Sir!' and raced off. The other men had already gone.

Johnson said, 'Thank you, Wendy. Gongs have been struck for less. See that Land-Rover? It's ours. Come on. Morgan!'

It was the only one left, and was the one we had come in. Johnson got there first, and hauled himself into the passenger seat. Hearing, Morgan broke into a run. I didn't. I halted. 'Sir Robert?'

Tall, solid, no longer insouciant, the head of Kingsley Conglomerates was standing alone in the emptying yard, staring at the falling mud as if mesmerized. He looked at me as if he no longer knew me. It was Morgan who said, 'We have a vehicle. You'd be safer with us.'

We pushed our former Chairman into the back, among a collection of objects we hadn't brought with us. I saw a hamper, and some boxes of cartridges, and a stack of new rifles. Sir Robert said nothing and Morgan, if he noticed, pretended he hadn't. He simply hopped round and took the wheel beside Johnson.

Except when my mother is there, the front bench of a Land-Rover seats three. Johnson gave me a hand, and I vaulted up and sat down between them. Then Morgan rammed his way through the gears, and gunned the Land-Rover out of the courtyard.

As we passed through the gates, I looked back. The place where Oppenheim had lain was quite empty. Nearly all the cars and the people had gone. Behind the yard a mountain of mud yawned and slumped, slowly digesting its banquet of majolica and mosaics and cedarwood, glass and slate, steel and crystal, enamel and silver. Swallowing the telephones and the photocopier and the fax, and the satin sheets and the pictures, and the tumble driers with the shorts, and the rows of shirts with B. on the pocket.

Somewhere along the bumpy road between the fort and the road to the south, I fell uncomfortably asleep. Slipping off, I was aware of Johnson's voice speaking over the radio, and voices answering. Among other things, he was no doubt conveying to the stupefied world that he had been discovered alive. It was before Easter, as well. I didn't wake until we reached the junction with the main road, and, pulling up, Morgan patted me and said, 'Hey!'

I opened my eyes. He said, 'Halt for major retooling; we're all knackered. Someone spoke of a hamper.'

'In the back,' Johnson said.

Morgan said, 'Wendy'll get it. What do you need?'

He got down, and I scrambled past him. I was aware, climbing in for the hamper, that Johnson hadn't replied. Sir Robert found the box and, shaking his head, pushed it towards me. He, of course, had had lunch. There were sandwiches in it, and fruit, and a bottle of wine and a corkscrew. Morgan said, 'Brandy? Or anything?' He sounded impatient.

I shook my head, on Johnson's behalf. His head sunk in the bench-back, he was fast asleep. I handed food to the front, and shared it with Morgan. He drank, but not much. We didn't talk. As I finished, I risked a low question. 'Which way are we going?'

'To Taroudant,' Johnson said. His eyes were still shut.

'But,' said Morgan, and stopped. I knew what he meant. But it's nearly two hundred miles. But we were supposed to be going to Rita's. But there are only two hours of daylight, if that.

'Nevertheless,' Johnson said. He opened his eyes, eased his position and, looking about, found the bottle in Morgan's hand and smoothly removed it. He took a sandwich and said, 'OK, Wendy? Sullivan.'

I thought what a lot of unnecessary words we use in an office. I said, 'Well, you heard that he killed someone in London and was all set to kill you. You know his friend Gerry went berserk at Asni.

287

According to Mr Oppenheim, Colonel Sullivan is working freelance for the men at the kasbah, and not for himself or Sir Robert. He says Sullivan likes beautiful cars, and can afford them from his past with some company. That was all, really.'

'Well, damn Sullivan,' Morgan said heartily. 'And damn Taroudant, if you ask me. Come on. Ouarzazate. Let's go see Oliver.'

'What company?' Johnson asked. He wasn't eating his sandwich.

'She doesn't remember,' Morgan said. 'She and I are going to retire to the bushes, separately or even together, after which I shall drive you to Ouarzazate.'

'I do remember,' I said. 'It was called after his first vintage car. I had an ashtray made of it once.'

'Dust to dust. Onyx,' Johnson said. He was good at puzzles. He seemed, with an effort, to brighten. 'Actually, you're right. We probably ought to go to Ouarzazate. Sir Robert could fly. Oliver and Wendy's mother are there. You could set up a base at the studios.'

'After which you will drive to Taroudant. Like hell you will,' Morgan said. 'If Sullivan could radio to the kasbah about Pymm, the kasbah could radio back to him that you haven't popped your clogs after all. Tell me I'm wrong.'

'Wendy and Kingsley?' Johnson said. I suppose because we were so tired, everyone was talking in shorthand.

I had forgotten Sir Robert could hear. He said, 'I owe Sullivan something I'd like to repay.'

'But Wendy?' said Morgan. He was looking at Johnson. 'Come on, pal. You're shagged.'

'That's all right,' Johnson said. 'You're going to do most of the driving. Wendy is getting out here. The police will give her a lift.'

'No!' I said.

'Why?' said Morgan. He said it quite gently.

'I'm your EA,' I said. 'I want to put in for overtime.'

I know he didn't like me as much as he did my mother or Rita. But he put his arms round me then, and kissed me soundly.

For the next hour Johnson slept, and no one wakened him. It was necessary, but it was also expedient. In daylight, on the busy road south, Sullivan wouldn't do anything.

I slept and woke, and so, in the rear, did Sir Robert. I saw him lying there on the bench, his body shaken, his hair unloosed over his face, and thought of Val, and his wife, and wondered who the other women were, who obliged when he felt like it. I felt, of a sudden, a rush of feeling for my mother that made tears come into my eyes. Then I fell asleep again while Morgan drove, his tough, scarred arms spinning the wheel.

I wondered, as I sank into sleep, what he was thinking. I wondered if, when I opened my eyes, there would be yellow stickers all over the dashboard, with brilliant ideas for the mechanism of bombs and missiles and rockets. The cause of everything that had happened was a man with a ferocious imagination and a pigtail who went climbing on Toubkal, sure as death, at precisely the same time every year.

Johnson woke, as if he had been programmed, when the Amerzgane junction was reached. Morgan drew in to the side of the road. He said, 'Don't you want to get out? I'll come with you.' The glasses looked at him. Then Johnson opened his door and stepped out.

While they were away, it was very quiet. I could hear a donkey braying, and birds I didn't know were singing in the silence. Sir Robert said, 'Wendy?'

I didn't want to talk. I didn't want an excuse, or an apology. Least of all, I wanted cajolement. I said, 'It's stopped. It never happened. Don't be worried: I'm not going to talk about it.' And he didn't speak again.

When the others came back, it was Johnson who sat at the wheel and Morgan who took the window seat. There were smudges under his black eyes. He sat with his right hand tucked between his threadbare knees, but I caught the gleam of his gun. They had tried to make me sit in the back but I wouldn't. I was fresher and younger than they were. I didn't have to wear glasses.

The road to Taroudant is classified as Pre-Sahara, and passes through only two fair-sized hamlets, Tazenakht and Taliouine. It runs southwards as far as the first, and then west through the upland plateau that forms the juncture between the High and the Anti-Atlas ranges of mountains. After that it descends, for the last

289

third of the journey, into the easy, lush valley of the Sous. Long before that, night would have fallen.

We drove into the eye of the sun. The traffic thinned in the passes and shepherd boys crossed the road, directing their flocks with shrill cries and the sting of small stones. The bends were easier now, sweeping round the flanks of the mountains; and all the snow was on the great bank of peaks to the right. I saw Morgan watching them, and supposed he knew what they were. Once he said, 'North end of the top ridge. Rotten rock.' And Johnson said, 'Sirwa? Yes.'

The rest of the time, we travelled in silence. Occasionally Johnson would brake without obvious reason, and I realized that he was only half concerned with the broken road and slow lorries: he was watching for other dangers. He didn't need to talk any more, because he had said it all at the beginning.

'In case you think Morgan and I are paranoid: I believe, although I've no proof, that the kasbah was set up as a trap, and Sullivan and his friend are here to mop up escapees. They've got radio. They must know I'm alive and Morgan's classed as expendable. The Gazelle d'Or is the end of their line: they've got to finish there with the rest of the Vintages. Hence they have to waylay us between here and Taroudant, and before it gets too dark to spot us. Whatever happens, it will have to look like an accident. They know we expect them. They don't know we have rifles.'

'How do they know?' Sir Robert had asked.

'They made no secret of where they were going. They guessed, if he got the chance, that Oppenheim would point us towards them. Everyone who knows anything,' Johnson said, 'knows that we have a score to settle with Sullivan.'

He spoke mildly. It made me wonder if he would relent, as he had done with Chahid. But if all the theories were right, Seb Sullivan had committed murder already, and was now keen to finish the job for his masters. And Sullivan was not a nameless assassin. He knew every one of us.

The sinking sun struck red through the windscreen and, as was its habit, lit Johnson's bifocal spectacles. All around us the hills, limp as blankets, glowed in soft reds, their milky hollows the colour of amethyst. The snow on Sirwa was tinged golden pink, and cast china blue shadows which were technically impermanent. A man walked by the road, a black goat like a scarf round his neck. Morgan said, 'We don't need to go all the way once it's dark. There's a hotel at Taliouine.'

'There's a kasbah at Taliouine,' Johnson said.

'So they'll stop us between here and there?'

'Within the next ten minutes, I'd guess. Unless the car that's behind tries to rush us.'

'Christ!' said Morgan. I hadn't seen any car, either. We both began to turn round. Then we both nearly crashed through the windscreen as Johnson jammed on the brakes, slammed into reverse, and shot the car sideways back and into the stump of a jeep road.

24

We didnt speak. We'd seen what he'd seen. The body of a man, flattened by wheels, lying across the road centre. And high above on the slopes, the splinter of light from a rifle.

We all knew the name of the victim, from the blood-drenched pale suit, and the crew-cut. 'Pymm Number Zero,' said Johnson. He reversed out of sight of the road and, turning off the ignition, put the keys in his pocket. He opened his door and jumped down. We had parked in the gut of a gully. Its scrub-covered slopes cut off the light on either side of the track.

'Dead?' said Morgan.

'What do you think? He'd become a problem for everyone. Kingsley to stay and look after Wendy: take a rifle. Mo, there are only two men up there. Cover me.'

'You're going to kill them?' said Morgan.

'Possibly,' Johnson said. 'But not until I've got some answers from Sullivan. If you catch Gerry, do whatever your whimsy dictates.'

'You want me to go all the way up that steep bit?' said Morgan. 'Carrying you?' A rifle over his arm, he was pocketing cartridges.

So was Johnson. He said, 'What do you know about climbing? Stay and cover me.'

'And you haven't sent for any help, because you don't want Sullivan killed. Why should I cover you?' Morgan said. 'All your bloody foals would be mental.'

A moment after, they took the nearest embankment slope at a run, side by side, no longer talking in undertones. At the top for a second the mellow light caught them, then the skyline was empty. Beyond, where they had set their faces to climb was the flank of the mountain; the boulder slope rising to cliffs and ridges and rockbands interlaid with tongues of snow, and scree-fields, and stony pockets of pasture. And further up, behind escarpment and terrace, the burning forepeaks of the range.

I had seen it all from the road. Somewhere there, already entrenched, already waiting, were Gerry and Sullivan, ex-SAS marksmen.

I was staring stupidly up when Sir Robert spoke. 'I'm going after them. They're going to bungle it.'

'They're both climbers,' I said. I was listening. I couldn't hear anything; not even a car on the road.

'I don't back anyone against Army but Army,' Sir Robert said. 'Stay.'

I wasn't a dog. I was the person he'd lied to most often. When he left the Land-Rover and began to forge up the side of the gully, I scrambled up after him. Then I knelt at the top and looked uphill.

By then, he was the only man on the boulder slope, moving swiftly among the tangled bushes and random stone outcrops. The others were already high in the rock, and after a moment, I had picked out three of the four. The highest was Sebastian Sullivan, still climbing and tauntingly visible. He knew, I supposed, that Johnson would come after him whatever happened. Since that first glimpse from the road, he had worked his way much nearer the headwall, passing the first of the ridges and reaching a point just below the middle crest. In the low, ruddy light from the west his big-featured face and bright hair moved from place to place like a coin of light in a lens. Tinker Bell. Tinker Bell with cord trousers and boots and a check shirt with a brilliant yellow silk scarf at the neck which he hadn't even removed: sucks to you, an undersized Arab and a reconstituted Academician with an undeserved reputation for girlfriends. If Gerry was there, I didn't see him. But I saw Johnson, and Morgan.

Widely separated, they were climbing in parallel, with the object of outflanking Sullivan. It was dangerous stuff, since he had the advantage of height and could, at the moment, pick them off whenever they showed themselves. Except, of course, that they mustn't be found full of bullets. I wondered how Sullivan was going to get over that, and then realized it would be easy. It occurred to me that, if Sir Robert could get up that slope, then I could. I rose to a crouch, and followed him quickly.

He stopped me where the first ridge began. I hadn't seen him. He said, 'Do you mind staying still? I should really like to move quietly. The fools seem to have lost sight of Owen.' He sounded exasperated.

I said, 'I'll stay here,' and watched him noiselessly leave. He and Charity went hunting quite often: he won medals for shooting. He had intervened to save Rita. Johnson had trusted him in the Land-Rover with the guns. He was going to help: I had to believe it. I stayed still by my outcrop and watched.

Gerry Owen had not appeared. I could see, in the flaming light higher up the faint movement that told me where Johnson was, and his stupid bifocal spectacles. He wasn't climbing especially wisely. Morgan had crossed a rib and seemed to be handing himself up a gully, his rifle slung on his back and his gaze divided between the two others. I saw him only when Johnson broke cover. Then Morgan swung into sight, striding over a gap; jumping for a new foothold. Morgan, decoy.

Sullivan, climbing higher and higher, looked down and seemed to be smiling. Now I could guess his objective: a rockband that ran part-way round the mountain, split with gullies and cracks that led to the bulging escarpments above. Before one of the cracks, Berber shepherds had once built a stone windbreak the size of a rampart, and the niche was further protected by an approach now broken sheer on all sides but for a cracked slabby ramp patched with snow, and a steep rake of rubble and debris.

Sullivan climbed it, not with Morgan's grace and precision, but with the determination of a powerful man at the peak of his training. He reached it, turned, and gesticulated. And as if in response, a new sound came to us in the silence: the sound of a powerful car driving west.

I saw the flash as Johnson's head turned. Morgan had halted. Above them both, Sullivan's smile became wider. The roar of the engine increased as it approached, and burst into full volume as it reached the unseen road directly beneath us. We heard the screech of its tyres as it braked at the sight of Pymm's body. There was a pause, then we heard it stop and reverse. There came a distant banging of doors. From the sound, more than one man had got out. A group of innocent travellers, aghast at a hit-and-run killing? Or the bodyguard of the lords of the kasbah, come to support their master's two agents?

It emboldened Gerry Owen to move. Sir Robert had been right. From his cover high on the mountain, he had watched and waited. Now he attacked.

It was Morgan he took, using Morgan's hill expertise to deceive him. Stopped by the sound of the car, Morgan was already looking down when the great fall of rock occurred far below, and the thud of a body heavily falling. It was no more, as it turned out, than a padded sack and a rope. But unthinking, Morgan obeyed his instincts and followed the sound, springing downhill, rifle slung, eyes intent. The blow when it came knocked him sideways. I saw him lose balance and stagger, and Gerry Owen seize him, one arm round his throat. With the other, he wrenched free his rifle and threw it out of reach down the slope. Then, before anyone could prevent him, he was secure behind Morgan's body, and I heard him drawl into Morgan's ear in a voice he didn't trouble to lower. 'Well, tiger; I guess no one ever knew you were such a bad climber. All those years scaling Toubkal, and here you are, discovered dead at the foot of a tiddler.' And he lifted the gun in his hand like a club.

I sprang to my feet. I couldn't shoot, but I could show him he had a witness.

Gerry didn't even see me. He stopped. Above and to one side there came a rumble of stones, and the patter of many light feet, followed by the cries of high, swooping voices. A huddle of black and brown goats came weaving and springing down the hillside, followed by three trousered boys throwing stones. The biggest was no older than seven.

They could have seen nothing precisely. They were, however, curious enough to slow and linger at the sight of two foreign men, one with his arm round the other. Gerry Owen took his threatening arm down, and changed his grip to a bone-bending lock that was invisible. He held his gun out of sight. The boys came nearer. He said, 'Go away!' The boys remained, their faces solemn, their eyes large and dark and inquisitive. 'Go!'

'You need to speak Berber,' said Morgan, croaking.

'Tell them to go,' Owen said.

'Why should I?' said Morgan.

'Because I'll shoot them if you don't. Then you and the painter. No hassle. The hills are full of tribes with old rifles.'

Morgan looked at him. Then he turned and called to the boys. It was a mixture of Berber and Arabic and I understood one word in three. But he was saying something very particular.

The children didn't do much at first. They listened wide-eyed, and flinched when Gerry made a threatening gesture. It was the insult of the gesture that decided them. They backed downhill, inclined to hurry, still looking. Then the eldest nursed the rag round his waist, and dipping absently into it, suddenly withdrew a small object and threw.

The child herdsmen of Morocco are the finest stone-throwers in the world. Fast and hard-pitched and accurate, their little missiles can put out an eye, numb a muscle, or kill. The boy's stone hit the back of Gerry's head like the blow from a spade, and he staggered. By the time the second and third stones found their mark, Morgan had pulled himself sideways and free.

Gerry turned, lurching. The boys, still throwing, raced down the hill and Sullivan's partner stood rocking, blood from open cuts streaking his face, his eyes hardly open. He would have fallen anyway, but Morgan made sure of it by kicking his feet from under him. He tumbled over the edge, and cartwheeled down the hill and into the darkness, where the boys and the goats had already scattered.

There was a single shot from above, aimed at Morgan. I heard it whine by. Then Johnson, from the rock he had chosen, fired shot after shot towards Sullivan: enough to keep him from aiming and let Morgan roll back under cover. I saw Morgan drag out his wallet and leaning over, toss it below. It bounded downhill, past the spreadeagled figure of Owen, and a small shadow, quick as a lizard, darted, snatched it and vanished.

'Give up, Sullivan,' Johnson said. Reasonable stuff: Sullivan was now alone. But down below were the men from the car, now alerted. Alerted to run away, or alerted to climb the hill and attack us.

Sullivan answered him with a second bullet, accurately aimed at where he had been. Planned accidents were a thing of the past. 'Why?' said Sullivan's voice. 'Morgan's weaponless, you're pinned down and Kingsley – is that Kingsley? – is coming, I hope, to give me a hand. Isn't that right, me old sport? Nothing for you in the land of your fathers except a club for old queens and the odd little handout from Charity. Why not join us for the hell of it?'

'Join you?' Johnson said. 'Trust a party of arms dealers, terrorists, mercenaries?' He was moving, testing one route or another. But Sullivan had been right. There was no way he could reach him, except by an impossible traverse up and across exposed ground. On the other side Morgan was climbing punctiliously. I couldn't see where Kingsley was. He could be within reach of Johnson. He could, with ease, shoot him or Morgan.

'Terrorists?' Sullivan said. 'Now, is that the image PR has spent so much cash to put over?'

'You don't leave Onyx,' Johnson said, 'once you've been in it.'

I crouched again, listening. I had no part to play. I was only a witness. The sky to the west held the afterglow but the darkness was creeping up the flanks of the mountain, and a wind had risen to stir the puffs of thorns and rustle the grasses, so that I could no longer hear footfalls. When Sullivan spoke, it was in a voice of discovery. He said, 'Kingsley's had nothing to do with this. You were after me.'

'Oh, Kingsley's had quite a lot to do with it,' Johnson said. 'But latterly, yes. I've been after you.'

'Because of Onyx? It's ten years since we broke up.'

'But some of you are still alive. You. Your chief? Perhaps others?'

'Ten years ago,' Sullivan said. 'So who were you then? The last job was a man with a woman.'

'That's who I was then,' Johnson said, and moved without warning out of cover, and up the exposed snowy slab towards the niche closest to Sullivan.

I saw the spitting red flame as Sullivan fired, and then two answering shots that came from the right, and a little further uphill.

They could have been aimed at either Johnson or Sullivan. Then Johnson said, 'Kingsley? I don't want Sullivan killed.' His voice came from a different place. He had reached the slot in the rockband he'd been aiming for. He sounded winded, but no more than I was. I let out my breath. Whatever else he had done, Sir Robert hadn't joined Sullivan.

Then Sullivan said, 'You don't want *me* killed? I have you in my sights now. Or I will have, when you can't hold that groove any longer. Then a bullet for Morgan.'

'So,' said Johnson, 'you may as well tell me. Who's left?'

'Me,' said Sullivan. 'And two hard men and himself, the CO. I'll tell them you were asking. You'd wonder that it took ten years before you noticed they'd done you and the lady that little disservice. Well, it's all over now. Have ye said your prayers, boyo? That's the bell for the end of the round.'

He was happily callous: a professional following his profession. And as he spoke, the waning light moved, and I saw the fissured rock against which Johnson was fitted, and further saw that he had a pressure-footing that could be measured in moments, and no possibility, with it, of using his rifle.

I don't know what he had planned when he made that heedless, unnecessary sprint. Perhaps to spring from his vantage point: but the gap between Sullivan and himself was too great. Morgan, his rifle gone, couldn't help him and Kingsley, for all he knew then, might have been Sullivan's man. Perhaps all he had wanted, more than anything, was to ask those odd questions of Sullivan.

Perhaps, also, he understood Sullivan better than I did. Time, to Sullivan, was an enemy. He couldn't be troubled to wait. I saw his head emerge, pale in the blackness; and saw his smile, and saw him take comfortable sight with his rifle. At the same moment Kingsley rose on the skyline. He called Sullivan's name. Sullivan swung his own rifle up, firing quickly. The shot went astray. He steadied, and made to repeat it. But before that, Sir Robert squeezed the trigger.

Springing out from the rocks, Morgan cannoned into him just as he did it. I heard Kingsley shout, and down below, Sullivan echoed it with a scream, his hand clapped to his shoulder, his rifle clattering out of his grasp. After the first second of shock, it was the loss of the rifle that revived him. He looked up once, before he turned to lurch downhill after it. His face, in the dim, opal light showed impatience, and pain, and a sort of preoccupied anger. I looked at the silent darkness below and wondered what he would find if he ran. A carload of frightened tourists, perhaps. Or perhaps not. If the silent newcomers were from the kasbah, they hadn't rushed to his rescue. If they were from the kasbah, they might even want rid of him, a liability like Sir Robert and Oppenheim. Then they would climb the hill and pick us all off. It wouldn't be difficult. Sir Robert could shoot, but Morgan and I were unarmed. Johnson couldn't do anything.

I think I got to my feet. I know Kingsley threw Morgan off. And Morgan himself turned, prepared to crash his way down. Loud and distinct and authoritative, a man's voice said, 'Stand clear.'

It came from high ground, and quite a different quarter, and was without passion, or effort, or urgency. Then a revolver fired once, and Sebastian Sullivan threw his arms up and fell.

Nobody spoke. The last of the light stole uphill, leaving us standing in darkness. For a moment Sirwa glowed still, and then was extinguished. I could hear men softly moving about me, but couldn't distinguish their dress: cap or turban or robes. I started to shiver. A torch clicked, and the brilliant light rested on Sullivan's lifeless body, and the waving gold hair, and the silk scarf that was yellow and red. Then it moved up and focused on Kingsley, the bantering lines turned into graffiti, and on Morgan, caught half-descended, with his narrow face gaunt, and finally on Johnson himself, still as a saltire, with his face like a teacher's behind the two dazzling lenses.

There were no ledges; only an unevenness in the stone. He had adhered to the crevice with nothing but pressure and willpower, but it was impossible that he could stay there much longer. Morgan, sliding and scrabbling, was coming as fast as he could.

Unmoving, Johnson said, 'How shall I thank you?' He spoke in English. The man who had killed Sullivan had spoken in English.

The torch didn't waver. The man who had killed Sullivan said, 'I make my own choices, Jay. Stop holding. We're here to catch you.'

I knew the voice now. I hadn't felt like weeping till then. I didn't wonder, then, why they hadn't intervened long before.

Johnson turned his head slightly. Every facet below him was sheer except the way he had come. The traverse up had been shocking, but to attempt it downwards was nothing but suicide. Morgan, the mystic idiot, said suddenly, 'There are rules about being a nuisance. It would stretch three good men to retrieve you, whereas I can bring you down in one pitch on my own. You!' His eyes steady on Johnson, he was calling the torchbearer. 'Are you who I think you are?'

'Probably,' said the man. He had been at Rita's last night. I recognized his voice. One from Frances, and one from Joanna, he'd said. Sir Bernard Emerson, I remembered his name.

'Then go on down,' Morgan said. 'Flash Gordon and I will come after you.'

Sir Robert found me where I stood trembling, and another man with a torch gave me his coat, and helped me down to the cars, where we waited. Sir Bernard's was a big Mercedes, and warm. There was a lot of efficient movement. They had Sullivan's body to carry down. I wondered if Gerry was dead. I remembered Pymm, and thought I was the only one who had, and what a pity it was. Then Emerson came with some brandy and made me drink it.

'They're down safely,' he said. 'Sir Robert is coming with me. Would you like to stay with me, or go back with Johnson and Morgan?'

Lumped together, they sounded like motor mechanics. He had used the intimate name, on the hill. I said, 'I'd like to go back in the Land-Rover.'

'Good. I'll see you at the Gazelle tomorrow. Here's Sir Robert.'

It was the formal bit of the parting that had already happened. We faced one another in the darkness and he said, 'I don't suppose we shall meet again. Have I made things frightfully difficult for you?'

'Yes,' I said.

'Oh, well,' he said. 'That's rotten old life, isn't? Look after yourself, won't you?'

And that was all.

The Land-Rover was to leave first. I walked to it on my own, rather slowly, and found Morgan by himself at the wheel. His face in the car light was yellowish. Then he saw me, and gave me a whole-hearted, open-pea smile that made my tears start again. He said, 'Come in, girl. You've been swilling brandy. Oh, my God, didn't you know what I wanted most in the world was a pretty girl stinking of alcohol?'

He had flushed with relief. I realized no one had comforted him. I said, 'Where…'

'Flash Gordon? Flaked out in the back. They gave him one of the jags he doesn't like. Another barracking tomorrow, no doubt.'

I said, 'You tried to save Sullivan.' I failed to shut the door twice. Finally he leaned over and banged it.

He started the engine. 'Yeah: and Emerson promptly shot him. Ever feel you've made a silly mistake? Ever feel you don't know what the hell is going on, and you wish all you had was a place of your own and a nice friendly girl snuggling up next to you?'

I looked at him, and he was smiling again, at the windscreen. 'It's all right, sweetie,' he said. 'Any sandwiches left?'

25

There were orange blossoms on my table at breakfast, which seemed a pernicious waste, since nothing that had happened that week had had anything to do with wedded or even unwedded love, unless you counted Val Dresden. I sat alone under their bony petals and brilliant yellow silk filaments. The scent of them was the first thing I remembered of my arrival at the Gazelle d'Or the previous night. A wall of perfume, hitting the Land-Rover and making Morgan sneeze until the windscreen started to drip.

We had travelled in silence, partly because Morgan was the only one wholly awake, and sometimes I had my doubts even of him. Now and then he glanced over his shoulder and once he drew off the road and went round to check, as he said, on his Mastermind. He returned with a nod, but without his anorak. Then, in due course, there came the odour of orange blossom.

The Gazelle d'Or is the kind of hotel made up of a palatial nucleus, surrounded by garden pavilions. We arrived at a side door in darkness, and were met by a number of helpers who went immediately to the back of the Land-Rover. By the time I got down it was empty, and Morgan was waiting to say goodnight to me. He looked exhausted; but wherever his charge had been lodged, he didn't want me to help, though I offered. He gave me a hug and a kiss before going. He is, as Rita said, a really nice man. Then the hotel staff came, and I was taken through the gardens, and into a private pavilion.

It was big enough to hold two apartments and furnished with everything, including a bedroom. They offered me supper, but I couldn't have eaten. I remembered the brandy, and had another.

I undressed while I drank it and fell into bed, huddling under the covers with my mascara all over the pillow. And slept like the dead, to waken to scent and sunlight and breakfast.

There was no one else there. I drank a lot of coffee, and washed, and walked shakily round the apartment. My dirty clothes of last night had all gone, and my luggage was in Ouarzazate. I made a kanga out of my bath sheet, and barefoot, stepped into the gardens.

The orange groves, in full and stifling blossom, were at the end. I turned my back on them and walked under trees, among dappled flowers. The silence was absolute. When I heard the ripple of water, I followed it. A channel led me up to the heart of the hotel. It looked like Designer Alhambra. Two ghosts in white headbands, slippers and robes appeared and vanished from a patio now empty and soundless. I felt like the person who survived the Black Death and took a homecoming trip to Pompeii. I climbed marble steps and began to search suites of reception rooms, as deserted as the *Mary Celeste*.

I was not without expectations. Only one person would keep ginkgo biloba and micronized marine algae in her bathroom, and a wet printed sheet headed 'What To Do When Your Boss is a Career Barrier'. I knew who had taken my clothes.

My mother wasn't in the main lounge, with its marble floor and its silken peach curtains. She wasn't in the rotunda, full of stucco and brass, with an inlaid zodiac floor, and a damascened bronze gazelle in an alcove. She wasn't in the corridor hung with inlaid and unloaded rifles. If she'd been in the unoccupied card rooms I couldn't smell her fags or see a trace of her socks, although I found a half-finished game of Monopoly. Someone had bought three hotels in Park Lane and the Waterworks. To Doris, that would have been both small beer and peanuts. I went the whole way back to the front porch, and emerged under a mat of bougainvillea. And I was alone in my towel no longer, but face to face with eight video cameras and five dozen fully dressed men and women, flushed with vintage champagne and exuberance. The cars had completed their rally.

It was Matchbox Day in Morocco. The vintage cars were drawn up in a row, their engines washed, their silver done, their leather buffed, their paintwork burnished like jewellery. Beside them, posing with a good deal of ragging and laughter, were their owners in period rig-outs. In the centre was the big '33 Chrysler with a bouquet of flowers on its bonnet, along with the wife of the owner in a cloche hat and strap shoes and silk stockings. The service men stood at the back looking happy, and the hotel staff had crammed into the yard, and quite a lot of casuals who were either gardeners or guests. Phrases sprang into the air: 'romped up the hill', 'cleaned the section', 'cranked her up that last bend', 'floor-boarded the bloody thing twice'.

I tapped a man on the shoulder. He was wearing plus-fours and a cap, and his collar was sodden. I said, 'The Frazer-Nash didn't make it?'

He turned, in high good humour, and was smitten by my sarong. He was one of the Bugattis. When his eyes got to my level he said, 'Poor old Tom, no. And Rupert's big end couldn't take it. And Chester spewed out a valve and got total brain fade over the tulips. CPSRP, poor old Chester.'

I asked him what he meant. It was the nearest thing to a talk with my mother.

'Couldn't Pull the Skin off a Rice Pudding, angel: burns his thumb on a plug change. Hey, didn't I see you at the Berber market? Not wearing that rig-out though, ha-ha-ha.'

I wished I'd also worn the free plastic shower cap. I said, 'Yes, I saw you there too. And what about the rest, then? The Lancia?'

'Crazy Yanks? Couldn't face it and went off home early. We did that this morning. Did you see us this morning? Did you miss that goddamned landslide? Christ, those two boys in the Sunbeam.'

Someone waved about another bottle of champagne and some of it went down my towel. I said, 'What happened?'

His face lengthened appropriately. I could see he really was sorry: I had just caught him in a moment of cheerfulness. He said, 'You didn't hear? Tried the Taroudant stretch in the dark, and copped a slide of those boulders. Nothing left. Not even the wreckage. At least that's what they say. I'm going to look. Actually, Charles dashed back this morning to see it, but the bloody police held him off.'

I said, 'There wouldn't be anything. Think of those houses.'

'Well, not much,' said the Bugatti. 'But unless you know cars, you don't realize. You know? Rudge-Whitworth Wire Detachables, even. Lovely single-plate clutch, those three-litres had.'

I said, 'It was a pity about Owen and Sullivan.'

If he went any redder, it was undetectable. He said, 'Bit of a fool, old Gerry Owen. That business at Asni. But Seb Sullivan was a bloody good sport. Game for any old prank. Got you out of a spot at Essaouiria, yes? Yes,' he said, slowing down his euphoria a little bit more, 'you must be pretty upset about Sullivan.'

'Yes,' I said soberly. 'But if he knew, he'd want you to finish the rally. What are you all going to do now?'

They were going to a public luncheon inside the town. He brightened: they were going to buy carvings. Taroudant, of course, was forbidden to Christians when R. Bontine Cunninghame Graham tried a long time ago to get into it; I could rather see why. I knew, now, where Johnson had picked up his alias.

The Bugatti man hadn't seen or heard of Johnson or Pymm, or he'd surely have mentioned them. He'd seen someone, though. Just as they all started to go, he called across to me. 'Hey, that little Scottie who swam with the boar? She's by the pool: saw her this morning. D'you think she should be told about Gerry?'

I knew where my mother was now. They must have driven in first thing this morning. 'Leave it to me,' I yelled after him. I knew he was hoping I'd wave.

I stood for a minute watching all the cars rev up and draw slowly away, some of them pinking. I thought I could get to like vintage cars, if it hadn't been for Gerry and Sullivan. Then I turned and ran back the way I had come, through the hotel, and out into the gardens, and along the shady way to the orange groves.

The swimming pool lay in the sun, surrounded by a lounging area shaded by trees, and a mass of unshaded sunbeds for grilling. Before the chambers for changing and massage stood a line of long tables, upon which covered dishes were being carefully laid. The starving herds for which the buffet was being prepared seemed to be absent. Two of the scruffy dressers from the front had returned to sit in drill shorts under the trees, reading books and sipping drinks at small tables: the kind of money vacationing here was not the kind

305

that gussied itself up in resort wear. The scent of hundreds of trees in full blossom filled the extremely warm air like a drug. I would have felt saner if I could have put the way I felt down to hallucinogens. There was no one here, and I wanted somebody. I went and looked into the pool.

A fully developed rhinoceros with a fag in its mouth was heaving its way from one end to the other, pulled forward by a brisk orange head in a sweatband. The mountainous form was my mother, and the retreating figure grasping her chins was the Chief Executive of the Marguerite Geddes Company, in a taut Lycra swimsuit and an air of amiable assurance. My mother saw me first. She looked up, began to cough, and swallowed water as the cigarette fell out of her mouth. Rita stood her on end and I saw the water only came up to her waist. They must have half emptied the pool. I said, 'What are you doing?' I could have cried.

My mother spluttered, and Rita thumped her and then waited while I got her a handkerchief. As she blew her nose, Rita waded with her to the steps. Rita said, 'We were just killing time until Mo came. Thought you'd be sleeping for ever. They've brought the cases in now.' She chucked a towel at my mother, who seemed to be wearing pyjamas and shark oil. Her bruise had got almost tanned over. She sat down with a wheeze, and inspected me as if checking for typos. She said, 'You want to know about Oliver? He's a strong boy. He'll do. Henry patched him up good with paper clips, and they're flying him straight to a clinic.'

I sat opposite. 'Henry?'

Rita, draped in a towel, was giving orders. She came back and sat down between us. 'That's our doctor. Hooker's Green and all that, remember? Wendy, are you all right?'

I remembered Hooker's Green. I said, 'Yes, I'm fine. Henry's in Ouarzazate now?'

'Was,' said Rita. 'Repairing Oliver, and giving out interviews on J.J.'s recent concussion and subsequent ammonia.'

She was wearing disco-ball earrings and a searching, if kindly expression. I didn't correct her, or ask where he was recovering from his ammonia. I was afraid to ask anything. I sat looking at the drink someone brought me. It looked like either whisky or brandy.

I wondered if I was a closet alcoholic. I took a gulp and said, 'So Henry's here, then?'

'Dropped in. He's gone,' Rita said. 'Probably in Agadir by now, stocking up *Dolly*. Lenny sailed her down the coast from Essaouira.'

I took another drink. 'To pick up Mr Johnson?' I said.

'Eventually,' Rita said. 'I suppose. Nobody's seen him yet. Go on. Drink up.'

'I'm all right,' I said for the second time. I sat up and looked at my mother. 'You know what happened?'

'Yes, Wendy. I know what happened,' my mother said. 'Short-term planning, that was. Poorly conceptualized strategy. High risk quotient for zero results. If you don't tell that fellow Johnson, I will.'

'He's been told,' said Morgan's voice. 'In extremely certain terms. Hello, Doris. Hello, Rita.' He touched my shoulder. 'Wendy?'

His T-shirt said *Die, Yuppie Scum* and had epaulettes on it, and his hair had been washed and thrust into a ponytail that made his face seem narrower than ever. He looked as if he had been up a long time. I hadn't been up long enough to know the answer to what he was really asking. I said, 'The Lancia's gone.'

'I know,' he said. 'It's all right. They know who the Americans are: they've got tabs on them. Exercise in debt reduction. They're all working like mad.'

'Who are?' I said. Birds twittered. A gentle splashing came from the pool. A white-robed man began placing things on our table: a bread-basket with a woven spired lid like the ones in the market; a red clay camel which couldn't run ahead of a Harley or it would have spilt the pepper and salt in its panniers. He went away to fetch silver and wine glasses. The scent of orange blossom was stifling.

'Who do you think?' Morgan said. 'Johnson was responsible for the whole bleeding massacre, so the least he can do is help fix it. The telephone wires are red hot.'

'What? How?' I said.

My mother tapped my hand. Hers had a freshly rolled bent cigarette in it. She said, 'Now you think what has to be done? *Sûreté* co-ordination; legal advice, consular help; messages to and from London, Toronto, Washington, Marrakesh, Ouarzazate,

Agadir, Rabat. Medical procedures; mortuaries; documents. A nice Sunbeam '26 to get rid of. And all on the *qui vive*.'

I have heard apter phrases. I said, 'I should have thought he did more damage at the kasbah. Doesn't that need some fixing?'

'A landslide?' said Morgan. 'Act of God dear. And the owners aren't going to charge anyone. Folded their women and stole away, they all did, after attending to Mr Daniel Oppenheim.'

'He went in an ambulance,' I said.

'He didn't get the chance,' Morgan said. 'Someone lifted him and chucked him back inside the kasbah. His friends or ours, I wouldn't know. He didn't survive.'

I saw that perhaps he hadn't been up so long after all. He just felt as awful as I did. I wondered when Johnson's jag had worn off. I said, 'He made a start on those arrangements this morning?'

'Must have done,' Morgan said. 'I reckon he got through an hour of it before Emerson arrived with the patch-and-mend specialists. They've rented a secure office: it's in a separate building. I'm to take you there.'

'Why?' I said.

'Because we've got to agree on our story, for one thing. And they'll need to talk to us, since we're mixed up in it. In fact, they ought to bloody well pay us, after all we've been through this last week, ending with the rock-folly shoot-out with Sullivan. Christ!' said Morgan; and his expression was one of awe. 'He'll never sodding well do *that* again.'

He meant Johnson. Rita looked at him. She said, 'The trouble is that he will. But next time, he'll make sure we don't know it.'

The door to the conference room was shut. I sat outside, now tidily dressed as for the Hotel Golden Sahara while Mo paced up and down jerkily. Once, a girl went in with a fax and, for a few minutes, left the door open. Inside, it was just an ordinary boardroom with a green-topped table with papers and men sitting around in shirts and ties, talking in French. Sir Bernard Emerson sat at the top. Beside him, taking notes, was Roland Reed, the MCG accountant. On his other side sat Johnson, studying some sort of checklist. There were two telephones at his elbow.

It was one of those days when his face consisted of nothing but bifocal spectacles. His shirt and tie looked as if they might be his own, but the linen jacket must have come from the Wardrobe. Although speaking only when spoken to, he didn't appear especially ragged, but rather a model of unemphatic officialdom. The assignment was damage containment, and he was not, for the moment, a person.

Sir Bernard took the fax, interrogated the girl, explained something to the most formally dressed of the men, and then asked Johnson a question, to which he replied. Then Johnson picked up the phone and put through a call, this time in Engish. As he waited, he looked up at the door. It was still open, but he gave no sign of having seen us. Then the girl came out, and the door shut.

Morgan stood and looked at it as if it had sworn at him. He said, 'They've got a bloody nerve, all of them.' He added, 'Including Johnson.' I thought he was going to walk out, but he sat down again.

The next time the door opened, the meeting was finishing. A knot of men came out, in the process of switching chat modes. The topics seemed to be the same as at home: summer holidays, children and golf. Another batch began to emerge, glancing at us and then away as *Die, Yuppie Scum* swam into their various kens. Then Rolly Reed came to the door. He looked worn, reassuring and friendly. 'Wendy? Mo? Will you come in?'

Emerson and Johnson were the only two left at the table. Emerson was presenting packets of stuff to his document case. He rose and sank as I came in, but Johnson only rested one preoccupied arm on the table and looked up and nodded to each of us. He didn't ask how we were, although he did seem to examine us both. Then he returned to studying papers.

Sir Bernard Emerson didn't ask after our blood pressures either. 'Please sit. This won't take very long. When you get back to London, I'll have to ask you to fulfil an appointment, but meantime a signature will keep everyone happy. Although I'm sure neither of you is a gossip.'

I said, 'My mother ought to sign something as well.'

'She has,' Emerson said. He waited while Reed produced two sheets of paper, and I read one, and wrote my name at the foot. Johnson didn't look up.

Morgan said, 'What if I don't?'

Johnson looked up. 'Don't be an idiot. It wouldn't change anything.'

'No, it wouldn't,' said Emerson sharply. He waited while Morgan signed, and then checked the result before Reed took the papers. The accountant put them in his briefcase, hesitated, and left. Sir Bernard Emerson sat back and surveyed us. I could feel Morgan resisting him.

Emerson said, 'Reed and I have to go. Morgan, we all have the future to think of. It's up to other people to talk to you about that, and Johnson knows enough to tell you something today. I hope it will work out in a way that will please you. All I want to do at the moment is thank you both for the extraordinary help you've given, in the face of considerable danger. Miss Helmann in particular had no idea what was going on, and was asked to do that most difficult thing, to transfer her loyalties. At the very least, it's up to us to make sure her career doesn't suffer. Morgan...'

He had smiled at me, but his glance at Morgan was on the grim side. He said, 'You helped us of course, quite immeasurably. Oliver probably owes you his life. I can't quite forget, however, that but for you, none of any of this need have happened. You realize that?'

'Free enterprise,' Morgan said. His jaw had set, but he had flushed.

'Oh, quite,' Emerson said. 'In its place, much to be commended. It seems to have infected my friend here, and resulted in what could have been your death and his own, if you hadn't been there to rescue him. I hope you will be satisfied with his apology. It is more, I must say, than I am.'

He was a big man, between fifty and sixty, with neatly waving grey hair and the style of a debater rather than a negotiator. He was a professor, I later found when I looked him up. Professor Sir Bernard Emerson with one wife, Frances, and one daughter, Joanna. Johnson sat hunched over his linked hands, and gazed at his thumbs as if they were rabbit's ears.

Morgan glanced at him before answering Emerson. He said, 'What's the big number? We chose to be involved. We could have gone to Ouarzazate: we took our own decision to travel with

Johnson. He didn't kill Pymm. I was the one who fixed Gerry. And it was you yourself who shot Sullivan. I tried to save him, damn it to hell. He might have said a lot more.'

'A mistake, I agree,' Emerson said.

Johnson laid his hands on his chair-arms and rose.

Emerson said, 'Where are you going? I want you to explain to Morgan what will be happening.'

Johnson stood still, a hand on the back of his chair. He still faced the door. Morgan said, 'Sir Bernard, tell me what's happening now. Why did you shoot Sullivan? Did you think he'd no more to say?'

'At the time, he wasn't sure he'd said anything,' Johnson said. He had turned his gaze to Emerson.

Emerson rose. He said, 'Is any of this relevant? I didn't intend to bring this up here and now, but the fact is that Johnson left to tackle these two men himself, without informing us or arranging for back-up. As it was, I didn't trust him and followed. But for us, Sullivan might have killed you.'

I said suddenly, 'You didn't help at all till the end.'

'He didn't want to kill Sullivan,' Johnson said. 'He wanted me to be forced to do that, before Sullivan talked.' He had released his hand and was standing properly, as if back in uniform.

'But—?' Morgan said. He remembered, as I did, what Sir Bernard had ordered at Marrakesh. Morgan said, 'But Sir Bernard *wanted* him questioned.'

'Not by me,' Johnson said. 'Sullivan answered the wrong questions, my questions. He might have had a lot more to say to the authorities. What he had to tell might have changed all our records. But Sir Bernard put an end to him, simply to stop him talking to me.' His eyes had never left Emerson's. He said, 'I suppose Kingsley told you later he *had* talked?'

'Yes,' said Emerson. Like Johnson, he was not standing casually.

'He asked me,' Johnson said. 'Sullivan asked me why I'd done nothing about Judith for ten years.'

There was a long silence. At the time, I thought they had forgotten us. Then Emerson gave an impatient sigh. He said, 'Frances thought this was why you kept working. So now what? Your suspicions prove

311

to be right. The Onyx team didn't all die. So you jack in all those years and go private?'

'I expect so,' Johnson said. 'You're not going to use public money to finance a one-man campaign against what's left of a bunch of mad mercenaries. They're a pin-prick in Europe. They'll be reaching senility soon, like war criminals.'

Emerson said, 'So do you blame me for scotching the Sicilian blood-hunt? An irreversible waste of irreplaceable resources, for what? What do they matter? Who was that unpleasant lout ten years ago? An apprentice mercenary: he didn't even remember your name. But you lost your head, and yesterday was the result: muddied thinking and needless destruction. I should get rid of you anyway. I thought I could trust you.'

'And you can't?' Johnson said. The passion clearly remained, but his voice, at least, was merely exasperated.

'Evidently not. You failed to tell me MCG were threatened by Kingsley's, and you further failed to tell me that you were freelancing to help them. Don't pretend your excuse was this other matter.'

'All right, I won't,' Johnson said.

Emerson waited. Then he said, 'Bystanders get killed in vendettas. You don't always work on your own.'

'No, that's right,' Johnson said. 'You teamed me with Daniel Oppenheim.'

He leaned over suddenly and picked up his papers. 'Would you excuse me then, sir? If you're staying after all, you might care to put Miss Helmann and Mr Morgan in the picture. If there is more to say, we could discuss it in London.' He had recovered the Senior Service style: quiet, respectful and civil. Translated, it meant go to hell.

He added, 'Wendy. Morgan. Excuse me.' Sir Bernard moved. Morgan began to jump up. Without waiting, Johnson walked to the door.

Filling the space like Stonehenge, my mother opened it from the outside. She said, 'I have come to be told what is happening today to my daughter. They are bringing lunch. We shall all sit down except Sir Bernard, whose car and chauffeur are waiting.'

She knew Sir Bernard by sight. Of course she did: she'd been at Ouarzazate. She had changed back to layers of cotton and her hair was lined up in hairgrips and she had her knitting-bag with her which, having sat down, she proceeded to open. Her feet were in Kentoh massage-sandals, planted apart like a Japanese wrestler's. She appeared not to notice the battlefield.

Morgan said, 'You bloody woman.'

Sir Bernard Emerson sent a glance round us all, ending with Johnson. Emerson said, 'I don't want you if your mind has gone fragile. If it hasn't, get on with it. This bit is your job, not mine. And for Jesus' sake, think what you're doing.' He measured Johnson up and down once and took a sharp breath, but let it go without speaking. He was rather pale. He said, 'You know where to find me,' and without another word, walked from the room.

Johnson stood as if thinking. Mo and I looked at each other. 'What a pleasure,' said my mother, inspecting her knitting, 'to move beyond barrier-ridden middle-management hierarchies and into the intellectual freemasonry of the privileged classes! So what is the problem, we ask ourselves? A serious difference, we perceive, which Sir Bernard must find a means to resolve. He acts, Mr Johnson. He isolates you psychologically. He rouses Mo to resentment. He encourages a personal bonding between you. He thinks, when Mr Johnson has fewer chemicals in him, that there is a very good chance you will both do as he wishes. He is right. You listen to words, you learn nothing.'

Mo's mouth opened. Johnson, startled out of his trauma, sat down on a handy chair and stared at her. Morgan said, 'Doris? How did you dream up that theory?'

My mother shrugged with her face. 'I follow Sir Emerson's reasoning. Am I right?'

'No,' said Morgan. 'Johnson's resigning.'

My mother glanced at Johnson out of the tops of her eyes. She said, 'Ah, yes. What man worth the name would do otherwise? He is an able fellow, this Emerson Professor St Bernard.'

'Professor Sir Bernard,' I said.

'So shortly he will overcome his pride and place his dilemma before you, and you will do what he wants. He needs you, Mr

Johnson, but he needs a lever to control you with. Or a little carrot. You know the girl is on holiday in Madeira? She flew there on an unplanned vacation just after the Sir left to come here.'

'What girl?' Morgan asked.

Johnson came to something near life. 'Shall I have hysterics now, or wait until after lunch? Doris, you are the daughter of the mother of whores, and translate that into Arabic if you like.' He laid down the papers and tried to smooth them. 'Who told you to come in and break it up? Rita, I bet.'

'Instinct,' said my mother.

Johnson looked at her. 'I knew it,' he said. 'You're into ESP and you've probably got a direct fax to Delphi. Do you mind if I ask you? What country do you really belong to?'

I'd always wondered. I needn't have. 'I am an Ealing,' said my mother. 'Once, of course, I was Turkish. Then Arab countries elsewhere, until I met Wendy's father.'

'He was Ealing too?' Morgan said.

'Always,' she said. 'But always merry, always good-humoured, always with the spirit to try something new, win or not, lose or not. And liking fat women.'

'We all have rotten taste,' Morgan said. Fortunately, she knows when he is joking. They eyed one another, then she turned back to Johnson.

'So now you will go, and take some pills, and do whatever Henry has told you to do that you have not done; and in a while we shall meet here to eat, and you and Morgan will decide what to do. It is the concensus.'

'You don't have a quorum,' Johnson said.

'Come on, pal,' said Morgan, advancing. 'It's not a democracy, it's a bloody dictatorship.'

'Well, I didn't vote for it,' said Johnson, with some irritation. He got up, watched by my mother's large, circled eyes, and strolled out, followed by Morgan. She looked complacent. I knew that look. I suppose she had reason. Whatever she had done, Johnson had temporarily re-opened for business.

26

This, the meeting called by my mother, was the last that I went to in Morocco. Of the four I had already attended, the most impressively equipped, I suppose, had been the one which took place in the kasbah. For this, the final agenda, they let us return to the room we had used in the morning.

For a working lunch it was late, the fault being as much mine as Johnson's. Dispatched to my room, I fell soundly asleep for the second time, and woke feeling both saner and hungrier. Johnson, when I overtook him in the gardens looked as if he, too, had slept, judging by his shirt and jacket. How I ever imagined him in uniform, I didn't know. Walking to the meeting, he laid an apologetic group of fingers round my shoulders. 'What an awful morning. Poor Wendy. Operas on every side.'

You learn when you are being trusted, and when you are intended not to ask questions. I said, 'Everyone was tired. I was. You look better.'

'There was room for improvement,' he said. 'Come on. Your mother will be waiting. A groaning board, and a groaning Morgan and lots and lots of alcohol, and there are still maybe futures out there waiting for somebody.'

We passed the pool on the way, and a red-headed water-wheel that turned into Rita, holding her nose. Johnson raised a hand and so did she: then her hand was replaced by her feet. He said, 'No, she's not coming. Only the victims.'

Only, as before, Morgan, my mother and me, sitting round a table; pushing out a raft into the wreckage of what used to be our career patterns. And Johnson. I wondered if he considered himself, too, a victim. I thought it unlikely.

Morgan, his hair down from a swim, greeted us with very few words and looked as if he'd been thinking. I couldn't see any stickers. My mother, unchanged in any respect, trod up and down the buffet table with a cigarette on her lip, dispensing prawns and salad and jellied titbits as once Rita had, at another board.

Johnson, swiping the winebottle, said, 'This is going to be short, because I am very shortly going to get plastered. Mohammed Morgan, you are about to be hauled out of Kingsley's whether you have the slightest desire to be hauled out or not. You can cut your throat, buy Manchester United or run a tea stall if you want. What you can't do is take your squad and start again on your own. Or you can, but only on certain terms, which I am empowered to put before you.'

He stopped to refill his glass. I hadn't even got my first glassful yet. Morgan said, 'In English. I want it in bloody English.'

'You'll get it,' said Johnson. 'So. Proposition. Government helps you finance a buy-out of your hardware design squad, and compensates for the loss of your earn-out. You get a 25,000 square-foot start-up workshop in England; build your own pre-production units and keep, license, or sell to your original equipment manufactuers as heretofore. The sine quae nix: a bowler hat on the board and first refusal of every new project, no matter who or what you bloody think you are making it for. End of proposition. They'd have done it this way in the first place, except that they thought everyone thought you made washing machines. So what about it? Yes, forget it or maybe?'

'I might give it a whirl,' was Morgan's reply. He threw it down like a platter of catfood.

'Whether I'm around or not?'

'Whether you're around or not.'

We had all, I think, expected an argument. Johnson himself waited a moment. Then he said, 'I see. I'll tell Emerson. Good.'

'Good?' Morgan said. 'Didn't you notice the wit? *Give it a whirl?* Wait, my boy, till you've seen my fighting Jacuzzis, my missile-tube hair-dryers, my limpet rollers with Semtex. Should we all go home, now you've got what you want? Or could you be persuaded – or, what's your name, darling Jay? – could you be troubled to tell us what's going to happen to Kingsley's and its entire international work force?'

He picked up his fork and attacked the mound of food my mother had just shoved in front of him. Johnson, leaning over, audibly stabbed a prawn on the same plate and lifted it, causing Morgan's eyes to lift also.

'Come on, Mo,' he said. 'I'm playing it as straight as I can. The truth about Kingsley's is that without you they're sunk, but they were going that way in any case. They'll have to be independently audited, and the nominees nitted out of the register. They're over-borrowed. Kingsley and his accountant suppressed that and more. It's a classic third-generation disaster: charming Chairman with public presence and a taste for high life, but nothing but average competence. The firm will be wound up or sold. Not your doing: it would have come, anyway.'

'I put him down as big scale,' Morgan said. He looked at me, and then back to Johnson. 'He had style. He was bloody attractive.' He said abruptly, 'My God, I loused it up for all of you. What will happen to Rita?'

It was a strange submission, and what had brought it about, I couldn't fathom. If Johnson did, he gave no sign. Only his manner, I thought, relaxed for reasons other than alcohol.

'Troon will drown one of these days,' he observed, 'but is otherwise fine. So is MCG, if it's survived a week without her and Rolly. Now I'm out of the cupboard, I might as well get myself on the board. You might want to poke your nose in. Kingsley put a crimp in her suppliers, but we'll soon get all that sorted out. It's really a very good firm. Otherwise the greedies wouldn't have wanted them.'

'Pymm and the Arabs,' Morgan said, returning a little to normality. 'So what about the Lord of the Kasbah? You made a cock-up of that bomb. They're having to rebuild half Morocco.'

'You do it next time,' Johnson said. He began, for the first time, to eat. 'It was a punk bomb with punk timing, but we did get everyone out. The village remains the world centre for goat cheese in oil cans. Chahid's in jail, and will languish there roughly for ever. Algeria, Canada, ex Foreign Legion; a fraudulent accountant before that. Except for the hard men he fell in with, Pymm might have stayed a role-playing mutt on the take. As it was, Sullivan caught up with him. We couldn't prevent it, but thanks to Wendy, we do know his principals, and we've also skewered the Arabs. Every name goes on file, and will save us all sorts of grief in the future. And one day, if we're blessed, we'll get an order from somewhere to waste them.'

'We?' my mother said, smoking and eating.

'Extended Editorial,' said Johnson shortly. She rose comfortably and refilled his glass.

'Extended New Flipping Testament,' said Morgan. 'Father, Son and Microchip of the Old Rolling Stone if I read the signs correctly. Doris is right. Once you get back into your skull, you're not going to leave Emerson. And you're going to make bloody sure that I don't.'

'Mo?' said my mother.

'Yes?'

'You are stating the obvious. So what about the late Daniel Oppenheim?' It was funny: that was what I had wanted to ask. And what about Muriel Oppenheim, I wanted to add, who had married her boss and ran the private side of his life to such perfection?

'Muriel needn't know,' Johnson said. 'Only that he died in the landslide.' He paused. He said, 'If he'd lived, they'd have put him away on a drugs charge.' It was probably true. It exonerated Emerson, at least, from that murder.

Morgan said, 'You partnered Oppenheim, but you didn't spot anything?'

Johnson gazed at his empty glass, and then at my mother, who was rolling a fag. 'Not at first. As it happens, I didn't much like him. It shouldn't matter, but sometimes it does. You lean over backwards.'

He didn't mention Muriel. I thought I understood. Whatever he'd been, he hadn't been jealous.

He said, 'Oppenheim was the best man for the job; I'd no right to blame Emerson. You know what happened. The MOD had come to its senses and noticed that you were pure bloody dynamite. I was to become your best buddy, while Daniel found out how to unbundle you. We needed real figures, and the bomb scare was to get us those, among other things. Of course, he had them already from Kingsley. He was silly to set off the bomb, and Sullivan was crazy to kill the safe-breaker, but it took me a while to cotton on.'

'You do this all the time?' Morgan said.

'Yes,' said Johnson. 'I get some real bastards for buddies. And of course, to forestall your next question, the figures were a great personal help in the MCG battle. Or would have been, if correct.'

My mother had begun to cut up tart like an astrologer. Then she refilled Johnson's glass, much more slowly. When you want her, she behaves like a waitress. I said, 'Then why filch the figures I had at the airport? A counter-check against Mr Oppenheim?'

'And against you and me,' said my mother. 'That's what they do in the movies.' Morgan rose pointedly and fetched his own bottle.

'The cinema,' Johnson said, 'has a lot to answer for.' He said it quite well, but I had a feeling he would be talking French soon, and that my mother would be the last to be astonished.

Morgan's eyes narrowed. He said, 'You freaking? I've got a question to ask before this meeting closes, and so has Wendy, and we both want an answer. Remember the special figures we got out for Emerson? The genuine, abysmal Kingsley position?' He waited. '*Johnson!*'

'This is a recording. Speak,' Johnson said, '*après le beep sonore.*' He wasn't all that drunk.

I said, 'Mr Morgan wants to know about that fax that came to the kasbah. It had the same figures in it.'

'And it nearly did for us,' Morgan said.

'But it didn't,' said Johnson. '*Le Jamesbonderie.*'

Morgan began to articulate faster, if not necessarily more clearly. He said, 'Will you damned well own up? No one could have sent that fax unless you told them where and how and what names to use. Where did it come from?'

I knew. Morgan had never seen the satellite direct-dial telephone on *Dolly*. I sat back and let Johnson admit it all. Then Morgan exploded.

'You've got a *fax* on that bloody gent's water-toy? You faxed the kasbah number to Lenny, and he faxed back that goddamned death notice? *And* the lie at the end about the Government taking me over?'

'I should think that was Emerson,' Johnson said. 'Lenny liked you.'

'It made me expendable!' Morgan exclaimed.

'Also Sir Robert,' said my mother, stacking priceless dishes prior, I suppose, to taking them somewhere and washing them. 'To place you in such danger, what was Sir Emerson's object?'

'Buggering up my personal relationships,' Johnson said. He got up as well, a shade uncertainly, and walked to the windows for the purpose of delivering a statement to the scenery.

'We've all been working to make sure of one thing, that Mo's brain cells don't end up with the bully-boys. So long as his work wasn't classified, the Arab group hoped to buy him with Kingsley's. Remove that hope, and they'd make sure no one else got to use him. The fax was sent to tell them he'd been security-parcelled. In theory I then put my cloak on and rescued him. If in further theory I botched it, poor Mo, the Arabs would strike, and the Grim Reaper would get the Jacuzzis.'

'And Sir Robert?' said Morgan. 'He was there. The figures made him a liar.' He was sitting opposite me. I could see the legend on his T-shirt rising and falling.

Johnson turned. 'By then, Kingsley was a simple no-hoper. No one cared whether he got out or not. I do like a good sporting game. What do you like?'

Morgan looked more solemn than angry. His eyes had narrowed on Johnson. 'You invited that fax. Dammit, did they think that I'd work for the Arabs?'

'They didn't know whether you knew that you wouldn't,' said Johnson, listening to himself. He looked gratified. He said, 'I knew you wouldn't. They'd hate your habits. They'd take you seriously. You might end up having to worry.'

Morgan gazed at him. I knew he had made up his mind finally about Johnson. I knew he was thinking, as I was, of the kasbah, and the bomb, and those moments when Johnson did take control, whatever anyone said, and brought us out despite Oppenheim and the Arabs. Brought out Pymm, even. Johnson was good, but in his way he was as ruthless as Sullivan.

My mother stacked the last of the dishes and stood with her arms at her sides, which in body language meant she was leaving. She also had her eyes on me, which meant she thought I was leaving as well.

I knew she was right. The questions had all surely been asked, but for the personal one I didn't know how to put to Johnson. Except that maybe it was easier to put it now, when he and Morgan might not remember it. I got up and said, 'Mr Johnson. The day the bomb went off in London, you'd already meant to make use of me? You took me to Sullivan's club and made sure I'd hear about Essaouira. You knew I'd... You knew Sir Robert would hear. You did use me.'

My mother shifted. I remembered Rita and Lenny, watching Johnson. I knew I shouldn't have asked, and I shouldn't expect him to answer.

He did, however. He even reverted to very clear English. He said, 'I needed your help very much at that stage, but we didn't know one another, and there was nothing I could actually tell you. I'd seen you were quick and observant, and whoever you reported to, you'd do whatever seemed good for your company. From that, of course, everything followed. If you're sorry, then of course I am as well. But I can't regret that very nice luncheon. I should have wanted to take you there anyway.'

He knew what I was asking, and had answered it. Whether he was speaking the truth, I had no way of telling. Far more people had known than I'd bargained for. I said, 'I don't blame anyone now.'

He studied my face, then he gave a slow, gentle nod and turned away from me. He meant, I think, to sit down, but Morgan prevented it. He was on his feet, his epaulettes set for a beam swell. Morgan said, 'Wendy ought to be told who *was* used.'

'Mo?' said my mother. 'Anything Wendy needs to know, her mother will tell her. Have you had all the wine you need?' She had a point. All the bottles were empty.

'He's had all the wine I need,' said Johnson obscurely. 'Goodbye, Doris.'

My mother had walked to the door. I joined her. Morgan stood in front of Johnson and, using his hand like a bat, hit up first one of Johnson's palms, then the other. As they fell, he stared glaring after them. Then he looked up. 'Sailing, is it?' he said. 'Well, Jesus Christ, aren't you tough! I thought they'd be meat.'

'Did you,' said Johnson. He spoke a shade drily. I'd forgotten. His hands were his cornerstone business. I remembered something else, that once had seemed so important. I stopped, bumping into my mother.

I said abruptly, 'Sir Robert's portrait. It never got finished.'

I saw my mother's face alter, and Morgan's. I saw the acrimony in Johnson's face lessen and melt into untrustworthy blandness. 'Well, not this version,' said Johnson. 'The one I did in London's all right. All expensively framed for the Academy.'

My mother bared her complete dentures. Wreathed in smoke, they perform like a pop group. Morgan said slowly, 'How?'

'I did two,' Johnson said. 'Stopped the London sittings, of course, with my tantrum, but the main portrait was kept in my studio. Finished it before going to Marrakesh. I didn't leave London till Wendy did.' He smiled at me. It was so rare that I stared at him. He said, 'Might do Sir Robert a bit of personal good. Too late, I'm afraid, for the Company.'

It was too late in more than one way. My training overcame my natural feelings. I said, 'The cheque! Mr Johnson, the cheque. Will they honour it?'

'No,' Johnson said. 'I tore the cheque up. Ethically, I took him as a subject, not a commission. And a good one: I was lucky to get him. The portrait I thought Charity might like as a gift. It's her money he's going to live on, unless he flutters off to the States with his title. I rather hope not.'

Charity. The name illumined, suddenly, something that Morgan had started to complain about. I said, 'Charity. She was the one Mr Johnson used most. He really exploited her goodwill. But she didn't mind, Mr Morgan. She did the right thing. In a real way, she was loyal to Sir Robert.'

Morgan sat, his eyes fixed on Johnson like press-studs. He didn't comment, and neither did Johnson. My mother answered, as usual. She took her fag out of her mouth and coughed as if she enjoyed it. 'That's right, Wendy; speak up for Charity. You too, Mo. *If it ain't broke, don't fix it.*'

She took a puff and viewed her blank, knackered audience. Then she exhaled the smoke like an offering. She said, 'Them Outward-Bound Weekends, would they be something like this, Mr Johnson?'

'Not so quiet,' Johnson said.

*

322

That afternoon, Johnson left for Agadir and his yacht, having written to Muriel Oppenheim. Neither she nor Mr James Auld would attend the Final of the Africa Cup *sous le Haut Patronage de* SM and SAR who, with various men from la Wilaya, were about to be charmed by the news that their portraits were going to be finished. As a victim of ammonia, Johnson himself looked quite authentic: as if he had been hit on the head and had not yet got himself fully together.

The Canadian journalists turned up in the Gazelle that evening and occupied the elegant bar of beaten copper and brass, hovered over by ONMT and RAM and the barman. They were shocked by Sullivan's death, but rather relieved by Pymm's absence on business. They were going home soon, and Canadian tourists would come in return to all the same places.

I hoped it would help the real bits of Morocco, all the endeavour of *Le Maroc en Fête*. The tennis, the skiing, the polo, the folk dancing and the Fantasia and all the events attended by Doris my mother in the company of the late Ellwood Pymm. I wondered what my mother really made of it all, a woman into her fifties, dreaming of Omar Sharif and Beau Geste and the Desert Song. I had to be pleased with the way she had managed.

I thought I should tell her quite soon that I had changed my career expectations. She had always done her best to help me up the managerial ladder: to learn to Plan, Organize, Direct, Staff, Co-ordinate, Report and Budget, or PODSCORB, as the proper term has it. To learn to run a sound business, that would never let anyone down. Also to make up to me, of course, for her own lack of trained business acumen. The skills denied to my mother, she had expected these courses to give me. In many ways, I still think them invaluable, although I notice she no longer samples them.

I had thought my judgement was good, but this week had shown me reason to doubt it. So perhaps Muriel Oppenheim doubted hers. Charity, from the same world as Sir Robert, had understood her partner better than either of us.

This week I had had the business opening I longed for: now I had lost my road to advancement. Another chance, as had been hinted, might come; but the road itself was no longer inviting. This week

I had done all that was asked of me. But all the acts of initiative, it seemed, had sprung from people whose lives were not structured at all, who didn't conform: who couldn't *spell properly,* some of them.

Not without pain, I reasoned out what this week had manifested. I couldn't be them, but they needed someone like me. I would make an excellent executive assistant to Mohammed Morgan's extradited division, and to its possible MCG cousin, with its brotherhood of unorthodox bosses. I was prepared to apply my problem-solving techniques to keeping their overheads down, and their offices properly run, and stepping in when they slagged one another. I wasn't going to miss Trish or Val. Or Sir Robert.

The night before we went back to London, I explained my decision to Doris and she listened, coughing and picking up stitches. At the end, she resumed knitting rapidly. 'I began to twig you was deviating, the day you accepted Mo's offer. Soft on this chip fellow, are you?'

'Mo Morgan!' I said.

'That's good,' said my mother. 'Swims a lot, doesn't he? Got his eye somewhere else, by my reckoning. If you ain't fussed about that, you could do a lot worse for a boss. Unless you thought of anyone else?'

'No,' I said. I said it after a pause.

'No,' she agreed. 'By the way, I got that girl business wrong. She didn't stay above two days in Madeira. And she didn't hop across to Agadir, neither.'

'What girl?' I said. After a bit I said, 'There was some girl he knew in the Balkans.'

'That's the one. Dubrovnik,' my mother said. 'Nothing to it, of course. Never could be, with the hole he's dug himself into. Did you ever get that photograph of yourself on the back of the Harley? We could make a Christmas card of it.'

I wish I were like Rita.

I wish I were like my stupid father.

Some day, I shall say that to her. To my mother. To Doris.

Some day, but not damned well yet.

Also available

Roman Nights
(Dolly, Book 5)

If Ruth had stayed on leave none of it might have happened…

An astronomer working at the Maurice Frazer Observatory, Ruth Russell is enjoying her time in Rome. That is until her lover Charles Digham, top fashion photographer, has his camera stolen and the thief ends up a headless corpse in the zoo park *toletta*. The enigmatic Johnson Johnson, in Rome to paint a portrait of the Pope, is on hand to unravel the mystery.

But as Johnson and Ruth begin the search for clues it soon becomes clear that more is at stake than the secrets of a couture house… something far more deadly.

Also available

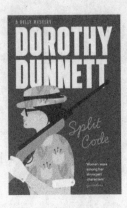

Split Code
(Dolly, Book 6)

To all appearances Joanna Emerson is a fully qualified, gold-medalled graduate of the world's finest college of nursery nurses...

Engaged as a nanny to Benedict, newly born heir to a vast cosmetic fortune, she becomes caught up in a complex kidnap plot. But the enigmatic portrait painter, yachtsman and former spy, Johnson Johnson is never far away – and he knows the dangerous game she's playing.

Before long, bullets are flying, and most of them in Joanna's direction.

OUT NOW

About the Dolly series

The Dolly mystery thrillers feature undaunted heroines in far-flung locations and plot twists sure to surprise.

In the background is the enigmatic and taciturn Johnson Johnson – famous portrait painter, secret agent and fixer of people's lives. Also an accomplished yachtsman, he's never far from his gaff-rigged ketch, *Dolly*, where much of the action takes place.

Yet the real focus of each adventure is the female narrator and protagonist. Singer, chef, doctor, astronomer, nanny or make-up artist, each is self-assured, independent, and whip-smart.

Dorothy Dunnett wrote the Dolly novels between 1968 and 1992, in non-chronological order of the story. The series is now re-published in chronological order of the story.

The full series –
Tropical Issue
Rum Affair
Ibiza Surprise
Operation Nassau
Roman Nights
Split Code
Moroccan Traffic

About the author

Dorothy Dunnett (1923–2001) gained an international reputation as a writer of historical fiction. She moved genres and turned to crime writing with the acclaimed Dolly books, also known as the Johnson Johnson series. She was a trustee of the National Library of Scotland, and a board member of the Edinburgh International Book Festival. In 1992 she was awarded an OBE for her services to literature. A leading light in the Scottish arts world and a renaissance woman, Dunnett was also a professional portrait painter and exhibited at the Royal Scottish Academy on many occasions.

Note from the Publisher

To receive background material and updates on further titles in the
Dolly series, sign up at farragobooks.com/dolly-signup